"Looking for someone?" Keeping his gaze on the instrument, he slowed his fingers and brushed them in one smooth stroke over the strings.

A rich, resonant chord sounded of sunset and the last days of summer. "No." She laid one hand on a handlebar and shook it.

"Stick around and I might charge admission."

Another chord followed with a tone so bright and true she felt her ribs sing in harmony. She snugged her arms against her chest to dull the vibrations. This whole evening was just too much—the class and the music and the dancing and now, this smart aleck cowboy with his filthy boots slung on her bike like he owned it. How typical. The English believed themselves entitled to everything. Those kindly old folks in the exercise class almost convinced her otherwise. How wrong she was.

She jerked the handlebar hard.

His feet slid, and he lunged sideways. With a twang, the music cut off, and the guitar banged against the truck bed. A loose strand of black hair flopped over his forehead.

He swiped it away and gazed sidelong with eyes the color of mossy stones. Seeming only now to clock her plain garb, his brows lifted. His gaze trailed down her body and back to her face, in a look more admiring than curious.

Praise for Wendy Rich Stetson

"Wendy Rich Stetson's writing is vivid, sharp, and alive with the beauty of rural Pennsylvania. I loved it."

~Ellyn Oaksmith, bestselling author

~*~

"With the lyricism of old-fashioned romance and the simple joy of a well told story, HOMETOWN is filled with whimsy and longing. A perfect escape into an older world made new again, and the journey of a young woman trying to find where she belongs."

~Gabra Zackman,
award-winning audiobook narrator and author

~*~

"Escapist romance at its very best!"

~Kirsten Potter,
award-winning audiobook narrator

~*~

"The Jane Austen sensibility set in Amish country makes for an addictive read."

~Julia Duffy,
Emmy award-winning actress and author

~*~

"If you want to know what true love is, read this book."

~S. Jackson, author

Heartsong Hills

by

Wendy Rich Stetson

Hearts of the Ridge Series, Book 2

Heartsong Hills

Cover Art by *Diana Carlile*

The Wild Rose Press, Inc.
PO Box 708
Adams Basin, NY 14410-0708
Visit us at www.thewildrosepress.com

Publishing History
First Edition, 2022
Trade Paperback ISBN 978-1-5092-4572-7
Digital ISBN 978-1-5092-4573-4

Hearts of the Ridge Series, Book 2
Published in the United States of America

Dedication

For Naomi, Julia, Micah, Cate, and spunky and curious girls everywhere.

Acknowledgments

To everyone in my hometown of Lewisburg, PA—my heartfelt gratitude for embracing the Hearts of the Ridge Series with such enthusiasm.

To my tap consultant, Micah Holly—thanks for bringing Shuffle Off to Fitness to life.

To everyone at The Wild Rose Press: my editor, the staff, and my fellow authors—you're the best team a gal could ask for.

To my sweet Pete and Cate—thanks for chocolate chip pancakes, gooey brownies, and endless patience and love.

Prologue

Holmes County, Ohio

In exactly three minutes, the pumpkin pie would burn. Nora sniffed again. Four at most. She didn't need to go look in the oven. The moment the filling caramelized, and the pastry darkened from buttery gold to the precise shade of brown that foretold not just a flaky crust, but a melt-in-the-mouth, dissolve-on-the-tip-of-the-tongue, better than *Grossmammi's* crust, Nora Beiler could smell that moment.

A shriek of laughter cut through the din, setting her teeth on edge. Perched in a stiff-backed chair by the sitting room sofa, she glanced toward the kitchen. Did those girls remember to set a timer?

Arms aflutter, her ten-year-old daughter Rebecca leapt over her feet and tiptoed to a gaggle of cousins playing charades around the woodstove.

Wee Isaac sprang to his knees and pointed. "You're a duck, you're a duck! No, a goose!"

Rebecca shook her head, gazed at the ceiling, and flapped harder.

Bellies full from the Christmas Eve feast, the old folks talked and laughed, their coffee cups and goody plates clustered on chair arms and end tables. Her brothers Samuel and Micah roamed from house to barn and back, doing whatever young men did on such a

1

night. With a swell of chatter, the women flocked into the sitting room. Red-faced from dish washing, they collapsed in gliders, smoothing damp aprons and tucking stray hairs into prayer caps, leaving the younger girls in the kitchen with the nearly burnt pie.

Outside, the holiest night of the year was blanketed in snowy silence. Inside, the house was a family-filled blizzard of chaos.

Sitting off to one side, Nora tugged a crocheted afghan over her bad leg, catching the toe of her shoe in a space between granny squares. Unable to stand for the duration of a large cleanup yet decades younger than her mother and aunts…where did she belong?

An explosion of girlish giggling heightened the ruckus.

Scowling, she shifted and craned her neck toward the kitchen. Like lightning, pain tore from hip to ankle, leaving behind an iron-heavy ache. Taking in a slow breath, she rubbed the heel of her hand down her thigh and darted a glance toward her mother. Had she noticed? No. For once, Nora's chronic discomfort evaded Verna Rishel's gaze.

"Good news! I found a buyer for Penny." Leaning back, Uncle Moses stretched his legs, wobbling the coffee cup atop his belly. He snatched it and slurped, dribbling a few drops in his chestnut beard.

With a disgusted snort, Aunt Martha tossed a napkin into his lap.

He dabbed the corners of his mouth with ladylike delicacy and winked. "She was a good horse—the best I've had since Lou. I hate to lose her, but 'round about Thanksgiving, she lost her pep. Don't want to see the old girl go lame."

Nodding, the men made murmuring sounds of assent.

In the kitchen, the girls almost screamed with laughter.

Nora squeezed closed her eyes. Their unbridled happiness felt like a slap in the face. Had she and her cousins been so boisterous when they were young? She didn't think so. Her generation was taught good Amish girls didn't carry on. Of course, the girls weren't trying to irritate her. She knew they barely thought of her, except on occasion, to request a recipe.

They'd do well to consult her now. A few minutes more and that crust would be char. She supposed they had enough dessert with the apple and bishop's pies she baked earlier. Her hip was always stronger in the morning. Plus, the eight—no, nine—dozen cookies in the pantry. After tonight's crowd, tomorrow's dinner for fourteen would feel cozy. But what was Christmas without pumpkin pie? She huffed a breath. "Are you girls watching the oven?"

Mamm shot her a look.

Maternally chastened, she clasped her hands and stared at her feet. Why did her every word sound like a rebuke? Even on Christmas Eve. No wonder the girls paid her so little mind. Still, one more minute and she'd take out the pie herself.

Uncle Eli popped two thumb cookies at once. "English family buying Penny?"

Moses interlaced his fingers behind his head and nodded. "Christmas gift for the children. A horse is a peck of work for a present, but I suppose they know what they want. She'll do for gentle riding—just can't pull a buggy no more."

Battery-powered candles flickered on the windowsills, making bluish flames dance in the foggy panes. She swallowed a sigh. Even after three years living with Moses and Martha in Holmes County, Christmas still didn't feel right. When she was a girl in Pennsylvania, her family lit real candles. She missed the golden glow and the simple Christmas Eve meal *Mamm* served. Her aunt's menu was as extravagant as an all-you-can-eat English buffet. Who needed three kinds of *stromboli*? She never even heard of the dish before moving here. It was fiddly to make and far too cheesy. Then six varieties of ice cream pie? Too much.

The gas lights hissed, and the roaring fire crackled, sending the temperature soaring. Ignoring the odor of burning pumpkin, she shoved the blanket from her lap. Her family bustled like bees in a hive. The instant one aunt sat, another rose. One cousin jogged down the stairs just as another bounded up. Never a moment of stillness. So many relatives and neighbors, she couldn't keep them all straight.

In Pennsylvania, Christmas Eve was a quiet, contemplative occasion. Especially those last few years when only she, Rebecca, and her brother Jonas gathered to light the pillar candle and read aloud the Christmas story, a few fresh-cut boughs suffusing the house with the scent of pine. Not that those were merry Christmases. If she were honest, each was gloomier than the one before, right up to the year her brother packed his bag and left their family and community forever, giving her no choice but to join her mother and younger brothers in Ohio. She clenched her apron and drove down the bitter memory with a huff. "That's enough, Nora."

Mamm and Rebecca turned in tandem, their blue-eyed gazes so similarly dark with concern they were like mirror images separated by sixty years. Nora's cheeks heated. As if her lame leg wasn't bad enough, she'd soon be known as the dotty widow who talked to herself.

A heavy knock at the door saved her the embarrassment of an explanation.

Rebecca twirled and scampered across the room. "I'm the Angel of the Lord, of course."

The aunts exchanged pointed looks.

Nora knew what they thought. Her father's daughter from head to toe, the child was too showy for her own good. Waving her arms in a manner more chicken-like than cherubic, Rebecca tugged the doorknob.

Arctic air rushed in like a locomotive, rustling wrapped gifts on the hearth. A single Christmas card launched from a garland and fell amidst the children who tumbled over one another, clamoring to catch it.

In the doorway, a young man hunched, shoulders and hat dusted with snow. He stomped heavy boots on the rag rug. Wet brown curls shivered at his temples, and his ruddy cheeks blazed in the gas light.

Her heart stopped.

Levi?

The boy doffed his black, brimmed hat, sending a snow shower onto Aunt Martha's linoleum.

Breath snagging in her throat, Nora clutched her skirt in tight fingers. Seven years. Levi had been dead for seven years. Yet, vision blurred by sudden tears, she could swear he stood in the entry this very second.

"Amos Mast, close that door before you let out all

the warm air." With effort, Aunt Martha rose to standing. "Katie! Your brother's here to fetch you home. Take the pie out of the oven and come along. And bring a dishtowel."

Amos stared at the slushy puddle. "Sorry for the mess, Aunt Martha."

"Never you mind." Martha offered a plate piled high with treats. "Have some fudge."

Amos. She blinked. *Not Levi. Amos.*

Flashing a gap-toothed grin, the boy took a huge hunk. "Merry Christmas."

His cheek was smooth and supple. His jaw was just starting to harden into a man's. He couldn't be more than seventeen years old—this boy—her cousin's son. If Levi were still alive, he'd be…what, thirty-five? Was such an age possible? She turned thirty-one last July so, yes. Thirty-five, indeed.

Flapping and whirling, Rebecca skated stocking-footed through the icy water. "We're playing charades. Guess who I am."

Amos crossed his arms over his heavy, wool coat and tilted his head. "A goose?"

Wee Isaac jumped up. "I told you!"

With a sigh, Rebecca rolled her eyes. "Don't any of you know the Angel of the Lord when you see her?"

"It's a good thing the shepherds did," Uncle Moses cracked.

Uncle Eli guffawed.

Nora could see Levi at seventeen as clearly as she saw this boy. He'd been taller than Amos and skinnier, with a long-limbed ease that made every gesture appear effortless. She swiped at her eyes with the back of a hand. Grief was a sneaky snake. It crept up when she least expected and sank its fangs deep in her heart. Shaking her head as if she could banish tears forever, she sniffed and clenched her fists. The pie. She'd take that pie from the oven or break her other hip trying. Planting both hands on the chair arms, she labored to her feet with no less difficulty than Aunt Martha.

Rebecca spun, her fair brows knit, and opened her mouth to speak.

With a glare and a quick flick of the wrist, Nora silenced her.

Great-aunt Ruth scrabbled for something under her chair. "For goodness sake, Nora. Take my cane."

The rubber-tipped monstrosity stabbed at Nora's face, narrowly missing her nose. She batted it away. "For the last time, Ruth, I don't want it!" A collective gasp sucked the oxygen from the room. If the candles hadn't been battery-powered, they would have snuffed at once.

Aunt Ruth recoiled, whacking the cane into a magazine rack, which toppled, spewing newspapers across the floor.

Lips pressed in a thin line, *Mamm* leveled her with a glare.

Blood thrummed in her ears. Twining her fingers in her apron, she reeled and stormed into the kitchen.

Like black-capped chickadees around a suet ball, five teenage girls knelt at the table, whispering and giggling, oblivious to the scene in the sitting room.

Catching sight of her, one bird stilled and nudged her neighbor. Instantly, the twittering ceased.

Nora placed a steadying palm on the counter. "Your pie is burning."

Katie Mast pointed at the timer. "It has five

minutes yet."

"In five minutes, it will be black as charcoal and just as tasty. Take it out now, or we'll have no pumpkin pie for Christmas dinner."

The girl lowered her chin and raised arched brows. "Shouldn't you be resting, Nora?"

Though spoken with concern, Katie's question was a blatant dig. Nora stiffened. "Shall I do it for you?"

Katie glanced across the table at her cousin.

The girl shrugged and swallowed a smile.

Another cousin picked a fingernail, while her stone-faced sister untied and retied her apron. The final member of the quintet stared Nora full in the face with a mixture of pity and contempt.

Glaringly bright, the ceiling lights hissed even more loudly than the ones in the sitting room. The timer ticked an erratic rhythm, signaling its uselessness as loudly as if the thing had spoken.

A trickle of perspiration snaked between Nora's shoulder blades.

Sucking her bottom lip with a smack, Katie slid from the chair, threw open the oven door, and dropped the pie onto a trivet. "It's fine."

The edges were dark as molasses, and the filling was a piebald mix of orange and brown. Edible...but barely. "It's burnt."

The girls contorted their faces too late to hide mocking smiles.

"Katie, your brother's come to take you home." Grabbing her coat from a peg, Nora flung wide the back door and fled into the cold, dark night.

"It's burnt," Katie echoed in a tone a little too like the one still ringing in her ears. Stifled tittering floated outside through the cracked-open window.

The three steps down from the kitchen felt like thirty—each more painful than the last. More painful even than being offered her great aunt's cane. Less painful, though, than the knowledge she needed the ghastly thing. The squall that dusted Amos's coat had blown eastward, leaving an inky sky pricked with cut-glass stars. Clinging to the banister, she descended the final stair on her good leg and swung the stiff one from behind.

Two inches of powdery snow lay over the barnyard, providing just enough traction to traverse the icy spots to the corral. At least she was alone. No one hovered for fear she'd fall. Moving with ginger steps, she took all the time she needed to make the trek. One foot…then another. The full moon lit her path like an overhead streetlamp in the parking lot of an English store. Clenching her jaw, she pursed her lips and eyed the ground for frozen ruts and icy patches.

Despite the frigid air, by the time she reached the fence, her palms were slick. Panting, she hooked her elbows over the rail and lowered her forehead onto her arms. How long before she couldn't walk to the barn? Or make it downstairs from her bedroom? How long before she'd have to accept that cane? Eyes closed, she sent up a wordless prayer, more feeling than thought. She tried to open her heart, but her chest squeezed tight. How long could she keep asking for strength? For guidance? For healing?

Mrs. Beiler, I can help you. A surgical procedure to replace your hip…

Penny nudged her cheek with a warm, oaty huff.

She lifted her head and gazed into the creature's

eyes, almost human in their kindness. This horse was the only living being to look at her without pity in months. She chuckled and pulled from her coat pocket a small, misshapen apple salvaged from the morning's baking. "You know me too well."

Whickering, Penny nuzzled her palm, snatching the apple in a velvety bite.

She ran her fingers over the horse's forelock and down her silky nose. "I'll miss you."

A surgical procedure to replace your hip...

Her sigh crystallized in a cloud.

The Christmas vigil was waiting. As a girl, she waited with jittery excitement for the annual Christmas program when she and her fellow scholars would recite poems, sing songs, and tell funny stories for their families before exchanging small presents with classmates and their schoolteacher. Then followed an endless night waiting for Christmas morning and *Mamm's* scrumptious breakfast. With maple-syrup-sticky fingers and the taste of bacon on their tongues, she and her brothers would dash upstairs to wait some more. Like wiggly puppies, they fidgeted on the landing, peeking over the banister while her parents deposited a gift at each of their places and games for everyone in the center of the table and covered everything with dishcloths. How painfully thrilling waiting was in those days.

Many years later, as heavy with child as Mary, she waited for the baby who would arrive only five nights hence. Unable to sleep, she had peeped out the window like she did as a girl, waiting for the Star of Bethlehem to appear in a flash of blinding glory.

Leaning heavily into the fence, she shifted more

weight onto her right leg and swiveled her left ankle. How quickly dampness seeped beneath her skin. Her elbow dug into the wooden rail, and she flinched. She was so skinny these days, her bones seemed constantly to jab doorframes and seat backs. Lifting her cheeks, she searched once again for the star.

And still, Nora waited. She waited for a dead husband to come in from the cold and for a daughter to cast off foolish ways. She waited to feel like herself again. She waited for miracles. She waited without hope.

A cheerful voice from the front yard shattered the stillness. It was echoed by another and yet another as her family bid farewell to Amos and Katie. The jingle of harnesses was followed by the muffled crunch of buggy wheels in the snow. The front door banged, and Amos's and Katie's laughter danced on the wind. Then silence settled over the farm again.

The air was crisp as a fresh-picked apple doused in creek water. The truth was crystalline as the stars. She needed no sign from Heaven or beacon in the sky. Her message came from within. She was lamer than this mare, and if she didn't want to be in a wheelchair at the age of thirty-two, she had only one choice.

Three years ago, as her daughter lay in a hospital bed, recovering from the meningitis she contracted right here on this Ohio farm, an English doctor pulled her aside. He just saved her child's life. Now, he claimed he could save hers, too.

Mrs. Beiler, I can help you. A surgical procedure to replace your hip provides a chance to recover full mobility. With rehab and a lot of work, you could walk as well as you did before the accident.

Planting both feet firmly, she moved her weight to her left leg, breathing through pain as she breathed through labor ten years before. Fingers numb, she gripped the splintered fencepost and decided.

No more waiting. Nora Beiler was going home.

Chapter One

Green Ridge, Pennsylvania. Nine months later

Between visits, Nora forgot just how cool the Covered Bridge Medical Clinic was. Walking into Dr. Richard Bruce's air-conditioned office after a morning of sweaty farm work was as refreshing as jumping into the spring-fed swimming hole behind the west field. Forgetting the relief of instant comfort was like forgetting the warmth of a husband's embrace. If she let herself remember, how could she live without it? Forgetting was the only way to leave it behind.

Dr. Richard released her left ankle and drew a sheet across her stockinged legs. "Excellent, Nora. You've regained much of your strength, and your hip is moving exactly as it should three months post-surgery."

She lifted onto both elbows and stared at her legs. They extended in straight lines like twin, snow-covered ridges. She flexed her left ankle and wiggled her toes, amazed by her body's ability to heal. Looking at it now, she could hardly remember how misshapen and short her left leg was for so many years after the accident.

The doctor sat on a stool, rolled to the desk in a smooth swoosh, and typed on a computer keyboard. "Never fear." He nodded toward a manila folder. "Your record will be updated in the paper file, as well as in our electronic system. Cindy, please help up Nora."

Nurse Cindy's expectant belly loomed large. A simple cotton shirt covered in pink and purple butterflies pulled taut over her girth. Clad in squishy-looking purple shoes, her ankles and feet swelled against the plastic strap and through the holes pocking the top surface. Her sparkly wedding rings cut into sausage-like fingers. Clasping Cindy's hand, Nora flinched, expecting a stab of discomfort when she rose, but with little help, she came painlessly upright. Relief unclenched her jaw. After years of worsening pain followed by hip replacement surgery, anticipatory wincing was a habit as automatic as squinting into the sun. She was still surprised when the slightest movement didn't hurt. As surprising, however, was how quickly the memory of that pain was fading. So, why did she still walk with a limp?

Bracing a hand on the small of her back, Nurse Cindy waddled to her husband and jotted a note on Nora's chart. She expelled a long, slow breath.

Dr. Richard shot his wife a concerned glance.

The woman's time was near. Gazing at Nurse Cindy, she struggled to remember what carrying Rebecca felt like. Now and again, when a muscle beneath her eye twitched, she remembered the sensation of a baby kicking.

Reading by the fire on those frosty autumn evenings, Levi had always noted the quick intake of breath that indicated a firm kick. He dashed to the kitchen and returned with the big old wooden spoon she used to make apple butter. Balancing it on her stomach, he watched, entranced, as it rocked like a boat on a stormy sea. Without fail, Levi flexed his arm muscles. "He's strong like his daddy."

Just as often, she had slid him a teasing smile. "Yes. She is."

She ran a hand over her firm, hollow belly. If anything, she weighed less now than she did when she was wedded. Ten years had passed since Rebecca was born. A whole lifetime. Now, the second her cheek stopped twitching, she forgot the feeling of life moving inside her. If she were honest, she hadn't felt alive inside for a very long time.

"Want to see your new hip?" The stool creaked, and the doctor rolled aside to reveal the computer monitor.

On the screen was a fuzzy, black-and-white image of what looked like a glowing mushroom sitting cockeyed atop a flagpole.

Dr. Richard pointed with a ballpoint pen. "A textbook surgery. Perfect."

She flushed and dropped her gaze. Photographs were forbidden in her community's *Ordnung* of Amish rules, but surely an X-ray was acceptable, albeit somewhat unnatural. She peeked beneath her lashes. Her insides shone, clean and bright. She stared at the smooth, ceramic dome of the artificial hip. After so many years, she, Nora Beiler, was perfect. At least, her bones were. "The operation worked?"

"Like a charm."

"And I won't need another one?"

With a smile, he shook his head. "The doctor who performed your emergency surgery did a fine job under the circumstances. He had every right to expect the pin would fix your break. But sometimes life throws us a curveball."

"A curveball?"

He chuckled. "I know an old Yiddish saying: 'Man plans, and God laughs.' " He held up a hand. "Not that I think God would ever mock us. Rather, life doles out one surprise after the next. When you and I first met, I never imagined the day I'd see you in my own clinic for a post-op visit after a total hip replacement. Yet, here we are." He caught Cindy's gaze and smiled. "Here we are."

Cheeks pinking, Cindy plopped her hands on her hips, and the gold hoops in her ears shimmied, catching the light. "You're good as new."

Dr. Richard swiveled back to the keyboard. "You have no residual pain?"

Nora shifted, and the paper atop the exam table crinkled. "Not much. Sometimes in the morning."

"Perfectly normal. Full recovery can take up to a year. Are you strong enough to work?"

Gelassenheit. Let it be. She'd been taught that principle from childhood. Accept with gladness. Don't complain. Be happy with your lot. Given the severity of her injury, a life without chronic pain seemed almost more than she had a right to ask for. To ask also for the strength of her youth and the endurance to stand at the stove as she did before the accident? She smoothed the table cover with a hand. Of course, if she really lived in a spirit of *Gelassenheit* she would never have had surgery to begin with. She nodded.

"Are you certain?" the doctor went on.

"Yes."

"All right then. Case closed." The computer keyboard issued a series of soft clicks, and tiny letters flashed across the screen.

She closed her eyes. The rhythmic sound was

strangely soothing. She heard a soft grunt, and the cushioned exam table dipped beside her. An exotic floral scent supplanted the medicinal smell of the office. Opening her eyes, she found Cindy gazing at her.

The nurse placed a gentle hand on her forearm. "How about your baking, honey?"

Nora would never dream of calling a casual acquaintance, "honey." Somehow though, when Cindy did, she didn't mind. The words rolled off her tongue in a sugar sweet accent that, though not belonging to the valley where Nora grew up, still warmed her inside.

Cindy's fingers tightened. "Can you stand in the kitchen as long as you need?"

That question cut too deep. Resisting an urge to pull away, she pursed her lips. "Well enough."

"You can bake all morning and still feel strong enough to do the rest of the cooking and cleaning? How many are you feeding?"

Nora swept a hand down her apron front, flattening the wrinkles. "Just my mother and daughter and my younger brother, Samuel. Sometimes the Lapp boys from next door or other folks who come to visit. But my mother and Rebecca share the work." She met Cindy's gaze. These two *Englischers* were different from the fancy folks she encountered every week at the Farmers' Market. When she first met Dr. Richard that horrible night he came to the farm and saved Rebecca's life, she thought he was exactly like the rest. He seemed arrogant and pushy, convinced he knew everything, and she, simple Nora Beiler, was an ignorant fool. But she soon discovered her first impression was wrong. He was a lifesaver. Oh, he was English through and through, and he still thought he knew everything. But he was kind. After working with her family, he opened this clinic to serve her Plain community and others like it. His heart was in the right place.

He spun, one dark brow raised.

She shifted her gaze from Cindy to Richard. They were rare, these two. Perhaps the only two *Englischers* who didn't think the world belonged to them and them alone.

Cindy released her arm. "Your hip feels fine through all that work? Not giving you a lick of trouble?"

She stared at the computer screen. A cluster of twinkling stars floating among iridescent clouds filled the monitor with such clarity she felt like she could walk right into it. "I hate to complain. My hip is head and shoulders better than when I first came to you. But I feel weak. I feel…" She started, surprised at sudden tears prickling the corners of her eyes. Blinking, she wiped a hand across her face and flipped the strings of her prayer *kapp* over her shoulders. She refused to cry in front of Dr. Richard and Nurse Cindy, no matter how kind they were. "I'm sorry."

"Don't you worry, honey." Nurse Cindy looped an arm around her waist and pulled her tight.

Nora flinched and scooted to the far end of the table, clasping her hands in her lap. Nurse Cindy was the type of person who flung an arm around people willy-nilly. Nora Beiler, most definitely, was not. She stared at her interlaced fingers. From the corner of her eye, she saw Dr. Richard shoot Cindy a look.

Cindy mouthed the words, *I'm sorry* and slid to the floor with a heavy thump. Thrusting her chin toward the door, she lifted an open hand.

Dr. Richard shook his head. "Nora, how bad is your pain? On a scale from one to ten?"

"Two? Maybe three? But I don't hurt all the time. Usually when rain's coming."

Standing, he put his hands on his hips and gazed down his nose. "Three?"

Feeling suddenly like a lightning bug trapped in a jar, she shrugged. "Four at the worst. The pain doesn't trouble me. What troubles me…" Her voice cracked. She put a hand to her middle and took a steadying breath. The artificially cool air smelled like store-bought cleanser and rubbing alcohol with a hint of Cindy's flowers. "What troubles me is that I don't have my strength back. I hoped by now I'd feel like my old self again."

Cindy shifted her weight, and her shoes squeaked. "Have you been doing your exercises?"

She nodded, and then stopped, unwilling to stretch the truth. "Occasionally. I don't have much time to myself."

Cindy sighed and rested her hands atop her belly. "Oh, honey, we women never have that luxury. But you need to take care of yourself for your family, as well as for you."

Dr. Richard picked up a pad and a pen. "I'll write you a prescription for ten weeks of physical therapy at the hospital clinic."

She thought of the driver waiting in the parking lot. He'd taxied her family for years, charging as little as he possibly could. Still, money was tight, and his service wasn't free. "I can't bike to the hospital without traveling busy roads." The image of a truck screaming down the highway flashed unbidden in her mind. She shivered and clutched the exam table.

Cindy snapped pink-tipped fingers. "What about the senior center? They offer all manner of fitness and exercise classes. The center is right off the town bike path—you can access that easily, right?"

The bike path ran half a mile from the family farm she, her mother, and brother had reclaimed after Jonas leased it to the Lapps and left. She could easily pedal the distance from home. But the *senior center*? Tears welled yet again. Did she endure major surgery and a painful recovery only to be lumped in with old folks once more? "But…I'm only thirty-two."

Cindy's glossy lips stretched into a smile. She giggled and tucked a bouncy, blonde curl behind one ear. "Oh, I know, but I'm sure they'll make an exception. My grandma attends a class every week, and she loves it. Why, those old folks would be so happy to spend time with a young person, your company would practically be a Christian service." She nudged Dr. Richard with her backside. "Move over, darlin'. Let me at the computer."

The doctor sprang to his feet. "And that's my cue. Nora, I leave you in my wife's capable hands. If you dedicate time to building up your strength, as I'm certain you will, we should have no cause to see you anytime soon." He smiled. "Though you're always welcome."

"Biking is all right? It won't hurt my hip?"

"Better than all right. You get back on your bicycle—safely, mind you—and into a fitness class, and you'll make a full recovery." He pulled a mobile phone from his pocket and studied the screen. "The afternoon's schedule is light, Cindy. Go home early. Soak your feet."

Cindy barked a laugh. "Not on your life, mister. This baby isn't coming for another two weeks. I'm not going anywhere."

Richard looked from Cindy to Nora and back again. "What can I say? I tried." He squeezed his wife's shoulder and left.

Cindy took the computer keyboard. "Men. Am I right? Imagine if they had the babies—the whole world would come screeching to a halt."

English women had no shame. Cindy talked about reproduction like she was swapping recipes. Nora gave a tight-lipped smile.

Squinting at the screen, Cindy tapped a nail on the desk. "Let me see… The center started their fall session last week, so you haven't missed much. At church on Sunday, my grandma was raving about her class. Can't remember what it was called, of course." She thwacked the side of her head with the heel of her hand. "Mommy brain. Please tell me it goes away." She laughed. "I know Nanny's class is Tuesday nights at seven… Ah, here it is—Shuffle Off to Fitness with Jerry Six Herbert—now that's a name to remember. Can I go ahead and sign you up?"

Nora hadn't attended a formal class since the eighth grade. Work was her fitness regimen. Chores were her exercise. If she couldn't regain her strength on a farm, she couldn't regain it anywhere. Fully prepared to decline, she slid to the floor, landing hard on her left foot. Her hip locked, and her knee buckled in a painful twist. With an awkward half spin, she caught herself on the exam table and drew slowly upright.

Cindy's expression softened. "Admitting you need help is hard, but if you don't rehab properly, you'll never get stronger. The class is free. Covered Bridge has a relationship with the Center—it's all taken care of. Nanny and her friends are sweet old ladies. You'll enjoy it."

Nora stepped into her sturdy black sneakers. She missed boots, but she had to admit the cushioned shoes she'd worn since the surgery felt like clouds on her feet. She stared down at the laces. They looked a mile away.

Cindy swiveled and yanked a stepstool, sliding it between her knees. "Give me your foot."

She hesitated. Despite her recovery, tying her shoes was a nearly impossible task. Still, to have someone do it for her was humiliating. She made a move for the chair on the opposite side of the room.

"Come on." Cindy patted the rubberized surface. "It's my job."

With a ghost of the limp that haunted her for seven years, she shuffled toward Cindy, shoelaces dragging, and lifted her left foot onto the stepstool. With a slight wobble, she reached for the laces.

Cindy shooed away her hands. "I got you." She executed an efficient double knot and patted the sides of Nora's foot. "Now, give me the right. I know this one's harder. Hang onto me for balance."

Nora hesitated.

"Don't be shy."

Taking hold of Cindy's broad shoulder, she teetered on her left leg and offered her right shoe. Lickety-split she was back on two feet. She met Cindy's gaze and smiled. "You'll make a wonderful *gut* mother."

"You think so?" Cindy reeled and fanned her eyes. "Hoo-ee, I'm sorry. I'm so emotional these days. Thank you. I needed to hear that." Pooching her lower lip, she blew out a breath. "Now, can I sign you up for class? I promise, you won't regret it."

Nora gave a quick nod and left the Covered Bridge Clinic for what she hoped was the last time in a long while. Stepping out of the air-conditioned building, she glanced at the printed paper confirming her enrollment in Shuffle Off to Fitness at the Green Ridge Senior Center.

Won't regret it?

She scrunched the paper and shoved it deep into her bag.

She regretted it already.

Chapter Two

The kitchen wall clock chimed six. Nora wiped her hands on a dish towel and looped it over the oven handle to dry. Her fingers trembled as she pulled at the bow behind her waist, accidentally tightening it into a knot. How had Tuesday night arrived so quickly?

In a rush, Rebecca swiped a plate and dropped it in the rinse pan where it clattered against another dish. "I'm almost finished. If I hurry, can I come, too?"

She tugged loose the ties and slipped off the work apron. "No."

Rebecca yanked the plate from the sink, spraying sudsy rinse water all over herself, the cabinets, and Nora's clean dress. "Please?"

Biting back a rebuke, she slung the apron over a hook and smoothed her skirt. "No."

"But I can do fitness, too. Want to see?" With a leap, the girl took off, racing in circles around the big oak table and chairs.

With every step, the china in the hutch shook, and the ceiling light trembled. Nora jumped aside as her daughter streaked, arms pumping, narrowly avoiding the corner of the stove.

"I can jog just like those English ladies in their track suits." She skidded to a stop, dropped the plate on the counter, and launched into energetic jumping jacks. "And I can do exercises, too. Please let me come."

She clasped her hands at her waist, closed her eyes, and counted. *Eens, zwee, drei, vier, fimf.* Lately, Rebecca's exuberance did nothing but annoy her. Where was the child's modesty? Then again, where was her own patience? She opened her eyes to a flushed face full of hope. "Don't slip on the wet floor."

Rebecca bounced on bare toes. "But, *Mamm*—"

Nora held out a hand. "Enough. Mind *Mammi* Verna and be in bed asleep when I get home."

"Fine." Rebecca slumped against the counter. "But can I go out back to Samuel's workshop when I finish the dishes?"

Even hunched over, she nearly bumped the bottoms of the upper cabinets with her white-blonde head. The child grew faster than summer sweet corn. "As long as you don't pester him."

Rebecca's eyes flashed. "Samuel doesn't think I'm a bother..."

Even if you do. Her daughter's insolent gaze completed the sentence without words. Nora held up a finger in warning, and an expression of docility just this side of impudence settled over the child's delicate features. Those robin's-egg-blue eyes came from her side of the family. But the rest of the girl? The quick, wide smile, the impish, upturned nose, and the impertinent, dimpled chin? They were all her father's. Rebecca was almost eleven years old. At her age, Nora needed no adult to admonish her into good behavior. She would no sooner have disobeyed as she would have leapt from a moving buggy. But this girl-child... To think, at one point, she prayed for a houseful of girls. She needed to consider future prayers carefully.

Very carefully. She prayed for God's healing hand,

and in answer, Nurse Cindy coerced her into a fitness class with a bunch of English senior citizens. If she could have sent her daughter instead, she would have done so gladly. She left the girl singing and drying dishes and fetched her bicycle. As she rolled open the door and wheeled her beloved, cherry-red three-speed out of the barn, she felt her stomach knot pretzel-like.

Sitting on the front porch bench, *Mamm* set aside a bowl of green beans. The late summer harvest was fat and woody, but it would serve for winter stews and soups. Still strong as a draft horse and almost as tall, the matriarch of the Rishel family came to her feet more slowly than she used. She pressed her hands to her lower back and rolled her shoulders. In the golden evening light, her blue dress against white clapboard was bright as a ripe blueberry.

Mamm shook her apron with a snap. "You haven't changed your mind, I suppose."

"I have not." Her stomach tightened. Could *Mamm* see her nerves, shimmering like heat off hot pavement? She needed to leave before her mother convinced her not to go.

"You look tired."

She pushed the bike between flower beds and into the drive. "This class will make me stronger."

"Dr. Richard said that, did he?"

Tucking up her skirt, she stepped one foot over the frame. "Nurse Cindy."

Mamm wrinkled her nose. "Pushy woman." She came down the steps and jutted her chin at the bicycle. "We're not in Ohio anymore. I hate to think what would happen if Deacon Elmer caught you riding. You'd be better off on a scooter."

She scowled. Those Lancaster-style kick scooters were essentially bicycles with no seats or pedals—only flat boards anchored low between the wheels. They were all she knew growing up and all her district *Ordnung* permitted. Why, she'd have to stand on her left leg and kick with her right the entire eight miles to the senior center. She shook her head. "I'd never make it."

Learning to ride a bike made those dreadful years in Holmes County bearable. Despite constant hip pain, the first time she pedaled out of Uncle Moses' steadying hold, accelerating all the way down the flat farm lane, she felt like an eagle soaring over an endless valley.

Never in her life had she knowingly transgressed the *Ordnung*. When she was growing up, the rules made sense, and she was happy to obey. The *Ordnung* provided order, simplifying life by eliminating confusing choices. Now? Well, if Deacon Elmer tried to take away her bicycle, he'd have to go through her first. Besides, Dr. Richard said she needed it to recover. All sorts of exceptions to the rules were made for medical reasons. She gripped the handlebars. "I better go. I'll be late."

Pushing up her small, round glasses, *Mamm* gazed out over the fields. "Never expected I'd see you willingly mix with the English."

"Well, things change." Her words came out more sharply than she intended.

With a deep sigh, *Mamm* let the harsh tone pass. "Believe me, I know. Now, Jonas on the other hand?"

A sharp inhalation hissed between her teeth. Her older brother's name was like a raspberry thorn piercing her skin. She stared at her feet, wishing her mother would stop mentioning him. Why couldn't she just let him go? She glanced up again. A wistful smile spanned her mother's cheeks like an upside-down rainbow. Then again, not every mother would have the courage to keep a shunned child alive in her heart. Verna Rishel had the strength of twenty men.

Turning, *Mamm* sharpened her gaze. "Jonas would go to an English class in a heartbeat. Samuel would be hot on his heels, and that daughter of yours would squeeze into his coat pocket to join them. But you?" She shook her head. "That you're here on your bicycle at six o'clock of a Tuesday tells me all I need to know. Take care of your hip, but be careful. Don't forget who you are."

The pretzel in her stomach added another loop. Why was she the only Rishel without an adventurous bone in her body? Setting her jaw, she met her mother's gaze. "I won't." With the September breeze at her back, still sweet and heavy with summer's bounty, Nora tromped on the pedals and set out to exercise with a bunch of senior citizens.

****

Slack-jawed, Nora stared at a pair of shiny black shoes with ribbons where the laces should be. The wall clock above the door to the exercise studio ticked off seconds with hollow clunks. She wanted nothing more than to dash beneath it, race out the front door, and ride home as fast as her legs would carry her.

"Can you make do with sevens?" The teacher, Jerry Six Herbert, wiped a smudge from the top of one shoe.

Nora glanced up, catching her own gray eyes in

28

floor-to-ceiling mirrors. She never in her life saw herself in a full-length mirror, let alone one that covered an entire wall. A few shades darker than her eyes, her dress was wrinkled from the ride, but the silver pins at her waist glinted clean and straight in the fluorescent light. A few strands of dark blonde hair escaped her bun and fell from beneath her gauzy *kapp*. With shaky fingers, she tucked them up. Eight faces, lined and wrinkled to varying degrees, stared at her reflection in the glass. She wet her lips, wishing she'd grabbed a drink from the water fountain in the hall.

"Is she in the right class?" a tiny, white-haired lady boomed.

How could such a large voice come from such a small person?

A bear of a man with a salt-and-pepper mustache scowled. "Turn on your hearing aids, Edna."

Nora took the shoes. They smelled of old leather and talcum powder. "I don't understand. I thought this was an exercise class." Her voice was small and breathy in the big, unfurnished room.

A woman with short, cinnamon-colored hair came beside her, her feet clicking with every step. She smiled. "It is, honey. Shuffle Off to Fitness is a dance fitness class. We tap dance."

"Dance?" Her throat constricted, and the single word came out as a squeak. Her bicycle was maybe permissible, but dancing was altogether too worldly for their Plain community.

Jerry Six Herbert flashed a smile. "That's right. We were delighted when Joan's granddaughter, Cindy, called and said you'd join us."

The woman who called her "honey" wiggled her

fingers in a wave.

"When done by professionals, tap is a strenuous workout," Jerry went on. "But I keep our class light and fun. It's a wonderful, weight-bearing exercise and great for your memory—of course, a young girl like you doesn't have to worry about that. We'll have your hip good as new in no time." With lightning speed, she executed a series of dance steps.

The rhythmic *rat-a-tat* of her shoes echoed like cheerful firecrackers. Her ankles looked to be made of rubber, and her feet moved so quickly Nora couldn't follow them.

Jerry finished with a twirl, opening her palms with fingers splayed and fluttering them like butterfly wings.

When the class burst into applause, Nora joined in.

Jerry wiped her brow. "Born before my time. Now they have girls of every color and background tapping on that big New York City stage at Christmastime. But back in the sixties and seventies? No, ma'am."

A woman with a poufy hairdo and a blousy floral top brushed aside the comment with a huff. "Their loss. Besides, if you'd stayed in New York, you would never have married Glen."

"And come to teach us," Joan added.

Jerry Six Herbert narrowed chocolate-brown eyes and nodded. "The Lord works in mysterious ways."

"Is she in the wrong class?" the tiny white-haired woman said even louder.

The grizzled man cupped his hands around his mouth. "Your. Hearing. Aids. Are. Off."

The woman opened her eyes wide. "Oh." She fiddled with a device in her ear, and a high-pitched squeal emanated from her head.

"Oh dear, Edna." Grimacing, the poufy haired woman covered her ears.

The piercing whistle amplified, rose in pitch, and then abruptly silenced. The ground beneath Nora's feet swayed. She rarely flushed, but blood rushed to her cheeks like a runaway train. "Perhaps I should go."

The poufy-haired lady pointed at the grizzly bear man. "Get her a chair."

He stuck a questioning thumb in his chest and drew his bushy eyebrows together.

"Yes, you, Hank McClure." The lady plunked balled fists on her hips. "Please bring our young friend a chair so she can put on her shoes, and we can start."

Grumbling, the man dragged a folding chair across the room and opened it. "Here you are, ma'am."

The class chatted softly in groups of twos and threes. Nora felt her shoulders creep toward her ears. What were they saying? Were they talking about her?

Jerry clapped her hands. "How about we all start seated? Pull up chairs, everyone."

A panicked impulse to run zinged in Nora's chest. Nurse Cindy signed her up for a tap-dancing class? How could she? Cindy knew her people didn't dance. Didn't she? She darted a look to the door and back toward her classmates, all of whom stared expectantly.

The gentleman who toted her chair cleared his throat.

She sat. Honestly, she wasn't sure she'd make it to the door without her legs giving out.

Joan took a seat beside her. "Don't worry. They won't bite. Well, I can't vouch for Hank." She nodded to the grizzled gentleman. "But the rest are pussycats. Do the shoes fit?"

The shoes dangled from her hand. She studied the women's feet. Some wore high-heeled shoes with shiny silver buckles. Some had regular shoes that looked much like the men's. Jerry Six Herbert's were silver and strappy and sported three-inch heels.

"My lands, it's hot." The poufy-haired lady lowered herself on Nora's other side with a muffled "oomph" and lifted her blouse from her neck. "I'm Marion Diefenderfer."

She gave off a scent like when the lilies were near to wilting. Nora forced a smile. "Nora Beiler."

"What are you waiting for?" Marion pointed at the shoes. "Try them on."

The class assembled, completing the circle she and the two women started. Her mouth was dry as cotton. She swallowed hard. Almost of its own accord, the toe of her right foot connected with the heel of her left and kicked off her sneaker. She slipped into the shiny shoe and pushed down, scraping her heel over the stiff back. Accustomed to spending half her life barefoot, she'd never put on a more uncomfortable shoe.

Joan peered at her feet. "Too small?"

Marion caught Jerry's attention with a wave. "Cinderella needs a bigger slipper. Do we have an eight in the supply closet?"

Jerry rose and skipped across the room in a series of hopping steps that rang with quick, cheerful clicks.

Though her dark skin stretched smooth over high cheekbones, Nora knew she couldn't be young. What did she say about dancing in New York in the nineteen seventies? Jerry was likely older than her mother and nearly as tall, but she bounced to the closet with girlish lightness. Oh, to float across a room. To feel airy as a puff of milkweed floss. To smile without a care in the world.

Jerry emerged from the closet with another pair of shoes.

Edna scurried across the room and joined her, tapping in perfect lockstep.

If anything, Edna was older than Jerry, but both women grinned ear to ear, looking like giddy companions skipping off to their first youth singing.

The replacement shoes were black leather loafers with regular laces. Aside from having metal plates on the toes and heels, they might have passed for shoes worn by any number of women in Nora's district.

"We keep a whole mess of spares in the closet," Jerry said. "Just in case."

The soft leather hugged her foot like the shoes were made for her.

Joan leaned close. "Better?"

She nodded. "But I can't—"

"Good." Jerry took a seat. "Let's begin."

An hour later, Nora flew from the senior center, more exhilarated than she'd been in years and certain beyond doubt she would never dance again. Mere moments ago, she'd thrust the tap shoes into Jerry Six Herbert's hands. "You've all been so kind, and I've enjoyed myself tremendously, but I can't—I mean—I won't…I have to go home."

Jerry's eyes rounded. "Are you all right?"

Even glistening with perspiration, the woman smelled of coconut oil and cinnamon—a friendly, welcoming scent reminding Nora of home. She pressed her lips and nodded.

Jerry took Nora's hand and gave it a soft squeeze.

"I'll see you next class."

Avoiding eye contact with her classmates, Nora bolted for the door.

"And Nora?" Jerry called.

In the doorway, she paused and looked over one shoulder.

"You've got rhythm. If I didn't know better, I'd say you've been dancing your whole life."

Nora blanched. Amish girls weren't supposed to have rhythm. She bobbed her head in polite acknowledgement and lifted her lips in a bittersweet smile. Then she fled.

Edna's booming voice followed her into the hall. "That Plain girl sure can dance."

In her haste to leave, Nora was only belatedly aware of how quickly she moved. Since when could she walk so fast? And so smoothly? She pushed out the door and raced across the parking lot, heart pounding in her throat. Now that September had arrived, the sun set earlier. The sky glowed violet, and an evening breeze cooled the sweat-slick skin above her collar. She'd get on her bike, ride home, and forget this night ever happened. Housework provided more than enough opportunity to strengthen her muscles. She didn't need any class.

Her footsteps across the gravel were drowned by cricket song. Never in her life had she heard so much secular music. Tinkling pianos and blaring trumpets echoed in her head until she thought she might try the dance steps again right there in the parking lot. She pressed her lips and drove the melodies from her mind, but her efforts were no use. Even the crickets sounded like music.

A forest-green pickup truck was backed up to the bicycle rack, blocking her path. The vehicle was boxy with shiny silver wheels and a thick white stripe along the side. Unlike Samuel, she made a point to learn nothing about cars, but even she could tell this one was old. The wide-spaced front lights and swooping, silver bumper almost seemed to smile. Still hearing music, she caught sight of the bike rack, and her breath caught in her throat.

Her bicycle was gone.

Did someone steal it? Lurching, she rounded the truck and searched again. A glimpse of cherry red frame offered momentary relief, giving way to simmering ire that bubbled in the pit of her stomach like a pot of half-cooked applesauce.

On the flopped-down gate of the truck, a lanky man in faded jeans and a plaid shirt hunched over a guitar. His legs extended long and crossed at the ankles. His dirty brown boots rested squarely on the seat of her bike.

Chapter Three

Nora balled her skirt in iron fists and stared.

Shaggy, dark head bent low, the man plucked a simple melody, the notes fading into traffic sounds from the nearby street.

What to do? She couldn't just yank the bike from under his feet. She darted a glance at the door. Her classmates would arrive any second, and she wanted to be long gone before they did. Sweeping her hands down her skirt, she spun back to the man. Her hip twinged, and ten unspoken rebukes ricocheted in her head. This whole evening had her completely rattled. All she wanted was to be back on the front porch with her mother, stringing beans. With two shuffling steps, she drew up beside the bike and laced her arms across her chest.

"Looking for someone?" Keeping his gaze on the instrument, he slowed his fingers and brushed them in one smooth stroke over the strings.

A rich, resonant chord sounded of sunset and the last days of summer. "No." She laid one hand on a handlebar and shook it.

"Stick around and I might charge admission."

Another chord followed with a tone so bright and true she felt her ribs sing in harmony. She snugged her arms against her chest to dull the vibrations. This whole evening was too much—the class and the music and the dancing and now, this smart aleck cowboy with his filthy boots slung on her bike like he owned it. How typical. The English believed themselves entitled to everything. Those kindly old folks in the exercise class almost convinced her otherwise. How wrong she was.

She jerked the handlebar hard.

His feet slid, and he lunged sideways. With a twang, the music cut off, and the guitar banged against the truck bed. A loose strand of black hair flopped over his forehead.

He swiped it away and gazed sidelong with eyes the color of mossy stones. Seeming only now to clock her plain garb, his brows lifted. His gaze trailed down her body and back to her face, in a look more admiring than curious.

His lips twisted in a wry smile. "Didn't like the song, huh?"

She swept a clump of dirt from the seat and brushed together her hands.

"I mean, plenty of people don't like my music, but none of them ever went so far as to knock me over."

"I didn't—"

"You know, you could have just asked me to stop." He swept back his hair and straightened, pulling the guitar across his body.

She opened her mouth, closed it, and then opened it again. "The song was fine—"

"Now, that's more like it."

"—but my bicycle isn't your footstool." Wrenching the handlebars again, she yanked free the bike. The truck was so close to the rack she barely had room to maneuver.

"My apologies." He tilted his head and gazed

upward. "Pretty sky, huh?"

The streetlamps flickered on, catching the two of them in a circle of light.

He struck a loud, jangling chord and began to sing. "My bike is not your footstool, the lady said to me." The chord died, and his voice trailed off. "You like that song any better?"

Was he mocking her? She clamped her jaw and glared. A rascally gleam flickered in his eyes.

"I believe you do." He launched into a fast and folksy tune. "My bike is not your footstool, the lady said to me. She whacked me with a ham bone and kicked me in the knee."

She gripped the handlebars with whitened fingers. "I did no such thing."

"Oh, I know." He let off playing. "But 'she whacked me with a ham bone and said she'd marry me' seemed kinda forward."

Outrage flared in her chest. Who did this man think he was? She wheeled around, slamming the rear fender into the rack and the pedal into her shin. Wincing, she muscled the bike in the proper direction, nearly bending the thing in half. Everything about her upbringing taught her to walk away from conflict, but this man... He was too insolent, too arrogant, and too sure of himself to go unreprimanded.

"Impressing the ladies as always, eh, Grandson?"

With a start, she whirled and discovered Hank lumbering across the parking lot. Though she hadn't noticed earlier, she saw that he, too, walked unsteadily.

Slinging the guitar over one shoulder, the young man sprang from the truck, closing the rear gate behind him. "Lemme help you, Hank."

Hank fixed his gaze on Nora. "Please forgive whatever my boneheaded grandson did to make you look like you want to bite off his head. I don't blame you. I feel the same way every day."

She darted the cowboy a look. Twilight made vision tricky, but she could swear his cheeks were red.

The young man extended a hand. "Come on now."

Hank batted him away. "Did he have the courtesy to introduce himself before he ticked you off?" One bushy eyebrow rose. "I'll go ahead and answer my own question. No." He swung open the passenger side door. "Nora, this is my good-for-nothing grandson, Tucker McClure. Tucker, Miss Nora…?"

"Beiler," she said.

"Miss Nora Beiler." Hank propped a hand on the open door and shifted his gaze between them.

Tucker gave a sheepish look. "Pleased to meet you."

Not remotely pleased to meet him, she did not return the courtesy. She glared in stony silence.

Hank cleared his throat. "Miss Beiler joined our class today."

Tucker looked from his grandfather to her and back again. "She's in Shuffle Off to Fitness?"

"She certainly is, and let me tell you, she's a regular Ginger Rogers."

Hank gazed with unfiltered admiration, and her heart warmed. He was an unexpected ally against this arrogant man.

Tucker lifted his chin in her direction. "But she's not—"

"Ancient?" Hank snarled. "Geriatric? Infirm? No, thank the good Lord. She's a breath of sunshine who'll be giving deaf, old Edna a run for her money before long. Miss Beiler is just what Shuffle Off to Fitness needs."

During the entire class, Nora didn't see Hank smile once. Now, he grinned like she lit the stars.

Tucker wheeled slowly, a crooked smile creeping into his eyes. "Well, I'll be darned. I feel a second verse coming on." With a deep inhale, he lifted his guitar.

Refusing to indulge another disrespectful ditty, she cut him off. "I've enjoyed meeting you both, but I'm not—"

"Coming back?" Hank finished.

A tendency to finish her sentences appeared to run in the family. She gave a curt nod.

Hank's expression softened. "Your hip, right?" With a nod, he patted his own hip. "Four years before she died, my wife had a hip replaced. You're recovering well—course you're young. Anyway, Lavelle's the one who got me coming to class. Thanks to Jerry, my wife walked again before she died. She not only walked...she danced." He gave a bittersweet smile. "Jerry will help you heal, too. You'll see." Turning, he hefted a foot into the truck.

Tucker hurried to his side. "Easy there, Hank." Ever so gently, he boosted the older man onto the seat. His grandfather safely stowed, he stashed his guitar and jogged to the driver's side.

With a muffled grunt, Hank settled back, closed the door, and rolled down the window. "See you next week, Miss Nora."

Not looking back, she vaulted onto the saddle and pedaled to the bike path as fast as her tired legs would carry her. Her breath came quick, stinging her lungs with sudden exertion. She'd have to hurry to reach home before dark. Next week she'd leave class right away—no lingering to chat.

Catching herself, she pulled hard to the right and dodged a fallen branch. Next week? Next week she'd be home, not at some crazy English dance class. Wouldn't she?

As her pedal strokes evened, the hum of the tires fell into a brand-new rhythm. Try as she might to shake it, it repeated again and again in her mind. *Shuffle ball change. Shuffle ball change. Shuffle ball change.*

****

Wide awake far later than usual that night, Nora lay in bed and stared at the ceiling. She stretched long like a cat, relishing the feel of muscles taxed to their limits. Though heavy with exhaustion, her body hadn't felt so good in months.

Candlelight flickered on the plain white wall, and the day's events played before her eyes like moving pictures. Shoving the infuriating *Englischer* from her thoughts, she clutched a pillow to her chest. Would she really return to class? Should she? A lifetime of obeying the rules told her dancing was forbidden. But was Shuffle Off to Fitness really, truly wicked? She shouldn't dwell, but she couldn't stop herself from reliving every minute and weighing each detail. Was it dance? Or was it therapy, as Nurse Cindy said?

Jerry began with a series of stretches in the chairs. Though the movements were unfamiliar, with every breath, bend, and twist, Nora's aching muscles loosened and lengthened so when she finally stood, she felt two inches taller than when she arrived.

With her students warmed up, Jerry stood before

them, eyes twinkling. "Since we have newbies as well as old-timers, let's kick it old school. Back to basics, ya'll." She skipped to a cabinet at the far side of the room and pressed a button. Music poured from the speakers.

For the first time in a long time, Nora listened to her heart. Pulse racing and nerves on edge, she joined the line between Joan and Marion and riveted her gaze on the teacher.

Counting out rhythms with a beat as regular as horse hoofs on pavement, Jerry demonstrated the steps.

Nora's borrowed shoes clicked with the cheerful tap of a hammer on a tin roof. Every step sent a shiver up her spine. Every *clickety-clack* widened her smile. Even the names of the combinations sounded happy.

Shuffle ball. Shuffle ball.
Brush strike. Brush strike.
Ball change. Flap-ball-change.
Heel step. Heel step.
Buffalo?

Covering her mouth, she let out a giggle. She studied Jerry's feet and imitated every move. The shoes let her know when she did a step correctly—the precise, rhythmic click its own reward. But even when she bungled a step, no one cared or even seemed to notice. She was surrounded by smiling faces and older bodies—some fleet of foot and some plodding as oxen. All were welcome.

"Now, we put them all together," Jerry announced, tapping to the stereo player and pressing a button.

The muscles in Nora's legs twitched.

Jerry clapped the rhythm. "Five, six, five, six, seven, eight."

One step led to the next like ingredients in a recipe. Nora felt like she was flying—her chest and arms were light as air, and her legs, wobbling from the unfamiliar strain, executed the movements with nary a misstep. As the sequence came to an end, she caught sight of herself in the mirror, *kapp* strings bouncing and skirts a-spinning. Her cheeks were rosy, and her forehead glistened. She almost didn't recognize the face looking back. The Nora in the mirror looked happy.

She *was* happy.

She was happy because she was dancing.

The music ended, and she stilled. Her breath came fast and high, and her ears rang. All around, the sound of laugher echoed. She had watched her classmates hug and clap one another on the shoulders, feeling the room spin and her heart swell.

Lying in bed, she felt that euphoria again, like sledding down the hill at Annie Amos's farm when she was a girl. Like taking the reins of the buggy for the very first time.

Tucker McClure's green eyes flashed in her memory.

Like falling in love.

No wonder dancing was forbidden.

Forgive me. She squeezed closed her eyes, but whom did she beseech? Her mother? Levi? God?

Forgive me but I must return.

Chapter Four

Amidst the hubbub of the harvest time Farmers' Market, Nora filled the empty spot in her display with the last apple pie. Considering less than twenty-four hours ago, she attended her first ever, tap-dancing class, she felt pretty good. She leaned into the table and stretched achy calves. Her hip didn't even twinge.

"You hurting from that exercise class?" *Mamm* called from the rear of the booth.

She jerked upward and grabbed the empty crate. "I'm fine."

"I don't understand the name Shuffle Off to Fitness. I thought the point was to stop shuffling. What sort of things did you do?"

Shuffle ball change. Shuffle ball change.

Her feet twitched. She rooted them and threw her mother a smile. "Oh, you know, stretches and whatnot. Exercises."

Mamm removed her glasses and huffed on the lenses. "What kind of exercises?"

She took a deep breath. The smell of butter and caramelized sugar always soothed her. Still, all the sugar in the world wouldn't make lying to her mother, even by omission, any easier. "I don't know what they're called. Exercises. Everyone is really old—even the teacher."

Frowning, *Mamm* buffed the glass with her apron.

Turned on one end, the empty crate made a good seat. Nora settled next to her mother and dropped her head against the wall. "They're grandmothers and grandfathers." She pictured the motley assortment of dancers and smiled. "I felt a bit silly among them, but they were kind."

A harried-looking mother hustled past, dragging a boy in each hand. One child squirmed free and, spotting Nora and Verna, gawked. Wiping the back of his wrist across his nose, he sniffed soggily, then plunged his thumb into a whoopie pie like he was smashing a bug.

Without fail, every time Nora softened toward the English, they irritated her. First, Tucker McClure and now, this boy. Old enough to know better, the boy stuck his thumb in his mouth and grinned a devilish grin. She jerked to her feet, ready to give the child the scolding he so clearly required

Mamm shook her head. "Leave it be."

She whirled. "But he—"

"No matter."

The boy's mother grabbed her son by the arm. "Come on, Jackson."

Verna crossed to them in two quick strides and picked up the squashed treat. "Why don't you take this home and share it with your brother?"

The mother whipped around her head, and her eyes went wide. "Jackson! Did you smush that whoopie pie?"

With a smile, Verna proffered the cellophane-wrapped goodie. "Call it a free sample, Jackson—so long as you share."

With a solemn nod, the boy took the treat.

The other boy scooted to join his brother. He

picked up a second whoopie pie and tossed it from hand to hand. "Why do you dress funny?"

Nora sealed her lips and took a deep, calming breath. Just when she thought these children couldn't be any more badly behaved, they outdid themselves.

Cheeks flushed, the woman wrenched the whoopie pie from her other son's grasp. "Max! Apologize to the lady right now." Open-mouthed, she appealed to Verna. "I'm so sorry."

Mamm waved a hand. "Well, Max, I wear what I do because I'm Amish. To be a part of our community, we all agree to dress a certain way. Simple as that. Besides, I like it. I don't have to waste time deciding what to wear every day." She inclined toward the woman. "Never you mind. I have four boys myself—each more outspoken than the next."

Color draining from her face, the mother dipped her chin. "Thank you."

Verna bent low, bringing her eyes level with the children. "You boys share the pie, then come back next week and tell me how you liked it. All right?"

The ruffians nodded.

Seeming eager to make an escape, the mother hustled them into the crowd. Nora clenched her jaw until her teeth could have crushed gravel. "Reward a child for bad behavior, and he'll never learn."

The folding chair squeaked beneath *Mamm's* weight. "Teach a child to be miserly, and he'll never share."

Speaking loudly into a cellular phone, another woman picked up a shoofly pie.

Spinning it on one palm, she examined the pastry like she was looking for bugs or mold. Nora jerked her head toward the woman. "These people think everything belongs to them," she hissed. "That mother didn't even offer to pay for the whoopie pie."

Verna sniffed and pulled her crochet from a bag. "She was ashamed. A pinch of kindness sweetens the bitterest cup. Mark my words; she'll be back next week and the week after."

The woman on the phone waggled a ten-dollar bill in Nora's direction. Without a break in conversation, she paid for the pie, took her change, and left.

Nora reeled and shook her head. "Unbelievable."

The silver hook flashed, and the crocheted chain folded in on itself in a perfect azure square. *Mamm* peered over her glasses at her work. "A smile would do you a world of good. And it wouldn't hurt business none, either."

Nora was not inclined to smile herself silly for no reason. Her baking spoke for itself—smiled for itself, even. Besides, the balls of her feet were sore. She pressed one foot into the ground and rotated her ankle. With every passing minute, the sweetness of this September day soured.

Glancing up, *Mamm* looked her over like a pig at auction. "Well, whatever you did in your secret exercise class, you'd best soak your feet when you get home. Even wearing those fancy sneaker shoes, you're hurting plain as day. I've a mind to go with you next week."

"Suit yourself." She straightened her spine. Hurting, indeed. Compared to the hip pain that plagued her for years, these little aches were nothing. "I'm going for lemonade. Can you tend the stand?"

Verna huffed and flapped her granny square at a pesky fly. "I can crochet an afghan, mind five babies, and tend the stand with one hand tied behind my back. I'll manage. Fetch me a bag of cinnamon pretzel sticks while you're at it."

Arguing with her mother was pointless. With a nod, Nora slid between tables and joined the crowd. She brushed a hair from her eyes and tucked it under her *kapp*. No matter how many pins she used, her hair was so silky it always slipped out of the bun, especially on a warm day. Early fall, and still, the indoor market was hotter than a skunk. At almost three o'clock, the building bustled with shoppers. When she was a girl, everyone arrived before dawn and left by noon, with the market building locked up tight by one p.m.

During the years she spent in Ohio, new owners took over, bringing new-fangled ideas to make the market a tourist destination. Stands selling all sorts of trendy foods popped up, and a new outdoor stage featured live music every Wednesday. More tourists meant more customers but also prying eyes and rude stares. Walking quickly, she glanced over the stands. What in the world was *kombucha*, and why would anyone bake a cake with no flour or butter? Some of these items made no sense at all. Feeling a headache coming on, she pinched her forehead between her fingers. And why was the music always so loud?

Even late in the day, the line at Annie Amos's pretzel stand went clear out the back door.

Catching her gaze, Annie waved and beckoned.

Jumping the line was tempting, but she received bitter looks the few times she dared to accept Annie's invitation. Forcing a smile, she shrugged and sidled out the door into an afternoon as hot as the inside of an oven. Taking her place at the end of the line, she stared at her feet, hoping not to be recognized. Though she loved her community, some days she wished she were invisible.

Enthusiastic applause echoed over the outdoor stalls, and a man's voice rang clear. "Thank you. Thank you so much."

Her heart hammered. She jerked up her head and squinted into the sun. The stage was surrounded by more people than she'd ever seen watching a singer. The crowd spilled over the wooden benches into several rows of lawn chairs.

"I love you, Tucker!" a woman in the audience screamed, waving her arms above her head.

The dark-haired man on the stage smiled and winked. "Wait 'til you taste my cooking, then let me know how you feel."

Laughter rippled through the audience.

A single chord sounded with a tone so true Nora caught her breath. The next cleared the muggy air like a breeze after a rainstorm.

"Excuse me, ma'am. The pretzel line's moving," said a woman behind her.

Nora shook her head and waved by the woman. Late summer sun beat on her shoulders, and she shielded her eyes. She sidled up behind the last row of chairs facing the stage.

Scanning the crowd, Tucker fiddled with something like small screws at the top of his guitar, plucking a few notes. "I've got one more song for you today…" He glanced up, and his gaze met hers. His brows rose, and the corners of his mouth twitched. "Well, shoot," he said in a low voice.

The strings sang a hello just for her. A smile

crawled from cheek to cheek, seeming to take up half his face. Before she realized what she was doing, Nora smiled, too. The grin rose from her toes, spread in a flush across her collarbones, and rounded her cheeks, reminding her in a flash what smiling with her whole self felt like. Once upon a time, she smiled so often her schoolteacher nicknamed her "Smiling Nora" to distinguish her from the other Nora at school. She thought that grinning girl died in a buggy wreck seven years ago, but as her lungs expanded and her heart warmed, Smiling Nora returned for the first time in…well, in quite some time.

Tucker tilted his head, and a lock of dark hair fell over one eye. He shook it back and struck another chord. "I was fixing to close with one of my songs, but all of a sudden…all of a sudden, I can't quite remember how it goes, because another song's knocking on my brain saying, 'play me, Tucker, play me.' "

Another laugh rose from the audience.

A giggle slipped past her lips. Nora was no simpering girl, and yet, she lingered, starstruck in a crowd of strangers watching an *Englischer* play the guitar. Hunching her shoulders, she darted a glance around the audience. She'd best leave before anyone noticed. She'd skip the lemonade entirely and tell her mother the line was too long, and she could get her own stinking cinnamon pretzels if she wanted them. Tucker McClure needed no encouragement from her—he had screaming fans galore. She knew she should do these things, but she didn't move. She stood rooted to the gravel and smiled even wider. Had she lost her senses?

"This is a tune by one of my grandpa Hank's favorite singers. I hate to make the old grump happy, if

I can help it, but I'm gonna play it anyway. I hope you enjoy it."

Lifting damp palms to her cheeks, she turned to go, but the guitar rang out again—a cheerful cascade of notes, tumbling one on top of the other like the footsteps of a child running down a grassy bank. He started to sing, and the voice that only yesterday seemed sour, was now sweet as spring water. His words poured over her, telling of a smiling face that turned him inside out. The earth tilted, and she slid a hand onto the back of a chair, steadying herself. She remembered this feeling.

Years ago, she stood in a crowd as a man led the Sunday singing and felt like his voice summoned her insides to the outside—like her heart was pinned to her dress along with her apron, beating for everyone to see. She remembered feeling like a song was a gift, meant for her and only her. But where Levi's voice had been rich and deep as a river, Tucker's soared like a hawk in flight. He opened his mouth, and his soul shimmered in the music. Listening, she knew Tucker's soul was good. Nobody with a dark heart could sing like he did. She hung on every note, and before she was ready, the song ended.

The audience hooted and hollered.

Tucker dipped his chin and flashed her a smile.

The crowd spun in a dizzying swirl, and she shook herself. She should probably clap, too, not stand rigid as a fence post.

With a wave, Tucker slung the guitar over one shoulder and bounded off the stage. Weaving through the crowd, he appeared, suddenly, to be coming right for her.

The sickening realization that she was directly in front of Lovina Lapp's produce stand crept over her. Talking to this *Englischer*—this *Englischer* with a guitar—while Lovina watched would never do. She spun and scurried toward the lemonade line.

"Hey, Nora!" a voice called from behind.

She winced. Just ignore him and maybe he'll go away.

"Nora!"

What to do? If she returned to her mother without lemonade and pretzels, she'd be peppered with questions. Questions for which she had no good answers. She stared at her feet, praying he'd take the hint and leave her be.

"Hi there."

His lanky form blocked the sun, casting a shadow over her sneakers. She peeked at Lovina.

Her old schoolmate poured a bushel of apples into a paper sack…all the while watching Nora's every move.

A gentle tap landed atop one shoulder.

She jumped and whirled.

"Whoa." He jerked back, lifting his palms. "Didn't mean to startle you. I thought you heard me."

"I did." She whipped around and advanced in the line.

With one long stride, he drew up beside her. "I know you're no fan of my music, but what did you think of that last song?"

He was like a mosquito she couldn't shake. Glancing again at Lovina, she edged toward the building. The woman was now deep in conversation with a customer. Nora released her shoulders. Maybe a quick chat could slip by unnoticed.

"I sort of thought you liked it." He matched her step, and his guitar bumped her shoulder. "From the smile on your face."

That smile—that dangerous, delirious smile threatened again. *Liked* it? She *liked* lima beans. She *liked* comfortable shoes. But his music… She clamped her jaw, swallowing yet another smile. The way his music made her feel all sparkly inside—such a feeling couldn't be proper, no matter how like an angel he sounded. "Seems you have plenty of admirers. Surely my opinion doesn't matter."

"I 'spose I like a challenge."

A group of young women in short shorts and sleeveless blouses hovered nearby, tossing glances at Tucker and tittering.

She jerked her head in their direction. "The real challenge will be fitting all four of those ladies into the front seat of your truck. However will you manage?"

Tucker's eyes rounded, and bright pink splotches erupted on both cheeks. He let out a laugh. "Did not see that coming."

Another step brought Nora right outside the door, nearing Annie Amos's stand at last. If only he would leave before Annie spotted them, too.

"Grandson! Leave off selfies with the fans and take me home before I stroke out in this heat." Catching sight of Nora, Hank let out a chuckle. "Well, if it isn't my new friend from tap class. Good Lord, is the boy tormenting you again?"

Not shushing the old gentleman like she did Rebecca in church took everything she had. She couldn't risk anyone overhearing. Still, the news

Tucker was about to leave was welcome.

Tucker thrust his hands in the pockets of his blue jeans. "Now, Hank, don't you have a bingo game to crash?"

"Jokes about my age." Hank snorted. "Aren't you clever? What brings you here, Miss Nora? I didn't expect to see you until next week."

"My mother and I sell baked goods at a stand indoors." She bit her tongue. Why volunteer information? This whole encounter had her flustered. When would they leave?

"Is that so?" Tucker stepped inside, right across the counter from where her old friend bent over, rolling out pretzel dough. "I look forward to sampling your sweets."

Annie jerked to standing and, spotting Tucker, her lips formed a tiny *o*.

"If not today, then I'll stop by next week. Old Hank here has me booked to sing through the holidays."

Nora scrunched her nose in a scowl. Could Annie tell he was talking to her?

Hank grunted. "Maybe next week you won't flub up and forget your own song. Thought that part of your life was over. You holding out on me?"

Tucker's expression darkened. "I didn't forget. I only said that because…" He caught Nora's gaze, and the cheek splotches flamed. "Well, because I wanted to play the other song, that's all. Besides, I thought you liked J.T."

"James Taylor played the Opry. You're no James Taylor, Grandson."

Tucker turned his gaze to Nora, and his eyes glittered hard. "See you Tuesday."

"Always a pleasure, Miss Nora." With a hitch in his step, Hank ventured into the crowd with Tucker on his heels.

A long, slow breath eased from her chest.

"What did he mean, see you Tuesday?"

She jerked around. Annie's dark eyes danced just as they did when they were girls in school. "Hm?"

"The handsome *Englischer*. He'll see you Tuesday?" With a smooth flick of the wrist, Annie twisted a span of dough into a perfect pretzel shape and slid it onto a cooking tray.

"I-I don't know. I suppose he was confused about market day." She pulled bills from her pocket and made a show of counting out five.

Annie sliced another length of dough from the long piece snaking halfway across the counter. "Didn't seem confused. Seemed pretty sure of himself—walking around with that guitar." She shimmied her shoulders in a manly swagger.

Nora couldn't help but smile. Tucker did ooze confidence…until Hank said what he said, and then Tucker's whole manner changed. What in the world was an Opry? And why did the mention make Tucker so mad? Shaking herself, she swiped damp palms down the front of her apron. "He's no concern of mine. May I have two lemonades and a bag of cinnamon pretzels, please?" Annie curled her lips in a manner suggesting she didn't quite believe her old pal.

What did Annie Amos know, anyway? They were thick as thieves as schoolgirls, but years had passed since they huddled together after youth singings, giggling and sharing secret dreams. Those girlish fancies ended only in heartache. Annie seemed happy enough in her marriage to good-natured, dim-witted Leroy. But for Nora, nothing short of true love…

Ach. Let it be.

Nodding a quick goodbye, she scooted aside, leaving behind thoughts of the past. The balls of her feet twinged, increasingly sore from yesterday's class and hours standing today. The idea Nora would have anything to do with an *Englischer*, let alone an *Englischer* who got up on a stage and sang songs, was absurd. After what her brother Jonas had done? Besides, what would a man like Tucker want with someone like her?

Tucking the bag of cinnamon sticks under one arm, she took up the lemonades, and headed for her stand. She'd indulge in a moment of frosty, tart refreshment, and then back to work she'd go. She had no time for unseemly and inappropriate nonsense.

No more classes.

No more music, no more dancing, and no more Tucker McClure. The matter was settled. She'd quit Shuffle Off to Fitness for good.

But as she weaved through the afternoon crowds, an echo of that smile still hummed. It bounced off the walls of her chest, threatening to pop out again. And if it did, she doubted she could do anything to stop it.

Chapter Five

The canning bath bubbled, and the kitchen timer let out a raucous *ding-a-ling*. Tuning it out, Nora gritted her teeth, and inhaling the scent of cooked apples, she strained tense fingers toward her shoelaces. The chair creaked, and knobby spindles poked into her spine. Just a few inches farther…

Leaving behind Saturday cleaning, Rebecca peeked into the kitchen, pale cheeks splotched pink and blue eyes clouded in concern. "Does your hip hurt?" The mop sloshed into the scrub bucket, and light footsteps tripped across the floor. "I'll finish the applesauce."

Nora waved a hand and bent her knee, hinging at the waist. Pain flared, and she winced. Had she reinjured her hip after only one class? Biting back a grimace, she snagged the laces and looped them into a firm double knot.

Barefoot, her daughter skipped to the counter and silenced the timer. In a jiffy, she grabbed a potholder and lifted the lid from the canning pot.

A warning to be careful died on Nora's tongue, as all seven jars alit on the cooling rack, and Rebecca reloaded the lifter and plunged it in for another round. "Don't forget to—"

"Yes, *Mamm*." Rebecca twisted the dial to twenty minutes, and the timer resumed ticking.

With one hand on the back of the chair and the

other on the table, Nora pressed slowly to her feet. Breath came with a struggle, but she sealed her lips and kept her expression steady. She remembered when she, too, could breeze through Saturday cleaning while making applesauce and doing ten other tasks at the same time. Between the class, standing market, and her regular chores, had she pushed her hip too hard? She felt so good all week, but now, she wondered how she'd endure three hours sitting on backless church benches tomorrow morning. She shooed her daughter. "Finish the mopping."

"But I can—"

"Go." Vinegar edged her tone, and she hid her face, a rush of shame rising from her belly.

Rebecca scampered into the sitting room.

She let out a long, slow sigh. Why was she always so short with the girl? Her daughter only wanted to help. Taking up the ladle and funnel, she set about filling the next round of mason jars. This year's Cortlands were so sweet the sauce needed only a dash of cinnamon for flavor and a few lemon peels for brightness. Not a pinch of sugar went in the pot. Planting her hands on the counter, she arched her back and twisted, feeling the muscles around her spine ease.

She'd made her decision on Wednesday, but she couldn't help but wonder if quitting the class was the right choice when she still had bad days. Dr. Richard said she required rehab to regain her strength. Could she really complete the recovery on her own? Dribbles of apple sauce collared the mouths of the jars. With a damp rag, she wiped them clean. The freshly sterilized lids were scalding, but her calloused fingertips long since lost sensitivity to heat. They were as numb as the skin around the scarlet scar on the back of her left upper thigh.

The tops threaded onto the jars with satisfying smoothness. She reached for a dishtowel and stared out the window, drying her hands. Her garden was lush and green, and the tomato leaves just edged with yellow. Despite repeated treatments, vine borers had their way with the zucchini, and she needed to pull the plants. The fall lettuce, spinach, and beets were growing nicely, but the peppers were nearly done, as well. The seasons marched through the garden with the same joys and frustrations as every other year. Each day in the kitchen was another round of baking for market and canning for winter. Each week brought cleaning galore. Nora's life was utterly predictable. Deep inside, a yearning to start afresh pooled like rainwater on a cabbage leaf.

She recalled the nosy gleam in Lovina Lapp's gaze. Even Annie's knowing glances made her un-comfortable—the expression on her sweet features suggesting a thrilling, but dangerous, connection. Unbidden, an image of Tucker came to mind as he met her gaze over a sea of onlookers and smiled a smile for her—for her, Nora Beiler. The sound of his guitar thrummed in her chest. His voice soared. Her own smiling face warmed her from the outside in.

"Are you humming?"

She started and spun.

Mamm's wide shoulders spanned the doorway to the pantry.

The woman was as red-faced and bright-eyed as her granddaughter—a picture of solidity and strength. Fine-boned and thinner than she'd been in years, Nora sometimes felt like the only one in the family who didn't radiate good health. "What? No." She hadn't been humming…had she?

Verna dipped a wooden spoon in the apple sauce and tasted. "Those Cortlands cook down so nice. Sweet as sugar." Her cheeks lifted in a small smile. "Just as your brother liked them."

Though she had four brothers, she knew immediately to whom her mother referred. Only one was spoken of in that wistful tone, though by rights he shouldn't be discussed, at all. Jonas was shunned—ripped from their lives as painfully and permanently as Levi. He made his choice, leaving her none. Three years later, the events of that horrible August still haunted her. The memory of her daughter's illness, Jonas's decision to leave the faith, and her forced move to Ohio clouded her head in a bitter fog of betrayal. She twisted the final jar ring so tight her knuckles popped. Why must her mother constantly remind her when she wanted only to forget?

Squeezing past *Mamm*, Samuel dropped another bushel basket on the table, heaped high with apples.

Nora's hip throbbed, and she sighed. Many hours of work lay ahead.

He grabbed a sugar cookie from the jar and downed it in one bite. "What about Jonas? Did you hear from him?"

With a sniff, *Mamm* shook her head, and the faraway look in her eyes lifted like mist from the fields.

Rebecca's elfin face popped into the kitchen entry. "Did someone mention Uncle Jonas?"

Samuel snatched another cookie and tossed it.

Squealing, Rebecca lunged, catching the treat in a tight fist, and crushing it. Crumbs rained on the floor.

"Rebecca! Samuel!" Nora balled her fists at her waist and scowled.

The two stilled, forcing twin looks of repentance.

She turned her cheeks to the window, longing for a breeze to cool the stifling kitchen—longing even more for a second of peace. The timer pealed again, its raucous screech kindling a headache behind her eyes. Wincing, she pinched her forehead between thumb and fingers.

Verna swatted the troublemakers with a potholder. "Clean up the cookie and hurry back to work."

Rebecca lunged for the dustpan and scuttled across the floor.

Spinning in the other direction, Samuel snuck two more cookies from the jar. "I'm heading to Elam Stoltzfus's. His brother's up from Lancaster where he's got a good business selling and installing solar panels."

Mamm caught him in a matronly glare. "Don't forget my washing machine."

"I'll fix it by Monday." Scooting around the table, Samuel slipped a second cookie to Rebecca.

Solar panels? Nora huffed. What next? Cars and mobile phones? Why wouldn't Samuel stay on the farm? Why couldn't any of them remain where they belonged?

Verna removed the processed applesauce from the pot, accidentally elbowing her in the shoulder. Droplets of scalding water peppered Nora's forearms, and she limped out of the way. As they cooled and sealed tight, the lids let out a chorus: *pop, pop!* Her family gyred around the kitchen like a dust twister on a blustery day, spinning dirt and dried leaves across fallow fields.

Crumbs rained into the trash bin, and Rebecca

brushed together her hands. "Uncle Samuel, will you drop me at the library on the way?"

"The library?" Nora shot out a restraining hand.

"*Mamm*, can I please check out the book I told you about? *The Lion, The Witch—*"

"The witch?" Head spinning, she gripped the countertop, feeling the sharp edge dig into her palms.

"*And the Wardrobe?* It's by Mr. C.S. Lewis, a famous Christian author who wrote many books about religion. Uncle Jonas said—"

"Uncle Jonas isn't here!" The shrill reprimand bounced off the kitchen walls like a siren on an English ambulance.

The whirling twister stilled.

Mamm folded a dishtowel neatly and draped it over the oven door. "Samuel, I'll see you for supper. Rebecca, the spinach and lettuce need weeding. I'll finish up in here."

Without a word, Rebecca and Samuel slipped outside.

Nora reached for a glass and filled it with water from the pitcher. Careful not to jostle her leg, she lowered into a chair and took a sip. The water was sweet but lukewarm. What wouldn't she give for buckets of ice from a freezer?

Hot jars clinked onto the cooling rack, and *Mamm* refilled the lifter. "You're too hard on her."

Nora choked, sending water down the wrong tube. Spluttering, she wiped a hand across her mouth. "You heard her. Lions and witches? We have shelves of appropriate books. Why can't she read those?"

"I've no quarrel with your judgment, but you'd best mind your tone."

"She's headstrong and willful—"

"And likely to jump the fence just like her uncle."

A stink bug, its shield-shaped body a bulky and cumbersome load, crawled along the rim of the bushel basket. She smashed it, and its distinct odor of overripe apples mingled with the scent of the fruit. Glancing up, she found her mother staring.

"I won't lose another child." *Mamm's* voice hitched, and she cleared her throat.

Was Rebecca at risk to go English? She couldn't bear the thought. Stomach tightening, she shifted and winced again.

"Your hip hurts—don't you deny it. Surprised as I am to say, I'm glad you have that exercise class. Dr. Richard will fix you right up."

Heaving to her feet, she grabbed the basket and lugged it to the sink, struggling to suppress her limp. "I'm not going back."

The tray of clean jars dropped onto the counter with a crash. "You're what?"

She dumped apples into a basin of cold water and swished them clean. "I have all the exercise I need right here—"

"But the doctor—"

"The doctor also said bicycling would get me strong. I'll ride over Tuesday night and tell the teacher I'm done."

"Deacon Elmer does not look kindly on bicycling. I invited him to dinner next Sunday. Maybe a slice of your shoofly pie will win his approval, but don't you count on it." Searching the counter, *Mamm* opened her hands.

Nora passed the ladle and funnel.

With a quick nod, Verna scooped sauce into the jars without a drop out of place. "Mervin and the *kinner* are coming, too."

An exhausted sigh eddied in her lungs. She closed her eyes and drained the apples. Within the last two years, Deacon Elmer Zook and his eldest son, Mervin, both lost their wives. As if bicycles and exercise classes were the primary reason for the invitation.

Yielding to her knife, an apple split into perfect halves, exposing russet seeds in their teardrop chambers. Enough talk. She'd deal with Mervin Zook when the time came. For now, quitting her exercise class and casting off all the complications that came with it—dancing and humming and nosy old people and above all, Tucker McClure—was her top priority. She'd feel much better once it was done. A sliver of Cortland lay on her tongue and crunched between her teeth, sweet and crisp.

Quitting was absolutely the right course of action.

Maybe if she repeated it often enough, by Tuesday, she'd believe it.

****

When Nora arrived at the studio Tuesday night, her tap shoes were waiting on a folding chair.

"Well, look who's here," said a pleasantly plump, gray-haired lady. Hand in hand with a pleasantly plump, gray-haired gentleman, she shuffle-stepped toward Nora. Her bright yellow shirt read, *I'm With Him* and had a big red arrow pointing at her companion. "I fetched your shoes."

The gentleman wore a matching shirt proclaiming, *I'm With Her*. He gave a red-cheeked smile. "Aren't you a sight for sore eyes?"

They looked for all the world like a set of salt and pepper shakers. Nora couldn't help but return the smile.

The pepper-shaker man jerked an elbow at a lanky fellow sprawled on the floor with his back against the mirror. "Isn't she a sight for sore eyes, Gene?"

The gentleman glanced up from lacing his shoes. "Indeed. To be frank, we feared you wouldn't return."

The saltshaker lady extended a hand. "We didn't get a chance to introduce ourselves. I'm Dot, and this dreamboat here is my husband, Bert."

Bert doffed an imaginary hat.

"And that..." Dot twitched a thumb toward the other man. "That there's Gene Stackhouse. You see, Gene and Marion always partner up. Bert and I are partners for life, as well as tap, of course. And Edna and Joan make it a darling twosome, leaving poor old Hank on his own." She stepped closer, tilting her head so a wispy curl brushed Nora's cheek. "Hank's been alone since Lavelle passed, of course, and grumpier than a hog on a diet. But now, here you are practically heaven-sent!"

Unfolding his legs like a stork, Gene came to his feet.

"I thought your people weren't much for dancing." Gene straightened his tie and gave the hem of his knitted vest a firm tug.

"We're not typically..." Nora scanned the room, her voice trailing off. Her stomach burbled a mix of nervousness and unease. She couldn't be Hank's partner. She needed to find Jerry and quit at once. "But sometimes exceptions to the rules are made for medical reasons." She bit her tongue. Why offer an explanation when in seconds she would leave?

Dot clapped and hopped from foot to foot. "See, fellas! I told you she'd come. And here you thought we spooked her."

Marion, Joan, and Edna burst into the room and clustered like hens, clucking about how happy they were to see her. She indulged their fussing with a patient smile and glanced toward the door. Where was Jerry?

Grim faced, Hank shuffled in. Spotting Nora, he lifted one cheek in a lopsided grin. "Well, good." He plopped down in a folding chair and unlaced his shoes.

"Jerry's running late—she just texted. All that Green Ridge traffic." Marion poofed her hair and cackled. "Ah, here she is."

Arms wide, Jerry sashayed through the door. "Shoes on, tappers! We have a lot to accomplish."

With a burst of music, class began, leaving Nora no time to pull aside Jerry and explain she wasn't staying.

The dancers assembled in a long line facing the mirrors.

Joan beckoned Nora to the spot between her and Marion.

As if every step was a slog through a muddy pigsty, she dragged into place. Her limp seemed to holler for attention. She stiffened her spine, struggling to even her gait, but the hitch only grew more pronounced. Jerry's stretches felt so good last week— so good she indulged in them several times in the intervening days. Certainly, a little stretching wouldn't hurt. She'd warm up with the class and then grab Jerry before dancing began.

Releasing her spine and bending her knees, she hinged at the waist and dangled her hands above her toes. She let out a sigh. The stretches were even more wonderful than they were last week when she'd been so tense and scared. Her heartbeat slowed. She followed Jerry's every move, twisting and extending, reaching for the sky and curling her spine like a fiddlehead fern until her nose touched her belly and her fingers brushed the smooth, shiny floor. The movements hurt a bit, but it was the kind of hurt that promised healing. Fearless, she embraced the pain, relishing how her muscles loosened and lengthened. Lunging, balancing, and bending, she felt the stress of the week ebb through the soles of her feet.

Jerry unzipped a velvety, purple jacket with embroidered, gold stars across the shoulders, revealing a black T-shirt with *Live to Dance* splashed across the front.

These English loved wearing clothes that talked.

"Grab a quick drink, tappers. Then we'll partner up and review what we learned last week."

Nora shook herself. *Right.* Now was the moment to make her exit. She sidled up to Jerry. "May I speak with you?"

Her classmates glanced up from water bottles and cellular phones. Dot's brows drew together, and Gene shot Bert an I-told-you-so sort of look.

Jerry met her gaze with a disarming smile that seemed to say in the friendliest tone imaginable, "I know what you're up to, young lady." Nora's belly churned like an ice cream maker full of sour milk.

Jerry picked up Nora's shoes. "Put on your shoes, baby. With me being late, we're already behind. Catch me after class, all right?"

The leather was as soft and supple as she

remembered. A scent of talcum powder mingled with lemon floor cleaner in a surprisingly pleasant combination. The metal taps rattled a *clickety* hello— the promise of cheerful sounds to come. Pressing her lips, she nodded, and the group seemed to sigh in relief. Baffled, she quickly changed her shoes. Why did these old folks care whether she stayed or went? They didn't even know her. Well, she'd come this far. One final lesson wouldn't hurt.

Jerry clacked to the front of the room. "Now, with Nora joining our group, we're an even eight at last. I know you'll miss me, Hank, but you'll be in good hands with the young lady. Let's stand next to our partners to get the feel of moving side by side, and we'll begin."

With a quick wave, Hank beckoned her to the rear of the class. "I like the back row." He focused his gaze on Jerry and didn't say another word.

At the oddest times during the past week, Nora had found herself shuffling up stairs or tapping out a beat while she hung the wash. After a quick look around to ensure no one was watching, she'd tried to tell herself the class wasn't so wonderful. Surely, memory exaggerated the buoyant freedom she felt while she danced.

She was wrong. The music swelled, and her body sang. She remembered every move—executing some as well as her more experienced classmates. New steps accompanied last week's combination, and when she put them all together, joining the chorus of lively clicks and clacks, she felt like she was flying. When the dance ended, she burst into breathless laughter, doubling over, hands to knees, just like the others. Lifting her chin, she glimpsed herself in the mirror, looking exactly as she did last week—cheeks flushed, eyes merry, and a smile as bright as Sunday morning. She caught Hank's gaze in the glass.

"Well, now. That was some fun." A grin cracked his grizzled face in two.

A soft tap landed atop her shoulder, and she turned.

Jerry dabbed at her neck with a turquoise hand towel. "Now, what did you want to see me about?" Her eyes narrowed. "Surely, you aren't planning to quit on us."

In a flash, Hank came to her side. "Of course not. Nora's my partner."

Nora gathered the fabric of her skirt in handfuls. "Well, I…"

Hank pivoted and raised one bushy eyebrow.

The dress pulled tight across her thighs. "I-I wondered if borrowing the shoes again was all right. Everyone else has their own." For an instant, Jerry seemed to look inside her just like the X-ray machine at Dr. Richard's office—as if she saw not only bones and sinews, but thoughts and feelings, too. Suddenly hot and itchy in her own skin, she squirmed.

Jerry's expression eased, and with a soft hand, she cupped Nora's cheek. "They're yours as long as you need them."

Her palm was warm and dry. Her voice was sweet as molasses. Forcing a quick smile, Nora unlaced the shoes, tucked them onto a shelf in the supply closet, and barely acknowledging the chorus of friendly farewells, once again streaked from the studio.

She hammered her thighs with tight fists and raced toward the door. Since when did she have so little courage—so little conviction? If Deacon Elmer found out…if her *mother* found out? With a disgusted grunt, she shouldered open the door.

Barreling into the parking lot, she drew up short and gawked at the green pickup truck blocking the bike rack. The strains of a guitar floated across the parking lot, and she clenched her jaw. Her cheeks sore from smiling and her toes still tapping a beat, she was all mixed up inside. Another encounter with Tucker McClure might scramble her senses forever. She had to get home and figure out how to face her mother again this week…and lie.

Sitting in the back of the truck, he bent over the guitar, bottom lip snagged between his teeth and eyes two dark slits.

He seemed unaware of anything but the music. Maybe she could sneak past and snatch the bike without notice. Her shoes crunched gravel, and she slowed, tiptoeing on achy balls of tired feet. She still had eight miles to ride.

A chord sang out. He flattened his hand against the strings, snuffing the vibrations with a thud. Another chord followed, slightly different from the first. Again he smacked silent the sound. He swept away the shiny dark hair that flopped over his eyes and strummed, tilting an ear to the guitar and singing under his breath.

This was her chance. Spotting her bike, she quickened her pace.

"No, no, no." He slammed a fist into the truck bed.

She let out a yelp and jumped.

Jerking up his head, he met her gaze, and a flush crept across his neck.

The streetlight buzzed, and moths made frantic

spirals in the glare. Dusk had fallen, but the sky still glowed azure and orange. She swallowed, wishing she had a thermos of water. "Are you all right?"

Shaking his hand, he huffed a bitter chuckle. "I'm a songwriter who can't write a song. Might as well cut out my tongue and feed it to the alligators."

The words sounded like a joke, but the tone was knife-edged. She smoothed the front of her skirt with damp palms. "Are you certain you're not hurt?"

He flexed his fingers and then rotated the hand at the wrist. "No such luck. If I were, I'd have an excuse not to write."

Nora never thought of writing anything. Levi was the storyteller. When Rebecca was tiny, he kept her in stitches with tales of his childhood. The goat that broke into the kitchen during Sunday worship and ate all the peanut butter spread. The rooster that tangled itself in the laundry and strutted around the barnyard, wearing ladies' underthings. Inside some people, stories seemed to spring. As if the truck was a skittish horse, she ran a hand along one side and approached. "But you've written songs before?"

He swung his legs off the back, kicking his heels like Rebecca perched atop the porch railing. "Hundreds. Ever since I was a boy."

The air hummed with cricket music. Though she grew up singing only hymns, the world seemed full of so many kinds of songs. She loved their traditional music, but it was nothing like Tucker's. When he sang, joy flowed from him like he was a spout connected to a hidden well. Surely, that spout couldn't simply turn off. She flattened a hand atop the side of the truck and rested her chin on it. "Maybe play your old songs until a new one comes to you. My mother always says, *Gott* doesn't close a door without opening a window."

He met her gaze. "I hope your mother's right."

His expression was so hopeful—like a little boy who heard his lost puppy was spotted in the neighbor's field. She lifted a shoulder. "She nearly always is." Try as she might, she couldn't suppress a dash of bitter humor.

A slow smile ambled across his face like it had all the time in the world. Suddenly, he didn't look at all like a boy. He looked very much like a man. With a quick intake of breath, she slipped around and took the handles of her bike. He'd left more space this week, and she easily rolled it from the rack.

He slid from the truck, landing softly beside her. "The old folks were practically taking bets about whether you'd show up tonight. The odds were not in your favor."

Aimed toward the trail, she threw a leg over the saddle. "They weren't the only ones surprised I came." Spinning the pedals, she planted a foot. "I was, too."

He laid the instrument into the truck bed and drew up beside her. "Hey, they let you dance? I mean, your…people and your mother. They think it's okay?"

"I'm not sure." Her fingers tightened around the handlebars. "We haven't discussed the finer details of Shuffle Off to Fitness."

Barking a laugh, he stumbled back a few steps. "You didn't tell them?"

"Not yet." The sky darkened. She wheeled out of the light from the streetlamp, not wanting him to see her face—unsure what her expression would reveal. Shame? Guilt? Rebellion? A smile tugged at one corner of her mouth. She glanced over her shoulder, catching his gaze. The turmoil in his face was replaced by surprise…and maybe a pinch of admiration.

He kicked at the ground with one boot and thrust his hands in his pockets. "I underestimated you, Nora Beiler." He winked. "You've got spunk."

Kicking hard with her left leg, she leapt onto the bike and took off toward the trail.

Night air cooled the perspiration on her body, making her shiver. As a girl, Nora Beiler was good. Nora Beiler was godly. She was obedient, compliant, and kind, and she always smiled. After her teacher dubbed her Smiling Nora, everyone in Shade Mountain District adopted the nickname, though no one called her that in years. But never in her entire life, did anyone say she had spunk.

Maybe, just maybe, Tucker McClure saw something in her no one else had ever seen before. And maybe, just maybe, he was right.

Chapter Six

Nora wedged the crate between one hip and the Farmers' Market table and made a neat pile of pumpkin whoopie pies. October was right around the corner, and the instant the foliage showed a hint of color, customers went nuts for anything pumpkin flavored. Nearby booths were laden with apples and winter squash and adorned with leafy decorations in shades of russet and gold. As she arranged the savory delicacies one atop the other, she kept her attention firmly fixed on two pretty, young women perusing her pies.

Seconds ago, one of them clearly said the name, "Tucker" and then giggled.

Nora had snapped up her head like someone yanked it with a chain and shifted closer.

"I'm dying to know what happened. I searched online, but the details were totally sketch." The dark-haired girl raised slender, tanned arms, palms skyward, and a dozen thin, gold bracelets jangled to her elbow. "He was scheduled to open for Jared Church at the Opry last June, and they up and replaced him with no explanation." She dropped her arms, and the bracelets clinked back to her wrists.

The other girl swung a long, yellow ponytail over one bare shoulder and made a spluttering sound. "Can you imagine firing Tucker McClure?"

"Please. That man could rob my grandmother

blind, and I'd still have his babies."

With a bubbly laugh, the blonde unzipped her purse. "Even if the rumors are true, he didn't do anything, like, super illegal. He's not gonna end up in jail."

Jail? Nora started, and the crate slipped from her hip. She snatched it, bumping into the table and jarring her entire display.

The brunette shot her a glance and fluffed long, wavy curls. "Not unless drugs were involved or something. I mean, who knows? Tucker's a bad boy."

"And bad boys are hot." The fair-haired girl pulled out a thin tube, unscrewed it, and swiped on pink lip gloss. "I mean, who'd have thought he'd end up here. I heard he was at the Hill Top last night. That bar is such a dive."

"Hey, want a whoopie pie?"

Shiny pink lips pooched in a pout. "I just put on lip gloss, and those things are like a zillion calories."

The dark-haired girl dangled a whoopie pie in front of her friend's face. "They're so bad they're good. Like Tucker McClure."

Nora shoved the crate under the table. Why wouldn't these girls leave and take their nasty conversation with them?

"Excuse me?" A dollar bill dangled from the brunette's tanned fingers. "We'll take a whoopie pie."

With a calming breath, Nora laid the bill into the money box.

"We gotta go." The blonde nudged her friend with an elbow. "He's on in five."

The girls disappeared before Nora could make change. The quarter clanged into the money box, and she closed her eyes, longing to escape the stuffy market air, reeking of sausage and fried onions…longing to unhear the conversation she just overheard. Bad boy? Jail? The Hill Top Bar? Every detail was more sordid than the last. She clasped her hands and rubbed one thumb into the thick muscle at the base of the other. When he talked about songwriting last night, he seemed like a different person. He was less brash and self-assured. His teasing was gentle…almost flattering. *You've got spunk.* Rolling her shoulders, she sighed.

"Do you feel all right?" *Mamm* turned sideways and squeezed between tables into the stand, holding a lemonade in each hand. She gave Nora a cup and removed two bags from under her arm.

"Well enough." She snatched a bag and withdrew one of Annie's pretzels. It was golden brown and baked to perfection.

Mamm sniffed. "Annie asked after you."

The pretzel was soft and buttery with a smattering of chunky salt she wanted to run her tongue over like a deer at a salt lick. She sipped lemonade and shivered at the bright combination of sweetness and tang. Then she heard his voice, and the shivering turned into a full-fledged shudder. The sound streamed in the open market doors like sunlight between barn boards, kindling her insides as if he had a match. The plastic cup was wet and slippery, and she eased her hold for fear it would slide from her hand. She swallowed a gooey lump of pretzel.

"I don't know about this music and whatnot." *Mamm* nibbled a cinnamon stick and pushed up the glasses on her nose. "Seems a body ought to be able to buy a beef roast without someone singing at 'em."

The guitar sounded, and her breath hitched. She ambled to the corner of the booth and peered out the opposite door. Through the glare, she could just make out the backs of heads above lawn chairs and the big speakers at the side of the stage.

"I've been thinking a lot about my music lately…wondering where it's gonna take me. Last night, a brand-new friend said playing my old songs might help me figure out what comes next. I think maybe she's right. Twinkletoes, this one's for you."

Nora couldn't remember the last time she blushed. At the silly word Twinkletoes, she felt her face flame as if Tucker McClure mentioned her by name in front of the whole town. She held the cool cup to one blazing cheek and hid the other from her mother. Fighting an irrational urge to dash outside, she rooted her feet to the floor.

"Did I mention Annie Amos says hello? Remember what good friends you girls were? Two peas in a pod."

If only her mother would keep talking so she couldn't hear his voice. If only her mother would pipe down so she could. If only she were home, safe in her kitchen where the only sounds were the ticking timer and the burbling creek.

"Annie still quilts every Monday at Sarah Stotzfus's shop. She invited you to join them…"

Her mother's voice faded into the market hullabaloo, and Tucker's soared above it, drowning all other sound.

"I wrote this song when I was sixteen years old, living on a potato farm in Northern Maine. Maybe some of you know it. It's called, 'The County.' "

The guitar sang, and the melody poured from the

speakers like the rush of water from a watering can. From deep in her belly surged a crazy urge to move to the music. Glancing down, she discovered her right toe tapping, almost on its own.

I'm gonna run from The County, leave my home far behind,

Take my hand, little darlin', and who knows what we'll find.

Pine trees blur the horizon, sunsets fire up the sky,

Nothin' left in The County for a boy who is learning to fly.

Restless and rolling, the song rekindled in her heart the longing for change she felt when she was canning applesauce. How she yearned for something different. How she craved a fresh start.

"So, what do you think?"

I love it. She blinked and gazed into her mother's round face. "About what?"

"Quilting with Annie."

"Sure." Like a bat, she tuned her ears to the only sound that mattered, and she'd say anything to stop her mother talking. "Let me sit a spell. Now you mention it, my leg is tired."

The woman with the naughty boys scurried to the stand and greeted them with a harried smile.

Her mother flashed the satisfied look of one who's been proven right for the thousandth time. Nora zipped to the milk crate by the wall where she could eat her snack in peace. Who knew beautiful music made delicious food even more scrumptious? But over the course of the next four songs, Tyler's melodies did exactly that. Convinced she'd never tasted such a delectable pretzel, she savored the last bite as the final chord died, and the audience erupted.

Seconds later, Tucker bounded in, red-faced and smiling with his guitar over one shoulder.

Bar…bad boy…jail…. The memory of the girls' conversation brought her back to reality. This man was trouble. She needed to send him on his way before her mother got wind they were acquainted. Like he had nowhere to be for the next forty years, he sauntered to the booth. Nora gave a tight smile over lemon sponge pies.

He ran a hand through his hair, and a ragged, white scar flashed through the stubble of a dark beard. "Afternoon, Nora."

She cast a sideways look at her mother who was busy with another customer. "Can I help you?" Her words were clipped. Her tone was cold.

Tucker tilted his head, gaze sharpening. "Enjoy the music? I took your advice—"

"As you can see, we're very busy. What would you like?"

He nodded, sliding a glance to the other end of the stall where her mother handed a customer change. "Well now, I want to take a pie to my grandfather, but as you know, he's a grumpy old son of a gun. Any suggestions?"

She grabbed the closest pie and thrust it at him.

He grinned. "Lemon sponge? That gonna make a sour old man any less sour, you think?"

How did he get that scar? An accident? A fight? Or worse? "Many of our customers enjoy the Shoofly."

"I'll take one of each." With a smile, he pivoted toward Verna. "Good afternoon, Mrs.—"

"Rishel. My mother." She gave a steely look she

hoped would quash further chitchat.

With a sniff, Verna refilled the empty spaces left by Tucker's purchases.

"Pleased to meet you, Mrs. Rishel. I'm Tucker McClure."

Verna sniffed again.

Somehow, her mother's sniffs conveyed as much information as a whole string of words. This sniff was a question directed at her. "Tucker's grandfather is in my exercise class." She gave special weight to the word *exercise*, hoping Tucker would respect what she told him in confidence.

Seeing nearly eye to eye with Tucker, Verna planted herself next to her daughter and crossed her arms over her ample bosom. "Good afternoon."

Tucker reached into his pocket and pulled out his wallet. "If you ever need a ride home after class, Nora, I'm happy to toss your bicycle into my truck."

Her mother's sharp breath whistled in her ear. The woman had lost one child to the English. The simple fear of losing another might kill her. In a fluid move, Nora snatched the proffered bills and returned change. "Thank you very much. Have a nice day." His smile faded like a rainbow, leaving behind dull gray sky. The pretzel hardened into a lump in her belly. Why did that icy tone come so easily? And what did she care if she wounded this rude and reckless *Englischer*?

With a brisk nod, he took up the pies and left.

"Watch your tone, *dochder*."

"But that man needs to respect—"

"That man is a child of *Gott* and a paying customer. You'd do well not to forget." Taking up her crochet, her mother planted herself on the chair and let her fingers fly.

Nora regretted nothing. Tucker's attention clearly made her mother uneasy. She needed to convey beyond the shadow of a doubt she wouldn't dream of fraternizing with an *Englischer*. Tucker needed a lesson in the same. Nonetheless, Verna's words stung. Lately, she received as much chiding as she doled out, almost as if she were a child. Though as a child, of course, Smiling Nora was never scolded.

Where was that cheerful girl? Was she hiding somewhere deep inside, waiting to be found? She remembered magical games of Hide and Seek, when all four brothers and innumerable cousins scattered around the farm, chasing each other until sunset. She remembered, too, the evening she hid in the old root cellar, waiting so long for a seeker who never came, she finally nodded off. Hours later, bleary-eyed and stiff, she stumbled upstairs into the empty barnyard to find everyone gone. Amid the bustle of a family gathering, no one had even missed her. Still feeling the twinge of abandonment, she tidied the pies in neat rows.

Let her mother scold. Reasserting steadfast loyalty was worth it. As for Tucker…well, if he never spoke to her again, then so be it.

On the outdoor stage, another musician struck up a jaunty tune.

Scoffing, she shut her ears. Tucker wasn't the only person on earth with the power to make her smile. Surely, someone in her community—someone appropriate—could find Smiling Nora curled up in her hiding place. If only he bothered to look.

****

Nora scooted into the corner of the front porch

bench and pinched her forehead between rigid fingers. Even filtered through yellowing leaves, the Sunday afternoon sunlight glared, and she felt a headache coming on. "I'm sorry, what?"

Mervin Zook took the move as an invitation to inch closer. "What did they replace your hip with? The bone of a horse or some such creature?"

With effort, she refrained from gawking. Could the man truly be so daft? "It's an artificial joint made of ceramic."

Mervin stroked his scraggly beard, thin lips sliding into a frown. "Ceramic? Like a teapot?"

She gave Mervin a tight smile. "Nothing like a teapot." With beady eyes, he assessed her, landing his gaze squarely on her right hip and looking as if he'd be happy to examine her like a mare at auction. Of course, a bumbling goof like Mervin couldn't be expected to have noticed which hip she favored. Not when he was busy devouring half a shoofly pie.

The man crossed spindly legs, making him appear even more like a lounging frog. For a person who ate so much, he had very little meat on the bones. Then again, without a woman in the house, regular mealtime offerings might be scant. Compassion twinged in her chest. She knew the agony of being left alone with a child. Mervin lost his wife much more recently than she lost Levi, and he had four youngsters to care for. He was a good man and a respected member of the community—a deacon's son. Mervin Zook was exactly the type of man she should marry. Except, of course, that he was a blockheaded bore.

Shrieking with laughter, Mervin's youngest, three-year-old Agnes, streaked across the lawn clutching a very agitated chicken.

Hot on her tail, Rebecca burst around the corner of the house. "Agnes Zook! Release that poor hen!"

Rebecca flashed Nora a look of exquisite agony. No wonder. After helping with the dinner dishes, Rebecca was given sole charge of Mervin's four children. Four devils, more like. Nora shuddered to think what the other three were doing. Likely someone should check the creek. Would Mervin and Deacon Elmer ever go home?

"You'll never catch Henny Penny!" Agnes screeched.

The chicken flapped and squawked in Agnes's iron hold.

Rebecca lunged for the girl, catching a handful of violet skirt. "Her name is Rosamanda Ingalls Wilder, and she doesn't like to be held."

"I'll hold her forever and ever!" With a shriek, Agnes wrenched free and disappeared around the other side of the house.

Mervin chuckled. "That girl could use a strong hand."

His children needed four strong hands at the very least. Softening her shoulders, Nora mustered sympathy. Could they really be blamed? "Oh, I don't know…"

Pressing a fist to his mouth, he let out a muffled burp. "Giving a chicken a name like Rosamanda such and such? It's indecent."

She jerked to her feet and braced her hands on the railing. How dare he criticize her daughter? Rebecca was nothing like his little monsters. Closing her eyes, she focused every ounce of energy on holding her tongue. *Eens, zwee, drei, vier, fimf...* Her breathing slowed, and she became aware of the oddest sensation in her feet. They tingled. Then they itched as if they wanted to move. *Shuffle ball change. Shuffle ball change.* In her head, a cheerful melody played, calming the storm inside.

When she opened her eyes, she was surprised to discover stubby fingers perilously close to hers on the railing. Mervin might be daft, but he moved like a cat.

He swiveled toward her, and the combined scents of dairy cows and cooked onions wafted in an odiferous cloud. "I'd be pleased to call on you, Nora Beiler."

She stared at her hands. Between her fingers, white paint cracked and splintered. Likely no one had painted the porch since Jonas three years ago. Was any leftover paint still in the barn? Perhaps she'd touch up the rail herself.

"Nora?" Mervin bumped her sneaker with his shoe.

She gripped the rail, wincing as a sliver dug into her palm.

The screen door swung wide, and *Mamm* burst onto the porch, holding her belly, and laughing. "And it was the sow all along?"

Deacon Elmer followed on her heels. "It was that rascal sow!" He slapped one thigh and hooted, his blue eyes dancing and his round cheeks red.

What a funny pair they were: her mother as big and broad as an oak and Deacon Elmer slender as a sapling beside her. They inclined their heads toward one another, and suddenly, Nora knew. One couple on the porch had a shine for each other, and that couple wasn't herself and Mervin.

Deacon Elmer wiped his eyes and sighed. "Verna,

your cooking was excellent as always. Thank you for having us."

Mamm glowed. "My daughter knows her way around a kitchen."

Deacon Elmer elbowed his son in the ribs.

Mervin flinched and rubbed his side.

"We'd be pleased to have you out again real soon, wouldn't we, Nora?" *Mamm* lifted her brows and nodded.

Not one itty-bitty bone in Nora's body was pleased at the notion of Mervin Zook and his rambunctious brood returning to her well-ordered home. They were probably trampling her vegetable garden that very minute. Her hip twinged, and she arched her back, wanting more than anything to retreat to the sanctuary of the kitchen and whip up a perfect pie crust. For her mother's benefit, she lifted tight lips in a smile. "Of course." Her mother's face shone with conviction all was right with the world. Most likely, Verna's thoughts were entirely for her daughter, and she didn't realize how taken she herself was with Deacon Elmer.

Years ago, her mother gently nudged her toward Levi Beiler, recognizing their suitability while Nora and her friends still tittered over anyone with a deep voice and his own two-seat buggy. Was her mother right again? Yanking the sliver from her palm, she set off to round up the junior Zooks. Maybe Mervin didn't make her smile from the soles of her feet, but he offered security and a good Christian home. Perhaps in time, she'd come to believe that's enough.

Chapter Seven

Nora gazed into the grinning face of Hank McClure. When he smiled, he looked like a different person. She blinked. "I suppose you're right." Coming smoothly to her feet, she executed a shuffle-step-heel-step with the swift proficiency of someone who'd been attending tap class for well over a month. The big wall of mirrors in the studio reflected a limber, young body with two equally strong legs.

"Attagirl. For weeks now, I watched you tie your shoes, and every time you reached for your toes, your mouth screwed up tight, and all the pink drained from your cheeks. But last week and then again today, tying 'em looked easy as pie. Told ya' Jerry would fix you up good."

Edna and Joan bustled into the classroom, peeling off colorful woolen scarves and hats.

October had arrived, and seemingly overnight, the maples sported red coats, and the grass awoke every morning beneath frosty blankets. When the air turned crisp and the temperature plummeted, Nora braced herself. For years, cold weather meant increasingly unbearable hip pain. However, as Hank observed, this autumn, the pain was minimal.

"If you don't mind my saying, that limp of yours plum disappears when you dance." He raised bushy eyebrows and tapped his temple with one finger.

"Something to think about."

Wearing a bright purple sweatshirt with the words *TipTop Tappers* emblazoned in sparkly gold letters, Jerry swept to the front of the class. "Good evening, dancers."

Jerry raised her hands and swiveled her backside in a manner that would have thoroughly unnerved Verna Rishel but seemed to Nora as cheerful as the gentle sway of a cat's tail.

Jerry pumped her palms toward the ceiling. "Ya'll ready to move?"

"You betcha," Bert and Dot chorused as one.

With practiced ease, the class assembled in two straight lines. Feet tingling and legs aquiver, Nora slipped into her customary warm-up spot between Marion and Joan and welcomed the feeling that came at the beginning of every class. She was so excited she could hardly breathe. And she loved it.

Dropping her hands to her waist, Jerry thrust out a hip. "Now before we get started, November's right around the corner, and you all know what that means."

"My annual colonoscopy," Bert said out of the side of his mouth. He groaned and hopped from foot to foot.

Dot thwapped him on one shoulder.

Jerry shook her head, but her smile was bright. "Time to get the TipTop Tappers back in action."

The class burst into excited chatter.

Nora looked from face to face, then sidled over to Joan. "Who are the TipTop Tappers?"

"Why we are, honey. Once a year, we perform in the annual Christmas show to benefit Dr. Bruce's Covered Bridge Medical Clinic."

Perform? At a show? The studio floor dipped, and

she hunched over, planting her hands on her thighs.

"Feeling all right?" Jerry laid a hand on her back.

Marion bounced to her other side. "Don't be nervous, dear. The show is a hoot and a half. We wear cute sparkly skirts—nice and long, of course. Only Mr. Diefenderfer gets to see these gams." She swept her leg in a big circle and popped her hip like a teenager.

Jerry patted Nora's back in soothing circles. "How about you and I chat after class, and I'll tell you all about the event? For now, let's just learn the dance."

Willing her heartbeat to slow, she breathed deeply and met Jerry's gaze. The woman's eyes shone with equal parts compassion and conviction. Not only did Jerry understand, she cared. Nora released her jaw and nodded.

With a jangle of gold and silver bracelets, Jerry sashayed to the front of the room. "Line up with your partners, TipTop Tappers. Let's rock around the old Christmas tree."

Jerry's reassurance coupled with Hank's encouraging smile buoyed her spirits. Class began, and almost instantly, her troubles lifted. She'd worry about performances and costumes later. For now, she surrendered to the joy of dancing. The cheerful *tappity-tapping* of her shoes made her tummy spasm with giggles. These English songs were ridiculous. They were silly and carefree and utterly irreverent, but every single face in the room shone with happiness and...dare she even think it...the light of the spirit.

She and Hank weren't perfect dancers. Honestly, they struggled to come close to Edna's and Joan's proficiency. But as she snuck glances around the room, catching stumbles, gaffs, and guffaws, she realized she wasn't remotely the worst dancer. In fact, she was one of the best.

Growing up, she never strove to be best at anything. Among the Amish, no prizes were awarded for personal achievement. All effort went to serving family, community, and church. Realizing dancing came naturally and gave her pleasure was a revelation. Her skill didn't diminish anyone, and excelling wasn't a sin…even if dancing was. She simply expressed a God-given ability to its fullest. And, if she chose, she could share that ability to benefit none other than Dr. Richard Bruce, the man who restored her to life.

As the class dispersed, Jerry waved her into the supply closet.

The space was large enough to function as a changing room, with benches and cubbies tucked beneath shelves lined with plastic storage tubs. The odor of leather and sweat was strangely reminiscent of the utility room at home.

Jerry sat and patted the bench beside her.

With tired but limber muscles, she accepted the invitation, bending over to unlace her left shoe. Hank was right. Her hip didn't holler even a tiny bit.

Jerry tipped back and surveyed her with narrowed eyes. "How are you, Nora?"

She stretched her left leg and wiggled her toes. The thin black stocking pulled tight, and she couldn't help but admire the graceful line of her calf and her slender ankle. "Very well, thank you."

Pursing violet-tinted lips, Jerry waggled her head and tutted. "I'm gonna ask again. How are you?"

When was the last time someone asked how she was? Her mother never did because her mother thought she knew. Often, she was right. Often, but not always, and certainly not lately. So how was she? Really and truly. Reflecting upon the last few weeks, she felt like a child in a mystifying world that turned out to be not at all what she was led to believe. "To be honest, I'm all mixed up inside."

Her gaze still fixed on Nora's, Jerry nodded. "I figured as much. You're a brave girl, you know that?"

First spunky and now brave? A bitter laugh escaped her, leaving a taste of sour greens. Quick as a wink, she untied the other shoe.

"You don't agree?" Jerry's lips tucked under at the corners. "Let me ask you this: do your people know what you do here?"

With a quick nod, she grabbed her sneakers from a cubby and slid the tap shoes into their place.

"Child, why do you make me repeat myself? Do they know?"

She felt her throat tighten. This conversation was a mistake. Jerry didn't understand—couldn't understand. Nora's fingers were suddenly sausages—thick and unyielding. She fumbled with the sneaker laces. "They know enough," she said with finality.

"Let me tell you a story." Slinging one knee onto the bench, Jerry reclined against the supply shelves. "When I was a girl, I didn't know many white folks. In those days, New York was a thousand different neighborhoods that kept entirely to themselves. My mama taught me to be careful and watch my back. Maybe even not to trust people who didn't look like me. But lord, girl"—she lifted both palms to the ceiling—"I loved to dance. It was all I wanted to do, morning, noon, and night.

"Now, I had Broadway-sized dreams and to let my light shine, I had to walk among folks my mama taught me to stay clear of. I moved myself to Manhattan and auditioned for every studio and class I could find. Most days, sitting there waiting my turn, I didn't see a single face that looked like mine. Not one. But dancing was in my soul. It was a gift from the ancestors, and who was I to refuse such a gift?"

A cheerful heart and a humble spirit were the gifts Nora was taught to value. When raised in praise at a singing or in church, perhaps a rich and strong voice like Levi's might be praised. She thought of her daughter's curious, creative spirit. The Amish community had no room for gifts such as hers. Let alone the gift to dance.

Jerry shook a purple-tipped finger. "I know what you're thinking. What does my story have to do with what you face right now? But every time I walked into one of those rooms full of pretty white girls, let me tell you, I was scared. When I went home for Sunday supper, and Mama asked what was I doing to pay the rent, and why I was not moving back to the neighborhood, I was scared. And when I fell in love with the white boy who delivered produce to the restaurant where I served fancy cocktails and waited for a break that never came? You better believe I was scared. Bravery comes in many forms. I know it when I see it."

Nora's belly tightened, and the corners of her eyes stung. Jerry smiled so kindly and smelled so comfortingly of cinnamon that Nora wanted to drop her head onto the woman's shoulder. She clasped her hands in her lap and pinched tight her mouth. "My mother doesn't know. I told her this is an exercise class—"

"And it is."

"But she doesn't know that I—that we…" She lowered her voice to a whisper, afraid that by saying the word aloud her whole community could hear her sin. "*Dance*. I should have quit weeks ago. I meant to, but I couldn't. Everyone is counting on me, and I just…"

"You just love to dance." Jerry patted her knee. "Oh, my girl, I can't tell you what to do. If you feel in your heart you need to quit, then you quit. You can do the stretches and exercises at home, and your hip will keep getting stronger." She jerked away and pursed her lips. "Now hold on a second. You ride that bicycle of yours. I might not know many of your people, but I've never seen a one on a bike."

She sniffed and dragged the back of her hand beneath her nose. "The bishop makes allowances for medical reasons. The doctor said riding my bike helps my hip."

"And dancing doesn't?"

A lump lodged in her throat, and she swallowed hard. "Oh, Jerry. Dancing is not at all like riding a bike. Dancing is a sin."

Jerry's eyes went wide. "Sweet Jesus, don't I know it." She let out a booming laugh, big enough to rattle the walls.

Unable to stop herself, Nora joined in. Shoulders shaking, she laughed until tears flowed, and she had to wrap her arms around her aching belly.

"Oh, I needed that." Jerry wiped her cheeks and sighed a long, musical sigh. "You follow your heart. The universe gave me the gift of being your teacher, and I'll always cherish it. You know we want you with us when we dance for Dr. Bruce, but if you feel you shouldn't, every one of these folks will support you. Even old Hank."

A weight like an ox yoke lifted from Nora's shoulders. "Thank you." She rose to leave and paused. "No one has spoken to me with such kindness for a very long time. Our people are expected to follow rules without question, but over the last few years, I've come to see…well, I suppose life is far more complicated than I ever imagined."

Jerry shook her head with a smile. "Amen, child. Amen."

When she emerged into the dusky parking lot, Nora was surprised to see Tucker's truck idling alongside the bike rack. The lot was empty. The other students were long gone, and streetlights flickered overhead. Chilly night air cut through the light wool of her coat, and she pulled the collar tight around her throat.

The driver's side window squeaked down, and Tucker's head appeared.

She caught his gaze. In the weeks since her icy reception at the Farmers' Market, he'd been cordial but distant, and she'd done her best to avoid him. His expression today was warm, and her legs wobbled. Steeling them, she quickened her pace.

"There you are," he said over the motor's hum.

Even speaking, his voice was music. In her head, she heard a guitar and the sweet strains of singing. Jerry's story had a happy ending. She'd be naive to think hers could, too. She hardened her shoulders and set her jaw against the mushy pudding feeling in her belly. "Why are you still here?"

He flashed a quick smile and jerked a thumb

toward the passenger seat. "Old Hank thought you might need a ride. I'm happy to toss your bike in the truck."

She pulled up short. No one was tossing her beloved bicycle anywhere. Seizing the handlebars, she jerked it from the rack and wheeled toward the trail.

"Oh, it was my idea, huh?" Hank let out a laugh and beckoned with a thick palm. "A chill's come on. Driving you home would be our pleasure."

The night was cold, and bicycling would be onerous. But she had a lot to think over—too much to let her mind be clouded by the presence of Tucker McClure. Slinging a leg over the seat, she shook her head. "I'll be fine, thank you."

Hank shrugged. "Suit yourself."

The tires whooshed, and the truck swung in a wide circle, bringing Tucker's open window to her side. "See you around, Twinkletoes."

Without saying goodbye, she pedaled hard for the bike path. Frigid air screamed into her lungs. Her legs heated, and her heart raced. No matter the temperature outside, her insides burned with the fire of a thousand unanswered questions. The most pressing of which was, would she dance in the Christmas performance for Dr. Richard's medical clinic?

Chapter Eight

No sooner had Nora pulled *On the Banks of Plum Creek* from the library shelf, than she felt a tap on one shoulder. With a gasp, she whirled. Clapping a hand over her mouth, she stared at the grizzled face. Though she occasionally happened upon friends during visits to the Green Ridge Public Library, Hank McClure was the last person she expected to bump into in the children's section.

Grinning, he stepped back and held up his hands. "Beg your pardon, Miss Nora. I didn't mean to startle you. Just wanted to give my regards."

Even for a sunny Saturday in late October, the library was busy. Only a few years old, the airy building provided plenty of shelves to browse and comfy chairs for quiet study. Today, children dashed between stacks gaily decorated for Halloween, and grown-ups greeted each other in louder-than-usual library whispers. Still, she hadn't been expecting the gravelly, hissed "hello" that tickled her ear and made her jump. Why did everyone seem dead set on startling her lately? She lowered her palm to her chest and puffed out a breath. "Rebecca, say hello to Hank. Hank attends exercise class with me every Tuesday."

Rebecca plunked her hands on her hips and studied Hank through slitted eyes. "What did you have replaced?"

Hank frowned. "Huh?"

"My mother has a new hip. That's why she goes to Shuffle Off to Fitness. What's new on you?"

"Rebecca!" This girl. Why couldn't she simply behave appropriately?

Hank dropped meaty paws to his hips and bent over, bringing his face level with Rebecca's. "Not a single, cotton-picking thing. Every part of me is older than the hills. My darned feet are so ancient I can't even feel them."

Rebecca dropped her gaze to Hank's brown loafers. "Is that true?"

"Yessiree, Bob. Those know-it-all doctors call it neuropathy—now, there's a nickel word for you. They say it's a sign of diabetes and won't let me drive my own car. All I know is my balance is all cattywampus, and I've got a hitch in my giddyup."

So that's why Tucker always drove Hank to class. Where was he, anyway? Nora snuck a glance over one shoulder. Not that she wanted to see him, even if her quickening heartbeat suggested otherwise. She simply didn't want to be ambushed twice in one day.

Rebecca's eyes went wide. "You know all sorts of words. You must spend hours in the library." She shoved a book at Hank. "Have you read Nancy Drew?"

Taking it, Hank lowered himself into an armchair. "Well, I can't say I've read one per se. I was more a Hardy Boys fella, myself. But my wife Lavelle had every single one of these here stories. She read them, and my daughter read them, and when they were both done, she lent them out to other children to read. I still have 'em all in my library."

Rebecca vaulted onto the arm of the chair. "You

have your very own library?"

Perched next to Hank, the girl looked like a bluebird sitting on the shoulder of a grizzly bear. A pang of longing for her own father pierced Nora's heart. He never had the chance to see his granddaughter grow.

"My mother won't let me read *The Lion, The Witch and The Wardrobe,* even though Mr. C.S. Lewis was a famous Christian theologian. She says witches are sinful."

Just like that, anger pushed aside melancholy. With Rebecca, she never had more than a few seconds of peace.

Hank slid Nora a glance from beneath bushy eyebrows. "Well now, mothers generally know best."

Rebecca recoiled, a look of betrayal creasing her brow. In an instant, her expression cleared, and she snatched the book. "Would you like me to read you some Nancy Drew since you never had a chance yourself?"

"Rebecca, Uncle Samuel will be here soon. We'd best leave Hank to his browsing."

Hank clapped both hands onto his knees. "Well, that's a shame. I was looking forward to hearing the story."

Hope shone in her daughter's gaze. Spine turning to spaghetti, Nora replaced the perfectly acceptable Laura Ingalls Wilder book and acquiesced. Every request from her daughter seemed to end the same way—with Nora reluctant but permissive and Rebecca a smidge too pleased. "All right, but only for five minutes, and stay away from the computer. I'll wait outside."

She left her daughter nestled in the chair with her

captive audience seemingly enthralled. How best to manage this child? She was a hard worker and clever, but she was never satisfied. If Nora gave an inch, Rebecca took a mile. Not content with the bottom branch of the tree, she inevitably scrambled to the tippy top. The pictures she drew of birds and bugs were colorful and full of exquisite detail...and yet always a bit, well, much. They had the look of the ungodly, somehow, as if the life force burned in their eyes for everyone to see. With a sigh, she pushed through the doors and squinted into dazzling afternoon sun. Then again, she herself was taking secret dance classes and pondering participating in a performance. She always attributed Rebecca's rebellion to her father. Maybe she'd been wrong.

"If I didn't know better, I'd say you were following me."

Outwardly, she froze. Inwardly, her heart rocketed into her throat as it did every single time she heard his voice. What was it about this man? Why did he rattle her so? And why, oh why, was Tucker McClure sprawled, arms outstretched and legs spread wide, on the only bench in front of the library? Running would be rude. Staying made the palms of her hands tingle.

He slid to one side of the bench. "You see Hank? I'm sure he'd want to say hello. The old grump won't give me the time of day, but to him, well, Twinkletoes, you must have set this old world a-spinning. He's smiled more since becoming your dance partner than he did the whole six months I've been in town."

Fuzzy, yellow dandelion heads poked through cracks in the sidewalk, tenacious and hopeful. How long would Samuel be at the hardware store? That morning, she got up earlier than usual to complete the day's chores before coming into town. All she wanted now was to rest, but sitting close to this man was dangerous. She hovered a few feet from the bench. "Hank is inside with my daughter."

A wide-eyed, slack-jawed look skittered over Tucker's features. Clearly, he never dreamed she was a mother, and the revelation unnerved him. For some strange reason, she liked it. "I left them reading Nancy Drew."

"One of my grandmother's favorites." He tilted his head toward the empty space on the bench. "How old is your daughter?"

Feeling momentarily like she had the upper hand, she sat, tucking into the opposite corner. "She's ten."

He nodded and stared across the parking lot. His truck gleamed green and shiny in the sunlight. High puffy clouds scudded over distant ridges. If the sun tucked behind one, the afternoon would turn chilly fast.

"Her father coming to pick you up?"

With a gasp, she jerked to her feet. How dare he ask…how dare he wonder…how dare he even think about her husband. "I should go."

He leapt up, thrusting out a hand. "Whoa, whoa, whoa. I'm sorry. Didn't mean to speak out of turn."

"I need to fetch my daughter." She spun and started toward the library.

"While she's reading Nancy Drew with Hank? Wait." With a few quick strides, he cut her off. "Nora. Please."

She paused and laced her arms across her chest like a shield.

Stepping back, he gestured toward the bench with a

slow sweep of the hand. "Have a seat. I didn't mean to pry."

Feeling tugged in twenty different directions, she hesitated. She wanted to sit, and she wanted to flee. She wanted her daughter, and she wanted her mother. She wanted nothing more than to be alone in her kitchen, her hands deep in soft, yeasty dough, and she wanted to hear him sing.

With a jingle of harnesses and a clop of hooves, Samuel veered into the parking lot. He pulled into the buggy space and jumped out, taking hold of Dan's reins. "Nora? Are you well?"

She nodded.

Striding with intent, Tucker held out a hand. "I'm Tucker McClure. My grandfather is in the Tuesday exercise class with your…with Nora."

Her brother was taller and broader than Tucker. All the Rishel boys were big. Her father had been a giant of a man. Whipping off his hat, Samuel ran a hand through his light brown hair in a manner so like their older brother Jonas, her heart ached.

With an easy smile, Samuel shook hands. "Samuel Rishel. Thank you for keeping my sister company. I was longer at the hardware store than I intended." He shot her a look. "Mr. Donehower doesn't stock brackets for solar panels, but he said he could order them."

"You in the solar business?" Shielding his eyes, Tucker lifted his chin toward the blazing sun. "I grew up on a solar-powered potato farm. We were off-the-grid before it was cool."

As they launched into an animated conversation about batteries and cells, the library door opened. Hand in hand Rebecca and Hank bounced through and skipped down the sidewalk, their feet tapping an unmistakable flap heel step.

"*Mamm*! Hank taught me one of the exercises from your class."

Her mouth went dry, and she swallowed hard. She spun to her brother and back to her daughter, and the library wobbled in her vision. Rubbing her eyes, she fought a wave of dizziness. From behind, her brother and Tucker shared a laugh. Coming toward her, Hank and Rebecca hopped like a pair of dancing rabbits. A car horn honked, and a dog howled, and in that instant, she knew. Her life was slowly and deliberately spinning out of her control. She sank onto the bench and lowered her head into her hands. Once and for all, this nonsense had to end.

****

Nora stood beside her mother on the porch and waved until the Zook's buggy rounded the bend. The sky was milk-bucket gray, and the breeze carried the scent of burning brush and rain. With the house finally empty, all she wanted was to curl up and read. Knowing she had no church service today, why hadn't she checked out a book yesterday at the library? Between Hank's dancing with her daughter and Tyler's prying questions, she got all tied in knots.

Mamm clasped her hands over her belly and sighed. "Can't imagine a nicer way to spend an off Sunday."

Nora could think of a hundred nicer ways.

The slosh of water and soft clink of dishes in the sink came through the kitchen window. Read a book, indeed. After the Zook family's tornado of a visit, Nora would be tidying up for hours. She turned toward the door. "Why don't you sit a spell? Rebecca and I can finish the dishes."

Verna snorted. "Piffle. I'm not so old as to be no help in the kitchen."

Far from it. Her mother was strong as an ox. She just enjoyed the ritual of everyone reminding her of the fact. "Of course, you aren't. I figured you might like a break. Those children are…energetic."

Mamm followed, wiping her shoes on the braid mat inside the door. "They're coddled and ill-mannered, but can you blame them, living in a house full of men?"

Amish children were known for excellent deportment. If Rebecca had behaved so after Levi's death, she would have been punished lickety-split. Did Verna really think Nora was the woman to train that litter of rascal pups?

Before he left, pink-cheeked and solemn, Mervin asked if he could call again in two weeks. What could she say? He was a good match. The community would bless their union. Unfortunately, apart from vague admiration for his general goodness, she still felt absolutely nothing for the man. Affection had not grown with acquaintance.

In the kitchen, she found Rebecca, a clean glass in each hand, tap dancing from the sink to the cabinet. Nora gritted her teeth, plunged her hands in the steamy wash water, and held them there. Her skin was bone-dry from fall cleaning. Sometimes, catching a glimpse of her hands, she mistook them for her grandmother's. She flexed her fingers and felt cracks split and burn where dish soap seeped into her skin. The pain was oddly calming, grounding her in her own body and driving out thoughts of Mervin, his children, and her daughter's tortured expression when once again she was tasked with their care.

Humming under her breath, Rebecca repeated the trip with two more glasses.

Mamm poured a cup of coffee and stirred in a heaping spoon of sugar. "Why are you bouncing around like a dizzy frog?"

Rebecca caught Nora's gaze and smirked. "I'm doing an exercise from *Mamm's* class. All that bouncing made her hip strong, and she smiles all the time now. Did you notice, *Mammi* Verna?"

Something in her daughter's expression unnerved her. Her look was entirely too knowing. "The floor's wet. Don't fall." Nora snatched the washrag and wrung it. It glided smoothly over the blue willow plates. By some miracle, the Zooks didn't break the good china. Mervin's father might be a deacon, but if she had her way, those children would eat from wooden trenchers. She lifted her cheeks to the cool breeze coming through the window. Did she really smile more? Right now, her old familiar companion, hot rage, summoned a scowl.

Mamm lowered into a chair with a muffled "oof" and sipped her coffee. "The deacon and I discussed the matter of your bicycle and the doctor's exercise class."

Stiffening, she gripped the plate so hard she feared she'd be the one to crack it. If that man forbade her to ride her bike, she didn't know what she'd do. She darted a glance over one shoulder.

A smug smile spread across *Mamm's* face. "Between bites of your shoofly pie, he agreed to both."

Relief softened her shoulders. Thank goodness. The fury demon retreated, and she slid the plate into scalding rinse water.

Rebecca switched from a shuffle to a skip and snatched a dishtowel. "Can I have a bike?"

Setting down the coffee cup, Verna folded her hands. "Do you have a new hip?"

The lightness in her tone suggested Rebecca might get her way, but beneath it lurked a message hard as iron. Despite herself, Nora smiled. She knew how this conversation would end.

Fair brows drawing into a *V*, Rebecca cast a glance at perfectly intact young legs. "No. Only the regular ones."

"Then walking will do very well for you."

Rebecca heaved a sigh deep enough to dry the dish in her hands. "Can I at least go to the exercise class? I'd love to jump around with the old people."

"Where do you get such notions?" Verna rose, scraping the sturdy oak chair across the linoleum. "I think I will sit awhile. I owe Martha a letter. She and Moses want us to come to Ohio for Christmas. I suppose we'll see."

Nora bit back a hasty objection. She was so looking forward to a Pennsylvania Christmas. "Maybe they'd like to come here."

"Can't see as Martha would make the trip." Her mother caught her gaze. "Unless, of course, a wedding was involved." With a meaningful look, she freshened her coffee and left.

Nora spun to the sink and hurled in the greasy roast pan to soak. If her mother mentioned Mervin Zook in a letter to Aunt Martha, she'd never hear the end of it.

"Who's getting married?" Rebecca asked.

"No one." The mashed potato pan followed, sloshing soapy water over the edge.

Rebecca dried a serving fork with focused vigor. "I don't want to be a Zook and have Zooks for brothers and sisters."

Nora wiped the cupboards with a damp dishtowel. "Hush."

"I want to be a McClure like Hank. Did you know he and his wife Lavelle flew airplanes in Alaska?"

"Don't talk nonsense." Snapping the dishtowel, she squatted to mop the floor. Her bottom nearly hit the ground before she realized what she'd done. She couldn't remember the last time she squatted all the way down without crying in pain. She shifted her weight from foot to foot, enjoying the open feeling in her hips. All that bouncing, indeed.

The serving fork clattered into the utensil drawer. "It's not nonsense. Hank and Lavelle delivered mail and books and medicine to families on faraway farms without electricity just like us. Hank lived the life of an adventurer."

She stood and leaned into the counter, stretching her calf muscles.

Rebecca eased the blue willow plates into the hutch, adjusting them until they were perfectly spaced. "Hank said his good-for-nothing grandson should go to Alaska. He said the wilderness makes a man see clearly and get his priorities straight."

"You and Hank certainly discussed a lot in a short time."

"We certainly did." Another knowing smile crept across Rebecca's face.

Sour queasiness rose in Nora's throat. She unhooked her favorite blue mug from the mug tree and poured a cup of coffee.

"Hank says I needn't borrow Nancy Drew from the library. He has a huge library at his house, and Lavelle had every single book in the series. He's going to bring them to exercise class one by one for me to read."

The coffee was muddy dregs. She choked down a bitter swallow and dumped in the rest with the soaking pans. Enough was enough. She'd waffled for two months. Between dancing and the Christmas performance and now her classmates putting ridiculous ideas into her daughter's head...between Tucker and music and smiling all the time like a lunatic...Nora Beiler was becoming someone she did not at all recognize. She grabbed steel wool and scrubbed the roast pan hard enough to tear a hole in the metal. "I'm quitting exercise class."

Rebecca whirled, mouth agape. "Why? You enjoy it so much, and your limp is almost gone."

Her question was earnest—innocent—infuriating. A stubborn hunk of grease clung to the pan like it grew roots in the metal. Grinding her teeth, Nora attacked it. "Hold your tongue. I'm done, and that's an end to it."

In a rush, Rebecca clung to her sleeve. "But—but—since you joined the class, you seem…"

She snapped around her head. Amazingly, she and Rebecca looked nearly eye to eye. In the months since they moved home, the girl had grown like a pea shoot. She'd be as tall as her uncles and *Grossmammi* before long. But her pale face was still as guileless as a child's.

Rebecca gave a lopsided smile. "You seem happy."

She jerked away her arm. "Enough."

Wobbling, but still latched to Nora's sleeve, Rebecca persisted. "You smile for no reason, and sometimes you even hum."

The grease gave way, and the pan slipped from Nora's hold, smashing into the mashed potato pot, and crushing her fingers. She yanked her hand from the water, wincing. "Go to your room."

"But, *Mamm*—"

"I said go!"

Rebecca dashed to the back door and flung it open.

Like an uninvited guest, a cold wind rushed into the kitchen, ruffling the wall calendar. Turning in the doorway, Rebecca met her gaze with a look of blazing defiance. *Levi.* Her husband stood before her in the form of this girl child, as plain as day. His eyes flashed from their daughter's face, and his wide, soft mouth hardened in defiance.

Rebecca pulled herself up tall. "If you quit that class, I'll tell *Mammi* Verna you've been dancing with the old people." A single shudder shook her, but she stood firm. "Don't think I won't." Then she whirled and fled.

The wind caught the open door, slamming it against the side of the house until the glass window rattled. Autumn herself seemed to lean into the door with a bone-chilling shoulder, and Nora barely found strength to catch the knob and muscle it closed. The hinges juddered, and the latch clicked, snuffing a noise that to her addled brain almost sounded like Levi's voice…laughing.

Chapter Nine

The following Tuesday night, Nora snugged her bike into the rack behind the senior center and huffed a breath into icy hands. She cast a wary look heavenward and shivered. Earlier, the sky was a solid gray slab with the look of snow. Now, the sun had set, and the air was unusually cold for the last week of October. Other considerations aside, how would she travel to class once the weather turned frigid, and snow coated the trail?

A red, compact car zipped into the space next to the bike rack, and Jerry jumped out. She gathered the collar of a puffy, plum-colored jacket beneath her chin. "Good evening, Nora. I hoped I'd catch you."

Nora studied the bug-splattered headlights. She had also hoped to see Jerry before class. Pot roast and green beans roiled in her belly. Why was she nervous?

Jerry hustled up beside her and gestured toward the warm building. "Did you have a chance to ponder our conversation?"

A familiar pickup rumbled into the lot. She glimpsed Tucker's shaggy head and Hank's snowy one. With a sharp nod, she quickened her pace. She wasn't ready to talk to either of those men.

Jerry stopped at the entrance. "Did you pray on it?"

She gulped a fortifying breath. "I did."

"The fact you're reaching for the door leads me to

believe the outcome is in our favor."

She nodded, unable to tell Jerry her decision had far less to do with heavenly guidance than her headstrong daughter.

"Wonderful!" Beaming, Jerry strode into the lobby.

"But about the performance." Her voice cracked. Simply saying the word made her mouth go dry. Dipping her head, she grabbed a quick drink from the water fountain and scurried down the hall behind her teacher.

"And what did the good Lord say about that?"

Her sneaker caught on the carpet, and she stumbled. The idea *Gott* would talk to her? Ridiculous. "May I think on it a bit longer? The decision is complicated."

"The best things in life usually are." Pausing outside the classroom, Jerry unzipped her jacket. "Take all the time you need. Come to class, learn the dance, and get your hip good and strong. Then, if you decide not to perform, I'll step in. Hank will make do."

Spirit lightening, she sighed. "Thank you." Through a window in the studio door, she spied Dot and Bert practicing the intricate combination that started the Christmas dance. Hands clasped, they glided across the floor like a young couple in the first bloom of love. Together, they were so much more than they were alone.

Bert said something, and Dot erupted in laughter.

Their faces shone with the simple joy of being together. She remembered that feeling. Would she ever feel it again?

Jerry chuckled. "Look at those two. They're two of a kind. Living proof there's someone for everyone."

Jerry might be right. But were two someones in a single lifetime too much to hope for? The elderly bodies moved with remarkable grace. What would dancing with a man she loved feel like? Sometimes when she and Levi worked together splitting and stacking wood, they found a shared rhythm that almost felt like dancing. Or when they rode out in the buggy on a sunny spring morning, singing a hymn in harmony, and watching the countryside roll by...that felt like dancing too. When Levi held her in his arms and kissed her alone in their room after everyone else was fast asleep—those private moments between husband and wife were a whole different manner of dancing. Her cheeks heated at the memory, and she uncoiled the scarf from her neck.

But to feel music rise from her feet like dough on a warm afternoon, and then to take the hand of a man who made her pulse race and her breath come quick and light...? A song about a smiling face tripped through her thoughts, and she shivered. The idea was almost too wonderful to imagine. Or was it simply too wicked?

Excitement about the December performance fizzed in the air. Amid men discussing the coming snowstorm and women chattering about their grand-children's Halloween costumes, Nora sat quietly on a chair and tied her shoes. She felt like the lone fixed figure in a snow globe surrounded by glittery flakes.

Hank sidled up. He sniffed and wiped his nose with a blue bandanna. "Evening, Nora."

She nodded, nibbling the inside of her cheek. Right then, she didn't know how she felt about Hank. She never said her dancing was a secret, and she certainly wouldn't expect him to lie on her behalf, but his loose lips landed her in a pickle.

His feet moved in an easy buffalo step. "That's some daughter you got. Smart as a whip and spunky, too."

Spunkiness must run in the family. She let out a long breath. "I suppose."

He traced his mustache with thumb and forefinger. "I bet she keeps you on your toes."

"She does, indeed." Annoyance prickled in her chest. Ready to leave behind this conversation and start class, she sprang to her feet.

Hank took her arm in a gentle clasp. "I don't know what Rebecca said to you, and I don't care for telling tales out of school. But first thing your girl did when you walked out of the library was to ask if this here class is a dancing class. Now I don't know what kinda…" He scrubbed a hand over the back of his neck and scratched behind one ear. "Well, what kind of arrangement you have with your people to be here, but I didn't feel right speaking false to a child. I told her she'd need to ask you."

So, Hank hadn't revealed her secret. Blinking into his watery gaze, she regarded him with new appreciation.

He released her arm and nodded. "As I say, I think that might have been answer enough for a clever girl, because then, of course, she asked me to teach her one of the 'exercises.' She likely has an inkling what we're up to."

She lifted one shoulder and let it fall. "I think she does. Thank you for telling me, Hank."

The warm-up music swelled, and Jerry sashayed to the front of the class.

Relishing an escape from her worries, Nora focused solely on her teacher and put aside all else. From infancy, she was part of a community. Her earliest memories were of helping her mother and aunts in the kitchen and playing among their ankles at quilting frolics. She'd seen a team of men raise a building in a single day more times than she could count, but she never imagined being part of a group whose sole purpose was to spread joy.

Jerry progressed methodically, teaching steps, and adding to them, until every dancer knew what part they played in the whole. She and Hank moved in and around the other couples, whirling and laughing as their feet kept time to the silly, jolly song. She never once opened presents under a Christmas tree, and she certainly never rocked around anything. But the melody and the movement and the company of enthusiastic, loving folks made her smile until her cheeks hurt.

She was still laughing when she burst out the door to find the parking lot covered in snow. A chill wind raced up her dress, and she pulled the light coat tighter around her shoulders. She didn't even have mittens. By the time she pedaled home, she'd be frozen solid.

Hank and Gene came up beside her and stared into the parking lot.

"The first snowfall of the year." Chuckling, Gene snugged on a pair of earmuffs. "Always makes me feel like a boy again. Say, maybe I'll get out the grandkids' sled."

Hank grunted. "Hope the roads are plowed."

Waving heartily, Gene ventured into the storm. "See you next week!"

A stocking cap emerged from the pocket of Hank's

overcoat, and he tugged it over his bushy hair. "Think you can bicycle home in this?"

She squinted into the wind. Truth be told, she wasn't sure. She hadn't expected the weather to turn so fiercely.

With a crunch of tires on snow, Tucker pulled up. Leaving the motor running, he hopped out.

Hank shuffled toward the curb. " 'Bout time."

"Easy there." Tucker reached out an arm.

With a grudging look, the old gentleman accepted it.

No use forestalling the inevitable. If she had any hope of getting home safely, she'd best make haste. Looping the scarf over her head and ears, she trudged across the lot. "Goodnight!"

"Now hold on a second." With Hank poised at the open door, Tucker jogged to catch up. "Can I give you a ride?"

She pressed her lips and slid a longing glance toward the heated cab. "No thank you."

Just as his grandfather had, Tucker took her arm.

Even through his glove and the layers of her clothing, she felt the strength of his grip and the gentleness of his touch. Her breath caught, and she tensed her arm without meaning to.

Easing his hold, he stepped closer.

The space between them narrowed until she felt the puff of his breath on her cheek. His voice was soft and low, warming her from inside, even as bitter wind stung her skin. She ran her gaze over the stubble of a dark beard. Men in her community either had full beards or clean faces. The swarthy shadow on his jaw made her insides as sticky as a cinnamon bun.

Forcing herself to look away, she surveyed the bike rack. Her seat was topped with a cloud of puffy white, and snowflakes dusted the red frame. The picture was lovely. Except for the fact she had to sit on that wet seat and ride eight miles home. She pulled free her arm. "I should go."

"Nora." He stepped in front of her, blocking her path.

Her name rolled from his lips like music. She gazed up at him, and her belly heated. Oh, but he was a handsome man. She couldn't pretend otherwise.

"Riding home in this weather isn't safe. Let me drive you. Please."

"Put her bike in the truck, and let's skedaddle." Hank clung to the door and beckoned. "I'm freezing my toenails off!"

Tucker was right, and she knew it. Although the thought of being so close in a small space made her head swim, accepting a ride was the only sensible decision. With a quick nod, she pulled her bike from the rack.

As gently as if it were a newborn calf, Tucker lifted the bike and laid it in the truck.

She bustled to where Hank waited like a gentleman, one hand on the door and the other extended. Taking his hand, she stepped up and slid to the middle of the seat. Dry heat spewed from the vents, toasting her cheeks. A tree-shaped thingamabob hanging from the mirror emitted the pungent scent of evergreen. Inhaling deeply, she sank into the seat, lulled by the mournful strains of a country song. Tucker scooted into the cab, and his shoulder pressed into hers, reassuring and solid. Taking a ride was absolutely the right choice. Even her mother would understand.

A bony elbow jabbed her ribs, and she glanced over.

Hank dusted snow from his shoulders. "Tell the boy where you live. The weatherman predicted ten inches. We'd best get a move on."

Shaking herself, she pulled upright. The cushion was as springy as the buggy seat, and all three of them bounced. She giggled and clapped a hand over her mouth.

Snow swirled in the headlights, and the song changed to an upbeat tune. A smile brewed like a cup of hot coffee in her belly. Why was she so happy? The roads were hazardous, and she was stuck in a truck with strangers. She glanced to either side, and her lips twitched. They weren't strangers. They were Hank and Tucker, and they cared enough about her to give her a ride home in a snowstorm, even if it meant prolonging their own trip. She couldn't squelch the smile if she wanted. "Head out Route 45 to Old Cowan Road."

"Yes, ma'am." Tucker nosed the truck onto the highway.

Now she'd admitted he was handsome, she couldn't stop sneaking furtive glances. He wore a tan, corduroy coat with a wooly collar and faded jeans. Wrapped around one wrist was a braided cord of dark brown leather. Her people didn't wear jewelry at all, let alone the men. The soft-looking band peeked from his sleeve, encircling a tanned wrist dappled with dark hair. Strangely breathless, she stared at his hands.

He tapped the wheel in time to the music and hummed under his breath.

A crazy notion to close her eyes and drop her head

on his shoulder tugged at her. She could almost feel the comforting firmness of muscle and bone beneath her temple. A quick calculation revealed she'd been up nearly sixteen hours. No wonder she was loopy. She straightened her spine and focused on the road.

Minute by minute, the snow thickened. In front of the quilt shop, Sarah Stoltzfus' pot of mums wore a fluffy white hat, and the new Mennonite church loomed behind a gauzy curtain. The truck trundled over the bridge, sluicing side to side in the grooved metal surface, and she pointed out the farm lane just beyond.

A ribbon of light glowed from beneath the shade in her mother's bedroom window. Otherwise, the big white farmhouse waited patiently in shadow.

Hank let out an approving grunt. "I like a nice tidy farm."

"Goodnight, Hank." Sliding past the steering wheel, she followed Tucker out the door and closed it quietly. Wet snowflakes *pitter-patted* on tenacious autumn leaves. If much more fell, her fruit trees risked losing branches.

With long-limbed ease, Tucker lifted the bike from the truck bed.

She reached around him for the handlebars, and her foot gave way on an icy patch. With a cry, she thrust out her arms, bracing for a painful fall that would surely undo weeks of healing.

Lightning fast, he lunged and grabbed her forearm.

Her shoulder bumped his chest, and she clutched at his coat. He was rock solid, one hand still holding her precious bike and the other supporting her. She leaned into him, anchoring her feet in the snow. Her fingers met muscle, and her pulse raced. Light as a feather, his cheek touched down on her head.

"Are you all right?"

His body was warm. His voice was a whispered breath. She hardened herself against temptation. Though night had fallen, they were out in the open where Hank or her mother might see. With a jerk, she pulled upright. "Fine. Thank you."

He released her and took hold of both handlebars. "Let me put away your bike. If you get hurt, Hank'll never forgive me."

By the light from the truck, she led him through the second-story entrance to the barn to where heavy equipment was stored when her father and brothers worked the land. Now that they leased the fields, the space was mostly empty, save some old machinery and tools. "You can park it next to the ladder." She gestured, and he wheeled past so close her skirt ruffled around her calves.

With the bike stowed, he took a long, slow breath. "I miss this smell."

She sniffed, wrinkling her nose at the fug of dung, must, and hay. How could anyone miss it? As a girl, she endured farm work, dutifully completing chores until her clothes and hair reeked. But any chance she got, she traded the barn for the kitchen and the homey scents of baking.

He tucked his hands in his back pockets and stared into the rafters. "I haven't stepped in a barn in…gosh, thirteen years."

Wind whistled through barnboard, but the structure provided haven from the storm. She padded closer, and darkness loosened her tongue. "I heard you tell my brother you grew up on a farm."

He nodded. "Way up north in Maine—almost to the Canadian border. We lived off the grid, not unlike yourselves. Never imagined I'd miss it, but I do."

She thought of Jonas. Did he miss the farm, residing as he did among the English? Why were some men compelled to roam? "I suppose for some folks farm life gets in your blood. Though I can't say the same for my daughter."

Chuckling, he shifted sideways, and the headlights through the door sliced him in half. "Hank couldn't stop talking about her. 'Curious and smart as a whip,' he said. You and her daddy must be very proud. I'd be pleased to meet him one day."

She swiped a foot over the floor in a heavy shuffle step. The rubber-soled sneaker thudded dully. "I wish you could. He died in an accident when Rebecca was three."

The wind ebbed, and the big, empty space went still.

She didn't know what compelled her to confide in Tucker right then. Was it the snow? The darkness? The memory of his warm presence in the truck? No matter the cause, having spoken, she felt jittery and brittle, and the night tilted out of control.

With a soft exhalation, he stepped closer. "I'm sorry."

She swallowed against sudden anger, and a bitter laugh snagged in her throat. "Don't be. You weren't driving the truck that hit us." Lashing out was wrong, but, oh, it felt good. She darted Tucker a glance. He didn't seem cowed.

His brows drew together in a deep furrow. "Us? Is that how you hurt your hip?"

The question was gentle, almost intimate, and she teetered on a knife's edge. Would she pour out her heart to a man she barely knew or scream and blow her top? Sharing secrets was perilous. Rage was likely to wound. Her lungs tightened. She had to get out of here. Now. She whirled. "My mother is expecting me."

Lunging, he caught her hand. "Wait."

A shudder seized her, rattling her bones and making her teeth chatter. Never had she been touched so often in one night by men to whom she wasn't related. What was wrong with these *Englischers*? What gave them the right to take and take and take some more? Closing her eyes, she let her arm go boneless.

"I am sorry." He ran his thumb over the back of her hand and slowly released her.

From below came the rustle of animal life.

She took in a breath that seemed to weigh a thousand pounds. His was not the apology she needed. That apology, she would never ever receive. In its absence, she tried to forgive the faceless creature who killed her husband and sister-in-law. She tried again and again. Her community and the laws of her faith required she do so. Only through forgiveness could she live.

Tasting rancor like bitter greens on the back of her tongue, she clutched her skirt and pulled it tight against her legs. Oh, but she didn't forgive him. She hated him. She hated him, and she hated the English woman who stole her brother, and she hated her brother for joining them, too. She hated ladies on phones and their ill-mannered children, and most of all, she hated men who drove recklessly in trucks.

Anger was easy. It worked quickly and made her

119

feel alive—the way she'd heard drugs discussed in hushed tones during her youth. Hate, on the other hand, took a toll. When fury abated, hate remained, coiled in her belly like a tapeworm. For seven years, it ate her from inside. Was she rotten at the core? Is that why she could no longer sing at church? Why every time she opened her mouth, her eyes welled, and her throat closed? Why she mouthed the words, pretending? Her thoughts reeled, and she yanked her skirt so hard she felt a seam pop.

"Nora? Are you okay?"

Tucker. She blinked and made out his shape in the dim light. Tucker wasn't the man in the logging truck. She didn't hate him. Gulping a breath, she nodded and unbound her skirt as the anger in her belly cooled. She was trapped on a nauseating merry-go-round of emotion, but he stood with feet firmly on the ground, a quiet presence, listening. She could still feel the rough calluses on his fingertips and the solid safety of his shoulder. The memory thrilled. For an instant, she thought only of him, and the merry-go-round made another turn. Everything inside, not only her bones and organs but also her rage and emptiness, turned to hot wax, soft and malleable, with the potential to burn.

Gott help her, she was already so far gone. She hardly recognized herself. She, who never broke a commandment. She, who would have happily stayed Amish forever. Smiling Nora now attended dance classes and dallied, weak-kneed, longing for the touch of an English country western singer—her thoughts wild and her emotions beyond control…

A horn blasted, and she jumped.

A sharp breath whistled through Tucker's teeth.

"Easy, old man." He strode to the door and waved.

The headlights glowed through the doorway, and when he turned, he looked almost otherworldly. Fleeing the shadowy barn where demons lurked in every corner, she scurried past him into the white. A blanket of snow softened the world's edges. Safe and familiar, the house beckoned.

With a hand on the car door, he turned. "Good night, Nora."

His voice touched a place deep inside she believed for years to be dead. With a rush of pins and needles, it came alive like a limb that had fallen asleep. She drew so close their shoulders brushed, the innocent touch as intimate as a kiss. If he reached for her, she had no idea what she'd do. "Thank you for the ride."

He swung open the door and climbed inside.

Warm air caressed her cheeks, borne on the strains of a country song that almost—almost—sounded like his voice.

From the front porch, she watched the truck fishtail into darkness. She clung to the railing and turned flaming cheeks to the wind. The blowing snow stung. It felt good. It cleared her head.

Surely her mother hadn't seen. Even if she had, never in a million years would she suspect anything Nora had done tonight. Or thought. Or desired.

She eased the latch and slipped into the chilly house. Confusing as they were, she'd keep those secrets and thoughts and longings securely hidden. She'd shove them into the rotten hole along with her hatred, if necessary. She would conceal all of it. She had to. No matter the cost.

Chapter Ten

Nora rested her elbows on the picnic table and stretched her legs, tapping her toes in muddy puddles. Circles of snow still ringed the trees, but scanning the Farmers' Market parking lot, she never would have guessed six inches fell the night before. Almost without realizing, she took up a catchy rhythm from class, alternating feet in an increasingly quick tempo. *Paradiddle, paradiddle, paradiddle.*

From where she sat, she couldn't see the stage, but the pleasant harmonies of a barbershop quartet floated on the wind. She squinted into the treetops, still stippled with yellow leaves. Sunshine warmed her cheeks, soothing the memory of last night's stormy winds and turbulent emotion. Welcome, too, was a respite from the crowds and from her mother's prying gaze.

Over breakfast, she told her family about the ride that spared her a dangerous pedal home.

Rebecca sulked over bacon, extremely miffed she didn't get to drive with Hank in the truck.

Her mother raised her brows, as if expecting more details. When Nora didn't elaborate, she hardened her stare and waited, the model of patience. Well, her mother could wait a lifetime. Nora would say no more. Truly, she wouldn't begin to know what to say. She couldn't possibly express how safe she felt in the cab of that truck...how she still tingled from the touch of

Tucker's hand…how when he glimpsed her ugliness, he didn't run away.

"Hey, smiley."

With a start, she whirled to discover Annie Amos clutching two insulated cups. Smiley? Was she smiling? Her insides were jumbled…but yes. Sitting alone in the sunshine, she'd been thinking about Tucker McClure and smiling.

Annie chuckled. "Didn't mean to scare you. Your mother told me you were outside. I brought ciders. Want one?"

Nora whiffed apples and spice, and her heart lifted. Annie remembered how she loved hot cider. She used to guzzle it nonstop at wintertime gatherings. Still smiling, she patted the bench beside her. "You bet."

Annie settled down and passed a cup.

Aromatic steam tickled her nose. How nice to have a friend at her side, even if more than a decade had passed since they shared each other's secrets. When they were young, they were inseparable. Maybe the smiling, hopeful girl Annie knew still lived somewhere deep inside. Maybe Nora was more than a rotted-out shell.

A flock of geese flew overhead, honking in noisy chorus. Shielding her eyes, she tracked them across the sky. Where were they going? Farther than she'd ever traveled. How small her world was compared to that of a Canada goose.

Annie giggled and stopped. She let out a muffled snort and giggled again.

Her laugh was exactly the same as it had been when they huddled in the back row of youth singings, trying not to crack up during endless German hymns.

Sometimes she and Annie giggled so hard they had to bite the insides of their cheeks to stop.

Annie let out another silvery laugh.

"What?" She sipped cider, holding the spicy liquid on her tongue.

"Do you remember when Mervin Zook got attacked by John Hochstetler's goose?"

Nora nearly choked on her drink and spurted it out her nose. Swallowing hard, she caught her breath and nodded. How could she forget the enormous white goose wandering into the schoolyard at recess?

A gang of younger boys hatched a plan to corral it, but Mervin Zook, then in his last year of school and feeling every inch the man, declared he alone would wrangle the beast.

Annie threw back her head. "He thought he was such a hero, but he was hardly bigger than those third graders!"

Mervin had puffed his chest and strode across the schoolyard like he meant to teach the goose a lesson. The moment it spotted him, it opened enormous wings and charged, nipping and honking like a mad devil. Feathers flew, and Mervin had streaked across the yard for dear life. Nora couldn't suppress her mirth. "That goose chased him in circles until Teacher Esther scared it off with a broom."

Annie nudged her in the ribs. "Best not remind him when he comes to call."

Her laughter ebbed, and she cast her gaze over the parking lot. No sign of Tucker's truck. "Mervin made mention of that?"

"Only ten or twenty times, according to Leroy. Seems he never got over you marrying Levi." Annie leaned until their shoulders bumped. "Do you like the man he's become?"

Did she? Mervin was a good man. He was a respected member of the community, and he made an honest living on the family dairy farm. Suddenly exhausted, she slumped and plopped her elbows on the table. No, she didn't like him. But honestly, did it matter? "Rebecca needs a father."

Annie slurped loudly. "Do you fancy him?"

A sigh slipped from her lips, puffing the cider's steam. "He's not Levi."

Nodding, Annie gazed at the clouds. "Your Levi was one of a kind."

Lowering her voice, she inclined her head toward Annie's. "Mervin can't carry a tune in a bucket."

"Not like that *Englischer*." A rascally expression flitted across Annie's dimpled face.

Eyes round, Nora jerked upright.

The quartet concluded with a resounding chord, and the crowd around the corner cheered.

Annie leaned out around the table and peered toward the stage. "And we're just in time to hear him."

"Give it up for the Third Street Singers!" A man's amplified voice boomed over the speakers, and the audience hooted again.

She downed the remaining cider in a gulp, burning her tongue. Returning to the stand would be prudent, but oh, she wanted to hear him sing.

"We've got a change to this afternoon's lineup," the announcer continued. "Tucker McClure had to cancel at the last minute."

Her stomach lurched.

A groan rose from the crowd.

"We all love Tucker, and he'll be back real soon. But we won't leave you hanging. Let's give a big Green Ridge welcome to Earl Zabek, the Polka King of Carbondale!"

An accordion wheezed, and she frowned. Last night, Tucker said nothing about missing his show. Why hadn't he come?

"Smiling Nora, where's your smile?"

Untangling herself from the picnic bench, she came to her feet. The market was still busy. She had work to do.

"I know that face." Annie pointed an accusing finger. "You used to get that look when Levi took Sarah Stoltzfus home from singing."

The accordion kicked up a manic melody. She pinched her lips in a scowl. Annie knew her too well, and yet, she didn't know her at all. A chasm of life and tragedy gaped between them. "Thanks for the cider. I should get back to work." She tossed the empty cup into the trash.

"You remember how when we were running around with the youth, I always had crazy ideas to buy a motorbike and go to New York City?"

Annie's words seemed to snag her by the sleeve. She curled her lips in a wistful smile and nodded.

"You alone kept me from making a fool of myself and crossing a line I might not have been able to uncross."

Nora scrunched her nose. "You said I was a stick in the mud."

Annie laughed. "Maybe you were, but you kept me safe. Didn't we have oodles of fun?"

Her insides softened. "The most fun."

The accordion quieted, and Annie's laughter trailed off. "You were so good, and you made it look so easy. Time after time, I flew out of control like a wooden top, but you steadied me." She took Nora's hand. "In a funny way, I think my turn's come—not to steady you, but to tell you to spin. Maybe we all need to spin wild sometimes just for the fun of it." Annie tightened her fingers in a gentle tug. "I'll be here to catch you, if you do."

Then she hopped up from the table and left, leaving Nora lightheaded and alone, wondering why Tucker McClure hadn't come.

****

With a giggle, Nora took Edna's outstretched hand and gazed at their reflection in the studio mirrors.

A week had passed since the Halloween snowstorm, and the other dancers stretched and chatted, awaiting the start of class.

After nearly tripping over Bert and bumping into a stack of chairs, Dot had asked for a refresher on a particularly tricky combination. "Before Bert winds up on his backside with me in his lap!" Doubling with laughter, she wiped away tears.

"Let's show 'em how it's done, Nora girl!" Edna counted and hummed the opening refrain for the Christmas dance.

Hand-in-hand, Nora was happy to oblige. Edna's skin was as delicate as an onion's, but her palms were warm, and her grip was firm. Nora snuck a look out of the corner of her eye. To say Edna looked young again took something away from her. She wore the experiences of a lifetime in the crinkles on her brow and creases of her smile. Her hair was the pure white of early-spring snow drops, and her cheeks were pale pink rosebuds. Dancing, she looked like Rebecca when the girl was younger and seemed almost not of this earth. Edna in motion was ageless.

Still humming, Edna spun slowly, holding Nora's hand.

Nora step-tapped a jaunty circle, and then they were side by side once again, facing the mirror in lockstep.

Bert and Dot joined the dance, just as the studio door swung open.

Reflected in the mirror, the lanky form of Tucker McClure filled the doorway.

Despite the cold, his cheeks were ashen, and dark smudges shadowed sunken eyes. He looked like he hadn't slept in a week.

The room went still and silent.

With an air of quiet confidence and a stride that said "don't you worry—everything will be fine," Jerry met him at the door. "Come on in, Tucker. What a nice surprise."

Edna plunked her hands on her hips. "Where's Hank?"

"Let the boy catch his breath." Jerry slid Tucker a folding chair. "You want to sit, baby?"

Tucker shook his head. "I'm afraid I have some bad news." He met Nora's gaze, and his lips twisted into a sad smile. "Last week after class, Hank fell and dislocated his shoulder. The doctor said he doesn't need surgery, but he can't tap until the spring."

With a little gasp, Nora shot a hand to the wall. So that's why Tucker didn't perform last Wednesday. Poor Hank. Was he badly hurt?

Edna scowled. "Clumsy old goat."

Tucker thrust his hands in his coat pockets and frowned. "Being laid up hasn't done much for his personality."

Dot clutched Bert's arm. "What'll we do? We need an even four couples or the whole performance will be lopsided!"

Nora felt as if her stomach knitted itself into a scarf, then looped into a knot. On one hand, Hank's injury provided the excuse she'd been waiting for. They couldn't perform with an odd number of dancers. She could easily withdraw, and none of her classmates would blame her. She grabbed opposite elbows and pressed her arms into her belly. Now the opportunity presented itself, the idea of quitting made her tummy ache. Hank's accident opened the door, but she didn't want to leave. She wanted to dance.

"We're all terribly sorry." Joan laid a hand on Tucker's arm. "How are you holding up, honey?"

Looking for all the world like he could use a hug, Tucker blinked down at the woman.

"I've been better," he said.

"I can imagine Hank's a handful. How's your cooking?"

Tucker shrugged. "I can boil an egg."

With a sympathetic nod, Joan gave his arm a motherly pat. "Hank loves his pot roasts. And isn't he on a special diet for diabetes?"

A pained grimace contorted Tucker's features. "I'm not sure."

"Oh, he is," Marion chimed in. "Mr. Diefenderfer is on the same one. Gotta keep that blood sugar under control."

"You know…" Joan tapped her bottom lip, and the diamond ring on her fourth finger glittered. "I just had an inspiration. Maybe we can help each other."

Gene stepped forward, tugging down his vest and interlacing his fingers behind his back. "I like the sound of this. Go on."

Joan beamed. "What do you say we come to an arrangement? Tucker, you need a hand with Hank—it's plain as the very handsome nose on your face. And the TipTop Tappers need a dancer. Without a partner for Nora, our performance goes up in smoke. Right, dear?"

Every face turned toward Nora. Palms suddenly clammy, she opened her mouth and closed it again. Dancing in Dr. Richard's show was one thing. Doing it with Tucker McClure at her side…holding her hand? That was another matter entirely. The knot in her stomach melted into hot custard.

Gene sidled up to Tucker. "Did you do much dancing when you sang with that big star down in Nashville?"

Tucker looked from Gene to Nora and back again. "Some."

Bert approached from the other side. "Ever had on a pair of tap shoes?"

Tucker made a face like Bert asked if he ever ate a peanut-butter-and-worm sandwich. Nora's throat tightened. Clearly, he didn't want to dance with her. She should quit now and go home for good.

He dipped his chin. "Can't say I have."

Marion pulled herself to her full height and eyeballed Tucker. "Let's put this whole arrangement into concrete terms. The TipTop Tappers are prepared to deliver diet-compliant suppers large enough for leftovers, four days a week. Agreed, ladies?"

Edna, Joan, and Dot nodded.

Marion plumped her hairdo. "In return, you agree to be Nora's partner. You show up at rehearsals, learn the dance to the letter, and perform at Dr. Bruce's benefit on Christmas Eve." She stuck out a pudgy hand. "Deal?"

Tucker's brows disappeared beneath the shock of hair on his forehead. He dug his hands into his back pockets and sucked his cheeks.

Was the idea of dancing with her so repulsive? Based on his behavior of late, she almost dared to think he liked her. But from his hesitation, she knew she'd been wrong. Her heart plummeted. She was an angry, hollow woman. Why would a man like Tucker want to spend any time with her? Unable to meet his gaze, she stared at her feet.

"Deal."

She whipped up her head.

With a cheer, her classmates thronged Tucker, thumping his back and pinching his cheeks.

He caught her gaze over their heads. Rolling his eyes, he smiled.

A flush surged up her neck, and she turned, only to spot Jerry, reflected in the studio mirror.

The woman tilted her head.

Saying yes to this arrangement was a covenant. If Nora gave consent, she couldn't back out in a few days or weeks. She glanced at her classmates who looked more like young people at a youth gathering than septuagenarians at a fitness class. In their midst was Tucker McClure, the first man to make her smile in years. Catching Jerry's gaze again, she nodded.

Jerry gave a thumbs-up and inserted herself into the crowd. "All right, this is still my class. Give the boy some space and take five while I find him shoes. What size are you? Eleven?"

Tucker unbuttoned his jacket and slid it from his shoulders. "Twelve and a half, ma'am."

Jerry fanned her face with one hand. "Lord, have mercy. I'll see what I can do."

Nora glimpsed her own form in the mirror and almost didn't recognize herself. Ruddy-cheeked and bright-eyed, she did not look like a person who danced simply to make some old people happy. She looked like a person...in love. She'd learned one thing from her weeks among the English. Mirrors didn't lie. For better or worse, she was about to take Tucker's hand and dance.

Chapter Eleven

Minutes later, Nora extended her arms like they floated on water and lifted her elbows high above her waist. Catching her bottom lip between her teeth, she slipped a hand into Tucker's, and a spark leapt between them, skittering up her arm, and lighting a little, crackly fire in her chest.

The silly, joyful music swelled, and Jerry counted them in. "One. Two. A one, two, three, four."

She caught sight of herself and Tucker in the mirror: he, tall and lean, his red plaid shirt open at the collar exposing a sliver of white undershirt and blue jeans cuffed over borrowed tap shoes; she, a whole head shorter in her gray cape dress, black stockings, and *kapp*. Together, they looked oddly…right.

The voice of a woman singing fifty years ago bounced off the walls, filling Nora's whole being like she was a glass jar full of fireflies. The rhythm took over, and she forgot everything but the dance. Buoyed by the music and the man at her side, Nora in the mirror moved with effortless ease. A smile made entirely of sunshine spread across her cheeks.

The singer left off, and horns took over the melody.

Jerry whooped and clapped. "Not bad, tappers. Not bad at all."

Tucker squeezed her hand and released it.

Stomach sinking, she darted a glance at the wall

clock. Could class be over already? She wanted to lunge for him and replay the music. She wanted to practice the first minute of the dance again and again until her legs gave out and she fell, panting, into his arms.

Bert let out a long whistle. "Hey, Fred Astaire, I thought you said you never tapped before. You trying to make us old timers look bad?"

Tucker pulled a red bandanna from his pocket and dragged it across the back of his neck. "I said I never wore of pair of these crazy shoes, but I didn't say anything about dancing. I was in a production of *Anything Goes* a while back. Guess I learned something in high school after all."

Though she had no idea what they were talking about, she joined the chorus of laughter. What was *Anything Goes*, and who was Fred Astaire? But she had to agree with Bert. Tucker mastered the first part of the dance in a single class and performed it with natural ease.

"All right, I'll see you"—Jerry gave Tucker and Nora pointed looks—"all of you, next Tuesday. Some practice at home wouldn't kill you. Christmas will be here before you know it."

With a burst of chatter and the chaotic clicks of nine pairs of tap shoes, the class dispersed.

She met Tucker's gaze and just as quickly looked away. Suddenly shy, she slid into a folding chair and unlaced her shoes.

In his sock feet, Bert lumbered to Tucker's side and thumped his shoulder. "Don't mind me. I was only joshing. We're right glad you saved the day."

Dot peeked around her husband. "I'm real sorry

about your grandpap, and I'll be by tomorrow with a lasagna. Don't you worry. Us ladies will keep our part of the bargain. You keep yours." She waggled a finger and scooted to the coat rack with Bert right behind.

Quick as a flash, Tucker had his shoes off. "Gimme a second to talk to Jerry, and then I'll walk you out? Hank sent something for your daughter. He'll have my hide if I forget it."

She nodded and glanced out the studio window. The sky was pitch-black, and rain spattered the glass. Biking home in this weather would be almost as treacherous as in a snowstorm. Would Tucker offer a ride? Should she accept?

The rack stood above the heating vent, and her damp wool coat was now warm and dry. She snugged a black bonnet over her *kapp* and hoped the rain would abate. Dressing for these late fall classes was nearly impossible. The ride might be bitter cold, but once inside the studio, she began to sweat. She threw a shawl over her shoulders and snugged it around her neck. Surely once she got moving, she'd be warm.

Tucker slipped his coat from a hanger. "You ready?"

She nodded.

"I'm trusting you, Tucker McClure," Jerry called from the storeroom doorway. "Don't let me down."

"Yes, ma'am." Tucker opened the door and gestured Nora into the hall.

Bulletin boards lined the walls, festooned with flyers advertising all sorts of goings-on at the senior center. If they were free to attend so many events, English old folks must not work much. Her mother would never have time. Then again, nothing in heaven or earth would compel her mother to darken the doors of this place, no matter how many spare hours she had.

Tucker let out a chuckle. "Those ladies drive a hard bargain."

"They mean well." Her mittens smelled like a wet dog. Why didn't she spread them out on a bench during class? As she coerced her fingers into soggy wool, Jerry's admonishment to Tucker bounced around her brain. Whatever they discussed seemed serious. "Jerry gave you a talking to there at the end."

"Maybe rightly so." He stuffed his fists in his coat pockets. "I'm going on tour for three weeks before Dr. Bruce's show."

Did he lie to her classmates to get free meals when he had no intention to stick around? She slanted a hard look. "You're leaving?" He thrust out both hands like he meant to slow a charging billy goat.

"Don't worry. I'm coming back. I have a weekend off in the middle of the tour, and I'll be here in time for the show on Christmas Eve. I learned a big chunk of the dance today. We'll have it down before I go."

His tone was reassuring, and she relaxed some-what. Surely, he wouldn't disappoint his grandfather's friends. "A vacation sounds nice. Where will you go?"

"I'm not taking time off. I'm performing. It's a concert tour." He banged one shoulder into the front door and hit the bar with his hip, pushing open the door and holding it.

Frigid air cut through her coat like shears. Lately, she was cold all the time. Was it because of all the weight she'd lost? Steeling herself against the blast, she stepped outside. Rain hammered the awning's tin roof, but Tucker didn't seem to notice. His expression was suddenly darker than the empty parking lot.

"Not that it's much of a tour. Not like…" He sniffed and squinted into the streetlights. "Well, not like other tours I've played." He jerked his head toward the pickup. "You're gonna let me drive you home, right? Besides, Rebecca's thing is in the truck. It's a Nancy Drew book."

A sudden gust drove rain in a horizontal sheet, dousing her skirt and stockings. By the time she pedaled home, she'd be drenched and lucky if she didn't catch a cold. Taking a ride was perfectly acceptable. Her friends and family did so all the time. What gave her pause was the memory of being inside the cab—the coziness of her shoulder against his—the way her belly pulled, and her breath quickened. Riding alone with an unmarried English man wasn't done. If Deacon Elmer found out…

Jogging from beneath the awning, he started across the lot. When she didn't follow, he glanced over one shoulder. "If Hank hears I let you bike home tonight, he'll have my hide." Hunkering into his jacket, he beckoned. "Come on. I won't bite."

Shadows obscured the entrance to the unlit trail. Bicycling tonight was more than foolhardy. It was dangerous. What harm could come from a simple ride? Tonight, she'd put away her own bike, precluding intimate conversation in the barn. She'd be safely home in no time. With a quick nod, she scurried after him.

Her bike was out of the rack and in the truck before she even reached the car. He unlocked her door and swung it open, holding out a hand as his grandfather had. Touching him seemed safe now. Sparks couldn't penetrate wet wool, right? She gripped his fingers, and heat radiated up her arm. *Wrong.*

No more touching, either.

In seconds, she was in the cab with the radio softly playing and heat pouring from the vents. Such comfort almost felt like sin. With a sigh, she melted into the seat. The windshield wipers shuffled and thunked a steady rhythm that made her feet itch to move. She tapped her soles on the rubber floor mat. *Brush step ball change, brush step ball change.*

Needing no reminder, he headed out a deserted Route 45 toward home.

Stopped at a traffic light, he looked at her hard and then turned away. His brows knit, and his mouth pressed in a firm line.

A feeling came over her like spiders crawling up her spine, and she licked dry lips. Did she say something wrong? Since leaving the studio, his cheerful mood seemed dampened with the weather. She'd pledged no intimacies, but pleasant conversation couldn't hurt. After all, he was going out of his way to drive her home. Maybe talking about music would make him smile. "Where will you perform on your tour?"

"Nowhere interesting. Big venues won't have me since..." He trailed off, scowling. "I'm playing honky-tonks from Elkhart to Wheeling, Twinkletoes. Dive bars someone like you has no business even thinking about."

His voice grated like a metal rake on rock. He was right. She didn't like thinking of gloomy taverns where people drowned misery in drink. Was Tucker McClure comfortable in such places?

He veered the truck onto Old Cowan Road and slid

his gaze to her face. "I've never seen you in that bonnet. You look so…"

"Plain?" At the brittleness in her voice, she winced. A spring poked into her back, and she wriggled, shifting closer to the door. Whatever connection they had was broken, and she had no idea why. Now, she wanted to be safe and sound, cuddled in a quilt in her quiet bedroom upstairs.

"I spent so much time on the road, it started to feel like home."

His voice was so quiet she strained to hear over the motor and the rain. The air thickened like when Rebecca forgot to open the flue before laying a fire, and smoke filled the room.

He latched onto the wheel until his fingers were white. "Cuz I'm one heck of a singer, and my star's on the rise. That's what the big dogs say."

His words seemed pointed—they pierced her like the pin that just then came loose from her apron and jabbed her hip bone. She tugged her waistband, dislodging the barb.

Was he angry about her behavior last week in the barn? She'd spoken so harshly—almost as if she blamed him for Levi's death. Then again, in class tonight, he'd seemed perfectly content. His demeanor only shifted when he brought up the tour…and her black bonnet. Men were meant to be strong and steady, but nothing about Tucker was even keel. His mood was as up and down as a teeter-totter. Even worse, when she was around him, she felt just as volatile. Her stomach turned. She wanted out of this car right now. "Our lane is right beyond the bridge."

He stepped on the gas, and the truck pitched. She

clutched the door handle, remembering how her brother's English wife was swept from this very bridge in a violent summer storm. If Jonas hadn't come to her rescue, the girl might have died, and her brother would be home where he belonged. Nora gnawed the inside of her cheek and tasted blood. What was wrong with her? Why did she think such terrible thoughts?

The tires sluiced over grooved metal, and he jerked the wheel. "Jeez, this place is remote. No wonder so much snow piled up by the time we got home."

The breath hitched in her chest, and for a moment she couldn't breathe. Last week, Tucker and Hank wasted over an hour driving her home in the storm. If they hadn't, Hank wouldn't have fallen. Her throat went thick. Hank's injury was entirely her fault.

Tucker revved the engine, accelerating off the bridge.

She jabbed a finger toward the window. "Turn there!"

With a screeching squeal, the truck skidded to a halt. Tucker rammed a thin stick protruding from the steering wheel.

The truck heaved backward and swung around so fast she bumped her head on the window. No wonder he was angry. She was a plain, little country girl with no place in his world, and she caused his grandfather's injury. A tear spilled down one cheek. She brushed it with a stinky mitten and clamped her jaw, determined not to cry. Why did she let him take her home last week? And why did she do it again tonight? The community rules existed for a reason. Transgression always resulted in punishment. She turned to the window, sighing when the house finally came into view.

He stopped in front of the barn and threw open the door. The overhead light glowed dimly.

Floundering, she dug her fingers into his arm. "I'll get the bike."

He jerked around, and meeting her gaze, he frowned. "What's wrong?"

More than anything, she hated to cry. Crying was weak and childish. But she couldn't stop. She scrubbed her eyes with damp wool and clenched her fists. "If you hadn't driven me home last week, Hank wouldn't have fallen. It's all my fault. I'm so sorry."

"Hey. Hey. Listen to me—Hank's injury was in no way your fault." He splayed his fingers on the dashboard and forced out a breath. "Hank has diabetes. He can't feel his feet."

"But if you hadn't delayed, the snow wouldn't have been so deep and—"

"His feet are numb, and his balance is off." He twitched his shoulders and pulled at his coat collar. "It was only a matter of time before he fell."

The words made sense, and yet, she didn't quite believe him. Why else would he have been so mad? "I should go."

His head fell back against the seat, and his chest lifted in a deep sigh. "Yeah, all right." Sliding from the truck, he dashed around and retrieved her bike.

Rain bounced off the hood like pebbles off sheet metal, and she plodded through mud to his side. Icy streams poured from her bonnet brim, soaking her stockings and shoes. The handlebars were frigid, even through mittens. "Thanks for the ride." She jerked toward the barn and felt a restraining hand on her elbow. Rain blurring her vision, she turned.

His face was inches from hers. His jagged breath condensed in steamy puffs. "The way I acted tonight had nothing to do with you, okay? I was a jerk, and I'm sorry." Releasing her, he buried his hands in his pockets and looked out over the fields. "I have things in my past—things I'm not proud of. Seeing you there in my truck, looking like you do and...just being the person that you are..." He shook his head, and water sprayed from his hair. "I don't know. I don't know anything except what happened to Hank wasn't your fault."

His expression was stormier than the night. Who was this man, and what had he done?

Wiping a hand across his face, he met her gaze. "You believe me, right?"

Shiver upon shiver wracked her body, and she nodded—not because she believed him, but because he seemed to need her to so badly.

His shoulders sagged, and turning, he staggered to the truck. He heaved his long limbs into the cab and was gone almost before she took another breath.

The bike caught in the mud, and she wrenched it around. As she headed for the barn, a creeping sensation, colder and clammier than the night air, slithered over her skin. Was someone watching? Had she and Tucker been seen? Hunching against the wind, she snuck a glance at the house. The windows were all dark, save one—her mother's—where yellow light glowed beneath a shuddering shade.

Chapter Twelve

The back door squealed, admitting a whoosh of brisk afternoon air. After a turbulent evening on Tuesday, standing market yesterday had been doubly exhausting. Now, with the morning chores done, Nora relished several hours in the kitchen, fiddling with a new recipe. The spicy gingerbread whoopie pies were nearly perfect and would make a wonderful addition to her Christmas offerings. Whiffing cinnamon and nutmeg, she glanced up from her mixing bowl.

Rebecca spun in a circle, a padded envelope clutched to her chest. "I got a package, and it's just for me!"

Lowering her newspaper, Verna peered in from the sitting room. "Did you hear from the Ohio cousins?"

Rebecca skipped into the kitchen and held out the envelope. "Nope! It says right here it's from Mr. Hank McClure—*Mamm's* friend from exercise class." She tore open the top and extracted a hardcover book. "*Nancy Drew and The Secret of the Old Clock*. How did he know I never read this one?"

Verna pointed toward an index card that slipped from the envelope and landed on the floor. "Don't miss the message."

Scrambling, Rebecca retrieved the note and read it close to her chest. "Hank says they forgot to give this to *Mamm* on Tuesday. He delivered it so I wouldn't have to wait until next week."

Verna folded the newspaper with a clean swipe and slanted Nora a look. "Why didn't he bring the book to the door? Surely, you're on good terms. He lingered long enough in the driveway the other night."

An egg smashed against the side of the mixing bowl with more force than Nora intended, sending bits of shell into the batter. "I wouldn't know."

"Come to mention it, I only saw one other person in that truck, and he lifted your bike pretty handily for an older man."

A shard slipped through the slimy white, evading her probing finger. "I'm not surprised you had trouble seeing. The night was dark and rainy. I was lucky not to have to bicycle home. I'd hate to hurt my hip again." Thus far, she'd avoided lying outright to her mother. Speaking an untruth now turned her stomach like she swallowed one of those raw eggs.

With a harumph, *Mamm* reached for her letter box and lap desk.

Hugging the book, Rebecca flew toward the sitting room, catching a foot on one of the kitchen chairs and sending it slamming into a table leg.

"Watch your step," Nora said at the exact same moment as her mother.

Rebecca snatched a pen from the writing desk and skidded to her knees at Verna's feet. "*Mammi* Verna, may I please have a sheet of stationery? I want to write a thank-you note to Hank."

Verna held a fresh piece of writing paper just beyond Rebecca's reach. "First, send that circle letter back to your cousins. You've had it nearly two weeks, and they'll think you forgot."

Groaning, Rebecca flopped onto the sofa. "Their letters are so boring. They tell silly stories about people I don't remember, and the poems they send are copied out of the newspaper—I know they are." Tossing the book on an end table, she bounced to sitting, eyes flashing. "I could make up my own stories, and they'd be much more interesting than real life.

"You'll do no such thing." *Mamm* added a second piece of stationery to the first. "Write to your cousins and then, you may write to your mother's friend."

Checking her notes, Nora added another half teaspoon of ginger. With a hint more spice, she was certain the cake would be scrumptious. Maybe if she lost herself in baking, she could tune out her family, forgetting lies and made-up stories, and most of all, a dark-haired man in a truck who most definitely drove her home unchaperoned. With a sigh, she adjusted the amount of ginger in her baking notebook.

"Any other mail?" Verna asked a few minutes later.

"I left it on the counter in the pantry"

Rebecca's voice was distracted. Who knew what nonsense she wrote?

"Who from?"

The rocker squeaked, as if echoing Verna's impatience. Dropping the wooden spoon, Nora stalked into the pantry. With a fistful of letters, perhaps her mother would finally stop chattering, and Nora could focus. The mail lay in a haphazard pile, and she riffled through as she ferried it into the sitting room. Catalogs…the latest edition of *The Budget*…another letter from Aunt Martha…

A step into the kitchen, she stopped. At the bottom

of the pile was a small blue envelope addressed in a neat, square hand.

"Anything interesting?" Verna glanced up from the lap desk and caught Nora's gaze. The crease between her brows deepened. "What is it?"

She stared at the familiar handwriting. By rights, her mother couldn't read the letter—shouldn't read the letter. With trembling fingers, she extended the envelope.

Mamm's cheeks went pale. "*Aai*."

Rebecca cast off her writing and crept alongside the glider, peering over her grandmother's shoulder. "Who's it from? I don't see an address."

Slowly, *Mamm* opened the envelope and pushed up her glasses on her nose. With a deep breath, she slid out the paper and read.

A soft cry escaped Rebecca's lips. "He's coming home!"

The floor seemed to crumble beneath Nora's feet. Stomach lurching, she clutched the doorframe.

With glistening eyes, *Mamm* passed her the note.

She'd know her brother's tidy lettering anywhere. A stinging started behind her own eyes, and the words swam on the page. Shunned or not, Jonas would be home for Thanksgiving. And he was bringing his wife and baby.

****

The full moon was so close to the horizon it looked otherworldly. Outside the senior center the following week, Nora stood beside Tucker and stared. When she was a girl, and the moon was enormous like this, her brothers tried to trick her into believing it would crash into their house. They told her to run to the cowstalls and hide until morning. Nora just laughed. The moon might be changeable, but *Gott* would never let it land on their snug, white farmhouse. He would keep the cows and the chickens and her whole family safe. She held that faith until the day a logging truck plowed into their buggy on a hilly stretch of road no truck had a right to drive.

She shook herself, digging rigid fingers into the tense column of muscle at the base of her neck. For the first time in months, the dream came last night. In restless slumber, she had seen Levi and her sister-in-law Elizabeth in the front seat of the buggy, returning from off-Sunday church service in Elizabeth's home district. Levi flicked the reins with the easy confidence that made her heart flutter. Heavy with child, Elizabeth turned to her brother-in-law, face flushed and round, rosy cheeks raised in a smile. With a hand on her own hollow belly, Nora peeked from behind where the children usually sat, wondering when *Gott* would send her another baby. She rejoiced for her brother's wife, but Levi so wanted a boy.

Nora's head nodded sleepily. Fragments of conversation drifted back. With a low call to the mare, Levi slowed to make a turn, and Elizabeth spoke her husband's name with tender concern. Had she sensed the restless spirit lurking beneath Jonas's skin? Had she feared it? Had she hoped a baby would quash his urge to roam, anchoring him to home in a way even she, his beloved wife, couldn't?

Then, a sound ended life as Nora knew it. To begin to describe it, she had to stray into Rebecca's imaginary realms, a place she did not like to go. It was the scream of a dragon with the roar of a freight train. The hissing howl of the devil and the thunderous laugh of a goblin deep in the bowls of the earth. Afterward, came not so much silence as nothing. A thick, black void lay like a wet blanket upon her soul until she awoke in a hospital bed, unable to move her leg, and certain beyond doubt that Levi was gone. She felt his absence like a hole in her heart before Jonas said a single word. The rotten void had made a home in that hole. It lived there still.

She blinked at the moon. Hovering mere inches above the ridge, it was almost too bright to look at.

Tucker tilted his face to the sky. "Hard to believe it's real."

The moon wasn't even near the top of the list of things Nora couldn't believe. She shivered and gathered her scarf around her neck. Winter had barely begun, and she was chilled to the bones. She really should try to eat more.

"Hey. Let me drive you home."

Tucker's voice was soft as a caress. The wind picked up, scuttling dried leaves along the curb. On the bike ride into town, she had wondered how she'd feel to see him tonight, given their strange and strained parting last week, made more awkward by the emotional conversation in the barn the week before. The memory of weeping in his truck triggered a twinge of embarrassed nausea. Dark intimations of a troubled past lurked in the corners of her brain. But when she got to the studio and found him missing, she was struck cold with fear he wouldn't come. As the clock ticked down, she retied her shoes into ever tighter knots, until finally, he breezed in with a quicksilver grin that instantly summoned her own.

Taking his hand, she began to dance, filled in a

breathless instant with the sensation she'd been this man's partner for decades. Catching sight of herself in the mirror, she stared at the smiling, young woman in tap shoes and let go of the last two weeks. If Tucker had secrets, well, she did, too. She released her shame and her worry, along with the fear she'd caused Hank to fall. Happiness was as active a choice as the decision to get out of bed in the morning. Why had she so often chosen misery instead?

Inspired by Tucker's presence, Jerry surprised the TipTop Tappers with a brand-new country and western version of "Rock Around the Christmas Tree," weaving in partner moves based on a dance called the Texas Two-Step. After class, Nora had departed the studio on a carpet of fluffy clouds, almost sashaying into the night. The air carried the smoky tang of a fall brush fire, and the moon hung like *Gott's* face in the sky. Standing beside Tucker, she let the nightmare dissipate and his voice fill the hollow in her heart.

He stepped off the curb, jingling keys in his pocket. "I'll fetch your bike?"

With a quick smile, she nodded, not needing to say a word. She slipped into the front seat, sorry Hank wasn't there, too, leaving her no choice but to snuggle against the soft corduroy of Tucker's jacket. Squarely on her side of the seat, she clasped her hands in her lap. What a silly notion. No need to moon like a starry-eyed teen. Tucker didn't care for her that way. The smiles he flashed her were no different from the ones that transformed Marion, Joan, and Edna into giggling girls. He signed on to this partnership for the casseroles. Period. His decision to dance had nothing to do with affection.

He turned the key, and music blared from the radio. Diving for the knob, he switched it off.

The song was the same one that played the first night he drove her home—the singer's voice so very familiar. Could it be his? The truck skidded onto the highway, and she slid toward him until, with a jolt, the seatbelt caught, digging into her neck.

He jerked the wheel back in the other direction. "Sorry."

Hot air streamed in a noisy rush. Heating and cooling might be the only comforts that would tempt her to go English. She pulled free her scarf and scootched toward the door. "Tucker?" she asked in a quiet voice. Somehow, she knew the matter was delicate. "That song on the radio...was that you?" Silent minutes passed, ticked off by mile markers on Route 45. She angled a questioning look. Did he not hear?

He moved a lever on the steering wheel, and a light on the dashboard blinked a melodic clicking sound. "Yeah." His mouth twisted in a tight-lipped smile. "Tucker McClure, one-hit wonder."

Only a fragment of melody escaped through the speakers, but his voice soared, sweet and true, sending a shower of sparks to her toes. "I'd be pleased to hear your song sometime."

He choked a vinegary laugh, and his eyes glittered, rock hard. Puzzled, she studied his profile, suddenly stony and brittle-looking. Upon her, his music had the exact opposite effect, softening every part into warm, gooey custard. "The song is beautiful. Why does it make you angry?"

His shoulders tensed. "You wouldn't understand."

The trees rushed in a blur, silver-tipped by moonlight. "Maybe not. Your music always makes me smile."

Ever so slightly, his fingers loosened on the steering wheel. He met her gaze for just a moment and turned back to the road. "I've never met a woman like you."

"I'm surprised. Maine has quite a few Amish communities—"

"Not because you're Amish, but because you say what you think. You wear your heart on your face."

She jerked her gaze to the window. If this man saw her heart, could he spy even deeper into the hate-filled hollow in her soul? Longing to conceal that inner darkness, she pressed her palms to her middle.

"Joy lights you up like a Christmas tree. I see it when you smile, and when you dance, and maybe, sometimes, when you hear me play."

He steered onto the grooved bridge, keeping on track with the same steady hand Levi had shown driving their buggy.

Nudging the wheel, he turned into the farm lane. "Just as fast, though, you turn it off. I've watched you do it."

Beneath her scarf, a hot flush raced across her collarbones. How dare he talk about her private thoughts and feelings? No one need ponder them but herself and *Gott.* This conversation was getting entirely too personal. She seized the door handle, ready to leap out the instant he slowed.

One cheek lifting, he slid a sidelong glance. "Let me tell you, I don't blame you one bit."

She stilled. "You don't?"

He shook his head. "After losing your husband and getting hurt so badly, you have the right to behave however you like. Now me? I made my choice. I got what I deserved. But you…oh, Twinkletoes. Life owes you a dance."

The notion life owed her anything was outrageous. It was so antithetical to Amish teachings she wanted to laugh. Tragedy struck with the random cruelty of a twister. The outcome was *Gott's* will. Nora Beiler, was not exceptional. Hers was not to expect recompense, but to move forward with acceptance, joy, and, yes, with forgiveness.

He rolled to a stop beside the barn.

The engine idled, vibrating her insides until they hummed. She shot a glance at the house. Every window, even her mother's, was dark. A madcap impulse tickled in her chest, fed by his kind words and perhaps by Annie's advice to let her top spin. Pulse quickening, she pointed to a space on the far side of the barn. "Pull up over there. Maybe we could go inside and practice our dance?" Her voice trailed off, and she stole a quick look. "We only have a few weeks before you leave, and you promised Jerry you'd be perfect."

His eyes were round, but a smile played across his lips. A low chuckle rumbled from his chest. "Didn't I say you had spunk?"

The truck tucked beside the barn like a foal nestling against its mama. The fields were fringed with moon shadows cast by spiky, leafless trees. She landed softly on ruts frozen in mud, closed the door with a quiet thud, and dashed into the barn. A shaft of alabaster light spilled in from outside, and she easily located the lantern hanging from a hook. The bulb cast a blueish glow, not nearly so cozy as an old-fashioned oil lamp, but far safer in a tinderbox full of hay. She set it on a milk crate and turned to find him silhouetted in the doorway, a slender figure, broad-shouldered and still. She took a cautious step. "We don't have music, but maybe you could sing?"

In two easy strides, he was at her side. "Long as you sing with me."

Her mouth went dry. She couldn't sing. Not anymore.

Standing tall, he scooped up her hand and met her gaze over one shoulder. "And a one, and a two, and a one, two, three, four."

With every exhale, her breath condensed in clouds, coming quicker and quicker as he hummed the opening bars. Even in wool stockings, her legs prickled with cold, but her palm heated where it pressed his. With a hop and a skip, she started to dance, shocked by her own voice when she sang. After years of silent mouthing, she expected a sound like sandpaper, but her tone shimmered as true as Tucker's.

She spun toward him, feeling his hand slide up her side to tuck beneath her arm. A tingling warmth flooded her chest like a million butterflies zipped between her ribs. No man had touched her so intimately in years. She rested her left arm atop his and clasped his hand, draping her fingers like a towel on a rack. Her face was inches from the opening of his jacket where his collar parted to reveal the notch at the base of his neck. He smelled of wool and something else—a fresh, musky scent no gentleman of her community ever wore. It was clean and spicy and very, very male. When she lifted her cheeks to gaze over his shoulder, the top of her *kapp* grazed his chin.

He broke into the verse, dancing her backward across uneven floorboards with absolute confidence. *Quick quick, slow, slow; quick quick, slow, slow.*

Never losing contact, she followed his lead into a couples turn, delighting at the zing in her belly as he spun her full circle. She sang louder, giggling at the goofy lyrics and the sheer bliss of gliding in his arms. Her muscles were strong and limber. Her feet were made of starlight. She half believed her toes really twinkled.

With a full-bellied laugh, he launched into the instrumental section, mimicking first the slip-slidey sound of the fiddle and then the tinkly piano cascade.

The two-step relaxed into a side-by-side tap dance. One hand in his, she tapped with loose-limbed gusto, her hips softening until her backside swayed like Jerry's. As if she weighed no more than dandelion fluff, she flapped her sneakers, imagining the crisp, cheerful tap of her borrowed shoes. Tossing back her head with joy she couldn't deny, she surrendered to the dance.

The verse kicked in again, and he whisked her into his arms, whirling across the floor. With the slightest pressure on her side, he guided her in perfect arcs in and around their imaginary dance partners. He sang louder as the song neared its finale, imitating to perfection the twangy voice of the recording as he grabbed her hand and twirled her to the end of his arm.

Laughing, she raised her voice, too.

When he crooned the final lyric about new old-fashioned ways, he departed from the choreography, tugging her hand and spinning her into him.

With a silly yelp, she threw her arms around his

neck, nearly falling over as her face nestled into the wooly collar of his coat.

"Yee haw!" His hoot echoed from the rafters, and he gasped and guffawed, relaxing into a gentle sway.

Head-spinning, she breathed deeply, filling her senses with the clean, English scent that turned her knees to jelly. How many years since she felt a man's chest rise and fall beneath her cheek? How long since her body thrilled to a touch? Her breathing slowed, and she let her eyelids close.

He twitched and eased his arms from around her waist, dragging the back of one wrist across his forehead. "Well, shoot."

Her surroundings returned in a rush. The musty odor of livestock and barnboard. The blue lantern light. Like a burbling brook, she giggled again and let the sound vanish into shadows. Did she dare look at him? What would he read in her features? Exultation? Fear? She lifted her chin, opening her lungs to hay-scented air, and met his gaze. Would he see desire? Because desire was exactly what she saw in his. Desire and deep, deep yearning that seemed to go beyond need for physical touch. Now, she caught a glimpse of *his* innermost soul, and to her eyes, it was as empty and longing as hers. A tiny "oh" escaped on a breath.

Dipping his chin, he lowered his gaze, shrouding his insides again. "Not bad for amateurs."

"I daresay almost perfect." She licked her lips and swallowed. What she wouldn't give for a sip of Annie's hot cider. Oh, how her fun-loving friend would delight to hear of this secret dance. Maybe, just maybe, Nora could tell her.

Wind whistled through cracks in the walls, cooling

the perspiration on her cheeks. She shivered. Any minute he would leave. The hour was late, and five-thirty a.m. would arrive before she knew it, bringing bacon and eggs to fry and mountains of tomatoes to can for winter.

If only she could freeze time, she'd linger in the barn for weeks. If only night would pass, and she'd wake to find him at the breakfast table with her family. If only she could drive away in his truck and never return. If only they could dance, hand in hand and cheek to cheek, until the past slipped away, leaving nothing but two beating hearts and a glimpse of eternity.

The rafters creaked. A critter rustled in the hayloft. He shifted his weight, and one boot scraped against the floor.

Like a page, the moment turned. The silly, dancing hilarity seeped into the walls, leaving them exposed in the eerie light of a battery lamp.

He lifted his gaze, and a slow smile crept across his face. "I'd like to kiss you, Nora Beiler."

Her heart whammed so hard she thought it might fly out of her chest. Her palms burst into flame, and she pressed them to her cheeks.

"If this was a different time in my life, say, oh, eighteen months ago, I might have taken that kiss. But not now. Not tonight." He shuffled back a step, scrubbing a hand over his chin. "Tonight, I'm gonna say thank you for the dance, get in my truck, and drive home."

Was the dizzy feeling quickening her breath and blurring her vision excitement or relief? Shaking herself, she snapped off the lamp and scurried behind him. Rusty wheels screeched, and the door slid closed. Hands clasped, she lingered beside the truck. A million unsaid words swirled in her brain, none of which made any sense at all.

Making nary a sound, he unlatched the door and swung it open. One foot inside the cab, he paused.

With the lightest of touches, he untwined her fingers and took her hand, tracing the delicate bones with his thumb. Now, the moon was far away—so high in the sky it could never ever crash to earth. The man in the moon smiled a teasing smile. They might be hidden in shadows, but he saw them. With her hand in Tucker's and the great, big, star-filled universe above, she felt at once miniscule and a thousand feet tall.

She blinked and met his gaze. The handsome lines of his face, usually quirked in a rascally grin, turned serious, and with delicious slowness, he lifted her hand and kissed it. His lips were warm and soft, and as he released her, his scratchy chin barely grazed her knuckles. Her insides pulled with longing like she hadn't felt in years.

"Goodnight, Twinkletoes."

She watched him until the taillights vanished, and the motor's roar died on the wind. Wrapping her arms around herself, she scurried toward the back door, desperate to creep to her room unnoticed. Because if her mother met her at the top of the stairs and asked what she'd been doing all night, she had absolutely no idea what she'd say.

Chapter Thirteen

Autumn surrendered to winter in a seemingly endless string of cold, rainy days. Wiping a baking sheet with a soggy towel, Nora peered out the kitchen window. The whole world was waterlogged. A little flame tickled her rib cage ever since the dance in the barn last week, but still, her spirit felt like a tub of wet laundry. She leaned over the sink, craning for a view of clear sky and hoping beyond hope she might get a break in the weather to pedal to class. Outside the window, the thermometer held steady at thirty-six degrees. Rain no longer pattered the fallen leaves. Sleet did. Riding to class was simply out of the question.

Pushing aside a jumbled collection of pans, she jammed the sheet into the cabinet, reminding herself that one short year ago, weather like this made walking unendurable. Tonight, her only complaint was that she couldn't ride her bike to an exercise class that would have been impossible to imagine before her surgery. She folded the towel and draped it over the oven handle. If she left now, she could scoot to the phone shanty and call Jerry. She didn't want her classmates to think she simply neglected to attend. Even more, she didn't want Tucker to think so.

Laughter rang in the sitting room. She snuck to the opening and peeked inside. Colorful cards thwapped onto the table punctuated by exclamations of triumph and despair. With her quick wit and even quicker hands, her daughter usually beat Samuel at board and card games. Given her brother's bleak expression, she guessed Rebecca's winning streak held. She swallowed a smile. A model of good sportsmanship, her strong and agile sibling won most everything he played—certainly if physical effort was required. He'd led his teams to more youth volleyball victories than she cared to recall. Seeing him lose a card game to her daughter was enormously satisfying.

On the other side of the room, *Mamm's* dancing crochet hook caught the light, and a baby blanket took shape before her eyes. Jonas's visit was fast approaching. She didn't know how, or even if, her mother would welcome her eldest brother and his family. Verna took Jonas's letter to her room and hadn't spoken of the matter since. Still, Nora noted more food than usual had arrived for the Thanksgiving meal.

Their Pennsylvania community practiced strict shunning. Cut off entirely, those in the *bann* were not welcome to table and were excluded from family functions. In Ohio, where her mother lived for years after their father's sudden death, rules were bent, and exceptions most definitely made. Whether Verna would greet Jonas according to her native or adopted customs remained to be seen. Honestly, Nora wasn't sure which outcome she desired. Through so many years of shared grief, Jonas was her comfort and constant companion. Could she blame him for pursuing happiness?

Cloudlike, the blanket billowed in her mother's lap—a lap that hadn't held an infant grandchild in years. How happy this baby would make Verna Rishel. The English woman Jonas married loved whoopie pies.

Perhaps Nora would add a batch to the Thanksgiving menu.

Recalling the advancing hour, she retreated into the kitchen and grabbed her coat, just as a heavy knock sounded on the front door. She turned.

"Now, who could that be?" *Mamm* craned her neck and looked out the window.

"I'll get it." Rebecca sprang from the chair. "Uncle Samuel needs a chance to catch up."

Samuel tossed his cards onto the table. "Braggart."

Nora scuttled across the kitchen and gazed through the living room into the front hallway.

The latch clicked, and the door opened with a groan, letting in a burst of wind and rain.

"Hey there. You're Rebecca, right? We met at the library."

Nora flattened one hand on the wall and the other against her ribs where the amber flame leapt up, searing her lungs. Why in the world was Tucker McClure at her front door?

Nestled close to the woodstove, *Mamm* leaned over her knees and peered into the entryway. "Who is it?"

"Hank McClure's good-for-nothing grandson."

Samuel strode to the door. "Rebecca, Tucker is our guest. Kindly address him with respect." He extended a hand. "Good to see you. Come on inside."

Taking her brother's hand, Tucker stepped into the entry and swept his gaze around the room. "Don't let me interrupt you. I came by to see if Nora needs a ride to exercise class." He spread his arms, displaying sodden sleeves. "This is no night to bicycle. She hasn't left yet, has she?"

"She's finishing the dishes." Dropping fists onto

hips, Rebecca narrowed her eyes. "Why does Hank call you good-for-nothing?"

Nora gasped. This child and her bottomless impertinence.

Balling the blanket, Verna hauled to her feet. "Rebecca!"

Tucker chuckled. "It's a fair question." He thrust his hands in his pockets and shrugged. "I guess I didn't make the same choices in life that Hank did. I took my own path, and not everything I tried worked out in the end. I think sometimes when we're different from our parents and our grandparents, they feel we're something of a disappointment. He means it as a joke. I don't mind."

Rebecca gazed at Tucker, unblinking. "I understand. I don't think Hank's joke is funny, and I won't repeat it again."

Rebecca *understood*? Years of harsh reprimands echoed in Nora's mind. Had she made her daughter feel like a disappointment? She should try harder to mask her impatience. Rebecca was only a child, and though she was mouthy, she was sensitive.

Tucker's expression softened. "Don't you worry. Even when Hank's gruff, I know he loves me."

"Go fetch your mother from the kitchen." Samuel shooed the girl.

Nora scuttled to the pantry and made a show of studying the shelves.

"*Mamm*, what are you doing in here?"

Nora straightened her *kapp*. "I thought I heard a mouse."

"If you let me keep Pumpkin inside as I requested, you'd have no such trouble. She's an excellent mouser." The girl huffed a sigh. "You're wanted in the sitting room."

Nora grabbed her coat and zipped to the entryway to find her brother and Tucker deep in conversation. Samuel's expression was as buoyant as the night was leaden.

"I hope to open my own solar installation business. I've got several families interested—businesspeople, mostly. I think I can make a go."

Nodding, Tucker swung his gaze to her.

Was it her imagination or did his face light as brightly as Samuel's?

"He's come to drive you to exercise class. Isn't that neighborly?" Verna gave a tight-lipped smile. "Where's your grandfather, Tucker?"

Nora's mouth went dry. Would Tucker reveal their arrangement?

"Home. I came early, hoping to catch Nora before she left. I'll fetch him later."

Best flee before her mother asked more questions or, heaven forbid, her daughter broke into a dance. She gave Rebecca a stern look. "Go easy on Uncle Samuel, and obey *Mammi* Verna." With an expression of uncharacteristic earnestness, Rebecca caught her hand.

"I will. Exercise well and enjoy yourself, *Mamm*."

Slick leaves carpeted the ground, and Nora dashed down the path with care. Inside the truck, a faint musty odor from the vents blended with evergreen and Tucker's spicy English smell that today seemed to emanate not only from his skin, but from his clothes, too. She let out a sigh. "Thank you for coming. I was about to call Jerry and tell her I couldn't attend."

One dark brow lifted. "You were going to call?"

He turned onto the road, and the cardboard pine tree swung in crazy circles.

"We have a telephone shanty, about a mile from the house—for business or emergencies."

"What category does this evening fall under?"

A silvery giggle escaped her lips. "Is there such a thing as a tap-dancing emergency?"

"If you hadn't shown up tonight, I think the TipTop Tappers would have declared one. Marion Diefenderfer might have called the cops."

She laughed. What fun to share silliness with a man. Every minute in the company of an unmarried Amish man was serious, weighted with the burden of finding a spouse. How she'd missed carefree companionship.

Sleet splattered the glass, making vision difficult. A nervous shiver skittered up her spine. She darted Tucker a glance.

Hands steady, he gazed at the road ahead.

At this hour, the streets were empty, she reassured herself. No buggies would venture out on such a night, and Tucker wasn't a reckless driver. They'd be fine. She settled into the seat, feeling the jostle of every pothole and bump. "I'm sorry you had to lie for me." She slipped her hands up into her coat sleeves and tucked them beneath her arms. "But thank you."

"Believe me, Twinkletoes, that little white lie's hardly the worst thing I've ever done."

She cringed at the biting tone that edged his voice whenever he stewed on the past. Pulling at a loose thread inside one cuff, she recalled the conversation between those girls at the market weeks ago. What had Tucker done? Surely it couldn't have been so bad.

Nothing about this man seemed wicked.

He cleared his throat. "Your daughter knows about our class, doesn't she?"

The sentence was a statement not a question. She nodded. "She figured out after talking with Hank in the library. She doesn't know that Hank's hurt and you're my partner or about the performance." She sighed. "At least, I don't think so."

"I hope she'd approve. She's a discriminating little thing."

"I think she would." Suddenly she didn't know what exactly they were talking about. He hoped she'd approve of what? Her stomach tightened, and she tugged at her waistband. She needed to loosen the pins. Was she finally gaining weight? She hoped so. When she saw herself in the studio mirrors, her cheeks did look fuller.

Tucker flicked the blinker and pulled onto a dirt road in the opposite direction of the senior center. She clutched the door handle. "Where are we going?"

"Oh, hey. Don't worry." He slowed the truck, skirting between fields stubbled with last year's corn. "We have almost an hour to kill before class. I thought we could hang out here."

Where, exactly, was here? She squinted through the windshield but couldn't make out much.

He turned off the lane into a field, and the headlights caught a long row of metal posts sticking out of the ground. Another row lay beyond, and beyond that, yet another. An abandoned cinderblock building with a bright-blue roof and wide windows sat in the center of the field, with seesaws, swings, and a metal climbing structure off to one side. The sleet on the windshield changed from a steady thrum to a spray, like a handful of pebbles landing in a lake. With a hard yank on the wheel, he swung around.

She wiped a circle of fog from the glass with the cuff of her sleeve. Directly in front of them towered the biggest wall she'd ever seen. She gaped at the odd structure, standing alone in the middle of a field. Streaked with brown and black stains, it was dingy white and pieced together like a quilt. One big panel had come loose and dangled askew over the section below, revealing a glimpse of wooden framework. "What is this place?"

The motor spluttered to a stop, and he leaned back, lacing his fingers behind his head. "A drive-in movie theater. Hank and Lavelle brought me here years ago."

With a gasp, she recoiled. "A movie theater?"

"Don't worry. It's abandoned. When the world went digital, people quit going to the movies. Heck, I guess they gave up on the drive-in years before." He swept a hand through his hair and tugged. "I don't know why. Drive-in movies are magic."

She took in the huge overgrown field. "How could you hear the movie from the car?"

He pointed out the windshield. "A speaker hung on each of those posts. You'd roll down your window and hook it over the door, and the sound came through. Then they figured out how to broadcast the audio through the car radio. Way better for keeping out mosquitoes. During action scenes, the whole car would shake."

Staring at the screen, she tried to imagine giant moving pictures and sounds loud enough to vibrate a truck. "What kinds of movies did you see?"

"All kinds. Comedy and adventure…romances." He glanced at her sidelong and waggled dark brows. "Classic black-and-white musicals with Ginger Rogers and Fred Astaire."

Tucking one knee beneath her, she swiveled. "Fred Astaire! That's the name Bert called you after class. Who is he?"

He gazed at her, unblinking. "Oh wow. Right. Sometimes I forget…you've never seen Fred Astaire dance, have you?"

She shook her head. "Have you?"

"Only in old movies. He was a huge star in the 1940s and '50s and probably the best dancer of his generation. Maybe the best male dancer ever." He arched his back and pulled a shiny, black device from his pocket.

The Farmers' Market customers couldn't tear themselves from their phones. They seemed constantly to stare, blank-faced, at screens. Yet Tucker had never once used his in her presence.

He pressed a button, and the device illuminated, revealing a photo of dense pine trees and a deep blue lake. "We're already at the theater. Would you like to see Fred Astaire dance?"

The truck windows were cloudy, making the massive screen shimmer like an unearthly mirage. Staring at it, she could almost see giants dancing in flickering light. She bunched her skirt in tight fingers. Watching a movie, any movie, was strictly against the rules, and she never ever broke the rules.

Until she started riding her bicycle. And dancing. And accepting rides with unmarried men. She flicked her gaze to him.

He tilted his head. Mossy eyes twinkled in the glow from the phone.

She was in a steamed-up truck in the middle of an empty field, far from prying eyes and nosy neighbors. No one would know, save her and *Gott*. She turned her gaze inward and sat in silent question. A teeny puff of the joy she experienced dancing in the barn filled her lungs like sweet summer wind. Peeping from beneath thick lashes, she nodded.

His thumbs flew across the screen. He slid an index finger over the glass several times and then stopped. "Ah, perfect—a video of him tap dancing with Eleanor Powell." He caught her gaze. "Are you sure?"

With a quick nod, she scooted closer, bumping his shoulder, and catching his fresh English scent.

He held the phone at eye level and touched the center. "Buckle your seatbelt, Twinkletoes. I'm about to blow your mind."

The gravelly rasp of his voice scraped over her skin in all the right ways. She shivered and focused on the rectangle of glass. Music swelled, the sound surprisingly full coming from an object no bigger than a mousetrap. Staring wide-eyed, she blinked. She thought the movie would be in color, but it was entirely black and white. The stage was a slick black mirror, shimmering like a moon-dappled mill pond beneath an inky background, studded with tiny, star-like lights.

A man and woman dressed all in white sauntered side by side to tooty, cheerful music. In motion, they looked to be made of licorice, lithe and bendy, but strong and sure-footed, too. *Tappity-tap-tap* went their shoes, striking ever faster, more complicated rhythms. Sometimes the dancers were in complete synchronicity, and sometimes they took turns, almost like the dance was a light-hearted, teasing conversation. The music stopped, but the couple kept dancing, their feet moving so quickly she couldn't even see them.

Tucker shifted closer, and his hair grazed her temple with feathery softness. A yearning pulled at her, and she inclined her head, her cheek so near his chin she could feel the heat from his skin. She parted her lips, as if to taste the air he breathed.

The music resumed with even more instruments deepening the sound. His breath quickened—his shoulder rising and falling against hers. The dancers' movements were effortless. Keeping a shared rhythm in their bodies looked as easy and natural as breathing. She could almost believe they were in love. Feet flying and smiles wide, they spun in tighter and tighter circles as the volume rose and the music accelerated to a sudden end. Before she knew it, the recorded audience burst into applause.

Never in her life had she seen anything so wonderful. Giggling, she clapped, too.

With a chuckle, Tucker shifted away, lifting one hip and returning the phone to his pocket.

She felt like baby Rebecca when Levi carried her on his shoulders. The girl would laugh and laugh, and when Levi finally put her down, she'd reach for him on tiptoes and say in her darling baby voice, "More, peas, Dada. More." Nora touched Tucker's arm. "More, please."

His forehead creased, and he caught her gaze.

Sleet *pitter-pattered* the windshield like tiny tap shoes. She scrunched her nose. "The movie was very short."

He gave a low laugh "Just one more. Don't want to be late for class." He brushed his finger across the screen again. "Let's see…"

A pang of jealousy cut through her. If only he'd touch her with such tenderness. Pressing her lips, she tamped down the ridiculous feeling. Imagine, being envious of a machine.

"Ah! Here's one with Ginger Rogers. She was his most famous partner. They don't tap, but I think you'll like it." He pushed the arrow in the center of the screen and lifted the phone once more.

Instantly, she was swept onto another darkened stage. Fred Astaire wore a black tuxedo now, and his partner was in a flowing, white gown. Hand in hand, they walked in front of a grand staircase as the orchestra played a melancholy tune. Violins swelled, and their walk became a dance—slow and graceful, their bodies barely touching.

Tucker scootched closer, and his hip met hers. He slid an arm over the back of the seat and inched the phone closer. The music brightened, and the dancers became weightless. They leapt like they were made of air. The filmy fabric of the woman's dress moved unlike any Nora had ever seen. It billowed like a gauzy sheet and frothed like whipped cream around her ankles. As she spun up the steps, the skirt became the petals of a flower—a lily cut loose and spiraling in the wind. Then the couple was in each other's arms, whirling faster and faster until Nora's head swam, and she leaned against Tucker's shoulder. Suddenly, the music slowed, and the woman twirled off the screen, leaving the man hunkered and alone like a lost soul bereft of its mate.

The video ended, and she read the words below the picture. The date was nineteen thirty-six. This movie was made nearly eighty years ago, yet it quickened her pulse as if she were the one dancing. She thought those long-ago times were innocent. Her mother and grandmother certainly spoke of the past in that way. But watching Ginger Rogers and Fred Astaire, she knew. Passion…love…desire…those emotions were timeless. After Levi's death, she believed she'd never experience such feelings again. Nestled against Tucker in a field of abandoned dreams, she knew she'd been wrong.

She lifted her cheeks. His face was inches from hers. His lips were close enough to kiss. She snagged her bottom lip between her teeth. "Fred Astaire looked sort of sad there at the end."

"Mm hm." He swallowed. His Adam's apple rose and fell, and the muscles of his neck worked.

Adam's apple. The forbidden fruit. The movie was just as forbidden as that Old Testament apple, but the feelings it aroused didn't make her feel wicked. They made her feel alive. "Funny how something made-up like that—a pretend story on an imaginary stage—funny how it can make you feel things. Deep inside." He inclined his head inches from hers, and for a heartbeat, she thought he really might kiss her.

"You feel a whole lot more than you say, don't you, Twinkletoes?"

In the unlit cab, he was painted in black and white like the man on the screen. She trailed her gaze from his high forehead, down his nose, and over his lips to the jagged scar on his chin, knowing as she did, he studied her, too. Could he really read her heart in her face? If so, what did he see? At that moment, she hardly knew herself. "Maybe I do." She flicked her gaze back to his.

His brow softened, and deep creases shot from the corners of his eyes. "The man you chose to share your heart with would be one lucky guy."

A deep, hungering breath expanded her chest. She remembered the feeling of knowing and being known. How she ached for a heart's communion. But was this English man worthy? Was he capable? Was he strong enough to hold her damaged parts? Or would he leave her, too?

Reaching for hairs tucked securely beneath her *kapp*, she slid to her side of the seat. For a second, she almost felt him follow—his chest seemed to strain toward her. Turning, she swiped a clean arc in the foggy glass and, dragging her wet palm over the velvety seat cushion, peered into darkness.

He slid behind the wheel and turned the key. "We'd best get a move on."

She nodded. A move on to dance class where Bert and Dot and Marion and Gene and Edna and Joan, and yes, she and Tucker, would rock around the Christmas tree like Fred and Ginger. Was her time with him just playing pretend? Were her feelings as imaginary as those shimmery black stages a century ago?

Could she trust the flicker in her chest and the heat in Tucker's gaze? Or would she wake up one day and discover he had left her, too?

Chapter Fourteen

"They're here." Nora's voice wobbled, and she cleared her throat. She filled a glass and gulped lukewarm water. Despite chilly weather, the kitchen felt more like it did in midsummer than on Thanksgiving Day. The oven had been in use nearly nonstop for seventy-two hours. It hardly had time to cool before they heated it again for yet another dish. Though only six would share the holiday meal, she and her mother prepared enough food for three times as many.

With a start, *Mamm* closed the oven door. Leaning over the sink, she peered out the window, and the turkey baster slipped from her fingers and clattered among dirty dishes. "*Ach du lieve.*"

Her mother's cheeks were red as tomatoes, and wispy curls gathered at her temples. *Oh my goodness, indeed.*

Hands on hips, Verna took a deep breath, puffed her cheeks, and let the air out slowly. Then she turned and marched to the door.

Footsteps pattered down the staircase, quick and light. "They're here!" Rebecca's jubilant voice bounced off the kitchen cabinets. "They're here! They're here!"

The latch clicked, and the door opened with a sharp squeal.

Nora swiped damp hands down her apron. How would this reunion go? Though she discussed the menu for the Thanksgiving meal at length, her mother made no comment regarding Jonas's homecoming. By rights, he and his family shouldn't join them at the same table. No matter the custom in Ohio, many members of their Pennsylvania church district wouldn't receive a shunned relative inside their homes.

But this morning, at *Mamm's* request, Samuel had toted the drop leaf table from the sewing room to the kitchen.

Without a word, Verna shoved it until a four-inch gap remained between it and the kitchen table. She threw a single long cloth over both, brushed together her hands, and returned to her sweet potato casserole.

Nora caught her brother's gaze.

With a shrug, he had disappeared into the pantry.

Her mother, it seemed, planned to welcome Jonas the Ohio way. Through the kitchen window, Nora spotted Samuel striding from the barn, a broad grin lighting his face. He, too, looked ready to receive their brother with open arms.

Sour uncertainty turned her stomach, and she balled the dirty washrag. Did she really want to share a meal with Jonas and that woman? Her life was completely uprooted when he left. She hurled the rag into the sink, splashing sudsy water onto the counter. Swiping the mess with a sponge, she thought back to the miserable days following Rebecca's hospitalization three years ago.

Over roast chicken one night in August, Jonas had declared his plan to leave.

Widowed, lame, and with a daughter to raise, she had no option but to join her mother in Ohio. An agonizing month followed in which she nursed Rebecca back to health and prepared to leave the only home she'd ever known. Her hip pain worsened by the day. As they closed the farm, she and Jonas spoke no more than necessary. During the endless van ride west, she couldn't even look at him. Loss compounded on loss. Loneliness had pitted in her soul, deep and dark as a well.

The sound of car doors closing called her back to the present. Apparently, her feelings mattered only to herself. Jonas would be welcomed with open arms. As he exited the van, she glimpsed close-cut, wheat-colored hair. Of course, he drove now. And he wore no hat. He was one of them.

She downed another glass of water. Why skulk in the kitchen? Head held high, she should go outside and greet her brother. She'd managed perfectly fine without him. She had a successful business, a healthy daughter, and an appropriate suitor any woman in the community would be proud to marry.

Water went down the wrong tube, searing a path to her lungs. Eyes burning, she spluttered.

And she had a secret life. And secret English, old-people friends. And a very secret man friend who danced with her in the barn and sang her special songs and made her smile from the soles of her feet. A friend she very nearly kissed in a pickup truck after watching a movie on his phone.

Maybe she was more like her brother than she cared to admit.

Lungs clearing, she breathed deeply and set her countenance. Unlike Jonas, she would never leave her family. And no one would discover her secrets.

Except Rebecca. But she could handle her

daughter.

With nary a trace of a limp, she strode through the sitting room and into the entryway. Framed by the open door, her mother and Jonas were locked in an embrace so intimate she fought the urge to look away. Her mother's back heaved with labored breaths. Her brother's eyes were squeezed tight, his expression mingling sorrow and relief.

Lifting his lids, he caught Nora's gaze over their mother's shoulder. His cheeks softened, and he smiled.

She should smile back. The day had arrived to forgive and welcome her brother with an open heart. But her face froze. Her insides turned to stone. She stared in bitter silence as time compressed until not a day had passed since she pulled that very front door closed and climbed painfully into a van against her will.

Brows creasing, Jonas eased his hold. "Nora—"

"And you must be Tessa." Verna withdrew from her son's embrace and crossed the porch.

Jonas spun and followed.

At the top of the steps, Tessa bounced a bundle in her arms. She'd pinned up her red hair in a bun and wore a long skirt, boots, and a forest-green, wool coat. Her cheeks flushed scarlet, and she nodded. "And this is Elizabeth. Elizabeth Grace."

Rebecca pulled back the blanket and peeked at the baby. "Uncle Jonas said they call her Lizzie for short."

Jonas came to his wife's side and gazed at the child with an expression of naked joy. Nora hadn't seen that look on her brother's face in many years.

"Elizabeth." *Mamm* repeated. "*Gott segen eich*."

"That means God bless you," Rebecca whispered.

Eyes shining, Tessa nodded. "Would you like to

hold your granddaughter?"

"Try to stop me." *Mamm* scooped the baby into her arms. "Come inside and warm up. We'll eat in no time."

Everyone bustled in, carrying the cold on their coats.

Samuel lingered and sauntered through the doorway last. "The Prodigal Son returns, eh?" He winked.

"You hush." She elbowed her younger brother in the ribs, filled with such sudden affection she could have kissed him on the spot.

As she struggled to taste the meal they labored over, the events of that awful night three years ago seemed to play out in front of her. Ghosts of their former selves flitted around the kitchen table. Tessa, garbed only in one of Jonas's shirts, pawing through Nora's kitchen drawers. Rebecca, pale and miserable, vomiting right there in front of the stove. Her brother, angrier than she'd ever seen him, threatening to cast Nora from the house forever. All the while, seated at a table separated from his mother and siblings by four inches, Jonas ate turkey and mashed potatoes and laughed as if he'd never left.

Balling her fists into tiny pink snails, the baby fussed.

Jonas handed her to Tessa.

Their gazes met over the squirming child, and their shared look was so tender that witnessing it, Nora felt like an intruder in her own home. Tonight was entirely too raw. Unable to sit another second, she shoved back her chair and sprang to her feet.

Jonas paused, a forkful of sweet potatoes in midair,

176

and watched. "Your hip seems strong. The surgery was successful?"

Rebecca flashed a brilliant smile. "Her surgery and the exercise class with the old English people."

The child gazed meaningfully on the word "exercise." Frowning, Nora yanked the oven door and reaching for the pumpkin pie, grazed her wrist on a rack. She jerked back her hand and deposited the dish next to a plate of whoopie pies. The burn would likely blister. Last summer, Rebecca's over-watering drowned her only aloe plant. Killed with kindness. Nora cursed herself for not having replaced it. "The doctor enrolled me in a rehabilitation class at the senior citizens center."

Between bites, Jonas chuckled. "I hope you can keep up with your classmates."

The knife slid through perfectly set custard. Slicing precisely equal pieces, she savored the spicy scent and willed her breath to steady. Why did her brother's happiness fill her with rage? She wanted to forgive him—*needed* to forgive him—but rancor eddied in the rotten pit in her soul. What was wrong with her? Had the accident broken her spirit, as well as her body? No surgeon on earth could repair such damage. She'd prayed, and she'd bided her time. When would she find grace? When would she be whole?

Flawless spoonfuls of whipped cream dolloped beside each piece. She served the pie and licked her index finger, seeking solace in sweet, silken smoothness.

Rebecca slurped her milk. "*Mamm* met all kinds of people in that class. One in particular is quite interesting—Hank McClure. He used to be an Alaskan bush pilot with his wife, Lavelle. He has an equally interesting grandson called Tucker who plays the guitar at the Farmers' Market and sings country western songs."

"Tucker McClure is in Green Ridge?" Tessa stared, goggle-eyed. "*The* Tucker McClure?"

Determined to keep her voice steady, Nora slid the plate of whoopie pies onto the table. "Do you know him?"

Tessa shifted the squirming baby to her other shoulder and took a whoopie pie. "Oh, gosh no. He's famous. Until recently, he was on TV all the time, but he...well, I read some rumors online. They're probably not true."

Rebecca came up on her knees and ogled the chocolaty treats. "What kind of rumors?"

With a firm hand, Verna guided the girl into her chair and passed the plate. "I don't condone gossip."

An awkward silence fell like a linen tablecloth onto a very long table with a four-inch gap in the middle. On the verge of boiling, the tea kettle hissed.

The wrapped bundle hiccupped and gave a loud squawk.

Verna peered over a bite of pie. "A hungry baby, if ever I heard one."

Brows drawn, Tessa patted her daughter's back in small circles. "She's usually so good."

How keenly Nora remembered feeling like everyone in a room knew how to settle her baby better than she. In those times, how she'd longed for escape. Softening her shoulders, she met Tessa's gaze. "Come with me. You can feed her in the sewing room."

Tessa puffed a curl from her eyes. "Thank you."

Nora led her brother's wife through the sitting room and into the sewing room on the far side of the staircase. Night had fallen, and the room was dark save for a shaft of light spilling through the open door. She lit the floor lamp, gestured Tessa toward a rocker, and turned.

"Please stay."

The quiet summons arrested her in the doorway. Much as she didn't want to linger, she wasn't eager to rejoin the family, either. She lowered stiffly onto a straight-backed chair beside the sewing machine, as far from the woman as was polite. The window rattled, and a draft seeped through cracks around the panes. She tilted her head and let the breeze cool her neck. Why hadn't she brought her pie?

Tessa pulled a blanket from her diaper bag and looped it over her head and shoulder. She snugged the baby beneath and settled into the chair with a sigh.

Instantly, the child hushed, and the sound of muffled suckling filled the silence.

Translucent skin beneath Tessa's eyes was smudged purplish-gray. Rebecca had been a terrible sleeper—colicky, fussy, and seemingly allergic to naps. Nora didn't get a full night's rest until the child was nearly three. "Does she sleep well?"

"Like an angel. I know I'm lucky, but even so, I'm exhausted all the time."

In the kitchen, laughter ebbed and flowed like autumn wind through the trees.

Beside the sewing machine lay pieces of a dress she was making for Rebecca. She ran a finger over the crisp blue cotton, feeling the prick of a straight pin. She'd let out her daughter's skirts until nothing remained to turn under. If the child took after her uncles, she'd be taller than Nora in a year.

Tessa shifted, and the chair creaked. "I'm glad your hip is better."

The pin jabbed deeper into the pad of Nora's index finger. Thank goodness she'd chosen to sit in the shadows. She didn't want this woman reading her expression, too. She barely knew herself what she was feeling tonight. As quickly as one emotion pierced her heart, another took its place. The feeling was eerily familiar. She swallowed, still tasting the sweetness of cooked onions. "Dr. Richard is a very good doctor."

"He certainly is." Tessa's freckled brow creased, and she caught her bottom lip between her teeth. "Is he well?"

Nora recalled that the doctor and Tessa courted not long before she became involved with Jonas. At the time, the rumor was just another black mark on the girl's character. Now, though, Tessa looked like an ordinary woman: not an evil, English shrew, or a scheming, remorseless brother-stealer, but simply a tired mother trying her best. Nora dropped an elbow on the desk and rested her cheek in her hand. "He is. He and Nurse Cindy seem very happy. They're expecting a baby any day now."

Tessa's eyes saucered, and she smiled. "Oh, yay. I hadn't heard. I've been out of touch with my Green Ridge friends since Lizzie was born, and with the time difference from Colorado, connecting is even harder."

The happy snuffles of a feeding baby quieted.

Tessa rustled beneath the covering and slid it over her head. "I think she's almost asleep." With the infant in one arm, she struggled to fold the blanket single-handedly.

Nora lifted partway from her chair and reached. "Can I help?"

"Yes, please." Tessa extended the swaddled bundle. "Would you take her?"

"Oh." She started. She'd expected the blanket—not the baby. "Of course."

Rising, she took the child and settled in the chair next to her sister-in-law. In the years since Rebecca was small, she'd held many babies. As a lame aunt, she could be relied upon for that task, if nothing else. But though most of the children were related, none was as close as a brother's—a dear brother's—child.

Lizzie nestled into her bosom, and a sense of familiarity stirred at the solid, comforting weight. Nowhere did one feel the life force more keenly than in a baby's quick, shallow breath.

"I'm glad to have a moment alone." Tessa folded the blanket in careful rectangles, smoothing the quilted fabric over her lap.

Someone made that nursing cover. Someone skilled with a needle.

Glancing up, Tessa caught her gaze. "I'm so sorry for any pain I caused."

Sudden tears pricked the corners of Nora's eyes, as sharp and stinging as the straight pins on her sewing table. Her sister-in-law might have gloated. She might have wielded the knowledge her quick actions saved Rebecca's life, and if Nora had her way, the Thanksgiving table might be missing a precious soul. But she didn't. She apologized.

"I don't know if you're aware, but after that night when Rebecca was sick and Richard—Dr. Bruce—

came, I left Green Ridge." Tessa shook out the quilt and draped it over her knees. "I drove until my van broke down in Colorado, and then I just stayed. I knew Jonas was needed here. I never thought I'd see him again." Her voice caught, and she took a trembling breath.

The baby wiggled and fluttered open her eyes. Nora rocked side to side, the soothing dance returning like riding a bicycle. She softened her tone. "With or without you, my brother was going to leave. After Elizabeth died, the only question was when."

Lizzie's delicate lids closed, and with a gurgle, she drifted back to dreamland.

"I didn't tell him where I was going, and once I was in Colorado, of course, I couldn't." Tessa lifted her shoulders and let them fall. "Somehow, he found me."

Nora met Tessa's gaze through the stark glare of propane light. She knew that while she and Jonas were at the hospital with Rebecca, Tessa cleaned the entire house of the messy remnants of illness. For years, Nora downplayed the toll that effort must have taken. Back then, she knew only that the woman had subsequently left town; she was ignorant of the circumstances. Discovering that Tessa labored all night only to walk away from the man she loved in the morning, Nora regarded the woman anew. If called upon, could she be so selfless? "Jonas made his choice. He loves you. A blind man could see how happy he is." She heard grit creep into her tone. She felt an unexpected kinship with this woman, but her feelings toward her brother still grated. Why was forgiveness so elusive?

Three quick raps came at the front door.

She turned with a jerk. Who would visit so late on Thanksgiving night? Still swaying, she stood and peeked out the window.

Mervin Zook's buggy was hitched up beside the barn.

Clutching the baby tight, she spun and slumped against the wall. She had no time. No time to hustle Jonas out the back door. No time to pretend they hadn't shared a meal. No time to concoct an excuse. Besides, she wouldn't want to.

With a quick word to Tessa, she reluctantly returned the baby and closed the door to the sewing room. "I'll get it," she called toward the kitchen, and straightening her spine, she flung wide the door.

Chapter Fifteen

Ten minutes later, Nora escorted Mervin outside onto the porch. "Are you sure you don't want a piece of pie? It's warm."

Mervin paced the length of the house. He hovered over the bench, knees bent as if he'd sit. Then he sprang up and planted his hands on the railing. "Never thought I'd see Jonas back here."

"His wife and child are resting in the sewing room." With cautious steps, she drew up beside him. "They named the baby Elizabeth."

Mervin's narrow shoulders sagged. Jonas's first wife was a distant cousin, and he'd mourned her death as deeply as anyone. As quickly, he stiffened his elbows again. "Unless my eyes deceive me, he appears to have shared the Thanksgiving meal."

A chill wind shook the naked tree branches, and she gathered the shawl around her shoulders. "The tables are spaced apart. In Ohio—"

"We aren't in Ohio."

His voice sliced the night like a scythe. She cringed. Mervin's father was a deacon. One word and her family could face serious consequences. In her head, she knew welcoming Jonas was wrong. Yet sharing a meal with her brother and his family felt right. A shiver convulsed her so fiercely her head swam. Moving from the hot kitchen, where Mervin gave a reserved holiday greeting to her family, outside into bitter cold was brutal. If Mervin noticed her discomfort, he didn't say. Hugging herself, she ran her hands up and down her arms. "My family lived in Ohio for many years. At first their customs seemed strange, even immoral, but once I saw how families could heal—how forgiveness could bring comfort—I changed. My mother has lost so much. Please, don't tell your father."

With a scoffing snort, Mervin hung his head. "Not tell him?"

Trembling, she laid a hand on his sleeve. "They so enjoy each other's company. I'd hate to see their friendship harmed."

Catching her hand, he turned and stepped closer. "As I enjoy being with you."

His fingers were thin and bone dry with nails bitten to the quicks. Was Mervin a nervous sort? His wide face, perched on a pencil neck like a pinwheel, loomed. He wasn't an ugly man. Soft brown curls fell from beneath his hat, and, though thin, his beard was neatly kept. His eyes were wide but in proportion with an equally wide mouth. Though not handsome, his face was kind. He wouldn't dare kiss her on the front porch, would he? And if he did, could she stop herself from wincing? Discretion was essential. If only for her mother's sake.

"For you, I'll keep this evening's events to myself," he said. "I know your family has seen hard times. We've had some pretty tough days on the Zook farm, as well."

His breath was hot on her forehead. The meaty scent of his own Thanksgiving dinner clouded the air. She forced a smile.

He pressed his fingers into hers. "Just be careful. I can't say how long folks will be so understanding."

Was he threatening or simply warning? Unsure, she gave a quick nod.

"After all, the future of your family means a lot to me." He cleared his throat with a high-pitched *ahem*. "My father said I should make my intentions clear. That's why I came by. May I call on you a week from Sunday evening?"

Encased in his fervent grip, her palm began to sweat. Mervin was a fine man. He came from a good family. For many women, such qualities would be enough. So why couldn't she open her heart? Spending the rest of her life hiding out with Tucker—dancing in barns and watching movies on his phone—wasn't realistic. She swallowed hard. "You may." Her assent came out a hoarse whisper. Seeming to mistake reluctance for girlish modesty, or worse yet, passion, Mervin darkened his gaze.

"Well, all right then. Good."

"Good," she echoed, dumbly. How utterly anti-climactic. She just consented to a visit that might very well lead to a marriage proposal, and all they could find say was "good." How Tucker would laugh over this scene. How she would laugh, too. To compare the touch of Tucker's hand to Mervin's was to compare a warm sweater to a block of cheese. But Tucker McClure was as much a fantasy as the man in the bright yellow moon. And this warning from Mervin was only a taste of what would come were she to become entangled with an *Englischer*.

At long last, he left. Free from the sour scent of his breath, she gulped crisp night air. All she wanted was a slice of pie and a cup of coffee and to put this whole day behind her. She waited until his buggy rounded the corner, trundling into darkness…and then she waited longer. She could imagine how her family would look when she returned: her mother eager but worried, her daughter pained, and her brothers both cautiously hopeful. Strangely, the only compassionate gaze would likely come from Tessa. Once she revealed Mervin's intention to call again, without his children and in the evening, they would see which way the wind blew.

Literal wind bit through her stockings, and she hugged herself for warmth. Oh, for a man's strong arms to hold her and a soothing voice to tell her everything would be all right. Instead, she had her daughter threatening to disclose her dance class and Mervin lording over her brother's return. From inside, a different kind of pressure pushed back against her arms—a mounting fear her secrets would only stay hidden so long. And then? Then who knew what would happen.

****

Nora layered the last dozen peppermint whoopie pies onto the table and tucked away the empty crate. Barely a week had passed since Thanksgiving, and the Farmers' Market was a riot of Christmas decorations. The second the turkey went cold, the English strung up a million lights. Every year they added more, and now the entire town was bedecked in a garish glow. The new market owners framed every door with fake greenery studded with colored bulbs. They set up artificial trees dusted in pretend snow and hung tinsel garlands from the rafters. English vendors followed suit, topping red and green tablecloths with Christmas cookies, wreaths, and gifts. The result was festive but gaudy. Seemingly energized by the pre-holiday bustle, patrons swarmed the booths like minnows around a dough ball.

Knowing the market would be busy, Nora increased her baking beyond even the robust Thanksgiving offerings, adding brand-new peppermint whoopie pies. She gazed over dwindling inventory, pleased with the pretty cream coated in sparkly crushed candy canes. Next week, she'd debut her gingerbread whoopie pies. Doubling the crystallized ginger was sure to bring the perfect spicy zing to balance the sweet molasses. If she made the final test batch in time, she could send some with Tucker when he set out on tour.

She checked the closest entrance for what felt like the thousandth time. Instead of Tucker's lanky frame, her mother's heavyset body filled the door. After weeks of steady exercise and an increased appetite, Nora filled out her dresses better than last summer, but her mother and brothers still dwarfed her. No doubt some fine-boned ancestor smiled down from heaven—a pony in a family of Clydesdales.

"Lovina Lapp sends her best." Verna tucked a bushel of winter squash into a milk crate and draped her shawl over the back of the chair. "She got wind Mervin is courting. In my day, couples kept such matters to themselves."

"I didn't tell anyone but you." The protest was unnecessary. A smug smile betrayed her mother's scolding. When Nora had returned inside Thanksgiving night, she immediately spotted her mother's dour face. As predicted, the revelation Mervin planned to call the following Sunday seemed to ease Verna's fears, and in the chaos of Jonas's departure, Mervin's untimely visit was forgotten.

Forgotten by all but Nora. Every morning brought her one day closer to his call and the inevitable declaration of his intentions. Over the course of the week, she felt as if her stomach crocheted itself into ever more complicated knots.

Last night's class had shimmered on the horizon like a beacon of hope, offering promise of worry-free fun. But yesterday was unseasonably warm, and when Tucker didn't arrive in her driveway an hour before class, she strapped the battery-powered light onto her bike and traversed the trail in the dark. The dance partner who arrived ten minutes late bore no resemblance to the man with whom she lost herself in decades-old movies. Distant and distracted, he executed the steps with perfunctory precision and zero joy. She went through the motions at his side, reassuring herself one bad practice meant nothing. Tucker knew the dance perfectly. The TipTop Tappers would be fine. Assuming, of course, he came back.

After a mumbled invitation, he drove her home as usual, but the silence was so uncomfortable she almost wished he hadn't. Though the idea was ridiculous, she couldn't help but wonder if, somehow, he heard about Mervin's visit. Mervin spread the news far and wide. Could the rumor have penetrated the English community? She fiddled with the big, black button on her coat. It slid smoothly against her fingertips. "Are you all right?"

"I leave for Akron on Saturday." With a scowl, he flicked the evergreen air freshener. "Just preoccupied, I guess."

Finally home and out of the truck, she grabbed the

door handle, possessed of an urge to close it with extra pepper.

Tucker stopped her mid-slam. "Hey, can you come by tomorrow afternoon and see Hank?"

Startled, she jerked away her hand, flinging the door wide. It emitted a raucous squeak and bounced on the hinges, bumping her hip. "Tomorrow? Tomorrow is market day."

He swung his gaze out the windshield and sucked his cheeks. "Right. How about I pick you up after you close? Hank has a business proposition to discuss."

In the distance, a barred owl hooted "who cooks for you." The eerie sound raised the hairs on the back of her neck. On the verge of Mervin's proposal, associating even more closely with the English felt like a bad idea. She cast a wary look toward the house. Light glowing around the edges of Samuel's shade offered the only sign of life. "What kind of proposition."

He swept a hand through his hair and jammed the truck into gear. "He can explain it better than me. Can you come?"

She had barely uttered "yes" before he sped out of the driveway, leaving her to ponder what kind of business proposition Hank possibly had in mind.

Clutching the remaining three peppermint whoopie pies, an elderly customer tendered payment.

Nora shook herself back to present and counted out change. Whatever the proposition, she'd take it. Saving money was a priority, and she needed work. Going into the next chapter of her life, whatever that chapter might be, she wanted a nest egg. Life was uncertain, and Mervin Zook didn't seem the type to permit his wife to labor outside the home. With the daily care of those wee monsters—wee *children*, she corrected herself, gritting her teeth—she wouldn't have time anyway. If she agreed to his proposal, of course. And that was one very big if.

Market day hubbub engulfed her, the chaos comforting in its predictable unpredictability. Gaudy decorations or no, she'd miss this place. She'd miss the baking and the bustle. She'd miss the customers. She'd miss the community.

Striding in Nora's direction, Annie Amos waved with an eager look that could only mean one thing. She, too, heard about Mervin Zook.

At almost the same instant, Tucker appeared. He caught her gaze from the doorway and flashed a smile as warm as a sticky bun fresh out of the oven. Her answering smile tasted just as sweet, scuttling momentarily her annoyance at his gruff behavior last night. Maybe he'd explain himself. He had in the past. She'd give him a chance.

Spotting Tucker, Annie pulled up short. She dropped her hands to slender hips, and a rascally expression dimpled both cheeks.

As a hidden flush raced across her collarbones, Nora shrugged. Tucker ambled to the stand like he was on a Sunday stroll. Unlike so many English, he never rushed.

He thrust his fists in his jean pockets and gave a sheepish, half smile. "Sorry I'm late. You ready?"

She nodded and peeked around him to check in with her friend.

Wide-eyed and grinning, Annie offered a thumbs-up before scurrying away.

Samuel ducked through the rear door of the stall, distracting her mother long enough for Nora to snatch her coat and slip away with a hasty farewell. Ever practical and with a level head for money, her mother hadn't balked when Nora floated the idea of working for Hank that morning over breakfast. She'd hardly be the first in the family to take a job with an English neighbor, and Verna knew too well the cost of raising a large brood.

In silence that wasn't quite strained but wasn't quite comfortable either, Tucker drove into a modest neighborhood comprised mostly of single-level homes. She wasn't the type to think houses had feelings. Such fanciful nonsense was squarely her daughter's domain. But peering at Hank's home through the mud-spattered windshield, she felt loneliness settle like fog. The one-story, brick house was tidy with wide picture windows bracketing the front door like unseeing eyes above a mustache of cleanly-pruned shrubs. Pursing her lips, she slid from the truck, turning her ankle on a patch of dead weeds sprouting from a crack in the asphalt. No wonder Hank had fallen. By the time she recovered her balance, Tucker was halfway to the front door. And he hadn't said a word to explain his foul mood.

Tightening her scarf, she scampered to catch up. Right before dawn, heavy rain had pushed the warm air east, leaving behind a sky like rolls of gray quilt batting. Damp wind battered her ears to a singing ache. She tucked her chin and ducked into the hallway on Tucker's heels, blinking into the dim foyer.

He tossed his coat onto a rack and rubbed together his hands. "Hey, Hank. I'm home."

From the living room, the sound of a television

newscaster increased to a deafening level.

"The other button!" Tucker called.

Muttered curses rumbled beneath the racket, and the house went suddenly silent.

She followed Tucker into a dimly lit living room. The space was orderly but in definite need of a deep clean. Piles of books and magazines covered the coffee and end tables, and crumbs littered the carpet around the recliner. A thick layer of dust coated the mantel and the framed photographs hanging in jumbled collections on the walls.

With a metallic squeak, the padded footrest retracted, and Hank pulled himself upright in the recliner. He rolled closed the top of a potato chip bag and wedged it on the end table between a dirty plate and a lamp. "Well, lookie here. If it isn't Miss Nora Beiler alive and in the flesh and standing in my living room." He tugged the front of a faded denim shirt, and a cascade of chip bits tumbled to the carpet. "Have a seat, Nora. Open the drapes, Grandson—it's dark as a sack of black cats in here."

She perched on the edge of the sofa. Thick curtains accordioned, giving off a stale, musty odor. Dust motes swirled in the gray glow coming through windowpanes very much in need of washing. Hank's arm was in a sling, but otherwise, he looked well. His cheeks were pink, and his blue eyes sparkled. She was sure a man like Hank didn't take to convalescence willingly, but he seemed not too much the worse for wear. Why in the world had he summoned her?

Peering from beneath bushy brows, he jerked his head toward Tucker. "How's my understudy? Can the boy dance worth a lick?"

She felt the warmth of Tucker's hand and the heat from his body as he held her in his arms. Her heart thumped, and a springy lightness lit her chest like jewelweed pods, ready to burst at the slightest touch. "He'll do."

"Don't just stand there, Grandson. Fetch our guest some fruit punch."

She held up a hand. "No need. I'm fine."

Ignoring her protest, Tucker ducked into the kitchen.

Hank ran his good hand over the chair arm. "As you well know, my grandson is leaving me in the lurch to go back out on the road. He's coming home Christmas Eve, of course, but December is a long, cold month, and I've gotten used to hearing another voice in this house besides my own."

"Cut the baloney, Hank. You need help." Tucker's voice was followed by the thud of the refrigerator door closing and the glug of liquid into a glass.

Hank dug his fingers into threadbare upholstery and twisted toward the kitchen, glaring. "Pipe down. I'm getting to it." He coughed and cleared his throat. "Joan and the gals bring my suppers, but the darn microwave is miles above the stove and the casseroles are heavier than sin. Truth be told, the laundry and vacuuming give me some trouble, and there's the matter of my memoir."

She cocked her head, certain she must have misheard. "Your what?"

Chuckling, Tucker sauntered in with a tray containing two glasses of cherry-red punch and a bowl of pretzels. "His memoir." He handed her a drink. "Don't get him started."

Ice tinkled in the frosty glass. "I don't understand."

Hank slurped and cradled the punch against his chest. "My memoir needn't concern you. I want the girl for that. Rebecca."

"My daughter?" The glass slipped, and she wedged it between both hands. The room felt suddenly stuffy. She toggled her gaze from Hank, calm as a cucumber in his recliner, to Tucker, sprawled in a chair by the fireplace. A look of unbridled amusement lit his maddeningly handsome face.

Hank nodded. "It's a package deal. Either I get the both of you or nothing. The girl's clever, and she makes an old man smile. Has she got good penmanship?"

"I suppose, but—"

"Excellent. This here bum arm is my writing arm, and I was in the middle of my life story when I busted it. Last couple of weeks, I've been dictating to Tucker, but he's a slow typist and has too many suggestions. Don't know who he thinks he is—not like he's written anything lately." He drained the punch and plunked the glass onto the end table, knocking the chip bag to the floor. He reached for it awkwardly, a grimace cracking his cheeks as his injured arm wedged between his chest and thighs.

She winced. Though a month had passed since his fall, clearly Hank was still in pain. Maybe the old gentleman really did need assistance.

Tucker started from the chair. "Sit down, Hank."

With a scowl, Hank snatched the bag and tucked it in his lap. "Now, if Rebecca writes out the book longhand, Tucker here can type it in the New Year." He swung his gaze to the collection of photos plastering the wood paneling. "I've had a heck of a life, Miss Nora. I want my story told before I forget it, and I'm prepared to pay very good money. As well for as the work around the house."

Never in a million years did she think Hank's business proposition would involve her daughter. "I suppose the content of your story is appropriate for a child?"

"For the most part—"

"One hundred percent." Tucker interrupted, cutting Hank a warning glance.

"I suppose I can skip the cussing and the juicy parts and add them when Tucker gets back. Now, I called the ladies from class, and they'll give you a lift three afternoons a week and Saturday mornings." He extended an open palm. "How about it, Miss Nora? Do we have an arrangement?"

She took a cautious sip of punch. It was sickly sweet but wonderfully cold.

"Hey, Old Man." Tucker stretched, and one elbow knocked a framed photo askew. "You forgot to tell her how much you'll pay."

She swallowed hard and, though she wasn't hungry, reached for a pretzel. Nibbling the salty snack like a squirrel, she turned over the proposition in her mind. Regardless of salary, could she...should she...say yes?

Chapter Sixteen

Rendered speechless by Hank's kingly sum, Nora gulped the remaining punch in a single breath. Tucking a stray hair into her *kapp* with shaky fingers, she rebuffed the offer, countering with a more modest sum.

Hank let out a guffaw. "Don't argue against your own best interest. The salary is perfectly reasonable, and with Christmas coming, you'd be a fool to turn me down. You folks exchange gifts, don't you?"

"A few."

"Well, pick up a few more. Or tuck away the money for a rainy day, I don't care. I made my offer, and I won't take no for an answer."

Tucker unfolded from the chair and retrieved the empty glasses. "I'd feel better, Nora, if I knew you were coming by."

Hank scowled, but he didn't mount an objection.

On what grounds could she refuse? Rebecca would be overjoyed to spend time with Hank. His stories would be all the Christmas gifts she'd require. Nora didn't know for certain what the New Year might bring, but whatever happened, having money tucked away would certainly ease her mind. She lifted her chin and thrust out a hand. "Thank you very much. I accept."

The sky had turned to charcoal gray by the time she was back in the truck. When she agreed to care for Hank, she figured Tucker's mood would lighten, but a somber cloud still shadowed his expression.

He toggled the radio from station to station before twisting the knob and silencing it with a grunt.

She licked her lips, her mouth gone sour from fake cherry sweetness. How was punch a nutritious drink for an elderly man? With what besides the ladies' meals did he fill his belly? He needed good healthy food to regain his strength, and she could help. While she was at it, she'd give that house the deep clean it deserved. Hank would be fine. So why was Tucker still sullen?

He yanked the wheel, and instead of heading west out Route 45 toward home, he steered the opposite direction toward town. They passed the English high school and entered the small shopping district, where grand Victorian homes converted into stores and restaurants lined Main Street. Puzzlement turning to irritation, she shot him a look. "The drive-in was fun, but I'm not comfortable with you taking me places without saying where we're going. I need to get home for dinner."

He drummed the wheel in a sharp, chopping rhythm. "I have to make a quick stop."

Swallowing annoyance, she struggled to keep her voice even. "I don't have time for a quick stop."

The truck idled at a stoplight beneath a banner spanning the width of the street. *Green Ridge Christmas Tree Lighting Tonight* was printed in fancy, old-style lettering, surrounded by painted silver bells and boughs of holly.

"Only a few minutes, I promise." The light turned green, and he proceeded onward.

"I don't have a few minutes, Tucker." Suddenly stifling, she uncoiled her scarf and balled it in her lap.

"Turn around, or I'll get out and walk."

"Please don't. I just…" With a sigh, he slumped against the car door. "I have to do this thing in a few minutes, and I'd feel a whole lot better if you were there." Pulling the truck into a parking spot, he peered through the windshield, and his jaw hardened.

She followed his gaze. Illuminated with what looked like a thousand strands of white lights, River Edge Park was packed with people, standing around the shadowy silhouette of a towering spruce. They huddled, faces aglow, and their collective attention riveted on a bandstand where a group of children stood in a wiggly arc.

He slid her a look. "I know I sprung this detour on you, and I'm sorry. Again. I was afraid if I asked, you'd say no. I promise I won't be long." The truck door slung wide, and the amplified voices of children filled the air. He smiled. "Come on, how cute is that?" Sliding an arm over the seat, he pulled his guitar from the rear of the cab.

Her breath came quick, coalescing in frosty puffs. The wind carried the brisk tang of snow. "You're singing?"

He nodded.

She hadn't heard him perform in weeks—not since the weather turned cold, and the outside concert series every Wednesday ended. The prospect made her pulse skip. Looping the scarf around her neck, she followed him.

He grabbed her hand and dashed into the park as the children sang a final, heartfelt note.

Mouths rounded in little *o's* and faces lifted heavenward, they were more angels than children, despite runny noses, overstuffed jackets, and snow hats akimbo.

The crowd cheered, and Tucker dropped her hand to join, his corduroy coat brushing her shoulder.

The TipTop Tappers' very own Gene Stackhouse bounded onto the stage, wearing a knit hat with a red-and-green pompom sticking straight up. Adorned with colored lights, the hat blinked cheerily. "Let's hear it for the First Presbyterian Church Cherub Choir!"

The children shuffled down from the stage, dragging mittened hands over the stair railing as they grinned and waved to the crowd.

Gene beamed broadly. "I tell you, the best part of being your mayor is presiding over the tree lighting every year. Spending this night with you is the highlight of my Christmas season."

She grabbed Tucker's arm. "Gene is the mayor?"

He nodded. "He ambushed me last night, in the bathroom of all places, and roped me into performing. I can't say no to those old folks."

Taking hold of the microphone, Gene crossed to the edge of the stage in a shuffle step straight out of class. "We're only minutes from the big event, but we have one final performer to ring in the holiday season in style. Lots of talented musicians have trodden this stage, but never one who hobnobs with country music royalty. Until tonight. The man needs no introduction. Ladies and gentlemen, Mr. Tucker McClure!"

The crowd parted like it knew he was coming, and without a backward glance, Tucker loped to the stage. A single snowflake fell, swirling in crazy eights as it seemed to follow him. The audience hooted, straining for a glimpse as he bounded up the stairs, taking his place under strings of crisscrossed holiday lights. Why did he want her there so badly?

Another flake fell and then another, sparked by stage light into lazy shooting stars. A yellow glow spilled into the first few rows of audience, illuminating the familiar faces of Joan and Edna, Bert and Dot, and Marion and a beefy man who must be Mr. Diefenderfer. Not a single black hat or bonnet dotted the crowd. Indeed, she struggled to remember that only fifteen miles away her whole community, her whole world, nestled into chilly farmhouses, snuffing the lights just as the English turned theirs on.

A chord rang out. "Good evening, Green Ridge."

The crowd cheered, and seeming to sense the solemnity of midwinter, they settled quickly. Out of the silence came notes like the plucked strings of a broken heart—mournful, soulful, and yet brimming with hope. All the bleakness of cold winter nights and the promise of bright Christmas mornings resonated in the sound. Tucker's sweet voice cut through with a tone as glassy as a frozen lake.

O little town of Bethlehem, how still we see thee lie
Above thy deep and dreamless sleep, the silent stars go by

Then, he glanced up abruptly and searched the crowd, wild-eyed. His voice wobbled. His cheeks went pale.

Nora caught her breath. She knew that look. She'd seen it on Rebecca's face during school Christmas programs when the girl stood at the front of the class, waiting to recite her part. With a reassuring smile from *Mamm,* panic ebbed, replaced by the inner peace of the holiest night of the year. Now, Tucker, a seasoned performer who usually seemed most at home in front of an audience, looked scared. Why was he nervous? Was that why he wanted her there? Did she make him feel safe, too?

She lifted a hand to shoulder level, summoning—beckoning him. Snowflakes prickled her palm. *I'm here, Tucker. I'm here.*

His gaze met hers, and his shoulders eased. Even as he sang, his lips curled into a smile.

How silently, how silently, the wondrous gift is giv'n.

Snow spiraled above the breathless crowd. With profound tenderness, he sang, each note stronger and truer than the one before. His smile widened. His lips parted, sending the song up, up, up—over the heads of the rapt audience members and straight to her heart.

Nora smiled, too, and from her crystalline breath to his, she spun an imaginary thread like sparkling lambswool, delicate as a spider's web and a million times as strong. Surrounded by hundreds of strangers and a few friends, too, she and Tucker were alone. He sang for her and her only. Each note vibrated the thread, sending a thrill that, if she didn't know better, felt an awful lot like love.

Before she was ready, the song ended. The final note hovered and drifted downstream with the river.

"The biggest miracles seem to happen in the smallest towns, don't they?"

His voice was barely more than a whisper.

The words were hers alone.

Striking a shimmering, upbeat chord, he stamped a foot. "It's Christmas time, baby!"

Another cheer rose. The tree lighting drew near,

and the crowd hummed with anticipation.

A second chord rang, familiar in its constellation of harmonies.

"Mayor Gene, are you ready to light this tree?"

With a smile as bright as his electrified hat, Gene held up two electrical cords, one in each hand.

Tucker jutted his chin toward the crowd. "How about it, my friends? Ya'll ready?"

The audience chorused approval.

Almost dancing with excitement, Nora raised her voice in concert. Like a child on Christmas morning, she could hardly wait.

"I've got one more song, and I'm pretty sure some of you out there know it. Sing along, won't you? One, two—a one, two, three four."

The rollicking melody from their tap dance poured from his guitar like not one, but six musicians, played together. How could a single instrument make so much sound?

Tucker's fingers flew, and the crowd burst into song.

On the side of the stage, Gene tapped his toes, and in the audience, Dot and Bert launched into a mini version of the dance.

Tucker's black boots kept the beat, and her sneakers crunched a fine layer of snow in time. He met her gaze again, and this time, he held her. She could almost feel his arms around her, and she laughed for the joy of being young and alive on such a winter's night.

Her whole life she felt part of a community. Never once did she face the world alone. Since the accident, however, people she knew from childhood spouted platitudes like hollow versions of themselves. Despite their good intentions, she felt isolated. Now, surrounded by the larger community of which she'd always unknowingly been a part, the loneliness vanished.

With a whoop, Tucker finished the song and beckoned Gene onto the stage. "Ten—nine—eight..."

The audience joined the count and, in perfect unison, chanted "three—two—one!"

The cord in Gene's right hand snugged into the one in his left, and the Green Ridge Community Christmas Tree revealed itself in an explosion of brilliance as dazzling and glorious as the angel who appeared to the shepherds on a night two thousand years before.

She gasped, pressing her palms to her cheeks, mesmerized by how the tree illuminated the whole park in soft, twinkly radiance. Yes, this light was worldly. Yes, it came from an electrical grid. But this particular electricity didn't separate the community. In a single beautiful moment, it made them one.

Someone squeezed her shoulder.

She swung around and discovered Jerry, incandescent in the Christmas tree's glow. She wore a purple knitted beret, fuzzy, purple gloves, and a matching puffy coat. Her lips were the color of plums, and gold hoops dangled from her ears, adding extra sparkle to an already sparkly night.

"I'm glad to see you out on this festive evening." Jerry looked from Nora to Tucker on the stage, and back again. "Mm hm. Mighty glad." She took the hand of the tall, handsome man for whom she left New York and sashayed into the snow.

The crowd slowly dispersed, and Tucker made his way down from the stage, shaking hands and posing for pictures with fans. Finally, he stood before her, eyes bright. "Walk with me?"

The night was cold, and the hour was late, and her family would wonder where she was.

He held out a hand.

She took it simply because she wanted to.

Away from the crowd, he led her toward the bluff. Shrouded in darkness, the river was a silent presence, pulling with palpable insistence toward the sea. She might have felt scared but for the hum of the crowd, the glow of the tree, and the warmth of the hand holding hers.

He wrapped both hands around hers. "Have you ever seen the tree lighting?"

She shook her head. She'd never seen anything like it.

"I wondered. Do you have a Christmas tree at home?"

"No. Our celebration is simple. Joyful, but simple." As the flurries ebbed, talking about their customs was easy. How different he was from the nosy *Englischers* at market. His curiosity rang sincere.

He tugged her hand, navigating around a big clump of rhododendron and toward a secluded bench overlooking the river.

The air smelled of moss and chimney smoke. To the right, a bridge arched to the eastern bank, lined by streetlamps ringed with lighted evergreen wreaths. To the left, the huge stone base of a long-unused railroad trestle hulked like a silent memory. She was part of this town—its past, its present, and its future.

Releasing his hand, she sat. Through her coat, the wooden slats were frigid. She'd been up since five, stood market all day, and called on Hank—all before attending a concert in the park. Even as her brain sparked a million thoughts and her heart reeled, her muscles slackened.

He leaned his guitar case against the bench and joined her.

His shoulder and side snugged against hers, and all she wanted was to slip into the comforting circle of his arms. She was too exhausted to question her actions and done with weighing the appropriateness of every thought. Tucker was a good man. Sitting with him felt like home. Nothing else mattered.

The clouds parted, revealing a slivered moon surrounded by stars.

He leaned forward, elbows on knees, and clasped his hands loosely. He wore black gloves cut off at the knuckles, exposing long, lean fingers with neat square nails. "Thank you for coming. The last couple of days, just knowing I was going back on the road made me edgy. I should have explained it all instead of moping around like a jerk, but somehow, I couldn't." He glanced at her over one shoulder. "You saw me lose my nerve there for a second, didn't you?"

She nodded.

"I covered okay, though, right?"

"You were wonderful. You're always wonderful."

With a bitter laugh, he jerked around his head. "Not always…" He tightened his fingers until the knuckles cracked. "The road is magic. Nah, it's more than that. It's home…at least, it was. For years, I felt most like myself when I was on stage singing. And when I wasn't performing, I wrote nonstop. Songs just came to me. They woke me in the night, knocking on my skull until I picked up my guitar." He pulled himself upright and leaned against the bench, burying his hands in his coat pockets. "Music was my ticket to freedom. As soon as I could, I got away—from the farm and my brothers and the potatoes. So many potatoes. I left and didn't eat a potato for three years."

She chuckled. "Too much of anything is never good."

"Once I got to Nashville, though, everything fell into place." He reached his legs long and rested his head atop the bench. "Success shouldn't come so easy. I got too much too quick, and it went to my head. I messed up, Twinkletoes. I blew it."

Sliding down on the bench, she settled next to him. "We all make mistakes."

"My mistakes could have killed someone."

His voice was acid, and her stomach clenched. What had those girls at the market said? Something about the police? About jail?

He shook his head, turning it side to side until his forehead grazed her cheek. "Feels like bad luck to even talk about it. When I get back to the clubs and bars, what if I do it all again? What if…" His voice hitched, and his words faded. He stared at the stars.

Cold, hard wood dug into her scalp, and her neck twinged. Rolling her head to ease the ache, she gazed at him. His profile cut into the sky like a mountain range. His high, handsome forehead. The aquiline nose he inherited from his grandfather. Soft lips and a strong chin. A pang carrying a memory of love shook her again. She steadied her voice. "Don't be afraid."

He turned and caught her gaze. "That right there— that's why I wanted you here tonight. I was afraid I'd get jittery and lose my nerve, and when I did, I wanted to see your face. Smiling. I'll take that smile with me, and when I get scared—scared I'm gonna fail or do the same stupid stuff I did before—I'll look out into the crowd and picture you. I'll be able to see you—exactly like you were tonight. Your smile is some kind of magic, Twinkletoes."

No man had spoken such words in years. From the top of her scalp to the soles of her feet, every inch of skin flushed like she'd slipped into a hot bath. She scrunched her nose. Who was she kidding? No man had ever spoken such words. Amish men didn't exhibit candor or vulnerability. At least, none of the ones she knew. Did her brothers talk so? Or Mervin Zook? She swallowed a giggle at the idea of a romantic overture by Mervin.

He lifted one dark brow. "What's so funny?"

"Nothing. Everything." The laugh slipped past her lips. "When I was a girl in school, we had two Noras. Nora Hochstetler was three years older than I and honestly rather dim-witted." She giggled again and raised a hand to her mouth. "I shouldn't say such things, especially at Christmas. Anyway, to distinguish between us, the teacher called her 'Nora' and me 'Smiling Nora.' For years, everyone called me that. I forgot how much I like to smile."

"I'd like to kiss you, Smiling Nora."

His voice was a sweetheart's caress. His breath on her cheek smelled of peppermint. She shivered. Wind gusted, and the rhododendron leaves gave a dry, papery whisper. Did he really ask to kiss her? Her? Plain, Nora Beiler? *Oh, yes, he did.* "I'd like that."

Lifting his chin, he touched his lips to hers so softly and so gently, tears sprang to her eyes.

Tenderness. She had no idea how much she missed the tender touch of a man until it was right there, nibbling with delicious delicacy.

A rush of warmth filled her chest, and she reached for him. The rough stubble of a beard tickled her palm, and she ran her thumb over his sharp cheekbone, trailing her fingers down his chin to his neck, relishing the warmth of his skin. A single tear rolled down her cheek.

He pulled away, frowning. "Are you all right?"

Another tear slipped its liquid bond. "Perfectly. I just…I want you to kiss me again."

A crease cleft the space between his brows. "Are you certain?"

"Oh, yes." With a breath of sharp night air, she pushed off the bench and came to him with passion stored up over long, lonely winters and endless summer nights. Her mouth crashed against his in a nose-bumping, cheek-smushing, chin-scraping doozy of a kiss, her smile turning to a giggle and then to a laugh as he twined an arm around her. She felt his lips lift in an answering smile as he deepened the kiss, and the silly, joyful fun of being so close threatened to summon a longing she might not be able to quash.

At last, they parted, and he snuggled her to his chest, letting out a sigh.

She laid her head against his shoulder and gazed at cut glass stars. *What have I done?* From far off, she heard laughter and the faint sound of jingle bells.

He dropped a kiss onto her prayer cap and another onto her forehead.

What in the world have I done?

Chapter Seventeen

The following afternoon, Nora stood on Hank's doorstep, grinning. Last night's dusting of snow still coated the grass, but the afternoon sun would soon dispatch it. The front walk was clean and dry. Tucker must have cleared it before he left that morning.

On tiptoes, Rebecca bounced at her side, a matching smile lighting her face.

She gave the girl a cautionary look. "Remember, we're not on a social call. We're here to work."

Rebecca spluttered a laugh. "If you call writing down Hank's remarkable stories work, then I suppose. Can I press the doorbell?"

She nodded. Though Verna was surprised when Rebecca accompanied her to Hank's, she'd certainly approved of the girl taking on proper employment. Of course, Nora hadn't mentioned the writing. Another lie by omission. Still, happiness filled her chest like bread dough. It rose in the warm oven of her joy until she thought she might burst.

Inside, a bell chimed.

The door swung wide revealing Hank in the entry, his injured arm in a sling over a spangled Christmas sweater. "What are you two smiling about?"

Why was she so happy? Cleaning Hank's house was a massive job. Long hours of baking loomed on the horizon. Tucker was miles away. Mervin would call on

Sunday. Her life was a mixed-up, muddled mess. Still, she smiled.

Rebecca took a slow step. "I'm honored you selected me to record the story of your life. My penmanship is excellent, I'm a hard worker, and I'll do my very best."

Hank frowned. "You realize you already have the job, don't you?"

"Oh, yes, but I want you to know I'm worthy."

He waggled a meaty finger. "I respect that, young lady. Come on inside."

Nora trailed Hank and her daughter into the foyer, wiping her sneakers on a tattered welcome mat. She cast a critical gaze over her surroundings. Cleaning the living room was the first task, and if she finished quickly, she'd whip up a batch of cookies—maybe even stick a dozen in the freezer for Tucker's return. He'd be away for two weeks, back for a weekend, and then gone one more week before he came home for Christmas. The season was busy. Time would fly. Still, missing him cut like an arrow through the warm, doughy joy inside.

"We'll work in my library, young lady. Follow me." Hank struck out through the living room.

Close on his heels, her daughter peeked at the walls. "Do you really know all these people?"

Hank paused and straightened a cock-eyed frame. "Every one. By the time we're finished, you'll know 'em all too."

"My goodness." Rebecca spun, sweeping a wide-eyed gaze over the expansive collection. "Photographs are wicked, of course, but I understand why you'd want them. You'll never forget these faces—even after

211

they're gone."

Nora's stomach lurched. On both counts, her daughter was right. A photo kept someone alive, and it was a daily reminder of heartache. Levi's face grew fuzzier every day. Was forgetting a blessing or curse? Rebecca was only three when her father died. Did she have any memory of him, at all?

Hank turned and caught Nora's gaze.

Seeming to read her thoughts, he gave a bittersweet smile. Of course, his beloved wife lived within these frames. As well as in in his heart.

He cleared his throat. "Cleaning supplies are in the laundry room. You should find everything you need." Scowling, he tugged at his spangly sweater. "My grandson forgot to do the laundry before he left. He seemed mighty preoccupied this morning. Come to think of it, he was smiling like a nincompoop, too! If you could see to the wash, I'd be much obliged. This crazy sweater was the only thing in my drawer. It makes me feel like…like…" He rubbed a hand over his chin. "What do I look like, girl?"

"Like a Christmas tree with a mustache," Rebecca said.

Hank snapped heartily. "Indeed. Now let's get started."

Nora hated cleaning. She loathed dusting, abhorred sweeping, and couldn't abide washing dishes. Having done chores for an English neighbor as a girl, she knew how to work a dishwasher and a vacuum—though their racket always gave her a start. Even so, as she tackled the living room, she couldn't keep from humming. Into the washer went the dusty orange drapes, allowing sunlight to slant into the room and kiss the heavy, upholstered furniture. A layer of grime vanished from the photos, revealing smiling faces in color and black-and-white.

As she cleaned, she examined them more closely. In nearly all the images, a younger Hank appeared alongside people holding giant fish, antlered deer, and even in some cases grizzly bears. A bonny, dark-haired woman with laughing eyes and a carefree grin posed in more than half of those, and a few featured only Hank and Lavelle. Rebecca had said he was a bush pilot in Alaska. Apparently, his work entailed hunting and fishing, as well.

Though she disliked cleaning, she loved the way the ceiling in a tidy room seemed to rise a foot or two. Almost finished with the living room, she swiped a rag over the mantle, inhaling the scent of lemon polish and chuckling for no other reason than the smell of citrus and wood was pleasing. She dusted ceramic polar bears and a bronze clock inside a glass dome.

Traversing the fireplace, she discovered a photo that made her laugh out loud. She snatched the tarnished silver frame in both hands and tilted the grainy image toward the light. It featured two chubby ruffians in knit hats and rubber boots, standing proudly on either side of a snowman wearing a lady's wig and scarf. Closer inspection revealed, however, that the face of the snowman was not ice but flesh. Fully encased, Tucker glared at the camera, tongue thrust out in fruitless protestation.

She studied the boy Tucker was. Much smaller and darker than his captors, he had clearly put up a fight. Matted clumps of dark hair escaped the wig and clung to splotched cheeks. Green eyes burned with ire. Free

213

of its snowy prison, one hand doubled in a fist. More than once, Tucker mentioned how glad he was to get away from home. Perhaps these bully brothers were among the reasons why.

Other than the photo, Hank's house revealed little of Tucker. Given the fact he lived there for several months, nary a trace was found in the living room. Another twinge of missing him shivered along her spine. The childhood picture was a surprise. What more might she find?

Emptying pockets as she loaded shirts and socks and trousers into the washing machine, she reassured herself she wasn't being nosy. Hank asked her to do the wash, and the items to be cleaned all seemed to belong to him. All except one. At the very bottom of the hamper, a red, plaid shirt lay crumpled. Whiffing spicy, English man smell, she ran a finger over one pearly snap. It was cool and smooth as a marble. Simply holding the shirt, she felt closer to him. She tossed it into the machine. Two weeks. In two weeks and he'd return. And then…?

With a gurgle, the washer sprang into action. The contraption looked almost as old as the one in her basement, but it seemed functional. She glanced at the mantle clock. Time for a bit more cleaning before she whipped up cookies and put Joan's macaroni casserole in the oven. Hank's muffled voice sounded at the end of the hall. Determined to ensure her daughter behaved, she tiptoed closer and hid behind the door.

A chair squeaked, and Hank sniffed. "The night was dark as sin—now that's all right for me to say, isn't it?"

"What's blacker than sin?" Rebecca asked.

"Not much indeed." Hank cleared his throat. "I had a three-hundred-pound mountain goat in my cargo, and oh, he was a beauty. The Hollywood bigwig who shot him was already sipping hot toddies back at the lodge, toasting his toesies and waiting for me to fly in his prize. Approaching from the west, I spied the camp, and my ticker about conked out. The temperature in the valley had risen fifteen degrees since morning, and the fog was pea soup. I couldn't begin to make out the runway lights. Where would I bring her down? I hated the thought of losing my plane, but even worse was the idea of that goat landing in my lap."

"What did you do?" Rebecca's voice quivered. "Did you crash?"

"Course not. I'm sitting here, ain't I? First requirement of a good bush pilot is a level head. I circled a couple of times, watching the gas gauge plummet and racking the old noggin for a plan. Then boom! Inspiration struck. I radioed down and told everyone at the lodge to drive their cars alongside the runway and turn on the headlights. When I saw those lights flicker on..." He let out a low whistle. "They were about the prettiest sight I ever saw."

"They must have looked like fallen stars all lined up in a row."

"Now that's fine prose. Go ahead and add that, too."

The washer let out a bang, and Nora jumped. She skittered from the library and came to a stop beside the open door to a small bedroom. Inside, a carved wooden trash can was ringed by crumpled paper balls. As she scooped them up, she spotted words in black ink, seeping through the pages. The air held the faintest scent of spice, and she knew with absolute certainty that the room…and the writing…was Tucker's.

She perched on the edge of the bed and dropped the wadded papers onto the coverlet. Tucker's writing was private. Even if he considered it trash, she had no right to read it. She twitched her fingers above a ball and jerked back her hand, swinging her gaze around the room. The furnishings were almost spare enough to be Amish—the dresser clear and the bed neatly made. The walls were light-blue, lined along the ceiling with a strip of wallpaper featuring whimsical birdhouses and sunflowers. Lavelle's doing? She couldn't imagine Hank picking out the feminine pattern. Otherwise, the room was unfussy.

She darted a glance at the pile. Time to toss the papers and get on with cookie baking. But she couldn't. The writing whispered in a voice like a page turning, tempting her to look. With a quick glance at the door, she snatched a paper and smoothed it over her knees.

Tangled in your bonnet strings, everything inside me sings

Her pulse tripped. She shot another look into the hall, but she was alone. She scanned the page again. Had Tucker written those words about her? Casting aside the paper, she reached with shaky fingers for another.

You're a dancing queen on a movie screen
I'm no Fred Astaire but you take me where
Stars light up the night on a stage so bright
From the black and white into technicolor

A thrill shimmered like sunlight off a snow-covered roof. These verses were about her…about her and Tucker…together.

No one ever wrote a poem for her. Levi was a tender and earnest suitor, but he would no sooner have given her a love poem than a diamond necklace. His courtship had been long buggy rides and bouquets of fresh-picked wildflowers. He played at her side in youth volleyball games and swooned over her pie. Reliable, good-hearted, and true, he wasn't the poetic sort.

She ran her gaze over the crinkled paper. Each phrase was on a different line, and capital letters topped some of the words: *C, F, G*. Screwing up her lips, she snatched a third page. It contained more writing than the others—three verses of four lines each. Her breath hitched. *Verses.* These lines weren't poems. They were songs. Tucker wrote songs about *her*.

He wrote them, and he threw them away.

****

The woodstove ticked like a kitchen timer. Arching her back, Nora wiggled her toes, toasting tired feet. Her hip twinged. Standing for hours in the kitchen was no trouble lately, but these December days were cold and damp. She supposed a wee ache now and again was to be expected. Compared to last year at this time…well, she could make no comparison. She was a different person than the one who limped across an icy barnyard to snuggle her uncle's horse. A smile as warm as the crackling fire inched from cheek to cheek. That Nora had forgotten how to smile. Forgotten what happiness felt like. Forgotten the feel of a man's embrace…

A flush bloomed from her toes to her neck. She flicked a glance at her mother, bent over a lap desk writing a letter. Her pen moved in smooth, even strokes. Verna and her cousins kept up a circle letter for over thirty years, replacing their last missive with a new one and sending the whole set on to the next in line. Did secret hopes and dreams fill those pages? Or were they simply a catalog of daily ups and downs? What would her mother write if she knew everything Nora had done? Almost of its own accord, her grin widened. She bit back the smile and refocused on her knitting. After all, Mervin's visit was tomorrow. What did she have to smile about?

Besides everything.

She shifted, rolling her shoulders and easing tired muscles in her back. From the table in the corner came the snick of her daughter's scissors. What was the child working on? She swiveled and glanced over the top of the chair.

"No peeking!" Rebecca flopped onto the table, hiding the project beneath open arms. "Uncle Samuel, I'm nearly finished with the design. Can we begin part two of my super-secret Christmas surprise tomorrow?"

Sprawled on the sofa, Samuel opened his eyes, and the newspaper slid from his lap. He snatched it and gave it a sound snap. "I promised, didn't I?" He lifted the paper and peered around it. "Though I don't think your *mamm* would approve of us building a rocket ship in the barn."

Rebecca's giggle was as bubbly as when she was tiny. Nora sighed. May her daughter never outgrow that laugh, and may she never have cause to frown more often than smile. An image of Rebecca sour-faced and panting as she chased Agnes Zook across the yard flashed in Nora's mind. Her decisions impacted not only herself. Rebecca's happiness—her future, lay in her hands. What choice was truly best for the child?

"Don't talk nonsense." Grunting, Verna scootched her chair closer to the floor lamp. She held aloft the letter and studied it. "I'll have to wait until tomorrow to finish. I can't make out my own words, even as I write."

Samuel caught her gaze and winked.

She answered with a sly smile. Noting the trouble her mother had seeing at night, her brother designed and had already begun to craft a magnifier with a built-in, battery-powered light. It would be a wonderful Christmas surprise.

The baby blanket puddling in her lap was soft and fine. She hoped Dr. Richard and Nurse Cindy would like the color—a variegated yarn in blues and greens. The knitting needles glided smoothly, clicking in chorus with the woodstove. She wasn't the knitter her mother was, but she was quick and competent. If she worked steadily, she could give Joan the finished product in class on Tuesday.

Verna tossed aside the lap desk. "What are you making?"

Nora glanced up. "A blanket for Dr. Richard's baby. They had a boy."

"Oh?" *Mamm*'s forehead wrinkled. "How did you hear?"

"Nurse Cindy's mother is in my exercise class. She told us last week."

"Well, isn't that good news. I can't imagine a nicer Christmas present than a *boppli*."

Samuel let out a chuckle. "Except, maybe, an engagement?" Catching her gaze again, he waggled his brows.

She glared. To her brother, everything was a joke.

"Are you planning to get married, *bruder*?"

Laughing, he tossed aside the paper. "Wasn't me I was referring to." He tucked thumbs beneath his suspenders and grinned. "What smells so good? Have you been baking?"

Her knitting needles flew. She sucked her cheeks like she'd swallowed Hank's vacuum. Samuel would not provoke her. Not tonight.

"An engagement would be a blessing. You baked something special, I hope," *Mamm* said.

She released her lips with a smack. "I'm trying a new recipe. Gingerbread whoopie pies." From the look on *Mamm's* face, she would have thought they were poisoned.

"For Mervin Zook? But he loves your shoofly pie."

"The whoopie pies are scrumptious," Rebecca chimed in. "I licked the bowl."

Samuel unfolded from the sofa. Grabbing the poker, he wrenched open the woodstove door. Sparks swirled like an eddy of fireflies.

Mamm gathered the cousins' letters splayed across the end table. "When a fellow comes calling, you make his favorite, plain and simple." She neatened the stack with a swift tap and slid it into a manilla envelope.

Samuel tossed another log on the fire. "If Mervin wants pie, he can buy one at Market same as anyone else."

Verna huffed a disgusted breath.

Nora scrunched her nose and counted stitches. Why didn't she bake a pie?

"I don't like this conversation. I'm going to bed." Shears clattered onto the table, and concealing her project, Rebecca sidled to the staircase and dashed upstairs.

"Don't let me catch that cat in your bed," she called to her daughter's shadow.

Tucking the envelope under one arm, Verna labored to her feet. She slanted a reproving look at Samuel and swung her gaze to Nora. "You've always been a sensible girl. I don't need to tell you what Mervin's courtship means. Knowing you and Rebecca are settled, and our family and the Zooks are bound in holy union…what more could a mother ask for?" She headed for the stairs, pausing next to Nora's chair to lay a hand on her shoulder. "Sleep well, *dochder*."

Her mother's door closed with a muffled thud, and Samuel let out a low whistle. "No pressure, huh?"

She scowled. "You're no help, Mr. Jokester."

Kicking up his feet, he leapt onto the sofa and landed on his back. "So how do you plan to answer ole Merv? If he asks, I mean."

Her stomach sank. "I haven't decided."

Samuel rolled onto one side, propping his head on his hand. "Don't tell me Smiling Nora would break *Mamm's* heart like her big brother did."

She stared at him—long legs extending over the arm of the sofa, tawny hair sticking out in all directions. Though he was slender and straight haired, he looked so much like Jonas. His brilliant blue eyes gleamed with the same rascally intelligence. His lips were always on the verge of a smile. She knew her friends thought him handsome. So why was she alone being hassled into marriage? "Why doesn't *Mamm* hound you to find a wife?"

The glimmer in his gaze faded. "I suppose I'm a lost cause."

His attempt at humor rang hollow. She dropped the knitting into her lap and gave a hard look. "I can think of ten girls who would marry you tomorrow."

"Ten? Nah."

She counted them off on her fingers. "Lovina Lapp, Anna Stotzfus, Jenny Glick—"

"She has a terrible overbite. She looks like a horse."

Yanking a throw pillow from behind her back, she hurled it at him. "Rachel Yoder—"

"She's barely twenty."

"Rose King, Leora Mast—"

"Okay, enough!" He clutched the pillow to his chest like a shield. "I can't get married, all right? I'm not baptized."

His words hit her like a twenty-five-pound feed sack. Mouth agape, she collapsed against the chair back. "You…you're…you never joined the church?"

With a deep sigh, he shook his head. "I was going to. Remember? Right before *Daed* died? Then *Mamm* was in terrible shape, and we left in such a rush. When I got to Ohio, everyone assumed I'd already joined, and I never said otherwise." He raked a hand through his hair and tugged the ends. "Then when we got back to Green Ridge…"

"Everyone here assumed you'd joined out there."

Flipping onto his back, he nodded.

She leaned forward and bundled the blanket in her lap. "You still could."

A bitter chuckle rumbled from his chest. "I'm twenty-eight years old, Nora. I'll look like a fool."

Samuel might be the family clown, but he was a proud man. The community welcomed all who truly

222

wished to join church, but to come forward now would certainly appear odd. Samuel had been playing the role of a church member. He'd seem like a liar.

He interlaced his fingers across his belly and stared at the ceiling. His chest rose and fell in a ragged rhythm. "Everything that happened—the accident and *Daed's* heart attack and Jonas leaving—those tragedies aren't yours alone. They affected all of us."

She tucked her chin to her chest. What had become of her family? She had one brother excommunicated and another apparently disgraced, all the while she'd been secretly dancing and kissing *Englischers* in the park. If the community found out...if Deacon Elmer found out...her mother would be devastated. When he left, Jonas broke *Mamm's* heart. Samuel surely added salt to the wound. If Nora refused Mervin Zook now, the disappointment might be too much for her mother to bear.

Her stomach clenched as if she'd pinned her apron six inches too tight. She hugged the blanket and forced a calming breath. If Mervin proposed tomorrow, how could she possibly say no?

Chapter Eighteen

The next night, Nora straightened the crocheted afghan draped over the back of the sofa and surveyed the sitting room. Everything was in perfect order. A fire crackled in the woodstove, cozy and inviting on a dreary winter night. Catching her wavy reflection in the picture window, she smoothed her apron with shaky hands and balled her fists at her sides. Best not to primp in the glass. Mervin was likely outside waiting.

In the air, the citrusy scents of wood polish and glass cleaner mingled. The house hadn't been so spotless since they hosted church the previous April. If he were so inclined, Mervin could eat the hotly-debated, gingerbread whoopie pies right off the floor. She closed the front shades, signaling her readiness, and spun, unsure what to do while she waited. The house was eerily quiet, her mother, brother, and child all safely upstairs. Her feet tingled, and she executed a nervous shuffle hop step, paradiddle combination, her weight bouncing left to right and back again.

Dropping onto the sofa, she pressed clammy palms to her belly. The whole charade was ridiculous. She was a thirty-two-year-old widow with a daughter, and this visit was no romantic rendezvous in the first flush of love. Romance and Mervin Zook barely existed on the same planet. The decision was purely practical, albeit with far-reaching consequences. As such, she had no intention of making it tonight. She would hear Mervin's suit, treat him with cordial respect, and postpone answering as long as she possibly could.

Two sharp raps were followed by two weaker ones, a pause, and a final thump.

Even his knock was unsettling. Steeling herself, she flung wide the door only to find herself staring at Mervin's back.

He held both arms behind him, one wrist caught in the other hand, and gazed into the drizzle.

The temperature was just above freezing—warm enough to keep the roads from icing, but so cold the dampness seeped directly into the bones. "Good evening, Mervin."

With a start, he turned, blinking rapidly through rain-dappled glasses. Droplets rimmed his hat and beaded his slender shoulders. He was taller than she, but only by an inch or two. Standing in the darkness, he seemed somehow even smaller.

He cleared his throat and gave a strained smile. "Nora Rishel—Beiler. Sorry." He dipped his chin. "Nora Beiler. Here I am on your porch. Here I am indeed, indeed." He lowered his hands and wiggled his fingers, rising onto his toes.

She bit back a smile. If she was nervous, Mervin Zook was petrified. A pang of compassion shot through her. "Would you like to come inside?"

"Don't mind if I do." Without waiting for her to step aside, he barged into the entryway, bumping shoulders, and knocking her into the doorjamb.

She flinched. His coat reeked of wet animal. She draped it over the rack, hoping the smell wouldn't seep into her family's garments. He marched into the sitting room and collapsed onto a glider so casually she thought he might rest his feet on the coffee table. He interlaced his fingers over his belly and studied the ceiling with squinch-eyed intent.

Nestling into a corner of the sofa, she clasped her hands in her lap and sent up a quick prayer for guidance. So many years had passed since she and Levi dated. She couldn't remember the procedure. What should she do or say? When she and Tucker were together, conversation seemed to flow—not that they were courting. She allowed her mind to drift. Where was Tucker now? Did he play concerts on Sunday nights? What would he say if he knew what she faced right this very second? And why hadn't she told him?

Mervin smacked his lips with a sudden, loud pop. "Have I told you about the new milker?"

Mervin! Yes, back to Mervin. Would he declare his intention immediately or work up to it? Twenty minutes into the tale of the new milking machine, she concluded in favor of the latter. Or perhaps she'd misread his feelings, after all.

"With any luck, I'll increase the herd to fifty cows by May. Leon and Luke won't be in school too many more years. I'll have plenty of help. That Rebecca of yours is a good strong girl, isn't she? Built like her grandmother and uncles."

He spoke of her daughter like another member of the barnyard. She answered with a pinched smile.

The tip of his nose pinkened. "I'm getting ahead of myself. Can't seem to keep the old nag in front of the cart!" He laughed.

Despite her unsettled stomach, perhaps now was the time for a snack. She stood. "Mervin, can I offer—"

"Say, do you like kites?" He bounced to the edge of the chair and rubbed together his hands.

Knees akimbo, with wide-set eyes and a gap-toothed grin, he never looked more like a curly haired frog. She settled back onto the sofa. "I like them fine."

His smile widened. "Not much I enjoy more than taking a couple of kites up Zook's Hill on a breezy summer afternoon. Sometimes I use a five-hundred-foot string, and they fly so high I think they might bump one of those airplanes passing over. Kites are about my favorite things in the world. You like them, you say?"

Swallowing hard, she nodded. So, Mervin was a kite enthusiast. Maybe he did have hidden passions with which she wasn't acquainted.

He clapped his hands onto his knees, "Well, I guess that about settles it."

He looked suddenly as though he had something important to say. A fire ignited beneath her backside, and she jolted to her feet. "Would you like a snack? I made something special."

A grin widened his already wide face. "You know I love your baking."

She led him into the kitchen where gingerbread whoopie pies dusted with powdered sugar were stacked in a pretty pyramid on her grandmother's rosebud platter. Two matching plates lay on the table with napkins and glasses nearby.

Frowning, he sat and studied the display. "Never seen orange whoopie pies before."

She filled the glasses with milk and joined him. "They're a brand-new recipe I created: gingerbread whoopie pies with lemon marshmallow frosting. I've been tinkering with the ingredients over the past few

227

weeks. You're the first to sample one." With delicate fingers, she placed the topmost treat on his plate.

Brows raised, he took a cautious bite and chewed with deliberation.

He looked like one of his precious dairy cows. She twisted the napkin in her lap. What she desired from this relationship remained up in the air with his kites, but she definitely wanted him to love her gingerbread whoopie pies.

Nose wrinkled, he swigged milk and coughed, pounding his chest with a fist. "They certainly are…gingerbready."

Annoyance sparked in her belly. Why wasn't he raving? Gushing? Swooning? The whoopie pies were exquisite. They were subtle and spicy, and anyone who didn't care for them had no taste at all. She scooted to the edge of her seat. "*Englischers* love special holiday flavors, and I enjoy creating new recipes. I think this item will be very popular. December is a good month for sales. The market stand is quite profitable."

The corners of his mouth turned down. "I guess I'm just a regular flavors kind of fellow."

He'd come expecting pie. Of course, he had. Would it have killed her to make one? She refilled his glass. "Nothing wrong with the regular flavors. They've stuck around for a reason."

"I stuck around, too, Nora—like good old chocolate and vanilla." His nose went pink again, and the flush spread to the tips of his ears. "I reckon you didn't know, but back in our school days, I had a soft spot for you. Ever since that mean old goose chased me around the schoolyard, and you were the only one who asked if I was all right. Do you remember?"

Good gracious. Mervin wasn't going to talk of love, was he? She thought this proposal was a purely practical arrangement. Nodding, she snatched a whoopie pie. The aromatic cake dissolved on her tongue, giving way to a layer of sweet and tangy cream. Mervin was nutty. The whoopie pies were divine.

"Then when you married Levi, and Fannie and I were wed, I suppose I put all that behind me. Never dreamed I'd be sitting here today." He shook his head. "Isn't life a wonder?"

For once, they were in complete accord. She never dreamed of sharing this moment with him, either. Nothing in life went the way she planned. She wiped sticky fingers on the napkin. "It certainly is."

He reached across the table and laid a hand over hers.

His palm was hot and dry. She stiffened but managed not to pull away.

"The way I see it, we're two peas in a pod. I've got a litter of youngsters in need of a mother, and you've a wild filly in want of a *Daed.* I'm a faithful, God-fearing man with a solid business. If you agree to be my wife, I'll take good care of you and raise your girl like my own." He leaned in close, and sweat glistened on his brow. "Now how about it?"

How about it? Was that his proposal? She thought of the lyrics like poetry Tucker sang straight to her heart. "How about it" was maybe the ugliest phrase she'd ever heard. Her shoulders tensed, and she shifted, unable to extract her hand. Her cape pulled at the waist, tightening around her neck. The second hand on the clock marked time with thunderous clicks.

Mervin anchored his gaze on hers and tapped the

fingers of his free hand on the table.

Upstairs, a floorboard creaked, and suddenly, an orange blur streaked into the kitchen and landed with a thud on the table, inches from the whoopie pies.

She gasped. "Pumpkin! You bad, bad cat!" Tearing her hand from Mervin's, she lunged for the animal.

The naughty critter wriggled free and leapt onto the counter. Crashing into the mug tree, she vaulted over the sink and skittered to the far end, whereupon she sprang atop the refrigerator and crouched, peering down at Mervin with slitted, green eyes.

Clutching her favorite mug, Nora whirled. "I'm so sorry. I've told Rebecca a thousand times to leave that cat in the barn, but she sneaks it in at night."

Mervin crossed twiggy arms and scowled. "That child is far too headstrong. When I'm her father, we'll put an end to such behavior. The first lesson I'll teach is obedience, and the second is humility, mark my words."

Nora clamped down on her cheek, struggling to hold her tongue.

Pumpkin flattened her ears and hissed.

She ran her gaze over Mervin's face. Thin lips like twin earthworms flattened into a pale line. Red-rimmed eyes narrowed in an expression of stern intent she struggled to take seriously yet feared at the same time. How dare he criticize her daughter? She'd rarely encountered more ill-mannered children than the Zooks. On more than one occasion, Rebecca had run herself ragged, trying to keep them out of trouble.

Oh, how she loved her bright and beautiful child—her fanciful, disobedient, miracle of a baby who was the living embodiment of the love she and Levi shared.

This man must have no hand in shaping her fierce and wonderful spirit. To say nothing of Nora's own fierce and wonderful heart. Splaying her palms on the table, she straightened her spine and met his gaze. "No thank you."

Eyes-bulging, Mervin jerked his chin into his chest. "What?"

"You're a fine man, Mervin, and I respect you tremendously. But I can't marry you. Thank you very much for asking." She folded her hands, set her jaw, and waited while Mervin's pain waged a piteous war with pride. His cheeks flushed, and he opened and closed his mouth like a fish flopping in the bottom of a rowboat.

"But I understood...I thought..." He gestured at the plate of treats. "You made special whoopie pies."

"I did, and I'm sorry you don't like them. I'll bake a shoofly pie and have my brother bring it by next week." His face crumpled like the balls of paper beside Tucker's trash can. Guilt dropped like a pebble in her stomach.

"I don't understand. With Levi and Fannie gone, I figured..."

She softened. He wasn't a bad man. He simply wasn't the man for her. "I truly am sorry."

He gazed at the table, red blotches spreading over his cheeks to his forehead. "You'd do well to consider my offer, Nora Rishel."

The words were quiet but knife-edged. The hairs on the back of her neck stood on end.

"Your family is...at risk. You all might have thought yourselves special in our youth days, but now? One brother shunned, another brother unmarried, and a rebellious daughter who doesn't know her place. You, yourself, attending exercise class with the English." He shook his head, sucking his bottom lip with a hissing squeak. "You're certainly not the same girl you were in school."

Anger seared her lungs as flaming as a hot iron. "Of course I'm not the same, and neither are you!" She gripped the seat of her chair and pressed her elbows into her sides. "You said it yourself: life happened—to both of us. The future didn't turn out as either of us was led to expect. Don't you see? Even a simple life can be complicated."

Sneering, he peered over the top of his glasses. "Spoken like an *Englischer*. Did you get these wicked notions from him? The man who drives you around in his truck?"

The floor heaved, and a wave of nausea engulfed her. How she loathed Lovina Lapp and the rest of the nosy gossips. Steadying her breath, she sipped milk. It was thick and lukewarm, and her stomach turned again. She swallowed and wiped her lips with a napkin. "What kind of a question is that? Who have you been talking to, Mervin Zook?"

He screwed up his mouth and, sighing, lowered his gaze. "I shouldn't have spoken so."

She relaxed her hold on the chair, but a slithery snake of worry coiled deep inside. Turning down Mervin wasn't only risky for her. If word leaked about any number of her behaviors, he'd likely make sure the whole family suffered. She hated the very notion, but this visit had to end as well as possible. She crept a hand onto the table, opened her palm, and forced a look of doe-eyed supplication. "I hope we can be friends, even after tonight…and that you'll keep what you saw on Thanksgiving between us, as you promised." A haughty look settled upon his brow, and the coating of milk soured on her tongue. He liked her to be indebted. She saw it plain as day.

He shook his head, tutting. "Does Smiling Nora Rishel want me to bend the rules?"

She lowered her gaze and honeyed her tone, disgusted with herself as she did. "Please, Mervin."

Huffing a bitter laugh, he shoved from the table. Heavy oak chair legs bumped the cabinets. "I'm a man of my word. You have nothing to fear."

A weight lifted, and she sagged. "Thank you."

"I'll see myself out."

His voice was a strangled croak. His footsteps were swift and regular. She heard his coat rustle and the front door creak. Then silence fell over the house again.

She spread her elbows and rested one cheek on the pillow of her hands. Closing her eyes, she breathed the dear, familiar smell of her kitchen and the delectable aroma of gingerbread whoopie pies.

With a thump, Pumpkin landed on the table. She smushed her face against Nora's temple and purred.

At least the cat was happy.

Her mother would be an entirely different story.

Chapter Nineteen

The smell of frying bacon always soothed Nora.
She stirred diced bits in the pan and stared out the
window into pre-dawn darkness. Since refusing
Mervin's proposal—such as it was—she'd barely slept.
She tossed and turned beneath her wedding quilt,
troubled by dreams in which Rebecca repeatedly
wandered onto the same half-frozen lake. In the dream,
she heard a dull crack, but when she tried to shout, no
sound came out. Her mouth seemed crammed with
warm, sticky dough.

The grease popped, and a pinprick of oil stung the
back of her hand. She winced and shied away. Her
mother loved breakfast casserole. She hoped it would
soften the blow.

Light footsteps padded down the stairs and across
the floor, stopping short of the kitchen. Glancing over
one shoulder, she spotted her daughter perfectly framed
in the wide entryway, hair neat, dress tidy, already
prepared for school. Weeks away from her eleventh
birthday, she was a curious mix of young and old. Her
limbs were long and lithe, but her face still held the
softness of babyhood. Pale-cheeked and unblinking, she
looked like a nervous patient awaiting a dreadful
diagnosis.

"I wish you much joy, *Mamm*. When is the
wedding?"

She dropped the spatula. "Oh, my dear *dochder*, I'm not marrying Mervin."

With a squeal, Rebecca dashed into her arms and pressed her face against her shoulder. "So, we aren't becoming Zooks?"

Closing her eyes, she rested a cheek on Rebecca's head. Her skin smelled like vanilla. "*Nee.*" Slower, heavier footsteps came to a stop.

"I knew you should have baked a pie," *Mamm* said from the kitchen entry.

Her mother's words weren't a reproach. Rather they seemed the pronouncement of a failed endeavor, doomed from the very start. Apparently, Verna always knew her daughter would disappoint, and Nora simply fulfilled expectations. What could she say to the contrary?

Untwining from her daughter's embrace, she seated Rebecca at the table and poured a glass of orange juice.

The back door squeaked, and Samuel tromped inside, wiping muddy boots on the mat. With a shiver, he doffed his knit cap and blew into his hands. "I suppose congratulations are in order."

Why was everyone up so early? She whirled to the stove, cutting the gas just in time to keep the bacon from burning. Perhaps she should be grateful no one rushed into the kitchen last night the second they heard the front door close. At least she had a few hours of privacy. Grabbing a slotted spatula, she removed the crispy bites, tossing them onto a paper towel and reserving the grease for her mother's favorite fried potatoes. Quarter to six was far too early for such a discussion.

Mamm slumped against the counter. "Mervin

didn't propose."

Samuel's tawny brows drew together. "Was it the whoopie pies?"

"The whoopie pies had nothing to do with it." She flung the bacon into the egg mixture and grabbed a stirring spoon.

He sidled close, frigid air clinging to heavy work clothes. "Did seeing Jonas at the Thanksgiving table change his mind?"

With a strangled huff, she reached around her mother for the casserole dish and dumped in the eggy mixture, sloshing over one side. Biting back a nasty retort, she snatched a dishrag and mopped the counter. "He didn't change his mind. He proposed." She folded the dishrag and hung it neatly over the faucet. "I simply turned him down."

Samuel staggered backward, eyes wide. Tilting his head, he regarded her, and a smile played at the corners of his mouth.

She snatched a mug from the tree and grabbed the coffee pot with her other hand. "Coffee, *Mamm*?"

With slow deliberation, *Mamm* pulled out a chair and sat. "Why would you refuse Mervin Zook?"

Offering the mug, Nora softened her tone. "I don't love him."

Verna stared at the ceiling and didn't take the coffee. "You could learn to."

Careful not to spill a drop, she deposited the mug on the table next to the sugar bowl. "Not the way I loved Levi."

Samuel spun and snatched his and Rebecca's coats from the hooks. "Rebecca, let's gather eggs."

Full juice glass in hand, Rebecca blinked up at her

uncle. "But I—"

"Now." He tossed the coat.

Agile as her uncles, she slid the glass onto the table and snatched the garment midflight. Rolling her eyes, she shoved her arms into too-short sleeves and followed Samuel into a charcoal morning.

The oven belched hot air, and the heavy casserole clanged onto the rack. Nora closed the oven door and caught her mother's gaze. "I can see you're disappointed, but my mind is made up."

Verna shook her head, glowering. "Rebecca needs a *daed*, and you need a *mann*. After all this family has endured, we need the Zooks."

A headache threatened. Ignoring the pain, she took a potato from the colander and a peeler from the crock. "We have the community for support. We have our faith, and Rebecca has her uncles for guidance. She has you."

"She needs a strong hand."

"She needs love!" Potato peels flew into the sink, and she inhaled deeply. Arguing served no purpose. "Rebecca's spirit is bright. As you said, if we aren't careful, we'll lose her." She darted a look over one shoulder. Without seeming to notice, her mother added first one, then a second, and then a third spoonful of sugar to her coffee.

Staring out the window, Verna stirred and sighed. "I so enjoyed visiting with Deacon Elmer."

The spoon clanged against the mug like a muffled bell. Guilt squeezed her chest. Her mother's friendship with the deacon was special—possibly very special. Did her rejection of Mervin endanger their bond? Gathering the potato, a grater, and a plate, she sat across from her mother. "Perhaps Deacon Elmer will still call…even without his family."

"Don't be ridiculous." *Mamm* slurped coffee and grimaced. Rising with a grunt, she dumped it into the sink, snatched her coat and scarf, and stormed outside.

Her mother was furious.

As if the whole mess was the potato's fault, Nora grated. It scraped across the blades, raining fleshy shards. Her mother was furious. Her brother was amused. Her daughter was relieved. And she *was* ridiculous. *Mamm* was right about that. A silly, rollicking Christmas tune played in her head. A quiet hum vibrated her chest. Her heatbeat slowed.

Scritch scritch scritch went the potato over the grater. *Paradiddle paradiddle shuffle ball step* went her feet on the floor. She gazed out the window at a streak of bright pink in the eastern sky…and despite the chaos in her kitchen, she couldn't keep herself from smiling.

****

Nora sat back on her heels, pooched her bottom lip, and puffed a breath. Why she had chosen to tackle this messy job the day after Mervin's proposal was anyone's guess. Was she punishing herself? Or simply taking out anxiety on oven grease? Wisps of silky hair snagged in her eyelashes, and she rubbed her face against one shoulder. From all appearances, Hank's oven hadn't been scrubbed properly since Lavelle died. She rolled her shoulders, loosening the crick in her neck. If only the tension in her household were so easily relieved.

After hearing of Nora's decision, her mother barely spoke. Her brother, on the other hand, went out of his way to be kind, helping with the busy holiday baking and downing gingerbread whoopie pies with gusto. She couldn't deny she felt relieved…despite nagging fears of the consequences. Her daughter was demonstrably overjoyed.

When they arrived at Hank's that afternoon, Rebecca had bounded down the hall like fawn.

The old gentleman raised shaggy eyebrows and jerked a thumb after her. "What's gotten into that one?"

She edged toward the kitchen. "Excited to get to work, I suppose." Watching the two disappear into the library, she'd heard Hank promise to loan Rebecca more books and her daughter's gleeful squeal. The girl was no demure giggler, tittering behind a hand. She laughed with her whole self. Rebecca did nothing halfway, and her enthusiasm for Hank's library was no exception. Well, no harm would come from Nancy Drew. As girls, she and Annie devoured those books.

She dragged a damp rag over the sides of the oven, raining gunky baking soda crumbs. Yanking up rubber gloves, she strained for the back corners. How she yearned for a real heart-to-heart with Annie like they had in the old days. She'd love to talk over the whole Mervin situation and, yes, even share her feelings for Tucker. Life was too complicated to figure out alone, and she knew Annie would never judge. She'd made a mistake by neglecting that special friendship. Was she too late now?

A glob of blackened grease protruded from the bottom of the oven. She caked on a thick layer of baking soda paste. This mess would require muscle and possibly multiple cleanings. The spray bottle squeaked, spritzing a vinegary mist. The tang summoned tears, and she sat back on her ankles. Baking soda and vinegar were remarkable substances. Each was powerful and effective on its own, but put them together, and they became something else entirely—something unpredictable, fizzy, and explosive.

She knew the proper procedure was to allow the baking soda to work for several minutes, scrape out the grime with a scrubbing sponge, and only then to spray the vinegar solution. Today, however, she felt fizzy and explosive herself. Taking aim at the baking soda and grease mound, she focused the spray nozzle and doused it with vinegar. With a steamy hiss, it bubbled and expanded like a foamy, brown monster. She reeled, goggling at the creature she created. It oozed toward the oven door, and she grabbed a rag. She'd rather not scrub the floor, as well.

Just then, the phone rang in the living room, the trilling beep adding to the bubbling chorus. She sprang to her knees and listened for footsteps. "Hank? Would you like me to answer?"

The phone rang again.

Maybe she should pick up. After all, she didn't want Hank to slip by rushing. She stripped one glove and had hold of the other when the ring suddenly cut off. The library door creaked, and Hank shuffled down the hall.

"Where are you now, Grandson?"

She froze. Was Tucker on the other end of the line? She thought back to the snowman photo. Perhaps one of his brothers called.

The recliner squealed, and the footrest flipped up. Hank grunted. "Sort of the armpit of Indiana, wouldn't you say?"

She really shouldn't eavesdrop. Trying to ignore

the conversation, she stared out the kitchen window to where a pair of cardinals perched on a feeder. She should refill it. Where did Hank keep the birdseed?

"No kidding. A whole museum just for Studebakers? I'd like to see that place. Maybe I should have come on tour." He chuckled. "Anyone turn out to hear you play?"

So, Tucker was indeed on the phone. With blood rushing in her ears, she crouched beside the oven.

"Not bad. You behaving yourself?"

She wobbled and wrapped her arms around her knees. She knew full well what Hank implied. Had Tucker returned to his old ways?

"Uh huh. Uh huh." Hank blew his nose with a loud honk. "Uh huh."

The palm still encased in rubber was clammy. She peeled off the glove, careful not to snap it. If Tucker had gone astray, she didn't want to find out like this.

"Matter of fact, they're here now. Rebecca's in the library, and Nora's cleaning something somewhere."

She couldn't listen a moment longer. She'd crawl into the laundry room, and Hank would be none the wiser.

"That girl is smart as a whip. I knew she was the minute I met her. The questions she asks." He whistled. "I don't have answers to half of 'em, but they get me thinking. I'm afraid she's put you out of a job, son."

How often had her elders reprimanded Rebecca? With dour faces, they ignored the girl's questions and quashed her ideas. Not Hank. His praise filled her with pride.

"Oh yeah, you should see the place. Looks like a million bucks. Hey, you want to talk to her?"

She started, bumping her shoulder into a cabinet.

"I think she's in the kitchen. Nora!"

Leaping to her feet, she scurried into the living room.

Hank thrust out the handset. "It's for you."

Butterflies flitted in her stomach like she'd swallowed an entire flowerbed. She hesitated.

"Come on now. The boy hasn't got all day." Chuckling, Hank handed her the phone and headed down the hall.

The plastic was warm, and the mouthpiece gave off a faint coffee scent. Often, she'd employed their community telephone for business and to arrange taxi rides, but never had she used it solely to talk to a friend. Such usage wasn't permitted by the *Ordnung*. If one wanted to catch up, one visited, plain and simple. She swallowed a lump in her throat. "Hello?"

"Hey there, Twinkletoes."

His voice was deep and throaty—intimate—like he was right beside her, whispering in her ear. Her knees turned to pudding, and she shot a hand to the back of Hank's recliner. No wonder the bishop outlawed telephones. "I'm cleaning the oven." Cringing, she wilted. She sounded dim-witted when she wanted to sound like a woman he'd kiss on a bench in the snow. That kiss was all she'd thought about for a week. Did he think of it, too? She fluttered a hand to her neck, trailing a finger into the notch at the base of her throat. "I'm glad to hear your voice. How are you?

"Fine. Tired. Hotel beds are awful, and the pillows make my neck hurt." He sighed. "The gigs are going well, though. Better than I expected. People love the old songs, and man, does that feel good. But…" His voice trailed off. In the distance, a siren wailed. "I miss you."

Her legs gave out completely, and she sank onto the arm of Hank's chair. Shooting a quick glance toward the library, she lowered her voice. "I miss you, too."

"What's that now?" he rasped. "I can't quite hear you."

She covered her mouth, holding in a giggle. "I miss you, too, Tucker McClure."

"How come you're whispering?" he hissed. "Hey, wait a second. Are you allowed to do this—talk on the phone?"

The worn upholstery was nubby beneath her fingertips. She traced an orange stripe through a patch of green. "Technically, no."

"Oh shoot. Goodbye then, Twinkletoes."

She dug her fingers into the cushion. "Wait. No. Don't go. I'm allowed to use the phone for work, so say you had something to tell me about the house or Hank. Then we could keep talking."

"Look at you, you rebel. Well, let me think. How about you clean Hank's nasty old oven?"

She snorted a chuckle. "Done. Mostly. Anything else?"

"Hey, I forgot my favorite shirt—the red plaid one. Could you toss it in with Hank's laundry?"

"Also done."

"Well, I suppose that covers work. Guess I gotta hang up now."

Joking with him, feeling his voice through phone like a touch on the cheek, she went all soft inside. She didn't want to stop. "Please don't. I like hearing your voice."

The other end of the line went quiet.

She swiveled to the window. Outside, the world was December gray. The sun slipped behind the ridge, and sky and street blended in shades of smoke and slate. A rustling sound came through as though he shifted the phone from ear to ear.

"I don't know much of anything about your people," he said. "But this...us...can this happen?"

In the house across the street, Christmas lights flickered on. Electric candles ignited in every window, and strings of colored bulbs traced the roofline all the way to a sharply peaked gable. She took in a breath, pressing a palm to her chest. How lovely it was—light shining through winter twilight. How hopeful. A matching flare lit in her chest like a beacon of irrational joy. From the soles of her feet, she smiled. "No."

"No?" He gave a grunt of disbelief. "Why do you sound so happy?"

Farther down the street, a jolly Santa Claus riding atop a polar bear grew as if inflated by the breath of the earth and burst into brilliant light. The decoration was so preposterous she couldn't hold back a giggle. "I don't know. You and I break all the rules I grew up following—rules I believe in—rules I vowed to obey when I joined the church." From down the hall came the tinkle of her daughter's laugher. "Right now, though, I just don't care."

"I do. I care a lot."

His voice was the scrape of fingernails on a washboard. Was Tucker McClure suddenly concerned about rules? About her rules? Her heart lifted. "I can't explain why, but since we started dancing together, I feel at peace. We'll be all right, Tucker. I have faith."

He rasped a bitter chuckle. "Faith?"

He was right to doubt. She could see no way forward—no magic resolution to their dilemma like in one of Rebecca's fairytales. Nonetheless, she relinquished doubt and all the tortured feelings that came with it. Surrendering heavenward a shard of the darkness that dwelled in her soul the last seven years, she gazed at the twinkling lights of a Christmas tree in a living room occupied by strangers who shared her hope in the face of a hopeless world. A path to happiness had to exist. If only she could find it.

Faith.

Chapter Twenty

Nora collapsed onto a bench by the Farmers' Market outdoor stage and stretched stiff legs. The ache was the good kind, earned by scrubbing Hank's oven on Monday, baking all day yesterday, attending dance class last night, and serving a steady stream of customers who snatched gingerbread whoopie pies with cries of delight starting at seven a.m. this morning.

With the lunch crowd gone and her brother providing extra help, she finally stole a few minutes to come outside for a breath of fresh air. She loved the market lunch counter, but the whole building reeked of sausage and onions. Her stomach grumbled. She should have swung by Annie's for hot pretzel sticks.

Thanks to milder temperatures, she sat among a sizeable crowd watching a special holiday concert. Bundled in puffy jackets and hats, they tapped their toes to the upbeat melodies of the Third Street Singers barbershop quartet. She turned her face to the midwinter sun. At almost three, it hung low in a powder-blue sky, but its rays heated her face with a tender touch. She let her eyelids drift. Speaking of tender touches, Tucker would be home in three days. Warmed from within and without, she lifted her lips and surrendered to a smile. Now that she'd rediscovered smiling, she couldn't seem to stop. Given how her cheeks hurt in the morning, she could only imagine she smiled in her sleep.

"Do you know that man?"

The question rasped, a hot whisper in her ear. She opened her eyes to Lovina Lapp's flushed, round face. Nora pressed a hand to her forehead and trailed it down her neck, giving tired muscles a soothing rub. "Who?"

Lovina pointed toward the stage as the audience burst into applause.

Decked in a green sweater with a sparkly sequin reindeer face splashed across his midsection, Gene Stackhouse waved enthusiastically. He spread his arms wide, pointed to his belly, and the reindeer's red nose lit.

She couldn't repress a laugh. Jolly Mayor Gene was everywhere this Christmas season.

Lovina plopped down beside her. "He certainly appears to know you."

"Gene Stackhouse happens to be the mayor of Green Ridge. He's also a faithful customer." She waved back. "And a friend."

Lovina's plump lips twisted in a smile. "Acquainted with the mayor? Well, well, well, I hardly know you anymore."

Lovina Lapp never knew her. And not just because she was ten years younger and ran with a whole different crowd.

Hands clasped neatly in her lap, Lovina gave a squinty-eyed look. "Then again, no one understands you these days."

The Smiling Nora of bygone days would have brushed off the comment with a laugh. Not today. Mature Smiling Nora felt the smile fall from her face like a cake gone soggy in the center. Ire gnawed her empty belly, and she levelled Lovina with a gaze. "Do you care to elaborate?" Lovina twitched like a spooked chicken.

"Why, Mervin Zook, of course! Everybody's talking about it!"

She reeled, raring to give Lovina and anyone in earshot a lecture on minding their own business.

"There you are, Nora."

Surprised again, she jumped and glanced upward. She seemed constantly to be startled these days.

Dangling a cup of steaming ham-and-cheese pretzel sticks, Annie Amos wrinkled her pert nose in a smile. "I've been looking all over. Your brother said you were outside."

"Samuel's here?" Hands fluttering, Lovina scootched to the end of the bench. "No one told me."

"I'm telling you now." Annie nodded toward the market building. "You should go in and say hello."

Pinching her cheeks, Lovina sprang to her feet. "I think I will. *Mach's gut!*" In a flash, she scampered away.

Gene blew a tinny note, and the Third Street Singers began a silvery, melodious version of "The First Noel."

"I guess your handsome brothers are good for something, after all." Annie sat and offered the treats.

The tantalizing scents of butter and yeast wafted. "*Denki.*" Settling against the bench, she took a bite. Sweet pretzel bread sandwiching gooey melted cheese and salty smoked ham exploded on her tongue. She let out a moan.

Annie chuckled. "You owe me one of those gingerbread whoopie pies everyone's raving about."

Groaning, she gave an exaggerated nod. "So, my baking is what's on people's minds?"

Annie's shoulder bumped hers, and the scent of cinnamon wafted from her coat. "Among other things. How are you holding up?"

She shrugged. "I'm not sorry I said no. Not for my part, anyway."

Annie took her hand in chunky knit mittens. "Oh, Nora, you couldn't marry Mervin Zook."

Flooded with gratitude, she held on tight. "I just couldn't." With a sigh, she let her face go slack. "My mother is devastated."

"She'll get over it."

"I don't know."

Scooting closer, Annie dropped her head on Nora's shoulder and gazed toward the stage, decked out in Christmas finery.

So many years had passed since they sat together like this. Once, Nora felt Annie was the sister she never had. Being close again, even for a short time, felt good.

Gene's high voice soared above the rest. "Noel, Noel…"

"Wishing someone else was on that stage?" Annie peeked up, her cheek dimpling.

A glob of pretzel lodged on Nora's tonsil, and she coughed.

Annie giggled. "Don't choke. I forgot your cider."

Swallowing, she sniffed and wiped her eyes. When she first kissed Levi, she couldn't wait to tell Annie. Today, she felt exactly the same. She chewed her lip, biting back a smile. "I kissed him."

Annie jerked to sitting, her chestnut eyes wide. "The *Englischer*?"

The wind gusted a cold reminder of December, and she nodded and shivered all at once.

"So, you and Tucker McClure are serious?"

A smile fought its way out, and she couldn't help but laugh. "How can we be?"

"If you love him—"

"Then what?" Pulling away her hand, she opened her palms to the sky, as if the answers she sought would fall into them like snow. "I can't leave. I won't break my mother's heart. Even after everything, I want to stay."

"Might he join us?"

The sweet simplicity of Annie's question stole her breath. She sounded so like Rebecca when the girl was tiny and certain the impossible was possible, simply because it should be. "Why can't I sleep in a cloud?" "When will the horse learn to read?" "How long until *Daed* comes to visit from heaven?" Uttered in Annie's gentle tone, the idea of Tucker joining the Amish sounded logical.

Except, of course, it was utterly absurd.

Exhaustion settled onto her shoulders, and she drooped. She barely had energy to shake her head.

"Why not?" Annie asked.

"You know as well as I what stands in his way."

Her friend tipped her head against the bench and stared into a cloud-streaked sky. "For three months, I listened to that man play. From the pretzel stand, I caught it all—every word. He sings like an angel. *Gott* touched his voice with a gift. But no matter what he sang, I heard the same two things again and again." She clasped her hands beneath her chin and wrinkled her nose against the glare. "First, I heard sadness. Even in the peppiest tunes, sadness hid beneath the words. But more than sadness—a kind of deep emptiness and the sound of someone searching."

"And the second thing?" she asked, a little breathless.

Annie shifted and caught her gaze. "Every song he sang was for you...Twinkletoes."

Her cheeks flamed, and she pressed her hands to her face. Her mittens smelled like wet sheep in a sunny pasture. "The idea of him joining the Amish...it's a fairytale."

"Is it? You were away a long time. Attitudes here are shifting. You need to fellowship with others and hear what they say. You might be surprised." Reaching over, Annie tapped her knee. "You're coming to our frolic Saturday, aren't you? Leroy expects a crowd to roof the new furniture showroom, and I need pie."

She hesitated. "Tucker will be home. He's been traveling for his music, but he's stopping through this weekend."

"Bring him."

Imagining country music superstar Tucker McClure hanging upside down from the rafters with Leroy, she choked a laugh. "What?"

Annie grinned. "Leroy's recruiting everyone. I wouldn't be surprised if he grabs folks off the street."

If she thought she was the subject of gossip today, what would people say if she showed up at a frolic with an *Englischer*? She nibbled a pretzel stick.

"Mervin isn't coming, by the way. He's visiting family up on Shade Mountain." Annie slid her a sidelong glance. "Bring him."

A nugget of powdery salt crumbled between her

teeth. She licked her lips and took another bite. "I might," she said through half-eaten pretzel.

"I should get back to work." Annie rose and tugged down her coat. "I've missed you, Smiling Nora. I'll see you Saturday."

The Third Street Singers bowed.

She joined in the applause.

Maybe you will, Annie Amos. Maybe you will.

****

Friday night, Nora scraped the bowl, dropped a final spoonful of sugar cookie dough onto the sheet, and sniffed. She needed no timer to know the batch in the oven was done. As she reached for an oven mitt shaped like a trout and opened the door, Hank's old kitchen timer dinged. The color of fresh-skimmed cream with a hint of brown around the edges, the cookies were beautiful. Checking an urge to dash to the window and scan the driveway for Tucker's truck, she swapped the trays and settled the fresh batch atop a trivet to cool. He'd arrive soon enough.

Hank liked his cookies plain: no nuts, candies, or sticky bits to catch in the teeth and yank out his fillings. She'd loved to have witnessed Tucker's reaction to the gingerbread whoopie pies, but Hank was the boss. Good, old-fashioned sugar cookies, baked to perfection, were the chosen treat for Tucker's welcome home. And coffee. And cocoa. She stopped short of baking a pie. She didn't want to seem desperate.

With a start, she spotted a dusting of flour spattered across her black apron and onto her skirt. How silly she'd been to wear her new dress to work. She only finished sewing it last week, and it was meant for good. Rinsing the washrag, she dabbed the fabric, trying not to smear the flour into paste. For seven years, every dress she made was gray. It suited her, and she saw no need for change. When she stopped by Sarah Stoltzfus's fabric shop a few weeks ago to get the stuff for Rebecca's new dress, on impulse, she picked up four yards of sky-blue cotton for herself. It was no splurge. Her old dress was wearing thin and fit snug around the waist and shoulders. She spread her skirt. It was wet but flour-free.

The spatula glided beneath the cookies. Peeking at the underside of one, she let out a satisfied sigh. In no time, the cookies were neatly arranged on the cooling rack, and the tray was plunged in hot soapy water. If she hurried, she could finish the dishes before the last batch was done. She tilted her head and rolled her shoulders. Though her body grew fatigued, she never tired of baking. The magic through which flour, eggs, butter, and sugar became dough, and dough plus heat became cookies was endlessly fascinating. Experimenting with recipes handed down through generations—a pinch more salt, a tablespoon less sugar, an extra dash of spice—never ceased to fascinate. She could discern the subtlest differences from batch to batch, which she recorded in a notebook, refining until her goods were more than good. They were spectacular.

Light footsteps zoomed down the hall. "He's here! He's here!"

Dropping the wet cookie sheet, she dried her hands and dashed into the living room. Her skirt was still damp, and her heartbeat skittered like a puppy's. Joining Rebecca at the window, she peeked through fresh-scented drapes at the old green truck in the drive and the long-legged man in a red Santa hat, sliding from the cab and stretching.

His coat rode up, exposing a denim shirt tucked into faded blue jeans.

She brushed her fingers across her lips, unable to look away. The kitchen timer jingled, and she jumped and ran. Jamming a hand into the fish mitt, she flung open the oven door. The cookie sheet clattered onto the stove, and she scooped cookies onto the rack with her bare hands, mindless of the heat.

Hank poked his head into the kitchen. "The boy's home. Say, those smell good."

"Try one." With a smile, she offered a cookie.

The front door creaked, and she heard tromping and rustling like a herd of cattle coming through a hedge. She peered around Hank for a better view.

The doorway was filled with the bottom half of Tucker and the top half of what appeared to be a bushy pine tree, slung over his shoulder.

"You came back!" Rebecca flung herself at him, disappearing among branches.

Tucker staggered, catching himself on the doorjamb. "I said I would, didn't I?"

"Why is this tree inside the house? It's prickly." Rebecca poked her head through the boughs, gazing at Tucker with saucered eyes. "Oh my goodness, is this a Christmas tree?"

"It is, and it weighs a ton. Help me get it inside, and we'll trim it."

Fair brows lifted and hands clasped beneath her chin, Rebecca turned. "*Mamm*?"

What was one more bending of the rules in a season of ever-increasing infractions? She sighed. "I suppose." In her daughter's radiant smile, she saw the girl she'd been before tragedy and loss shadowed her life. Was a happy child an obedient child? Would saying yes to her daughter's whims foster peace at home? If Nora gave an inch now and again, could she prevent Rebecca from following her Uncle Jonas to Colorado? Maybe.

Tucker and Rebecca disappeared inside the tree, which shuffled to the wall on four feet. Pinesap cut through the scent of baking with a sharp tang.

Craning around branches, Tucker met her gaze, and his expression softened. "Hi, Twinkletoes."

"You call her that because of dancing class." Rebecca brushed together her hands in two brisk swipes. "Nicknames are fun. Can I have one?"

Facing a world gone topsy-turvy, she shook her head and smiled. "Welcome home. Are you hungry? I made cookies, and I think we have some of Joan's hamburger casserole in the refrigerator."

"I'll grab a cookie, and we'll get going on this tree." He tossed his coat onto the rack and laid a hand on Hank's shoulder. "Decorations still in the basement, old man?"

Settled in his recliner, Hank watched the action like a volleyball game, his gaze bouncing from Tucker to Nora and back again.

A grin tugged at the corners of his mouth. "Same as always."

Tucker dashed into the kitchen and returned with a fistful of cookies. He took a bite and moaned, clutching his chest. "Best thing I've eaten in two weeks." The basement door flung open, and he waved Rebecca along. "Come on, kiddo."

Rebecca scrunched her nose and followed him

down the stairs. "I don't like 'kiddo.' Let's try another nickname."

Hank chuckled.

"I suppose all this seems terribly amusing." She gazed at the trail of pine needles and cookie crumbs. "The quaint Amish family's first Christmas tree."

"No." He rested a hand over his injured shoulder and rotated the joint gently. "I think it's wonderful."

In a jiffy, Tucker had the tree bolted into a stand and nicely positioned before the living room window. Soon, the family across the street would feel the same shiver of delight she did when the lights in Hank's house twinkled a message of hope. Funny, she always imagined Christmas trees to be garish symbols of a holiday that lost its soul, becoming only about the buying of gifts. But the way these English people put their trees in windows and shared the happy glow was generous. Christmas decorations could be a gift in and of themselves.

Rebecca pawed gingerly through a crate and pulled out an old cardboard box containing fat, colored bulbs the size of quails' eggs. "I found the lights."

Tucker extracted the strand and located the plug. "Looks like these have been out of action for a couple years. Better test them." He plugged in the cord, and the bulbs flared in brilliant shades of red, blue, green, and yellow, casting a splotchy rainbow across his face. He grinned just as brightly and beckoned. "Lights are a two-person job." Unplugging the string and sliding the bundle of cords and bulbs into Nora's grasp, he kept hold of one end and reached way up into the branches. He teetered, and his body angled toward her.

The woodsy smell of evergreen mixed with that

spicy Tucker scent, and she nearly teetered, too. If he lowered his arms right now, he'd have no choice but to wrap them around her. Her insides melted like a stick of butter on a woodstove.

He secured the end and draped the string around the topmost boughs. "Come along behind me," he said in a soft voice.

As Rebecca dug in boxes and Hank shuffled to the record player, Nora tiptoed behind Tucker until they were smushed between the tree and the curtains. Needles pricked her wrists, but she didn't care. Finally, they were alone.

"I missed you," he murmured.

A flush crept over her neck. "I missed you, too."

"Help me keep the bulbs away from the drapes." He gave a quiet chuckle. "These lights must be sixty years old. Don't want to torch Hank's house."

"What is this?" Rebecca asked.

Still trailing Tucker, Nora emerged from behind the tree.

Her daughter held up a small, round quilt that slitted open to a hole in the middle.

"That there's a tree skirt," Hank said.

Rebecca wrapped the quilt around her waist and swished side to side. "Why does a tree need a skirt?"

"Who knows?" Hank opened a cabinet jam-packed with record albums. "Lavelle made it. Said the tree looked naked without it—pardon the vulgarity, ladies."

Crouching, Rebecca circled the skirt around the trunk and spread it flat. "Lavelle was an excellent quilter."

Her daughter was right. The pattern was a giant Lone Star, an intricate, eight-pointed star made of diamond shaped patches in red, green, and gold prints. She handed Tucker the lights and knelt to examine it. The quit was pieced by a seamstress of notable skill and beautifully finished. "What a wonderful heirloom."

Tucker circled the tree again, nestled the final lights into the bottom boughs, and threaded the cord to the nearest outlet.

Rebecca sprawled on the tree skirt and stared up into the branches. "Can we plug in the lights now?"

"Not until the star's on top." Tucker dragged the crates closer and threw open the lids, releasing a decades-old scent of musty tissue and candle wax. "Time for ornaments."

Rebecca scrambled to his side and lifted a paper-covered bundle from the top of a crate. With careful fingers, she unwrapped crumbling tissue to reveal a shiny blue ball. The words *Silent Night* were printed in glittery white paint above a steepled church surrounded by snow. "How pretty." She tilted her head, eyeballed the tree, and then hung the ornament right in the middle.

"Don't take all day, girl." Hank waved toward the crate. "We've got about three thousand more."

Rebecca scampered back to the box. "They're like tiny presents from the past." She extracted another bundle and unwrapped it to reveal a miniature airplane with a wooden peg angel flying it. She dangled the ornament from one finger. "Is this Lavelle?"

Hank stared at the plane, and his eyes went misty. "Let me see that."

Rebecca perched on the chair arm and dropped it in his hands.

He turned it over, running a thick finger along the

wings. "Yessiree, this here's Lavelle. She was an angel of the skies."

So, Hank's wife had been a pilot, also. Nora glanced at the woman's photo on the wall, suddenly eager to read the memoir Hank and her daughter were writing. *Thank you for the ornaments, Lavelle.*

Rebecca gestured to the crate. "It's a box full of memories, too. Tucker must know all your stories—like the time you and Lavelle got marooned in a swamp for two whole days and counted ninety-two moose. Or the time you toted a noisy walrus for the San Diego Zoo, and when the air traffic controller asked what was making all that racket, you said he wouldn't believe if you told him."

Hank shook his head with a laugh. "I'm sure he's heard some."

"What's the point of having such remarkable stories if you don't share every single one?" Rebecca propped an elbow on the back of the chair and rested her cheek in her hand. "I guess that's why we're writing your book."

Hank jerked a thumb toward Rebecca. "What'd I tell you, Grandson? Sharp as a tack."

Nora gazed at the mismatched twosome. She vividly recalled sitting on her grandfather's lap, combing his voluminous beard with a tortoiseshell comb. Her mother's father was a jolly man, as burly as a bear and as gentle as a newborn calf. Nora's father died when Rebecca was four, and Levi's parents moved to be near family in New York not long after the accident. Rebecca had many great uncles and cousins, but the bond between grandparent and grandchild was special. Seeing her cuddling with Hank gave Nora a bittersweet ache.

With a scratch and a crackle, Christmas music poured from big speakers on either side of the fireplace.

Tucker grinned. "Bing Crosby on vinyl. Very nice, Hank. Now, let's get this tree trimmed!"

Tissue piled at their feet like snow. Ornaments old and new bedecked the tree. Gleaming glass balls and sparkling bells cavorted with colorful felt fish and tiny wooden canoes. Finally, when not an unadorned limb remained, Tucker handed Rebecca one final wrapped item.

She removed the tissue to reveal a silver star with big white bulbs on the ends of each point. Red block letters spelled out *Merry Christmas* right in the middle.

It was large and clunky but simple, and rather perfect in a peculiar way.

"That star was my mother's." Hank's voice caught, and he cleared his throat.

"You want to do the honors?" Tucker asked.

"Nope. Your turn, Grandson."

Tucker beckoned Rebecca. "What do you say we do it together?" Wrapping his hands around her waist, he lifted her until her *kapp* brushed the ceiling.

She leaned over the tree and settled the star on the topmost pointy branch. "Now is it time to turn on the lights?"

"Almost." Tucker connected the star to the other electrical cords. "To do this right, we have to turn off every light in the house."

Rebecca flitted from switch to switch, extinguishing lamps and overhead fixtures until the room was totally dark but for light spilling in from outside.

Just as Gene had done in the park, Tucker held a

cord in either hand. "Ready? One…two…three!"

Music swelled, and the tree ignited. Lustrous glass balls caught the light, sparking a glittery rainbow. The star shot a kaleidoscope across the ceiling like a heavenly spiderweb, and the room shimmered as if in lamplight, making each face shine. Hank looked half his age; Rebecca might have been a fairy, indeed; and Tucker… Seeing Tucker in the tree's soft glow summoned thoughts of an existence in which she gazed at him across a lamplit table every single night for the rest of her life.

With a gasp, Rebecca clasped her hands beneath her chin and stared. "Are all Christmas trees as pretty as this one?"

The recliner footrest flipped down, and Hank came upright. "Nope. We've got the prettiest because we had the best decorators. Can't remember the last time we had a tree in this room. Does my old heart good."

She felt movement at her back, and Tucker's voice crooned in her ear, echoing the old-timey sound of the man on the record player. Tilting her head, she giggled, and his breath tickled wispy hairs on the side of her neck.

Tucker hitched his thumbs in his belt loops and hopped around boxes in a silly jig.

Laughing, Rebecca bounced on stocking toes, copying his steps. "What's a Killarney?"

Tucker crooked his elbow in the girl's direction. "A town in Ireland."

Rebecca looped her arm through his and skipped in a circle. "It sounds wonderful. We like to spend Christmas with the folks at home, too." She and Tucker cavorted, kicking up tissue and bumping into furniture.

Nora wagged a finger. "Careful, you two." The admonition turned to a whoop as she felt Tucker's other arm catch hers, sending her spinning. Soon she was stepping in time—the lighthearted music like a fourth partner in their goofy dance.

When the song ended, Tucker launched Rebecca with a spin.

The girl whirled like a top and collapsed onto the sofa, arms flung wide, panting for breath.

With a quick flip of the wrist, he turned Nora into him, wrapping his arms around her waist as they both stumbled a step. His hold tightened, and her feet left the ground. The lights blurred in colorful streaks, and her heart skipped not one but several beats.

Ever so gently, he set her back on the floor. "Merry Christmas, Twinkletoes." Releasing her, he shuffle-stepped sideways and clapped his hands. "Who's hungry? I could eat about a dozen more cookies."

Rebecca rolled off the couch, landing on all fours. "Me! Me!"

"Race you to the kitchen!" Tucker took off, with Rebecca hot on his tail.

Still reeling from the dance and the deliciousness of being in Tucker's arms, Nora glanced around the room. Cardboard and wrapping littered every surface. "English Christmas sure is messy."

Hank met her gaze and flashed a rare smile. "Don't be afraid of messiness, Nora. Messiness is where the good stuff lives."

The hour was late by the time Tucker dropped her and Rebecca home. Sitting between the two adults, Rebecca chattered the entire way, fiddling with the radio knobs and asking what every button and lever in the front seat did.

Tucker patiently explained, shooting Nora smiles over the girl's head.

Snug in the cozy cab, she watched Christmas lights stream past, and a feeling settled over her that was equal parts sensation and memory. It was warm and heavy—like waking to find a cat sleeping on her chest. A man, a woman, and a child together not only in body, but in spirit. This moment felt like family.

Tucker pulled up in front of the barn and turned off the lights.

She appreciated the small kindness. Her mother wouldn't enjoy the glare cutting through windows in the dark. He was a man who thought of such things.

Rebecca bounced in the seat, pointing out the rear window. "What's in the back?"

Tucker glanced over one shoulder. "The truck bed."

"A bed?" Rebecca hitched a knee beneath her and faced him. "Can I go see?"

"If your mother agrees."

The hour was late, but granting the child's request would give her precious minutes alone with Tucker. She nodded. "Quickly."

He jumped out to let the girl pass and slid back inside. Slumping sideways, he laid his head against the seat and blinked drowsily.

Smudges like ashy fingerprints shadowed his eyes. A shock of hair fell over his brow, and for the thousandth time, she fought the urge to brush it aside. How she longed to smooth his forehead with a cool palm and watch him fall asleep.

"Penny for your thoughts, Twinkletoes."

Even his voice was tired. Scrunching her nose, she dipped her chin. She couldn't speak the thoughts in her head. She was tired, too, and her judgement faltered. If she wasn't careful, she'd say something she'd regret. She lifted a shoulder and fiddled with the button on her coat.

A clang came from behind, followed by scuffling as Rebecca scrambled around the empty truck bed.

"I wish I could whisk you away." He flopped a hand onto the seat, inches from her thigh. "This visit is too short."

His long and graceful fingers were callused like the hands of so many men she knew. And yet, they were different somehow. Her insides pulled toward him. She wanted to be together, too. Annie's invitation tickled in her thoughts, and before she could stop herself, she spoke. "Would you like to go to a work frolic tomorrow? With me?"

His brows drew together. "A work frolic? Isn't that kind of a contradiction in terms?"

She laughed. "Not really. It's a work party. The community comes together to perform a job for a family in need."

"Like a barn raising?"

"Yes. But we hold frolics for many tasks. My friend Annie's husband is expanding his furniture business with a showroom. He needs to install the roof before the winter snow."

A smile played at the corners of his mouth. "What makes you think I know my way around a job site?"

Very gently, she laid a hand on the seat, her fingers nearly grazing his. "You don't need to. Even children help. Besides, a big part of frolics is the singing."

He tapped her index finger with his. "Lucky for you, I do know how to build. Not much for singing, though."

A knocking came from the back of the cab. She turned.

Rebecca smushed her cheek against the window.

Tucker shook a fist in mock ire. "Don't smudge the glass, you rascal."

With a smile, Nora shooed the girl. "Get down from there."

Rebecca whirled and vanished.

She swung her gaze to Tucker. "We should go."

In an instant, he slid a hand to her shoulder and leaned close. "I'd love to frolic with you, Twinkletoes."

His lips brushed hers in a sugar-cookie kiss so quick and light she might have thought she imagined it, but for the warm tingling left behind. Her belly tripped, shooting fizzy sparks into her chest. In another time and place—another lifetime—she'd have stayed in that truck and chatted all night. With a heavy hand, she opened the door and climbed out. Did this evening really have to end?

Rebecca ran her fingers along the side of the truck. "Motorized vehicles are endlessly interesting."

"What do you say we take another ride tomorrow?" she said.

Rebecca looked from her to Tucker and back again. "Really?"

She nodded. "Tucker's coming with us to Amos's frolic."

Rebecca's smile faltered. "But he doesn't speak German. How will he know what to do?"

Tucker leaned out the window and cupped one ear

with his hand. "*Ich werde zuhören.* If I listen very closely, I think I can figure it out."

Nora stared, agog. Would a day ever come when he stopped surprising her?

Chapter Twenty-One

Snugging the wicker pie basket into her lap, Nora scootched to the middle of the seat and flashed Tucker a grin. The sun hovered above the eastern ridge, casting a misty golden glow over the gray landscape. Still gobsmacked over the revelation he spoke German, she stared at his face, half in shadow, wondering what other secrets he contained. "Are you fluent in Chinese, too?"

His yawn turned into a laugh. "*Nein*, Twinkletoes."

She clicked the seatbelt around her waist. "But you do speak German?"

He held up a hand, thumb and forefinger an inch apart, and leaned close. "*Ein bisschen.* I've listened at the market, and I can make out the gist of what you say, but your German is not what I learned in high school." He dropped a quick kiss on her cheek. "Morning."

His chin was scratchy, and his skin smelled of soap. She cast a quick glance toward the barn. When the temperature dropped, Rebecca pleaded to bring Pumpkin inside for the night. Feeling oddly like she had the cat to thank for avoiding a disastrous marriage, Nora acquiesced, but Rebecca was under strict orders to return Pumpkin to the barn before they headed to Annie's. She toasted chilly fingers in the current from the heating vents. Hearing the soft, familiar sounds of her native tongue roll from Tucker's lips made her feel like a brownie—crispy on the edges and positively

267

gooey inside. "But why study German?"

A quiet Christmas song came through the stereo, and he drummed a light rhythm on the wheel. "Most kids in Northern Maine studied French, of course. I know a little, but I never liked the sound. When I came here in the summers, Lavelle and my great aunts spoke German. Her grandparents emigrated when she was young and opened the airplane engine factory near Williamsport."

"And you still remember the language?"

"Hey, high school wasn't that long ago." He nudged an elbow into her side. "Besides, I pick up languages pretty quickly, if I do say so myself."

Bringing a blast of chilly air, Samuel flung open the door and leapt into the seat. "I've wanted to ride in this truck for weeks! Morning, Tucker."

Tucker nodded, stifling another yawn.

Clutching the basket to her chest, she jerked toward her brother. "You're coming, too?"

"You better believe it."

"*Mamm's* idea?" she asked.

Samuel blew into cupped hands and rubbed them together. "Can't have you two showing up un-accompanied. Especially after…" Tucking his chin, he gave her a pointed look.

"After what?" Tucker asked.

She hadn't a good opportunity yet to tell Tucker of Mervin's proposal. Not that she was in any rush. Did she really need to tell him since she'd said no? Still, she had a nagging feeling she was concealing something.

Little knuckles rapped on the passenger's window. "Where do I sit?"

Samuel swung open the door and hoisted the girl

inside. "On my lap, wiggle worm."

Rebecca exploded in giggles, jutting elbows and knees in all directions as she flopped into Nora, nearly bumping her head on the pie basket.

Nora scooted closer to Tucker. "Careful, you two." Her daughter's cheeks smelled of vanilla and her coat of the barn, but underneath was another smell—the ripening smell of a girl who'll be a youth before long. At Rebecca's age, Nora had care of three younger brothers, yet Rebecca was the lone child in a house full of adults.

"Will I look after any Zooks today?" Rebecca asked as the truck pulled away.

Tightening her hold on the basket, she shook her head. "Plenty of Amos *kinner*, but no Zooks."

"Thank goodness." Smiling, Rebecca raised her voice with the hymn on the radio.

In perfect harmony, Tucker joined in, the sound vibrating through his shoulder into hers. Nowadays, families came in many shapes and sizes, didn't they? When that truck driver tore a hole in her world, her dreams of a normal Amish life unraveled, too. Did she dare to hope love could knit new bonds from the broken strings of the past and the delicate threads of the future? The sun burst from behind a cloud, painting the world in bold splashes of yellow. Since when were her thoughts so poetic? And had she ever seen a more beautiful sunrise?

She directed Tucker to Annie's lane, admiring the neat white fence and well-kept yard surrounding her friend's one-story, brick home. How many years had passed since she visited Annie? The thought cut through the beauty of the morning and settled heavily on her heart. Too many. She remembered so well the excitement surrounding Annie's wedding, just one year after her own. Leroy was a middle son and a furniture maker. When the two married, they bought a modest English house with a large, detached garage that converted nicely into Leroy's shop and retrofitted the buildings and acreage for Amish life.

Tucker pulled up next to the line of buggies. Leroy had already framed out the new showroom, and a dozen men clustered around the work site.

She slid Tucker a glance, a twinge of nerves zinging through her chest. He'd never been among so many Amish. Would he fit in? For his part, Tucker seemed perfectly relaxed. He swung out of the truck with loose-limbed ease and hefted a tool belt from the back. The twinge faded, and a smile lifted the corners of her mouth. She'd never met anyone so adaptable. Did nothing frighten this man?

Idling beside the truck, she watched Samuel and Tucker walk side by side, gravel crunching beneath nearly-identical work boots.

Sandy-haired Samuel, big and broad, clapped Tucker on the shoulder.

Tucker, equally as tall though wirier, laughed and yanked a navy-blue hood from beneath the fleece collar of his coat.

Raised in a climate far colder than hers, he knew to dress in layers. The man could take care of himself.

Inside, Annie's kitchen hummed like a beehive, smelling of coffee and cinnamon rolls. She'd just had breakfast, but still, Nora's mouth watered. Somehow, sweet treats always tasted better when eaten among friends. "*Guder mariye.*"

Annie looked up from chopping and flashed a dimply smile. "Good morning, Smiling Nora." Her brown eyes streamed tears, and she dragged a sleeve across her face. "*Ach*, these silly onions have me crying like a *boppli*. Leroy loves his meatloaf, and I'm happy to make it, but the onions will be the death of me."

At the sink, Annie's mother, Lydia, paused from peeling potatoes. "I've told you a thousand times, hold a slice of bread between your teeth when you chop."

Annie scowled. "Seems a waste of perfectly good bread."

Rebecca hung her coat on a peg by the door. "You could use a cinnamon bun. When you were finished, you'd have no choice but to eat it."

"Now that's a sensible idea." Sarah Stoltzfus sat at the table, rolling a pin over a clear plastic bag full of butter crackers.

Annie's meatloaf was beloved. Her not-so-secret recipe called for crushed crackers to be mixed with the beef, ketchup, and seasonings, creating a mouth-wateringly moist texture. Flashing her old schoolmate a smile, Nora tucked the pie basket into a corner of the counter. "Go look after the girls, Rebecca. Unless you want to help with cooking?"

Clustered like a patch of daisies on the floor, Annie's and Sarah's daughters rummaged through a box of paper dolls.

Spying them, Rebecca bounded into the sitting room. "I'm a better storyteller than meatloaf maker."

Dark eyes focused on her work, Sarah attacked the crackers with the same intention she brought to her studies as a girl and now to her bustling fabric and quilting shop, which had garnered a fine reputation.

Sarah waggled the pin at Rebecca's fleeing figure. "Clever girl." Rotating the bag, she came at the crumbs from a different angle. "Is she good with numbers, Nora?"

Nora snatched a cinnamon bun. It was warm and gooey and smelled like paradise. "Her mind is quick as a rabbit. Too quick for her own good."

The crackers crunched, spreading into a fine layer under Sarah's hands. "Business is brisk, and I could use help at the shop. After the New Year, maybe Rebecca could work a couple of hours on Saturdays. If she takes to it, we could consider a permanent job once she finishes school."

A permanent job? Her daughter was still so young. But Nora knew how fast those final years of school flew. Soon, Rebecca would attend singings and run around with a gang. Sarah was a good friend during their youth days. Though she was serious and sober, she was kind. Perhaps Rebecca would enjoy helping in the shop. After all, the girl already had a job, and Hank seemed delighted with her work. In a few short months, she had gone from a source of nearly constant worry to nearly constant pride.

Nearly. She couldn't forget the threat to disclose the true nature of Shuffle Off to Fitness.

Had Rebecca changed? Or had she? She leaned against the counter and peered into the sitting room.

Rebecca pulled Joanna, Annie's youngest, into her lap, held up two paper dolls, and narrated an animated conversation.

With chubby fingers, the toddler clutched Rebecca's arms and giggled.

Sarah's youngest leaned her head on Rebecca's

shoulder, eyelids drooping.

Nora sighed. The image of her daughter sur-rounded by children pulled at her heart. For years, she'd been so blinded by grief and anger, so she hadn't noticed how the loss impacted her daughter. Even among a vibrant, loving community, the child led a lonely life. No wonder she was prone to flights of fancy. Compared to the happy chaos of Nora's childhood home, the quiet atmosphere of a bunch of grown-ups going about the grown-up business of ordinary life was almost unnatural. Rebecca should be surrounded by siblings, day and night. Was such a life still possible? Nora was only thirty-two. Her mother gave birth to Samuel when she was thirty-five.

Peeling a doughy strip from the bun, she shifted her gaze past neatly tied-back curtains and out the window. The men spread out all over the showroom, perched like grackles on ladders and struts. Together, they'd have the building roofed and possibly sided before dinner. Squinting, she searched for Tucker and spotted him, balanced atop a wall. Her stomach clenched.

With Samuel's help, he hoisted a roof truss from men on ladders.

She crammed the bite of pastry into her mouth. Sugar and cinnamon crunched between her teeth. He'd be fine. He grew up on a farm and knew what he was doing.

Arleta, Sarah's eldest daughter, pulled back the curtain. "Who's the *Englischer*?"

The girl was dark like her mother, with dancing blue eyes and full, pink cheeks. Seventeen and coming into her own, she was all the coquette her mother had never been. Dough fused to the roof of Nora's mouth and gummed on her teeth.

"Samuel's friend," Annie chimed in. "Tucker McClure—the fellow who's been playing music at market all fall."

Arleta came up on tiptoes. "Oooh. I heard about him."

Nora gave Annie a grateful look. "Let me help with those onions."

Annie's son Zane dashed into the kitchen trailed by a gaggle of boys. They skimmed between the women like minnows and circled the girls who clutched the dolls to their chests. Amid shrieks and laughter, the boys barreled back into the kitchen, grabbing at snacks and each other.

"Run along outside." Sarah flung open the back door. "You're needed by the men."

Zane thrust a fist into the air. "Come on, boys! Last one on the roof is a rotten egg."

The tykes thundered across linoleum, grabbing coats and hats before streaming out the door.

In the thick of the scuffle, Zane bore no resemblance to the shy tot who lost his hearing to repeated ear infections. Nora strained for a glimpse of the boy's hearing aid. As he streaked past, she spied the device beneath a mop of hair. She bumped shoulders with Annie. "Who is that rascal? I hardly recognize him."

Still red-eyed, Annie sniffed and laughed. "I can't believe how he's changed. Dr. Richard said he would, but I didn't quite believe him."

How well she knew the lure of the doctor's promises and the wonder when those promises came true. She nodded, popping in a final bite of cinnamon bun, and wiping sticky fingers on a damp rag. "Dr. Richard is a blessing, plain and simple. Did you hear they had their baby?"

"A boy," Annie's mother chimed in. "Grayston? Grayson?" She huffed, flinging a potato peel into the colander. "English names."

"At least they aren't all Jacob and Sarah," Sarah muttered.

The morning was a laughter-filled blur of boiling potatoes, peeling carrots, and baking rolls, as the savory scent of the midday meal supplanted the homey smell of breakfast. Nora whisked brown sugar into the meatloaf glaze. She liked a good, sweet sauce on meatloaf. Soon, the meal would be ready, and the men would gather around long tables they'd set up in the living room. She swallowed a sip of coffee, savoring the bittersweet, milky taste. How would she feel to have Tucker in their midst?

Rebecca perched in the glider with the younger girls at her feet. She held up four dolls. "The two brothers and two sisters climbed to the tippy top of the hayloft. The light was dim, and the air was full of tiny flecks like gold dust. Suddenly, they saw a big wooden door they never noticed before. Lucy grabbed the doorknob and pulled as hard as she could."

Sarah's youngest gazed at Rebecca in wide-eyed wonder. "Who was inside?"

Rebecca hunched down, and the glider squeaked. "Standing in the midst of a raging blizzard was a creature who was half goat and half—"

"Jesus," Annie's mother interrupted. "They saw Jesus up in heaven."

"Is that really any better than a goat man?" Sarah muttered, a smile twitching her lips.

Nora silenced Rebecca with a look. She knew the girl's head was full of fancy, but some might interpret such stories as wickedness. Where did she get these foolish notions?

Annie pulled two trays of meatloaf from the oven, ready for glaze. "Rebecca, can you run outside and count the men? I want to make sure you girls set enough places."

"I hope the boys haven't tied the *Englischer* to a rafter," Arleta giggled.

Checking on Tucker was an excellent idea. Nora shooed her daughter toward the door.

Minutes later, Rebecca dashed inside, panting. "Fourteen. And Tucker's on the ridge pole. He climbs like a monkey."

Annie's mother ladled applesauce into a serving bowl. "Good heavens. I hope he knows what he's doing."

Rebecca wove among the women and came to Nora's side. She sniffed the contents of the pot. "Leroy said he's not a bad carpenter for a potato farmer."

The meal bell rang, and the men trooped in, rinsing hands and faces in a steaming bowl on a bench in the hallway. They brought with them a camaraderie like that of the women but somehow more expansive, as if they wore the winter sky along with heavy boots and whiskered chins. They took their seats at the table, passing sly smiles and knowing looks.

"Eleven...twelve...thirteen." Arleta's snub nose wrinkled, and she stared at the empty place. "All right, boys, where's the *Englischer*?"

"Who?" her brother Mattias asked, elbowing Leroy.

"Tucker!" Rebecca ran to the door and peered out. "What have you done with him?"

"Ach." Samuel bonked the side of his head with an open palm. "I knew I forgot something."

Nora peeked out the window. There on the very end of the ridgepole, legs dangling far above the ground where every single ladder lay flat, sat Tucker. She bit back a smile. Joshing with Tucker was a sure sign the men had accepted him. Liked him, even. She slanted her brother a smile.

Samuel wriggled free from the bench. "I'll be right back."

Ruddy cheeked and smiling, Tucker entered the house, washed his hands, and took a seat.

Leroy cleared his throat, and every head bowed in silent prayer.

Nora lifted one eyelid a fraction of an inch. She and Tucker hadn't spoken of faith, and yet, despite all she knew of his past, she felt in her heart he was a God-fearing man.

Hands clasped and head bowed, Tucker sat shoulder to shoulder with the men of her community.

His features softened in peaceful contemplation. Throat tightening, she closed her eyes. Did she dare think he could become one of them? That he would *want* to become one of them?

Leroy shifted and sighed, signaling the end of the prayer, and the midday meal began. Several juicy meatloaves, mounds of mashed potatoes with gravy, fresh baked bread, applesauce, and tossed salad vanished in seconds. Amazed as always how the fruits of hours of labor disappeared so quickly, Nora dined with the women at the kitchen table, savoring every bite and keeping an ear tuned to the boisterous chatter from the sitting room.

Tucker ate heartily, wiping his plate with a fluffy roll.

His eyes were bright. He looked happy. He looked…at home.

Conversation flowed in a mix of English and German. She noted her brother speaking in English more than usual, and gratitude bloomed in her chest. Samuel was more than the good-natured jokester he appeared. After the confession regarding his church status, she was certain. With Jonas gone and Micah and Hannes in Ohio, she could use a brother who was also a friend. She vowed then and there to get to know Samuel not just as family, but as a person.

"How many acres does your father own up in Maine?" Leroy asked.

"About a hundred." Tucker forked a bite of shoofly pie. "Course the moose think most of it is theirs." Catching Nora's gaze, he gave a quick wink.

Her pulse skipped, and she took a long sip of lemonade. Did anyone see?

The men chuckled.

Leroy's grandfather leaned toward his grandson. "*Ist der Englischer gheiert?*"

Lemonade went down the wrong tube, and, eyes watering, Nora stifled a cough. What did Leroy's grandfather care if Tucker was married?

Downing a big bite of pie, Leroy shrugged.

"Not for lack of trying," Tucker drawled, taking a long swig of coffee. "Guess English women don't care much for potato farmers."

Silence settled over the room as one by one, the men's jaws dropped into their pie.

In her highchair, baby Joanna hiccupped.

Then, an eruption of laughter shook the walls and rattled the windowpanes.

Leroy's face turned bright red, and his grandfather guffawed so hard his false teeth slipped out.

Fortified, the men clamored to their feet, thanked the ladies, and headed back to work.

Halfway into his coat, Tucker caught her gaze over the mess of dirty dishes and flashed a lopsided smile.

You're terrible, she mouthed across the room.

Joining in a rousing chorus of "Oh Come All Ye Faithful," he sauntered out the door.

As she scrubbed grease from meatloaf pans, Nora barely noticed the sting of hot water on winter-chafed knuckles. She was a big mossy rock in the middle of a creek, and the women eddied around her. Their chatter was the rush of wind and the burble of water. The girls' laughter was twittery birdsong. Sun-warmed and steady, she thought of nothing but the increasingly solid feeling her life was beginning again.

"Who's come so late?"

Arleta's chirping question snapped her back to reality. Peeping outside, she spied a buggy rolling to a stop beside Tucker's truck. Steel wool dug into her fingertips, prickly as a burr. Her mouth went dry.

"I thought he wasn't coming," Annie said under her breath.

"Me, too." The spatula slipped from her grasp and clattered into the sink as Mervin exited his buggy. "Me, too."

Chapter Twenty-Two

So close to the window she could feel the cold like an icy breath on her cheek, Nora watched Mervin unhitch his horse. Was he following her? She gripped the dishtowel, and the splits in her knuckles pulled at the edges. Fourteen men were more than enough to finish a roof. They'd be done within hours. Maybe Leroy would send Mervin home before he had a chance to…what? To stir up trouble? Mervin Zook was as likely to stir up trouble as a hamster. Still, dread thickened on her tongue.

Scowling, Mervin looked long and hard at the green pickup truck.

Her towel circled the rim of the roasting pan until it was bone dry. She'd done Mervin no wrong. She had nothing to fear.

Leroy greeted Mervin with a clap on the shoulder, pitching the slight man forward a step.

Mervin righted his hat and gazed at the roof where Tucker sat atop the ridge pole, fastening a slab of red, tin roofing.

With a quick nod, Leroy made for the house.

She jerked from the window, sliding the roaster onto the counter, and taking up a wet pitcher.

"Any pie left?" Leroy called from the hall. "Mervin could use a piece. You know how he loves Nora's shoofly."

Annie dropped the pie plate onto the table and gave Leroy a firm look. "We *all* love Nora's baking."

Leroy's smile vanished. "You can say that again." Coughing, he tugged his trim black beard. "Turns out Mervin's aunt is poorly so they made a quick trip over Shade Mountain. He came back early and thought he'd swing by to lend a hand."

A wedge of pie large enough for two men plopped onto a plate. "How kind." Annie tucked a fork into a napkin, poured a cup of coffee, and gave everything to her husband.

The delicate plate and cup looked tiny in Leroy's hands, as if he were a bear serving tea at a fancy restaurant. The kitchen went silent, save for the clink of silverware and the gurgle of the coffeepot.

"All righty then." Leroy scanned the room. Without another word, he fled.

With the slam of the door, the kitchen buzzed back to life. Again, Nora was a stone in the middle of a creek, but now, the current rushed wild and out of control, and she feared she might drown. All the while she cleaned, she kept her gaze trained out the window.

True to form, Mervin lingered over his pie, scraping the plate from all angles before abandoning it on a stump. He ran a hand over the wiry scraggle of his beard and, sipping coffee, joined the men cutting and hoisting roofing panels up to Tucker and Samuel. Her shoulders eased. Maybe Mervin had moved on. Maybe she could let herself be happy.

Fueled by meatloaf and pie, the men worked quickly, and as clouds thickened and the sun sank, they installed the ridge cap along the peak of the roof, finishing the job.

Bundled in coat and mittens, she gathered her pie basket, extracted her daughter from the girls and dolls, and joined the women outside to admire. With its white siding and bright-red roof, the showroom was pleasingly simple. Snug and solid, it was a well-built structure and would be a tremendous asset to Annie and Leroy. She snuck a glance at her brother and Tucker standing shoulder to shoulder, regarding their work. Tucker had been right there among everyone—his skill and good-nature earning him smiles and friendly ribbing. Home for a short time, he'd given up a whole day of rest for people he never met, simply because she asked. Pride and gratitude warmed her soul.

Snow flurries danced on the wind. The men dispersed, gathering tools and heading toward buggies and home.

Her stomach turned. How could she avoid Mervin seeing her leave in Tucker's truck? Likely, he had been introduced to Tucker as Samuel's friend as everyone else had. Why would he think otherwise? A biting breeze chafed her cheeks, bringing the smells of barnyard and woodsmoke. She laid a gentle hand between Rebecca's shoulders. "Run along and fetch your uncle and Tucker." Like a colt, her daughter dashed surefootedly over ruts frozen solid in the mud.

Annie drew up beside her. "They did a wonderful *gut* job, and your pie was scrumptious as always. You'll share that recipe before you die, won't you?"

She gazed into bonny brown eyes. Annie's friendship was a blessing. Never again would Nora let their bond loosen. "When you least expect it."

"*Denki* for the pie." Glasses fogged and cheeks splotched pink, Mervin extended the empty plate and cup.

Nora jumped. Yet again, she hadn't heard him approach.

Annie accepted the dishes with a smile. "Give our best to your aunt. And *denki* for coming."

He took off toward his buggy with short, springy strides. "*Mach's gut!*" he called over one shoulder.

"You see?" Annie nudged her with a hip. "Mervin's fine. Besides, I hear Leora Mast has her eye on him. He'll have a *mudder* for those horrid *kinner* before Easter."

She giggled. "I left the rest of the shoofly pie on the counter."

"I watched you do it, and I didn't say a word." Eyes dancing, Annie tilted her head toward Tucker. "Now go take a ride in a truck, you hussy."

Nora squished into the seat between Tucker and her brother. Rebecca's knobby knee slung over Samuel's leg knocked against hers. Christmas music filled the cab. She tucked a loose strand of hair behind one ear, and her arm pressed into Tucker's, warm and solid. Exhaustion weighed heavy on her chest, and all she wanted was to rest her head on his shoulder and close her eyes.

The upbeat song ended, and a bittersweet Advent hymn unspooled like a velvety ribbon made of smoke.

Tucker cleared his throat softly. "Thanks for inviting me today. I've never been a part of anything like what we did for Annie and Leroy—never seen people work so hard without getting something in return. You have these frolics often?"

"When they're needed." Samuel slipped his arms around Rebecca's waist. "We do get back something, though. Next time we need a new fence or buggy shed or anything really, we know folks will come. Not because they owe us, but because their grandparents came for my grandparents, and their uncles for mine. And they know Rebecca here will come for their daughters and granddaughters. It's what we do."

"I've never seen anything like it...and I've seen a lot in my time." Tucker squinted into the wintry twilight. "A whole lot."

The voices on the radio sounded like angels. Nora stared through the windshield at snow streaking through the headlights like a zillion shooting stars. She was almost afraid to breathe for fear one of these men, who were so dear and seemed suddenly so vulnerable, would crack a joke. Though vastly different, Tucker and Samuel both laughed through life—often, she suspected, to keep from crying. Or to keep their demons at bay.

Rebecca's head lolled to one side, her eyelids heavy. "This song is so sad and so Christmassy. How can any one thing be two opposite things at the same time?"

"Most people are." Tucker's cheek lifted in a half smile. "At least the interesting ones."

Oh, but this man was so very interesting. The most interesting person she'd met in years. Reclining, she allowed her own head to roll until her cheek nuzzled the seat and her gaze landed easily on his hands, so sure and steady on the wheel. With her nose inches from his shoulder, she drank in the smell of damp corduroy and good honest sweat. Right now, she'd let this man take her anywhere. Which was funny because he seemed like he wanted to stay right here. Yet, come morning, he'd be gone. Back in the world of which she, simple Nora Beiler, knew nothing.

He pulled up beside the barn and cut the headlights.

She couldn't let him go. Not yet. But under what pretense could she keep him? "Tucker, I have something to show you," she blurted. Her cheeks flamed, and she swallowed hard. "In the barn."

Rebecca perked up. "What's in the barn? I want to see."

"You can't, silly. It's a surprise. A Christmas surprise."

Samuel opened the door and swung Rebecca to the ground. "Speaking of secret surprises, we have our own project to finish, don't we, Rebecca?"

Thickening snow swirled as Rebecca jiggled on tiptoes. "Did you finish cutting out the—"

"Shh!" He took a runner's stance. "Race you to the workshop."

"I wasn't going to tell!" Laughing, her daughter flew around the barn, her narrow skirt bright as a robin's egg in a world of winter gray.

Samuel hefted his toolbox from behind the seat. "Good working with you, Tucker. Take care out there."

With boyish enthusiasm, her brother took off in pursuit, vanishing into shadows as quickly as Rebecca. Steeling her nerve, Nora slipped from the car and hurried toward the barn, beckoning Tucker with a glance. Inside, a whiff of exhaust mingled with the musty scents of hay and animals. Scurrying, she switched on the battery-powered lantern and turned to see Tucker in the doorway—a tall, dark figure, sinewy and lithe.

He stomped snow from his boots and rubbed together his hands. "What did you want to show me?"

Closing the distance between them in a heartbeat, she pulled him inside, threw her arms around his neck, and kissed him.

He jerked upright, but then his shoulders eased, and his lips curved against hers with delicious slowness. He was smiling.

He wanted her to kiss him. And more than anything in the world, she wanted to kiss him, too.

With a sigh, he slid his hands around her waist, deepening the kiss with the gentle strength of a man who knew how to take what he needed while giving all he could.

A tingly flush crept across her collarbones, but she was no simpering youth sneaking a kiss behind the barn. She was a grown woman, as sure of herself and what she wanted as he. And though it made no sense whatsoever in her Amish world, she wanted this country music singer who spoke the language of her grandmothers and knew how to install a roof and made her laugh like no one before. Tucker McClure filled the hole in her soul with a love song. He made her want to live.

Pulling gently away, he raised one dark brow. "Do you have a special gift for Rebecca?"

His voice was a husky drawl. A sliver of guilt poked at her conscience. Scrunching her nose, she shook her head. "Just a new dress."

"You better come up with something else quick." He lowered his lips to the sensitive spot beneath her ear where her pulse pounded. "Something great," he murmured against her neck.

Shivers twitched up her spine, but from the chilly air or his warm breath, she couldn't tell. She tilted her head, giving full access to the tender skin beneath her chin, giggling as the stubble of his beard tickled.

He let out a throaty noise and gathered her close.

Her toes left the ground, curling at the sound rumbling in his chest—a sound that mingled love, longing, and a dash of frustration, too. She pressed her cheek into his shoulder, relishing the feel of velvety corduroy and wooly fleece. Drinking in that spicy scent that would forever be Tucker and only Tucker, she strengthened her hold. What did he want? What could she give? Maybe more importantly, what in this great, big, complicated world could they possibly have together?

Her feet touched the ground, and her lips found his, and a rush of love surged from her center like the underground springs that fed her childhood swimming hole. It bubbled pure and clean—steaming hot and bracingly cold all at once. No longer was she an empty shell of a person. She was a full vessel, overflowing with love that lightened her step and filled her soul with sunshine. "Dance with me," she whispered into his lips.

"What? Why?" He breathed. "Let's keep doing this."

Laughing, she pulled away and dashed to close the barn door. "Please. You have music on your phone, right?" The strand of loose hair came untucked and fell across her face.

He caught it and held it to the light. "I've never seen your hair."

She snagged her bottom lip between her teeth and gazed from beneath her lashes.

The lock looped around his fingers in a golden, silky coil. "I've imagined it—yellow as cornsilk." He eased away his hand, and the strand slipped free.

"A woman's hair is for..." Her body went all trembly, and her voice shook. She took a deep breath and struggled to slow her skittering heart. "Her husband."

Releasing his hold, he stepped back. "I see."

Down below, animals shifted in their stalls, huffing and clomping hooves. Snow snuck through cracks in the walls. Her stomach churned. Had she said too much? Fingers trembling, she extended an open hand. "Dance with me?"

He took it and pulled her close. His chest rose and fell in quick heaves.

His face was so near she saw tiny shadows in the crinkles at the corners of his eyes and a flash of the white scar beneath his chin. He gave a smile that could have liquefied every snowflake in a twenty-mile radius and then some.

He dug a hand into his pocket, pulled out his phone, and tapped the screen. The strains of that silly country Christmas song blared from the device, and he let out a laugh. "Yee haw, Twinkletoes." And with a quick kiss, he broke into the opening sequence.

The steps were familiar, but the dance was entirely new. The air crackled, and love seemed to spark at every touch. Spinning and tapping, she felt her stomach zing like she leapt from the highest bales in the hay loft. The instant she drew near, Tucker stole a kiss. As she spun, arms outstretched like a whirligig, happiness erupted inside, forcing any remaining bitterness into her fingertips and launching it into space. The man who drove the logging truck that horrid day…the English who seemed to take and take and take…..the brother who abandoned her…even the beloved husband who died…finally, she found strength and grace to forgive them and the courage to love again.

Laughing, she sang along with the music—her voice soaring clear and true. Two-step shifted to tap, and she and Tucker became those flickering movie icons, lit by magic and lamplight, surrounded by swirling snow.

He sang, too, his honey-sweet voice embracing her as warmly as his arms, his laughter moving over her skin like ripples on a pond. The music swelled to a giddy climax, and they whirled into the final rip-roaring sequence and struck a pose.

The music died. Wind whistled through cracks in the walls. A hinge creaked, and she jerked around her head.

Standing in the doorway, arms crossed and eyes ablaze, was Verna Rishel.

For weeks, she'd lived in fear of this moment. Though she'd lied and sneaked around, its coming was inevitable. Why, then, was she so utterly unprepared for its arrival?

Chapter Twenty-Three

As if his fingers were fire, Nora dropped Tucker's hand—cursing herself as she did. She loved him, and she'd stand by the simple, good truth of that love for a lifetime. But all the love in the world didn't change the fact that she lied to her family for weeks. Shame burned in her cheeks.

Hardening her gaze, *Mamm* gave a slow nod. "Now I understand," she said in clipped English. "You refused Mervin's proposal for an *Englischer*. Did he tempt you into this wicked dancing?"

The sordid insinuations landed like a slap. Nora steeled herself and turned the other cheek. "I refused Mervin because I don't love him, and I dance because I choose to—because it makes me happy. Dancing healed me."

"It poisoned you," *Mamm* spat. "It made you foolish and vain."

She sprang at her mother, balling her apron in tight fists. "I dance for myself, not for show. And I dance for Doctor Richard. Our class is performing at a program for his medical center. We're raising money for the clinic so others get the care I did. Hank was my partner, but when he got hurt, Tucker stepped in." Her mother's face went as white as the snow-covered fields. In anger, she seemed to grow five inches.

"A performance?"

"A charity event—a community celebration—with many participants," she stammered, eyes burning. Every attempt to clarify just compounded the initial transgressions of dancing and lying. As a child, Nora often sat by as her disobedient brothers suffered their mother's reprimands. For the first time, she took the full brunt of Verna's wrath, and it curdled her resolve.

With a curled upper lip, *Mamm* scoffed. "I've heard enough, *dochder*. You know your sin. I trust you will make the right choice." She turned and strode stiffly into the night.

In her absence, a small, dark form came into focus.

Arms wrapped around her middle, Rebecca huddled against the door, pale and shivering. She streaked into the barn and grabbed Nora in a fierce embrace. "If you go away, take me. Please don't leave me behind."

Nora's throat burned, and she struggled to speak. "No one is going anywhere. Run along. I'll be right inside."

Rebecca buried her face in Nora's shoulder. "Promise?"

She laid a quivering hand between her daughter's shoulder blades. They jutted through her coat, sharp and bony. The girl was still so young. "I promise."

Sniffling, Rebecca squeezed her hard and fled.

Once, as a child, Nora fell off Annie's pony. She collided with hard-packed earth and lay unable to move or breathe for so long she wondered if she would die. Waiting now in leaden silence, she felt her stomach spasm and her lungs turn to concrete, and was laid out again. She was afraid to look at Tucker—afraid to speak. High above, the rafters creaked in the wind. The lamplight dipped, its bluish glow eerie in the airless

291

cavern of the empty barn. Minutes passed. Snow eddied around her ankles, and her blood thickened. Finally, she slid Tucker a glance.

Hands on hips, he hung his head and stared at his feet. "You turned down a marriage proposal?"

The hurt in his voice rasped her insides like sandpaper. Licking her lips, she summoned the courage to answer. "Yes."

He met her gaze. "Why didn't you tell me?"

Pain twisted his features, and she longed to cry out—to run and embrace him—to explain everything. He had no idea what her life was like—what surviving the last seven years demanded every single day. But she couldn't touch him. A wall stood around him now, as impenetrable as if made of stone.

She forced a ragged breath. "When Mervin proposed, you were already gone, and when you came home, we had such a short time, and we were so happy, I didn't want to ruin it. Besides, I turned him down." She reached for him, arms open and palms splayed. "I don't love Mervin Zook, Tucker. I love you. I thought you knew my heart. I thought maybe…you felt the same."

Wide-eyed and twitchy, he retreated into shadows. "Do you think because I can hammer a nail, I'm like you? Because I speak a little German?" With a bitter laugh, he jerked his head to one side, and his neck cracked. "We're nothing alike. I'm a performer, Twinkletoes. I smile for the people and put on a show because that's who I am—that's what I do. I don't belong here anymore than you belong at a dive bar in Tennessee."

Lurking in darkness, he was a different person. She

struggled to mesh this presence with the tender man she kissed only moments ago. The man she loved. "I-I don't understand." Had this bitter, menacing person always lurked beneath the surface? She refused to believe it. "I know I lied, but we can work it out—we can explain—the dancing and the performing..." A floorboard dipped, and she stumbled, nausea souring her belly. "My mother wasn't at the frolic to see and hear how well you—she just doesn't know you. We have to have faith, remember?"

Snorting, he jutted his chin, and lamplight cast ashen shadows over the sharp planes of his face. "Faith don't pay the rent. Someone has to live in the real world, and that someone is me."

Outrage incinerated her insides. Did he really regard her and her community so poorly? "I live in the real world."

"Do you?" Burying his hands in his pockets, he rounded his shoulders and kicked at a post. "Because all this seems kinda like a fairytale—like a reality show that never ends. You can't hide from the world, Nora. The world always finds you."

The pain and loss of nearly a decade quaked her whole being, leaving her taut as a rubber band about to snap. "I know all about your world. Your world murdered the person I loved most and left me with a child to raise." Trembling, she confronted him, coming so close she could smell the tang of his sweat. "You know what's real? Grief. And loss. The kind of loneliness that makes every night a test of how much you want to wake up in the morning. I didn't choose those things. Your world forced them on me, and this life that seems like a fairytale to you is the only thing that saved me. I didn't quit. I didn't lose my faith. I kept going." Venom seeped from a crack in her soul that hadn't quite healed, and she thrust her face upward. "Can you say the same for yourself?"

He recoiled, clipping the post with one elbow. Wincing, he shook his head. "I don't belong here." His voice cracked. Tears glistened in his eyes.

Rage dissipated in an instant, leaving her weak-kneed and gasping. What had she done? She lunged, reaching for him. "Tucker, wait."

With a growl, he brushed her off. "See you around, Twinkletoes."

Unable to move, she watched him stagger out, looking like a deer shot by an arrow but not taken down. Bile rose in her throat, acidic and sour. "Tucker!" His name tore from her body. She bolted for the door and grimaced at the blinding glare of headlights.

The motor revved and slammed into gear. Spewing rocky slush, the wheels spun, and the truck careened into the storm.

She wanted to go after him. She wanted to beg his forgiveness and hear him do the same and know in her heart they could work through any barriers standing in their way. Love was stronger than the hurt they had suffered. It was stronger than any hurt they could give.

Icy wind lashed through her coat, and she slumped against the barn door. Her buggy could never catch his truck. His world ran twice as fast and three times as far as hers could even dream. She—plain Nora Beiler who'd never been farther west than the state of Ohio, never seen a city bigger than Harrisburg—was helpless. The motor faded before her own gasping sobs. In the speed of an electric current—a computerized message—a particle of matter whizzing through space in a way she never learned in her embarrassing eighth grade education...in the speed of thought, he was gone.

She told him she loved him. She dared to speak truth. To sing her heart's song. She told him, and she drove him away.

Her belly heaved in a shattering cry. Blinding snow sliced her cheeks until she thought they'd bleed.

How could she face her mother? Her daughter? The TipTop Tappers? How could she face anyone ever again?

****

Two days later, Nora hugged the foil-wrapped pot roast to her belly and watched Marion Diefenderfer drive down Hank's street and round the corner. A headache lurked behind her eyes, and she rolled her shoulders. During the entire car ride, Marion chattered nonstop about tomorrow's dress rehearsal and the benefit performance that weekend. Nora couldn't squelch the sick feeling congealing in her stomach like overcooked porridge. Surely, Tucker would come back. He promised.

Saturday's storm yielded four inches of wet snow. Here in town, the banks were already filthy. She gazed over Hank's modest neighborhood. It was completely drained of color—a world as black and white as the movies Tucker played on his phone on a night that felt like a million years ago.

Three hulking crows clustered in the highest branches of an oak. She tried not to interpret their cries as ominous. Rain or shine, crows crowed.

With an exasperated huff, Rebecca pressed the

doorbell again.

Since witnessing the scene in the barn, her daughter was skittish and sullen. In truth, none of the adults knew how to act, either. Having spoken nary a word over Sunday breakfast, her mother left for off-Sunday services in a neighboring district and returned late. Verna's Bible reading this morning was a baffling reminder to judge not lest you be judged—ironic given the fact her mother seemed to have done a bucket full of judging already. Samuel appeared eager to talk but kept leaving abruptly midsentence. She sighed, peeking in the living room window for a glimpse of Hank. The roast wafted a sweet smell of cooked onions and root vegetables. How she longed to hole up in her kitchen for a single day of peace. Maybe she'd bake Hank a pie.

Finally, the latch clicked, and the door swung wide.

Hank's gaudy Christmas sweater stood in stark contrast to his somber expression. "My good-for-nothing grandson called," he said by way of greeting. "He's not coming back."

"Don't you call him that ever again!" Rebecca pushed past the old man and bolted into the house.

"Rebecca!" Nora lurched weakly for her daughter.

"Leave her be." Hank stepped aside and flicked on the hall light. "Come on in. I'll fetch you a fruit punch."

Perched on the edge of the sofa, Nora stared at the photo of Tucker and his brothers. She clung to the cushion with rigid fingers, certain if she breathed too deeply, she would crack.

With a grunt, Hank handed her a glass and settled into the recliner. He nudged a bowl of pretzels in her direction. "Jerry can step in. She could have taken my place to begin with, but she liked to see you two dance."

She licked dry lips and sipped. The sickly-sweet liquid slithered down her throat, leaving behind the taste of artificial cherries. "Did Tucker tell you what happened?"

Hank shifted in the chair, positioning his bad arm carefully across his chest. "I got a little out of him before he drove off like a demon." He held up a hand. "Now don't you worry. The boy's fine. He called this morning from somewhere down in West Virginia. From what I could gather, you rejected a marriage proposal and never told your mother you were dancing."

"I did all that and more." Unable to look at him, she stared into the half-empty glass. Specks of dust floated atop the punch. Hank must have used glasses from the back of the cabinet. "I drove him away, Hank. I was a horrible person. I said dreadful things."

"Quite the opposite, my girl. Quite the opposite."

She swirled the drink, and the dust motes spiraled. "What do you mean?"

"Never for a single day did that boy think he was good enough for you." He jerked his head toward the library. "As the spitfire down the hall rightly points out, I didn't do much to disabuse him of the notion. He tell you about his troubles? Down in Tennessee?"

At the mention of trouble, she felt her stomach heave. For months she'd dreaded the truth—the scandal the girls at the market whispered about and her brother's wife alluded to at Thanksgiving supper. She didn't want to know, and she couldn't go on not knowing. She met Hank's gaze and shook her head.

The footrest squealed, and Hank reclined in his chair. "You wouldn't be aware, living as you do, but our boy was a songwriting sensation. Last spring, he was opening for a big country music star and about to sing in the most hallowed hall down there in Nashville. But success came too easy, I guess. I don't know. Maybe it didn't sit right in his heart, but he started drinking. He drank way too much."

She'd known boys who drank to excess before they joined the church. Running wild with their gangs, they cavorted in semi-secret at weddings, bringing shame to their families. Sometimes they repented. Sometimes they were lost. With quivering fingers, she slid the glass onto the coffee table.

"I only know what I saw on the Internet and what he said when he first arrived, but eventually, he started performing drunk and forgetting his words. Then down in Memphis, on the night before he was to make his big Nashville debut, he drank so much he passed out and missed the show all together."

Pity and anger burned in her cheeks. Was his life so hollow he turned to drink? How could he have been so stupid? She understood, and yet, she didn't. If only she'd been there, as impossible as the notion was.

"He came to just in time to see the tour bus leave without him." Tracing his moustache with a thumb and forefinger, Hank exhaled forcefully. "The story doesn't end there, I'm sorry to say. He wasn't alone in that motel room."

She clamped her jaw so hard a muscle in her neck twinged. Snatching the punch, she gulped.

Hank reached out and placed a thick hand on the arm of the sofa. "I know, it's not easy to hear, but it's the truth. He got in that girl's car and chased the bus like greased lightning. Didn't make it a half mile before he plowed into a daycare center."

A strangled gasp seared her lungs. "Did he hurt anyone?"

"Not at one in the morning, Nora girl. That son of a gun is lucky he didn't kill anyone. But no matter the details, just the fact of it was enough. The optics, as they say. The big star dropped him from the tour, the record label cancelled his contract, and he came to me clean and sober after going cold turkey alone. Best of my knowledge, he hasn't touched a drop since. But the boy's hurting."

She sank back into the sofa. "He's forgotten how to write songs."

"It eats at him." Hank reached for a pretzel, and the recliner groaned. "Day and night, he works at it. More than once, I found him asleep on the couch with his guitar across his chest."

Despair settled over her like a leaden blanket. She let her eyelids drift and stared into a world of infinite gray. But even with her eyes closed, the lights from the Christmas tree penetrated, and a scent of evergreen filled her. "Why? Why did he throw away his life?"

Hank sniffed. "Even with all the money and excitement, I think that life left him feeling empty. Since he was a boy, he's been different. He's been searching and searching for something…or some-one…to make sense of the world. His talent is a gift, but he's never known how to use it. Sometimes, I think he fancied he might join your people."

So Annie wasn't the only one who thought so. But a musician joining the Amish? Sure, she'd heard of a fellow or two out in Ohio who sang songs at hospitals and prisons. But as Mervin Zook said, she wasn't in

Ohio. She shot Hank a dismissive look. "Ridiculous."

"Is it?" Hank cranked the lever and pitched forward. "What's keeping him here? He can't stand his brothers and hasn't seen his mom and pop for years. He does love that truck but..." He scoffed, swatting at nothing. "A fella can forsake most anything for love."

"Love?" The word pierced her heart. "I don't know." Longing to put the whole affair behind her, she jerked to her feet and grabbed her glass. She gestured to his punch. "Are you finished?"

With a bittersweet smile, he handed the cup. "Go fetch your girl, and I'll call Marion. You look like you could use a day off."

The headache pounded, and she let her shoulders sag. "Thank you."

She rinsed the glasses and hurried down the hall to Hank's library. "Rebecca? I don't feel well. We'll go home early today." Nudging open the door, she peeked inside. Curled up like a cat in an overstuffed chair, Rebecca sat reading.

In a circle of light from an arching floor lamp, the girl's face shone red and tear-streaked. Catching sight of her mother, she gasped and clutched the book to her chest.

Nora had seen that look before. Many times. Squinting, she made out part of the book's title. *Lion...Witch...Wardrobe*. "What are you reading?" Her voice was granite.

Through slitted eyes, her daughter glared. "Why are you the only one who gets to break the rules?"

Pain hammered her temples, and she pinched her forehead. "Watch your mouth, *dochder*."

Heavy footsteps sounded from behind. "Take it

easy on the girl." Hank's voice was gruff. "I gave her the book. C. S. Lewis is a renowned Christian writer—"

"I don't care who he is!" The words scraped her throat like broken glass. "I trusted you, Hank. I gave you my daughter."

Rebecca scrambled from the chair, hugging the book tightly. "I'm not yours to give and take!"

Nora wrenched it free and slammed it onto Hank's desk, toppling a pile of yellow writing pads. "Wait for me outside." With a sound like a wounded bird, Rebecca stumbled into the hall.

Hank leaned heavily against the doorframe. "Don't blame the child."

"I don't." She stabbed a stiff finger. "I blame you."

"I understand." He frowned, his bushy eyebrows cutting a deep crease in his brow. "But let me ask you this: how is her reading any different from your dancing?"

The question landed like a horse kick to the stomach. She doubled over, struggling for breath. She was a hypocrite of the worst kind. Hank knew it. Her daughter knew it. Likely Tucker knew it, too, and that's why he could never love her. At length, she gathered herself, straightened, and caught his gaze. "You're right. I don't blame you, Hank. I blame myself. This whole mess is my fault. And it's time I put it right."

Chapter Twenty-Four

"Thank you for the ride." Head throbbing, Nora closed the door her daughter flung open before barreling out of Marion's car and disappearing into the barn.

Marion rolled down the window and smiled. "A big glass of water and a nap, and you'll be right as rain."

Nora could drown in water and sleep for a week, and the absolute catastrophe that was her life wouldn't be an ounce better. Messes needed cleaning, one by one.

The kitchen enveloped her in the scents of coffee and baking. A deep longing to collapse in a chair, sip warm milk from a too-hot mug, and lose herself in the comforting bustle of aunts and grandmothers was so overwhelming she thought her knees might give out. But she was no longer a girl, and the kitchen was empty, save for her mother.

Stooped over the counter, Verna crimped a pie shell with brisk efficiency, her knuckle and fingertips sculpting a ring of perfect dimples in the dough. "You're home early."

Oh, but she needed that glass of water. Cotton batting seemed to layer her mouth and throat. "I'm sorry I lied. I was selfish and wrong, and the consequences of my actions have punished me thousandfold. I've no one to blame but myself." She clutched the back of a chair until she thought the wood might splinter. "My dancing put our whole family at risk. I'm quitting. I should have done so weeks ago."

Intent on her work, Verna pricked the bottom of the pie shell and layered in a round of parchment. "Since I found you with the *Englischer*, I've thought and prayed—prayed and thought. What would your father say? What would he do?" Looking up, she caught Nora's gaze. "Do you love him?"

Pain stabbed behind her eyes, and she drove a thumb into her temple, rubbing in deep circles. "I…"

Mamm tilted her head, and her cheeks rounded. "You do. It's written all over your face."

Gripping the chair, Nora lifted the back legs and slammed them against the floor. "I'll stop. I'll stop loving, and I'll stop dancing and—"

"Good heavens." With a start, *Mamm* scurried to the kitchen window.

Nora darted a look and froze. Her repentance came too late.

Deacon Elmer and Bishop Mordecai strode across the snow.

Younger and haler than Mervin's father, Bishop Mordecai had a thick brown beard and beaklike nose bracketing a deep frown. He was reasonable but unbending. Deacon Elmer's fond feelings for her mother would likely do little to soften the blow of this meeting. Her vision blurred, and she thought she might be sick. Why were they here? They had several transgressions from which to choose. Which would they address?

Bracing herself, Smiling Nora strode toward the

door prepared to face discipline, whatever it might be.

Mamm hurried behind. "Run upstairs, *dochder*. I'll tell them you aren't well."

"I'm fine." Chin high, she reached for the knob. "I'm a grown woman, and I'll speak for myself."

"I know your head hurts, and that pain's nothing compared to the ache in your heart." *Mamm* laid a hand on Nora's cheek. "You've borne more in your years than most do in a lifetime. As a girl, you never seemed to need me. Let me help you now."

Her mother was not given to affection, and Nora leaned into the touch. The urge to be small and cared for surged, and she nodded. Besides, the headache was now so intense she could hardly stand. "Shall I fetch Samuel?"

Brushing flour from her apron, *Mamm* shook her head. "I'll face them myself."

Verna might be a woman, but she had age and stature on her side, and Deacon Elmer cared for her. Nora jumped at the loud rap on the door. Halfway up the stairs, she leaned over the banister. "*Denki, Mamm.*"

With a sniff, Verna opened the door.

She hunkered in shadows on the landing as she and her brothers did so often in their youth. The entry echoed with the stomp of boots and cordial greetings.

"We're sorry to visit so late, Verna—terrible sorry—but we felt the matter was best settled quickly."

Deacon Elmer's voice was as high and fluty as his son's, and she shivered at the similarity. How like some parents and children were, and how different others. Would anyone meeting strong and stoic Verna Rishel ever guess Nora Beiler was her daughter?

"That's a fine smell. One of Nora's shoofly pies?"

The Bishop's voice was deep and resonant. Would pie soften his demeanor? She'd gladly make him twenty.

"My *dochder* has a sick headache. Shall we talk in the sitting room?"

"We'd like very much to speak with Nora," the bishop said.

"You'll have to make do with me. Rest assured, I'll convey the message. Come inside." Declining to offer refreshment, her mother gestured toward the sofa and took a seat opposite in the glider.

Sitting straight-backed and proud, Verna looked like she'd summoned the men instead of the other way around. Oh, but she was a force. Heart swelling with gratitude, Nora scootched closer to the stairway, gaining a clear sight of her mother and a slant view of the gentlemen's knees.

Peering over her spectacles, Verna placed one hand atop the other on her thigh. "What can I do for you?"

Elmer cleared his throat. "Now, Verna, I'm sure this is all a dreadful misunderstanding—"

"Your daughter has been fraternizing with an *Englischer*," the bishop interrupted. "A country western singer. She rode unchaperoned in his truck on multiple occasions, and he accompanied her to Leroy Amos's frolic last Saturday."

She dug her fingernails into the railing deep enough to leave a mark. That squealing rat, Mervin, tattled to his father like a schoolboy! Or maybe he went straight to the bishop. But did he know about the dancing? The headache crushed her skull like a vise. If she got through this evening alive, she'd make sure Mervin Zook never tasted her shoofly pie again.

Verna pushed up the glasses on her nose. "As you're well aware, Elmer, at Doctor Richard's orders, Nora participates in an exercise class at the senior citizens center. You'll have noticed how her limp is all but gone. When the weather turned cold, a classmate offered a ride. Simple as that."

"You see, Mordecai?" The deacon's skinny knees jiggled. "I told you she'd have an explanation."

"The *Englischer* is not elderly," the bishop went on. "He's a young man. Given your family's history, naturally, we're concerned. When one child departs, he often leaves the door open for younger siblings. Weaker members of the family—"

"Ones mixed-up perhaps, through grief—" Deacon Elmer cut in.

"—might be tempted to follow."

Nora clutched her skirt, wishing she could take the men by the backs of their necks and toss them out the door. How dare the bishop call her weak? He might have held her as a babe, but the man had no idea who she truly was.

The glider squeaked a steady rhythm. "I see. Do you require church confession?"

A spasm of shame wracked her body. In her lifetime, she'd witnessed many confessions. Though designed to allow errant members an opportunity for public repentance and restoration, to her, they seemed like needless public spectacles. She would never subject herself to such humiliation. She'd prove the bishop true and go to Colorado first.

Mordecai tapped his knees with fingers as hairy as his chin, "We're weighing the option—" he began.

"Oh no, not yet—" Elmer said at the same time.

The men's' voices trailed off, and the only sounds were the crackle of the fire and the hiss of the lamp.

Frowning, Verna sniffed again. "Are you acquainted with the gentleman? Tucker McClure? Have you spoken to him?"

The bishop ceased tapping. "No."

"Did you know his name before I spoke it?"

"I can't say I did. Did you, Elmer?"

Deacon Elmer's knees jiggled faster. "Ah…no. No, I didn't."

Mamm looked from one to the other. "Then I daresay you don't know the man's heart."

"Only *Gott* knows the contents of a man's heart," the bishop intoned.

"Indeed." Verna planted her feet, stopping the rocking chair mid-glide. "My son, Samuel, worked side-by-side with Tucker McClure at the frolic. Were you aware the *Englischer* speaks German?"

The question was greeted with silence.

Nora held her breath.

"He grew up on a potato farm in Northern Maine," *Mamm* continued. "He was a church member in his youth, and he knows his way around a construction site. As you say, *Gott* alone knows the contents of a man's heart, and only He holds the divine plan for our lives. He saw fit to call home my husband before his sixtieth birthday. He took my daughter-in-law and her unborn babe, and in so doing, He took my eldest son." Lifting her chin, she stared down her nose. "Through healing my daughter from the very same accident that claimed her husband, He brought this *Englischer* into our community. Perhaps *Gott* sent Tucker McClure so we don't lose my daughter and granddaughter, as well."

Slack-jawed, Nora stared at her mother. Did *Mamm* truly believe Tucker was sent by God?

The bishop ran his hands up and down his thighs. "We cannot know the mind of *Gott*, but he chose me to lead the church—"

"With compassion, with wisdom, and with love." Lacing her hands over her belly, Verna rocked back in the glider. "Times have changed since your sisters and I were among the *youngie,* and you were still in school, Mordecai. Our community survives by adapting to change while holding tight to what makes us *us*. Don't judge my daughter and Tucker. Not yet. Be patient as I, too, struggle to be. Perhaps instead of losing a child, this time, I'll gain one."

Nora's throat constricted, and tears stung the corners of her eyes. Stumbling upon them in the barn, *Mamm* seemed furious. Had she misread her mother's feelings? Or did she have a change of heart?

Deacon Elmer's legs stilled. "You speak wisely, Verna. We'll keep your family in our prayers and visit in a few weeks to see how you're faring, won't we, Mordecai?"

Nora's heart went out to Deacon Elmer. He must be disappointed on behalf of his son, yet he showed such grace and generosity. She'd underestimated the man. Perhaps, he was worthy of her mother's affection.

Bishop Mordecai coughed and cleared his throat. "We certainly will."

Mamm's expression relaxed into a smile. "Well, now we've got that out of the way, who'd like pie?"

Nora slipped into her bedroom, downed two aspirin with a huge glass of water, and collapsed onto the bed, listening until she heard the front door close and her mother's deep sigh. On legs as strong as they were when she was a girl, she flew down the stairs and wrapped her arms around her mother's waist, utterly unable to speak.

Mamm stiffened but didn't pull away. "All right now. They're gone. Everything will be all right."

She tightened her hold, pressing her cheek into her mother's shoulder. It smelled of laundry soap and talcum powder. "Did you mean what you said?"

Mamm laid a hand on the small of her back. "I won't abide lying, and it's never been like you to break the rules. You surprised me, and you disappointed me, *dochder*."

Ducking from her mother's grasp, she hung her head and swallowed the taste of bitter guilt. "I'm sorry."

"I forgive you." Verna slid an arm around Nora's shoulders and led her to the couch.

Headache easing, she sank into the cushions and let her mother drape the crocheted afghan over her knees.

"When I saw you in the barn, I was angry, yes, but anger wasn't all I felt." *Mamm* sat by her side and pulled free a crease in the blanket. "I'd have to be blind to miss the change that's come over you, and I had my suspicions as to why. I don't mind saying I've watched you out the window several nights, coming home from your class. You're my smiling girl again. I hoped it was due to your body healing, but once I saw you with that boy, I knew. Love gave you back your smile—love and dancing."

Tucking one foot beneath her, she jerked toward her mother. "I'll stop! I'll quit the doctor's performance and stop loving Tucker and—"

"After what Doctor Richard did for this family? You'll do no such thing. Not another word, only pray, *dochder*. Pray for that English boy with all your heart."

She poked a finger between granny squares and twisted the yarn until her fingertip went white. "He's gone, *Mamm*. Tucker's grandfather said he left for good."

Verna frowned and pulled her close. "Then we'll have to pray harder."

For her mother's benefit, she forced a smile. With Verna's blessing, she could keep her promise to the TipTop Tappers and to Doctor Richard. No matter how much it hurt, she would smile, and she would dance. She wouldn't let those good people down.

As for Tucker, she'd never forget the searing sting of his words and the haunted look in his eyes. She'd been healed, but he was still deeply wounded. Maybe irreparably. She heard again the hollow resignation in Hank's voice when he said Tucker was gone—as if he'd always known his grandson would break his heart.

She let her eyelids close and quieted her mind. She'd pray all right. But would all the prayer in the world be enough to bring Tucker home?

Chapter Twenty-Five

The last place Tucker belonged was a bar. Every ounce of sense told him to crawl back to his crummy motel and hit the sack. Two days back on the road, and already he felt his fingers twitch, itching to hold a bottle. He pressed them hard into his palms. Then again, when did Tucker McClure ever do what he should?

Even for a dive, the place was grim. Neon flickered hazily above stock car posters, framed photos of a local lady boxer, and yellowed signs reading *Cash Only* and *Beer to Go*. Christmas lights dangled from the mirror above the bar like someone threw them without looking. The air was rank with cigarettes and despair. He was living the high life all right.

"You drinking, McClure?"

The bartender hulked like a mustached grizzly bear in faded flannel. What he wouldn't give to be eating cookies with Hank and Nora in that faraway living room, the Christmas tree twinkling and Rebecca smiling like he hung the moon. He licked cracked lips. "You got any punch?"

"Punch?" The bartender snorted a laugh. "Like fruit punch?"

Tucker nodded.

"No, man. No juice boxes, either."

"How about OJ?"

The guy dragged a gray rag across the bar, clipping Tucker's elbows. "Do I look like some kind of mixologist? You want a bespoke cocktail?"

"Yeah, all right. Gimme a seltzer."

With a whoosh, seltzer jetted into a glass, drowning out the tune that tickled at the edge of his brain. Almost a week now, the melody gnawed like a forgotten dream. Lyrics bubbled up and receded. Why couldn't he remember the song? A strain shot through his consciousness and faded like a falling star.

I used to tap a keg, tap a key,
Tap on the glass between you and me...

With fingers moving almost on their own, he strummed empty air and stared at the tin ceiling. What was the next lyric? The next chord? Fisting the seltzer, he took a long pull and grimaced. It tasted like watered-down, flat cola.

"Easy, cowboy. Don't drink it all at once," a husky voice drawled.

Tossing a glance over one shoulder, he came face-to-face with a dark-haired, blue-eyed beauty right off the pages of a swimsuit calendar. She nursed a beer, cherry-red lipstick staining the glass in a perfect imprint of plump lips. Just a year ago, he would have drunkenly taken this woman back to his room and left her without a second thought. A year...and a lifetime ago.

The woman tossed back her head, exposing a long neck and a low-cut top. "I caught your set. Sounded even better than when you played here three years ago. You remember that night?"

Uh oh. Should he? Had he in fact taken this woman home in the before times when dive bars were sanctuaries and the road felt like home? Where was he again? West Virginia? He gave a half smile. "Sure, I do."

She tipped her head to one side and slanted a look, her lips curling into a slow grin. "Liar."

He blinked and stared at her face. Her mouth moved, and she spoke, reminiscing about a night he could no more recall than the song dancing on the edge of his thoughts. How did it go again? Maybe drinking fried his brain, after all.

Tap my fingers and tap a vein, tap on your door in the pouring rain…

She oozed closer, silky hair sliding over one bare shoulder with a whiff of fruity shampoo.

A woman's hair is for her husband.

Lukewarm seltzer burned his throat, granting no relief. His brain was a sadistic son of a gun. He couldn't recall a simple song, but he remembered every detail of Nora's exquisitely beautiful face when she said those words…soft, pink cheeks more alluring than the acres of flesh on display in this bar. He remembered everything about that night. The shock and disgust in her mother's face. The terror in Rebecca's voice. The tears in Nora's eyes—tears he caused. Hurting her shredded his insides, but he had no choice. He was a ticking time bomb. Sooner or later, he detonated everything in a hundred-mile radius.

The brunette nursed her beer.

He could almost taste it. One drink wouldn't kill him, right? Just one? He drained the seltzer and wiped a hand over his jeans. The idea of him joining the Amish was a freaking fantasy. Pushing away Nora gave her a chance at a good life. That Mervin guy seemed decent. She'd be okay. He balled a fist against his thigh. He'd told himself these things a thousand times since he left. Why couldn't he believe them?

Red-tipped fingers raked through his hair. "Come back, cowboy. You're a million miles away."

He blinked scratchy eyes, and the bar and its inked and boozy patrons, hunched like the haunted over bottles, came into focus. His belly pulled, longing for a touch, but not from this woman. The woman he loved was a world away, wrapped in an apron he'd never unpin and a bonnet he'd never untie. He remembered a flash of silver in lamplight and the realization nothing but a few slivers of metal held up her dress. Again, the melody nagged. He swiveled on the barstool. "Hey, do you know this song?" Bringing his mouth to the woman's ear, he hummed the melody that wouldn't leave him alone.

She turned, hovering her face inches from his. "I don't think so." Red lips stretched in a languid smile. "What are the words?"

Her breath smelled of hops and her cheek of something flowery. She was close enough to kiss, but kissing her was the last thing he wanted. "I can't quite remember. Something like 'I was just about to tap out, but then you tapped in, and tapped down into my heart.'" Lips parting, she lifted her chin like an invitation.

"Sounds like one of your songs."

Everything—the crowd—the bartender—the old school jukebox blaring Hank Williams in the corner—everything froze. Smoke eddied in fixed spirals above shaggy heads of bikers and coal miners. Dust motes suspended like comet tails amid orange globe-light suns. Rising slowly to his feet, he dropped a twenty on the bar, slipped between statues, and shouldered the door to the street. A tinny bell jingled. Sleet pelted his face, bouncing off cars with a sound like fingernails tapping glass.

It sounded like his song because it *was* his song.

A new song.

The song he was just about to write.

****

Nora slipped an arm through a red, green, and gold plaid vest and peeked into a full-length mirror. Catching a flash of red satin lining, she cringed. The night of the performance had arrived, and her costume was miles beyond fancy. She scrunched her nose and sighed. In for a penny, in for a pound.

Minutes before, nurse Cindy had toted the mirror into the Sunday School room of First Presbyterian Church for the TipTop Tappers. With her baby strapped to her chest in an intricate carrier, she gave Nora a sideways embrace. "Thank you for the sweet blanket. Grayson loves it." Cindy looked at her clipboard, checked an item off a list, and bustled into the hall where performers young and old darted in and out of adjacent classrooms.

The air was electric with the excitement of a Christmas Eve show. Singers warbled scales, and actors repeated tongue twisters as children in candy cane outfits chased one another like puppies. The scent of Annie's cinnamon sticks drifted in from a hallway refreshment table providing snacks and cider. Turning, Nora regarded herself from all angles. She couldn't deny how cheerful the vest looked atop the emerald cape dress she borrowed from Annie. Though she didn't exactly match the other ladies in their sequined green skirts, red turtlenecks, and vests, she blended in, and her classmates were all smiles.

Reflected in the mirror, Bert and Dot sashayed around the room, while Marion, Joan, and Edna reviewed one of the more intricate tap sequences. Doing double duty, Gene was upstairs performing with the Third Street Singers. A perennial favorite, the TipTop Tappers were scheduled for the end of the program, and Gene assured them he'd have ample time to change into the blue jeans and matching red-and-green-plaid bow ties the male tappers donned.

Strains of a jazzy "Jingle Bells" came over the speaker in the hall, and Nora poked out her head for a better listen.

Poised by the refreshment table, Dr. Richard held a cinnamon stick to his wife's lips.

Giggling, she took a bite.

Brushing sugar from her chin, Richard laughed, too, and dropped a tender kiss atop his son's head.

Pierced with bittersweet longing, Nora slipped back into the room. Oh, how she missed those private moments. A small, but loving, gesture…a heated gaze meant only for her. Her heart ached, and she lay a soothing hand on her middle. For a few weeks, she dared to imagine such a special bond was possible again. For a few weeks, she was happy. Though Tucker's departure shattered her dream of love, it didn't rob her of a newfound sense of peace that softened the edges of sadness. The gift of forgiveness persisted. It was hers and hers alone, and because of it, she was free.

Gene's tenor rose in a shimmering version of "It Came Upon a Midnight Clear," and she ran her gaze over walls festively adorned with popsicle stick stars and paper plate doves. She'd never been in an English church. How similar the decorations were to those at the Amish school, where that afternoon Rebecca participated in the annual Christmas program. Though her daughter once again assumed the role of the Angel of the Lord, her recitation this year was different. No longer jittery, she spoke the familiar text with a steady voice, creating a calm and, yes, angelic presence amidst wiggly young shepherds. Watching her, Nora was filled with pride. When they finally had a heart-to-heart talk, she would be sure to tell Rebecca.

Slumping a shoulder against the wall, she stared at her borrowed tap shoes, buffed until they shone. Hank's question still nagged. Did her dancing differ from Rebecca's reading? Of course, it did. She was a full-grown adult, and Rebecca was an impressionable child. Closing her eyes, she pictured her daughter's sweet face, her features guileless yet knowing. She was a child with a fertile imagination and wisdom beyond her years—a lonely child for whom books were solace. Was Verna right? Could the rules be amended in ways that preserved their values but acknowledged they inhabited an ever-evolving world? If trees didn't bend in the wind, they'd surely snap, no matter how deep the roots.

"I knew you were tough, Nora Beiler, but I didn't know how tough until tonight. I'm honored to be your partner."

Opening her eyes, she met Jerry's gaze. "I honestly thought he'd come. Even when Hank said he wouldn't, I hoped, and I prayed and…" Nora lifted her shoulders and let them fall.

Jerry slid an arm around her. "The good Lord

always answers prayer, but sometimes, the answer is no."

With a sigh, she rested her head on her teacher's shoulder. Despite the heartache, knowing these people—these *Englischers*—was a blessing, and she'd never regret it.

Jerry gave her a gentle hug. "And sometimes we're so busy asking God for things, we forget to listen for an answer."

An enthusiastic round of applause came through the monitor followed by a single guitar strum. The chord was rich and sweet...almost familiar. Staring at a rainbow-hued Mary and Joseph on a coloring page, she pricked up her ears.

Another strum, and the hoots and clapping ebbed. Then a melody sounded, pure and simple. Knuckles knocked the body of a guitar, and the tempo quickened, chord after chord tumbling one upon the next.

And then came a voice she would have known anywhere.

Jerry's chest vibrated with soft laughter. "Well, butter my butt and call me a biscuit. I guess the answer was yes."

Nora jerked to standing. She dashed out of the room and tiptoed up the stairs to the back of the church social hall. Heart pounding, she slipped around the corner, flattening herself against the wall. The room was long and narrow. Between her and the stage were rows and rows of folding chairs, packed with gaily dressed folks enraptured by country music star, Tucker McClure.

In a pool of white light, he stood with eyes closed and head tipped back as his fingers flew. He stepped up to a microphone, and a lock of shiny black hair flopped over one eye.

He tossed his head, the familiar movement so dear she struggled to breathe. She ran her fingertips over the grooved wood paneling, reassuring herself this be-wildering night was in fact real. Alone on the stage, he was bigger than life—like something out of a dream or a movie played on a giant screen. As he sang, he sounded like the star he was.

The song was unfamiliar. The lyrics stopped the world from spinning.

I used to tap a keg, tap a key,
Tap on the glass between you and me, girl.
Tap my fingers and tap a vein,
Tap on your door in the pouring rain.
Gotta tap into love, tap into life,
Turn on your smile and make you my wife.
I was just about to tap out, but then you tapped in,
and tapped down into my heart.

He kept his promise. He came back. Up there on the stage, he couldn't see her. She was certain. But as Annie said, he sang to her and her alone. Her heart ballooned until she thought it would burst.

When he finished, the crowd leapt to their feet.

Tucker's song still ringing in her ears, she scurried down the stairs. He sang plenty of love songs, but this one seemed different. Did she dare to believe the message was meant for her?

She bumped shoulders with Nurse Cindy. "I'm so sorry."

"Don't you worry, honey." Cindy checked her list. "Next up are the Gingerbread Grannies, then the Cricket Creek Cherubs and then you're on. Break a leg!"

Completely befuddled, she stared. Why would Cindy say that?

Bonking her head with the clipboard, Cindy laughed. "I'm such a goose. 'Break a leg' means good luck to a performer. Last thing I want is for you to break a leg, honey!" Still chuckling, she patted Nora's arm and hurried down the hall.

Nora's head spun. Did she eat dinner? Suddenly, she couldn't remember. She snatched a cinnamon stick and ducked into the room with the other members of her group. They huddled like livestock around a feeder. She entered, and every head turned. "Guess he's back."

Marion took a big breath and then snapped shut her jaw. She squinched her eyes and peered over Nora's shoulder. "Well, look what the cat dragged in."

A shuffling sound came from the door. Nora's back tingled, and she nibbled the cinnamon stick.

Jerry stepped away from the group and opened her hands. "Just in the nick of time."

Edna's hearing aid squealed. "We figured you were gone for good."

Nora bit her lip to keep from laughing. These old folks looked like they would tear Tucker limb from limb for almost missing the show. She sidled closer, turned, and lifted a brow.

Tucker cleared his throat. "I deserve that."

"You bet you do," Marion snapped. "After all those casseroles?"

"I'm sorry." He leaned his guitar against the wall and slid a duffel from one shoulder. "I don't have any excuse, other than I needed to get my head on straight." He unzipped the bag and pulled out a pair of tap shoes.

"I know I'm late, but I'm here now, and I'm ready to dance." He met Nora's gaze. "If you'll still have me."

No one spoke, and Nora wondered if they were waiting for her response. From the hall, the speaker crackled with a kazoo version of "Rudolph the Red Nosed Reindeer."

"Of course, we'll have you." Jerry swooped in and wrapped Tucker in a voluminous hug.

The other tappers crowded around, clapping him on the shoulder and welcoming him.

Nora hovered on the outside, unsure what to do. The shock of seeing him was like leaping into an icy lake—invigorating and paralyzing all at once. She had so many questions. Why did he come back? How long would he stay? Did his return and that song *mean* anything?

"That was a catchy tune," Joan said. "I don't think I've heard it."

Tucker met Nora's gaze. "I just wrote it."

"You did?" Her voice was high and breathy. She bounced on tiptoes like her daughter.

Grinning, he extended a hand. "Nora, may I speak to you?"

Her belly flipped, and she slipped her fingers into his.

"Make it quick, buddy. We're on in five," Gene called to their backs.

She skittered behind him, ducking through a doorway at the end of the hall.

Dropping her hand, he scanned the room. Colorful, felt banners with appliqued messages of hope and praise covered the walls. He chuckled. "This is not where I imagined we'd have this talk."

Unsure she wanted to have "this talk" at all, she hovered inside the door. "You wrote a new song. I'm so happy for you."

"I wrote a couple, and I have lots more bouncing around in here." He rapped his skull like he rapped the guitar on stage. Pacing in a wide circle, he pulled out a child's chair and sat, his knees almost level with his shoulders. He yanked another chair to face him and gestured toward it.

Fighting an impulse to giggle and a simultaneous fear she might cry, she sat. The emerald skirt ballooned, and the tips of her tap shoes poked out beneath the hem. "I guess everything worked out then. You can go back to Nashville and pick up where you left off. You've changed, Tucker. I'm sure with hard work and persistence—"

"I don't want to pick up where I left off." Elbows on knees, he scooched to the edge of the chair until it tipped, and he had to lean back to right it. "My new songs aren't regular country songs. They're about something bigger and deeper. And they're simple, too. Almost from another time."

"I liked the one you played tonight." Her collarbones heated, and she lowered her gaze.

"That song is the first one I wrote in more than a year, and it's a love song, pure and simple." Sliding off the chair, he came to his knees. "The song is for you, Twinkletoes, and I meant every word."

"But you said—"

"I know. And I'm sorry." He closed the distance between them until he knelt right in front of her. "I was hurting and scared, and I lashed out. When your mother found us together and said what she said...it confirmed what I knew all along. I could never be good enough for you."

She gripped his shoulder, fingertips digging into rock hard muscle. "No! She was just shocked to see me dancing and looking so happy. I think she was scared, too—scared she'd lose me."

He sat back on his heels, fisting his hands against his thighs. "I want to be worthy of you, Nora. I want to stay here. With you."

Her heart rocketed like the great soaring fireworks she saw one summer out in Ohio. As quickly, though, it snuffed and fell into her chest. "I won't leave the Amish. I can't."

"I'd never ask you to." He rose again to his knees and opened his palms. "I want to join you, Nora. I'm ready."

Hardly daring to believe him, she studied his face. Moss-green eyes burned with solemn intensity. His jaw was set firm. With a deep breath, she took his hands, shivering at the electric tingle his touch sent to every part of her body.

"Here with your family and the folks in your community, I feel at home." He brought his face to within inches of hers. "I belong here. I want a life here. With you."

His spicy, delicious, uniquely English smell flooded her senses, and she breathed him in, wondering if he'd still smell the same when he was Amish. She met his gaze, searching for the catch—the "except"—the hesitancy behind his eyes belying his words. She found none. A giddy urge bubbled from deep inside, and she nuzzled her nose against his in a playful invitation for a kiss.

His mouth hovered a feather's distance from hers. "*Ich liebe dich.*"

"I love you, too" she whispered and lost herself in his kiss.

His arms threaded around her waist, and he pulled her to him, tiny child's seat and all.

As the chair legs *thump-thumped* over the floor and her body nestled against his, she laughed, surrendering to the wonder of being in his arms, in a miniature chair, in an *Englischer* church, about to tap dance on a stage. Her heart thudded so hard she was sure he could feel it—every beat pumping life and love from her once-hollow heart to her once-injured hip. She was a different woman from the one who just a year ago snuggled a horse on a frigid Christmas Eve and made a decision that would change her life forever. She liked this person a whole lot more.

A gentle but pointed "ahem" came from behind, and she turned. Jerry's beautiful face peeked from the doorway.

Burnished bronze, her cheeks lifted in a wide smile, and her brown eyes sparkled.

"All right, you two, you'll have time for that later. Right now, you've got to dance."

Nora's life was messy. Her relationships were complicated, and her future was still unknown. But in Tucker's arms, she was whole again. She was healed. Bounding her feet, she wiggled her backside in lighthearted imitation of Jerry and fired off a tap combination that would have done Edna proud.

Tucker and Jerry hooted, and she laughed for simple joy of having a body to move and a heart to love.

Christmas Eve was a time of new beginnings. And this holiest night of the year was one of a kind. Tonight's performance would likely be her only appearance with the TipTop Tappers and the last time she ever laced on a pair of tap shoes. But for this night...

She gave Jerry's hand a grateful squeeze, smooched Tucker on the cheek, and scurried to join her friends.

For this night, Nora Beiler would *dance*.

Epilogue

Green Ridge, Pennsylvania. One Year Later

Nora arched her back, pressing one hand into tight muscles along her lower spine and flipping breakfast bacon with the other. Forget dancing. These days she was a circus performer, juggling ten balls at once. Laying the tongs on the kitchen counter, she swiped her forehead with the back of a wrist. She shifted her weight, easing the burden on her left ankle. Her leg felt strong as ever, but she was so very tired. Given how she'd kicked all night, maybe the baby would be a dancer, too.

Tucker insisted they were having a boy, but Nora knew better. After enduring four miserable months of nausea, she'd eaten more Christmas cookies than she had in years. Her mother decreed morning sickness plus a sweet tooth meant a girl child. She looked down at her belly. Her pointy, bony body was long gone, replaced by an ever-expanding physique that somehow didn't seem like hers anymore. Though she remembered little from carrying Rebecca, she did recall feeling her body was no longer her own—that it was in service of something bigger.

A yawn convulsed her from head to foot. She didn't care whose body it was. She just wished it wasn't exhausted all the time. Maybe she could grab a quick nap between the school Christmas program and their guests' arrival for the Christmas Eve meal.

Heavy steps thundered down the stairs accompanied by men's laughter and the sounds of good-natured ribbing.

Pulling black suspenders over an emerald-green shirt, Tucker strode into the kitchen and gave Verna a firm kiss on the cheek. "*Guder mariye*," he said in flawless Pennsylvania Dutch.

Verna shooed her son-in-law with a good-natured swat.

Her mother had grown used to Tucker's many *Englisch-isms* as she called them but was still squirrely about frequent shows of affection. Having surrendered much to assimilate into Amish culture, hugs and kisses were one habit her husband refused to forsake.

He propped his guitar against a cabinet and plopped at the table next to Samuel. "I'm playing in the children's ward at the hospital this morning, but I'll help with the solar installation over at King's this afternoon."

Samuel attacked his breakfast in a businesslike manner. "I can use you. Lucas King's operation is growing, and it's a big job. If we do well by him, we'll get plenty of other businesses to sign on."

Nora placed heaping plates of scrambled eggs, bacon, and biscuits in front of the men. "Don't be late for the Christmas Eve program at school."

"I wouldn't miss it." Rising partway, Tucker planted a kiss next to her ear. "Sit, and I'll get you a plate."

With a giggle, she squirmed free. "I had an early breakfast."

Mamm lifted a brow over the rim of her coffee cup. "Cookies again?"

"The baby likes sweets." Popping a strip of bacon, she shrugged. "And pork."

Light footsteps pattered across the sitting room floor, and Rebecca bounded in like a long-legged foal. Nora gazed at her daughter and was filled with mingled gratitude and relief. Still teeming with questions and too smart for her own good, Rebecca seemed satisfied of late. Though Nora didn't dare hope her restless streak was gone, for all outward appearances, the child was content. She'd make a wonderful *gut* big sister.

"When do Uncle Jonas and Tessa arrive with little Lizzie?"

Verna's cheeks glowed. "I told you twenty times. His letter said tonight."

Outside, a horn honked. Nora leaned over the sink and waved out the window.

Tucker's truck idled in the driveway with Hank at the wheel. His recovery was truly amazing. His shoulder was healed, and his diabetes was well under control. Fresh off this year's performance with the TipTop Tappers, he would join them for holiday festivities.

Rebecca grabbed a biscuit and a piece of bacon. "Shake a leg, Tucker, or we'll both be late."

"Now wait a minute!" Verna boomed over the chaos. "This might not be a proper family breakfast, but we will pause for prayer."

Instantly, the swirling craziness ceased.

Nora dropped into a chair and bowed her head. Resting clasped hands on her swollen belly, she sighed. She had so much to be thankful for.

With a sniff, Verna ended the prayer, and the kitchen exploded back into life.

Swapping Rebecca's makeshift breakfast for her coat, Nora slid the garment over slender shoulders and dangled the food in front of her daughter. "What kind of expression is 'shake a leg?' "

Rebecca snatched the biscuit. "Hank says it all the time. I like it. It's got energy." She flung open the door. "See you after school!"

"That's my cue." Tucker pushed back from the table. "Be right there, Short Stuff."

"Nope!" Rebecca hollered from the yard. "Don't like that nickname, either."

Nora laid a hand on Tucker's shoulder. "You hardly ate a bite."

"From what I've heard, we'll eat nonstop for the next two weeks. I'll be fine."

She sliced another biscuit and layered in eggs and bacon. Wrapping it in foil, she met Tucker at the door. "You'll be glad for it later."

Slinging an arm around her waist, he bent and kissed her belly and then brushed a soft kiss over her lips. "I'm glad right now. Merry Christmas, Twinkle-toes." With a final smooch, he sauntered out the door.

Nora leaned against the doorframe, drinking in the shape and rhythm of his stride. Like his distinctive smell, it hadn't changed. It still rendered her jelly-kneed.

The low winter sun cast long shadows over her mother's snow-covered flower beds. By this time next year, their little house in the east pasture would be finished—complete with the beautiful, latticed window boxes Samuel and Rebecca made her last Christmas.

Then, she, her daughter, her husband, and their baby would be snug in a sweet new home, outfitted with this year's gift: a second kitchen for baking.

With another honk, Hank drove down the lane, white exhaust billowing. How Tucker adored that truck. He told her once that home was the open highway. Yet, for love, he gave it up and built a new home with her on the farm. He could no longer drive away when times were tough. He surrendered his truck and his dreams of stardom and his life on the road. He gave them up for her. And for himself, too.

Closing the door, she turned her attention to the long list of preparations for Christmas Eve supper. Her life was chaos and laughter and a song that echoed from one green hill to the next. Sighing, she bit into a buttery biscuit and let her feet tap a gentle shuffle step. Smiling Nora wouldn't want life any other way.

A word about the author…

Wendy Rich Stetson is a New York City girl who still considers the back roads of Central Pennsylvania to be home. Now an author of clean and wholesome romance, Wendy is no stranger to storytelling. She's a Broadway and TV actress, an audiobook narrator, and a mom who enjoys little more than collaborating on children's books with her artistic teenage daughter. And coffee. Wendy lives in Upper Manhattan with her family of three and Maine Coon mix kitty, Tessa. For book news and more, subscribe to Wendy's newsletter, "Manhattan Farmgirl" at: http://wendyrichstetson.com

Another Title by the Author
Hometown, Hearts of the Ridge, Book 1